Fusion

Candace Sams, author of *The Peacekeeper's Soul*

CRIMSON
ROMANCE
F+W Media, Inc.

This edition published by
Crimson Romance
an imprint of F+W Media, Inc.
10151 Carver Road, Suite 200
Blue Ash, Ohio 45242
www.crimsonromance.com

ISBN 10: 1-4405-6903-7
ISBN 13: 978-1-4405-6903-6
eISBN 10: 1-4405-6904-5
eISBN 13: 978-1-4405-6904-3

*For Lee and for anyone who ever looked
to the stars and imagined! Good reading to you.*

Chapter 1

Reisen Four
Behind enemy lines
Earth year 5037

To save what ammo she had, Lyra Markham jammed the butt of her photon rifle into the face of the charging Condorian. The resulting thud was exceedingly gratifying.

Her foe fell into an awkward heap. His head lolled to one side and his eyes immediately assumed a deathly, hollowed glaze.

It'd been a very good hit.

She tossed her empty rifle aside. It was added weight she couldn't afford.

A quick search of her dead foe's arsenal proved pointless. Though the fool was out of ammunition he'd still had the balls to charge, brandishing a horrific looking, ten-inch boot blade. Aside from that weapon, which she summarily shoved into the barrel of her tall desert boot, there was nothing else to be scavenged from his body. No ammo. No grenades. Nothing.

Scrambling sounds made her glance backward.

Unfortunately her dead enemy's nasty-looking friends witnessed her attack from about a hundred yards away. They grouped for the chase.

As they ran toward her, firing, she ducked and took off northward, as fast as her body armor allowed. She now counted seven Condorians breathing down her neck.

Sweat poured down her face as she gazed ahead, hoping to get to the far, rocky hills where she'd have the advantage of being on higher ground.

As Lyra ran, she was forced to jump over the bodies of Delloids, Capricans, Startsur warriors, and Freermen. All of them were

Earth allies in the war against the Condorians. All were spilling blood just as freely.

No matter how many allies came to the front, intending to beat back the enemy ravaging the entire galaxy, the Condorians kept bringing more. The only thing that kept her world and other allied planets from being overrun were these desperate stands in space—diversions meant to slow the enemy while allied commanders fell back and reassessed battle strategy.

Annihilation was only a matter of time. She knew it; so had all the dead lying around her. But no one was giving up. The Condorians wouldn't take hostages. Innocent inhabitants from hundreds of allied planets would die horrible deaths. It now came down to a matter of how one died. Her course was in battle.

She rounded an outcrop of rock and stopped to lean against it, dragging air into her lungs while she could. Every detail of this stinking, blood-soaked battleground blended together.

There were almost no colors on Reisen Four. Sepia-tones obscured some of the rocky escarpments in shadow. There was no grass, sparse plant life of a higher order, and precious little water. Whatever the cost, Lyra vowed not to be taken alive.

Approaching boot steps signaled her brief respite was over. She gripped her sidearm and ran again. She'd have taken her helmet off for better maneuverability, but the only long-range transmitter she had was built inside. Even though she was sure her superiors had given her up for dead, she couldn't relinquish the last communication device available. And some part of the helmet might deflect incoming fire.

As one of thousands of Class M planets, Reisen Four's air was breathable. Lyra and other allied fighters had been given orders to leave air packs behind. In this environment, the oxygen canisters would have weighed fighters down. That brilliant foresight helped her make good time now. But without filtered oxygen, the dirt in the air penetrated every part of her uniform, including the damned helmet. Still, she clung to the last hope that a signal might come from an allied vessel. With her own fighters scattered to the four winds, Earth Forces deployed in this battle were quite gone or dead.

There'd originally been three other women in her platoon. She was the last and had seen the remains of her friends and what had been done to them. That image was burned into her brain and was the only thing keeping her from turning around and shooting into the pack chasing her. Her pursuers had picked up the pace. She was pretty damned sure they knew she was female.

Hours went by. She dodged, hid, and ran but it made no difference. After only a few precious moments to rest in every few hundred yards of running, her foes kept up the pursuit. Their persistence had less to do with losing their friend to her rifle butt, and more to do with catching a woman and slaking their lusts before slowly slaughtering her.

It was now late into what passed for a Reisen Four night. The sepia-tones were only a little darker to delineate the passage of time. She had no idea where she was and didn't care. The Condorians were still running her to ground like hounds on a blood trail.

With her body and wits taxed, she turned into a small, narrowing canyon. Without energy reserves, she suddenly realized she couldn't climb up its side fast enough to keep from being hauled back down the rocky slope. It was there she turned to make what she assumed would be her last stand.

I'll take a few of you bastards with me.

She squared her shoulders, determined to save one last round for her head. She'd be dead before they actually began tearing her apart.

As she raised her sidearm fear gripped her soul. It was then she realized she really wasn't ready to die. A noise from behind signaled she wasn't alone.

In an instant someone from behind clamped a large, strong hand on her shoulder. She was hauled off her feet and bodily thrown into a dark, cavernous space. Her weapon fell from her grasp and she scrambled to retrieve it.

Her attacker pulled her backward. That was the last thing she remembered.

• • •

It might have been hours or minutes later when she opened her eyes. She felt her neck being massaged by huge, gentle hands. When her foggy wits cleared, she eventually pushed herself away from the enormous, crouching figure next to her. Since she'd be dead if he was a Condorian; the reasonable assumption was that this darkly uniformed fighter was an ally. He'd most likely saved her life.

"Wh-what the hell happened?" she murmured through her helmet mouthpiece.

Her helmeted savior stared at her.

The huge megalithic creature before her tilted his black, armored head, as if he hadn't heard her correctly. She repeated her question and added more.

"I'm Lyra Markham…Master Sergeant, Tenth Earth Regiment. Who are you and what happened?" she demanded again.

When he kept staring down at her—his face as invisible as hers behind the anti-glare plexi-shielding—she kept trying. "Is your communicator working?" She tapped her head to indicate a communication device that should be located within his helmet.

Since learning that other races occupied the outer reaches of space many centuries ago, universal communication technology had been developed for the benefit of all who wished to speak freely. Unfortunately, better communication hadn't worked with the Condorians. They had but one desire—to take everything and kill anyone who wasn't one of them.

Lyra's comrade continued to stare at her without making a single sound. "Can…you…understand…me?" she asked one last time, enunciating every word quite clearly.

He finally stood and backed away.

From where she sat, she felt at a decided disadvantage. The figure towering over her had to be nearly seven feet tall, as wide as a hatch on a cargo frigate. His shoulders, even without the black, unmarked armor, spanned the distance of a full yard and then some. Unlike her headgear, *his* had a pronounced front-piece that appeared very avian in nature. It was as if the designer was trying to emulate the head of a very large predatory flying creature. She'd never seen its like before. Still, there was no doubt in her mind that he was an ally.

Finally, she hauled her tired frame to a standing position then removed her helmet so he could see her more clearly.

Sometimes these alien beings didn't take to speaking without eye-to-eye contact. She couldn't afford to piss this mountainous person off. He represented the only help available.

Her companion simply tilted his head the other direction and kept staring down at her. She knew she wasn't the most attractive human at the moment. Grime and sweat ran in rivulets over her face, neck, and body. She could feel it even if she couldn't see it. Without oxygen canisters, the body armor was left unsealed so the user could breathe. That resulted in every bit of dirt getting in.

He seemed to study her uniform markings carefully. Even from a great distance, anyone as familiar with allied patches could tell she was an Earther and was ranked Master Sergeant. She'd only announced that fact along with her name and unit designation as a matter of habit. Still, the painted emblem of Earth, surrounded by its telltale starry circle, was clearly emblazoned on her right shoulder and over the left breastplate of her armor. Her helmet had the same emblem plastered all over both sides. He couldn't mistake her origin, but he just wasn't communicating.

She stood for a long moment considering what to do. Her last thought before blacking out had been of death. Not rescue. And this silent giant wasn't helping her overtired brain make sense of the situation.

• • •

Soldar Nar had heard of Earth women being sent to fight on behalf of their world. But her sudden appearance in this desolate, lonely place was utterly astonishing.

Women from his home world of Craetoria simply didn't battle.

Indeed, women in most of the Allied Forces were rare. *This* one was not only in the middle of a very deadly confrontation, but happened to be quite arresting despite the dust and sweat all over her face. Once her helmet was off, he took full stock of a suddenly beguiling sight, something surreal and incomprehensible in this horrible combat zone. Her eyes stared up at him questioningly. Because of the hazy, dirty atmosphere he guessed they might be bright blue. For a moment, he found his mind consumed with the hue. Then he mentally shook himself and considered the rest of her appearance. She didn't seem harmed by his having jerked her into the cave.

Her short brown hair curled just beneath her chin and fell over her forehead in long, wavy wisps. She had a straight, perfect nose that spoke of fine breeding. Her cheekbones were high and elegant. Moreover, her full lips were slightly parted, as if she was about to speak again. Clearly she was as at a loss as he.

Right before he'd grabbed her, the woman had turned to fight her last. Her steadfast inclination to accept fate was apparent in the way she'd leveled her weapon against the oncoming enemy. She'd spread her legs and assumed a stance of absolute resolve.

The exhibition of courage cemented his determination to save this noble ally. At that time, however, he hadn't known this valiant fighter was a woman. He'd believed *her* to be a *he* of very small stature. Now he knew her gender, everything changed.

He felt parts of his body respond magnificently. Except for the absence of a left cheek mark, she could be any woman on his world.

More to the point, he had hadn't seen a woman of *any* race in more than a year. If the Condorians had gotten their hands on this one, he couldn't imagine what she'd have suffered.

Thoughts of his sisters, his mother, and other kinswomen came to mind. If anyone had touched them the way the Condorians would have ravaged this stunning creature, he'd have butchered every last one of them no matter how long it took.

How could Earthers allow their most prized citizens into the middle of battle? Were they really as foolish as others claimed?

He'd seen their men as gallant fighters. Why would they so risk their women? Why would this questioning beauty be in this Creator-forsaken wilderness, fighting all alone and with no hope for survival?

"It's clear there's something wrong with your communicator," she told him. "There are no markings on your uniform but I know damned well you're no Condorian." She suddenly coughed to get a thick layer of dust out of her throat and mouth. When she recovered, she tried to communicate her intentions. "Look…I'm checkin' outta here. You can try to get back to your unit or you can follow me. That second option is best since two of us are more likely to survive." She raised one gloved hand and pointed toward the cave entrance. "We…can't…stay…here. It isn't safe. Those Condorians might be back and the sniveling cowards will come with company. Do you understand?"

He remained silent. His mind just wasn't absorbing her presence. Something deep in his head told him she wasn't supposed to be there. He kept searching for an answer to her presence but his intuition revealed nothing.

"Leave or stay…what's it gonna be?"

He mentally shook himself back into reality and finally responded.

"The Condorians are all dead," he electronically blurted in perfect English. "They didn't call for backup or reinforcements would have been here by now." His helmet speaker blocked more of his voice than hers had. His mouthpiece made his response sound quite automated.

It was her turn to be taken aback. He saw her brows rise. Her pretty, bow-shaped lips fell open, probably shocked to hear him speak her language so proficiently. He was still struck by the twisted situation. Her presence was wrong. He couldn't dispel the shock of it.

Finally, he haltingly raised his hands and considered removing his helmet. This Earther might have never seen a Craetorian's face. His people were ordered to keep their helmets on and speak as little as possible to allied brethren. It was thought that fraternization might prove demoralizing. His superiors believed it was hard enough watching those from one's home world die. How much more difficult would it be to have troops inflicted with the site of newly befriended, slaughtered allies. All this considered, the circumstances surrounding his presence—and hers—called for creativity. His mission came first. He must do what he must. She wouldn't find his face shocking. His features would be the same as her human countenance with but a singular difference.

• • •

Lyra couldn't place his armor or helmet at all but that really wasn't unusual. With so many different worlds fighting the Condorians—whose silver and metallic armor was arrogantly meant to be visible—it didn't matter where any allied warrior originated. All that mattered was that they kept fighting.

There were a few planets, including Earth, whose dignitaries and generals regularly conferred as to battle plans. At Lyra's low rank she wasn't privy to their strategies. She just took orders. So if there was a new, friendly race in the battle she welcomed their presence. It wasn't as if the enemy was running out of fighters.

When her comrade took off his helmet, Lyra barely saw his face in the half light. He seemed to realize his body was shadowed and quickly stepped into a brighter area. This was how she got her first good look at a race that was at the front of every battle. She'd heard of them but had always been sent to fight in areas they weren't present.

"I'm Colonel Soldar Nar, Fifth Planetary Pulsar Unit for Craetoria. At least, my rank translates to Colonel in your language," he announced.

She shook her head in vague recollection. Earth English was rumored to be one of several dialects spoken on his world. Since it was the most universally broadcast, a lot of other races used it. His unexpected familiar greeting made her feel easier. It was a relief to know that neither of them would need any translation devices.

"I've heard of your race," she congenially acknowledged, "but I'm afraid I've never seen one of your people, sir." With that being said, she'd still have recognized the piercing eyes and long blond hair that spilled onto his shoulders when his helmet was removed. The black slash mark originating from the corner of his left eye down his strong cheekbone bore further proof of his heritage. That feature was one of the Craetorian attributes about which her Earth colleagues regularly gossiped. As they'd described, it *did* look exactly like a black electric bolt.

"Where is the rest of your platoon?" Soldar asked.

She briefly lowered her gaze.

"I see." He gestured to the empty cave around him. "My insertion team met the same fate when we landed. I heard the howling of those brutes chasing you and knew some allied fighter was their target. I took position in this cave and waited, but you'd turned to fight off the whole pack by yourself." He waited for her response, but she made none. "I apologize for having incapacitated you, but it was necessary. As I said, I don't believe they had time to call for backup or we'd have been attacked." He sighed, pushed his hair away from his face, and turned his head away to spit dust out of his mouth. When he gazed on her again, his words conveyed his admiration. "You're quite the bold one, Sergeant. The cowards had you at seven-to-one."

Lyra snorted. "Sir, couldn't you have just called out that you were here? Then we could have taken that pack together."

"I hadn't time. And I'm not supposed to be seen by anyone, not even one of the allies. I've told you, I was part of an insertion team. I'm under top secret orders. That means *you're* under those orders now."

"Excuse me?"

"I'm pulling rank, Sergeant. General Elias Shafter sent us here. I'm in his command. That makes me, as ranking officer, your superior. And no, you may not ask why an Earth general is issuing orders to a Craetorian colonel."

"Christ! I don't even want to guess," she readily confirmed as she straightened her body armor and shook her head in amazement. "Whatever the hell is goin' on...I don't mind you being responsible. I'm just here to fight." She shrugged and stared up at him. "So what're our orders?"

"I suggest you get some rest. We sit tight for another hour. Then we move due east."

She watched him lean against a far wall and toss back the thick blond hair that, even in the dim light, draped down his body like a shimmering cloak. She surmised his helmet would be back in place before they left the cave, otherwise that glowing pelt would be plainly visible in the half light of the Reisen Four evening. The presence of such long hair was another unusual characteristic of his race. Locker-room gossip had bestowed some very godlike characteristics on his people.

Was it true they were stronger than almost any other ally and could fight like madmen? Could they go without water for days, and did they have no problem eating rodents and insects they found under logs and rocks?

She tried not to smile as she recalled other, more intimate gossip concerning his race.

Was it true they made love with all the stamina of a photon infusion engine? Were they able to please their partners so thoroughly that their mates stayed by their sides for life?

She looked away before he caught her staring, but lifted one hand to her own short locks. They were matted and dirty. She was sure they didn't shine the way his thick mane did.

When she'd first left Earth as a cadet, she'd had her entire head completely shorn. Over the years, she'd let it grow and now kept it below ear length. It fit uniform codes, was easy to maintain, and didn't obstruct her view. Nobody out here cared what she looked like. Even the Condorians didn't give a damn. That she was a woman was enough for them.

For some odd reason, she wondered about the women of *his* world. Was it true they were as tall as the men? Did they crave Earth chocolate so much that they'd really smuggled it through blockades?

She shook her head. The inappropriate nature of these queries was obvious. What did any of that matter? None of them would live long since the Condorians couldn't be stopped. There were so damned many of them. They'd taken over almost half the galaxy and were on their way to finish the job.

As she leaned against a wall and slid to the ground, she looped her hand on her now empty holster. The hole where her weapon *should* be made her go rigid. She gazed down at it and felt her heart begin to pound.

"Son-of-a-bitch! I lost my sidearm. It's still out there somewhere." She stood and quickly began to search the immediate area around her before making her way outside the small cave.

"You didn't lose it," he advised as he pulled her weapon from under his armor. "I picked it up after rendering you unconscious. I only had three volleys and hoped you had more. Luckily you did."

"Sir?"

"I took out seven Condorians so we now have two volleys left. Both of them are in my weapon. The men chasing you had no remaining laser power. It appears they intended to do you in with one of these."

He showed her a long knife within his right boot top, then carefully handed back her empty sidearm.

She angrily slid her empty pistol back into its holster. The top of the Condorian blade she'd liberated still stuck out of her own boot. "I know you must have been firing fast, sir, but couldn't you have left me one round…in case I get caught?"

"Master Sergeants who lose their weapons don't deserve spare rounds."

She scowled. "Sir, you clearly saw my uniform. You could have stood beside me and helped. Instead of acting like any other ally, you rendered me unconscious, emptied the only weapon I had, and are now insinuating I was careless in losing my sidearm. I hardly think that's a fair summation—"

"Cool off, Earther. It was a joke."

"By the way…what *did* you do to me?" she asked as she rubbed the back of her neck.

"I used a lateral vascular neck restraint. I think that's the politically correct term nowadays for a choke hold." He smiled. "Its effects are only wearing off, or you'd have been questioning me about my actions sooner."

She put her hands on her hips and glared at him.

"I am sorry about taking you to the ground," he apologized. "But when I grabbed you, you turned to fight. I had a few seconds before that pack came barreling down the canyon. I didn't have time to answer questions."

"I suppose this is the part where I'm supposed to thank you?"

"Your sarcasm isn't welcome, Sergeant. I should have left you safely in this cave, coming back to consciousness on your own, without seeing me." He shrugged. "I had a surge of conscience and couldn't leave a comrade alone in this wasteland. You've seen me now and I've conscripted you for a mission. My actions make me responsible for your safety."

"Really? I thought that was *my* job."

"Get over it," he shot back. "We're a team now, whether either of us likes it or not. But to set the record straight as to your ability to look after yourself, I require an answer to just one question."

"Sir?"

"Why did you run into a canyon with no outlet? Were you not properly briefed about how many were present in this area? You're a supervisor. Did you not check maps before landing to fight?"

She rolled her eyes and let out a long, frustrated sigh. "Okay...I made a wrong turn. I screwed up!"

"I can live with the explanation, though you may *not* have. Let's just say we've both had better days. You and I have survived to learn lessons."

"What lessons?"

"You won't run into dead-ends...and I won't lose my weapons, inclusive of all the ammunition, or my entire team!"

He stood, angrily thrust his helmet back on his head, and stalked toward the cave entrance. Once there, she saw him gaze outside.

She finally understood.

He was feeling guilt over surviving. When she'd run toward him—being chased by Condorians bent on peeling her skin off— he saw his chance at vengeance. She'd just been in his way.

This cave, wherever it was, was probably the place where he and his team were supposed to have waited until later in the night. Then, they'd probably have gone about finishing whatever mission they'd planned. But, like so many plans the allies composed, nobody could maneuver against twenty-to-one odds. As she saw it, they were both lucky to be alive.

She almost let the incident go. However, her rescuer now had two shots in his weapon. He'd used hers on the enemy and that situation had to be addressed. She pulled on her helmet and approached him once more.

"Sir?"

"What now, Sergeant?"

"If we get caught you've got all our firepower. Will you make sure they don't take me alive?"

He turned his helmeted head toward her. "Count on it, Sergeant Lyra Markham!"

The corners of her mouth lifted.

His powerfully worded promise to see her die painlessly was acceptable. They now had the makings of a team. For however long they lasted.

Chapter 2

They trudged past the bodies of the Condorians Soldar had killed and into the night.

Lyra automatically reached for the side compartment in her hip armor. But once she opened it, grabbed the marked flask of water, and recalled she'd emptied the container hours ago, she angrily shoved it back. She had enough bio-tabs to clarify any kind of cesspool. There just wasn't a drop of even foul water in sight. Nothing lay before them but rocky, sepia-toned hills and shadowed dirt.

Soldar stopped, opened his own armor compartment, and offered her a fresh water flask. "Stop here. We'll rest a while." He pulled his helmet off as he spoke.

"Thank you for the water, sir."

"How long had you been running from those warriors?" he casually asked as he knelt, shook his hair back, and sipped from their shared container when she offered it back.

"I don't know for sure." She shrugged and checked her wristband readout. "Maybe three hours before I ran into that canyon. Which reminds me," she said as she took the container again and sipped, "thank you for saving my life. I owe you one."

"Before we're out of this, I'm sure you'll repay the favor."

"Any time, sir."

"I was thinking of sooner than later."

She tilted her head and stared at him, scooting closer to his location while still kneeling. "Sir?"

"As I told you, you're now on my team. While landing much earlier today, our light-pods were shot down along with all our supplies. I was the only survivor to crawl from the wreckage. There should have been four men with me. If I'd failed in my mission and hadn't made it back to a point where they were supposed to wait, one of them would have taken my place. That was to have kept up until one of us succeeded or all of us were dead."

"Should I be hearing this, sir? I mean, I don't have security clearance for any field op of this nature. I may be on your team but this sounds way over my head."

"As I see it I don't have a choice. I need a backup plan. You're all I've got."

She arched one brow. "Thanks…I think."

He shook his head and smiled. "I *meant* that I need help. This plan must succeed. It might be a way to save thousands of lives."

That caught her interest. The very nature of the words and the way he uttered them meant this was something big. "How, sir? What's goin' on?"

He huddled closer and pointed due east, toward a small pile of rocks and an escarpment on the other side of them. "About two clicks away, there's supposed to be an oasis. At least it passes for one on this damnable rock-of-a-planet. It's located just on the other side of that outcrop. We'll find water, food, and some civilian clothing there."

Lyra moved closer and was almost mesmerized by his silvery gaze. Even in the hazy light, the brightness of his eyes was striking. "So this is an undercover operation?"

"It is. Though my contact was expecting five men, she'll get one man and one woman. Before going in we'll have to come up with some different story than planned."

She sipped more water and nodded for him to go ahead with his explanation. Whatever "going in" meant, it didn't sound like her idea of fun.

"About three clicks past the oasis, a pleasure cruiser has landed on the surface. She's called the Venus and she's now officially listed as a Condorian haven. One of our enemy's commanding officers took her over as his base of operations. He did this while his ground forces slaughtered ours."

"Sir, how do you know all this, or should I ask?"

He gazed into her face for one long moment. "If you're captured out here, you'll need that spare round in my laser. I'll need one too. We can't be forced into talking."

"I-I understand," Lyra insisted when he hesitated.

Soldar continued. "The woman who owns the pleasure ship is an allied spy. Her name is Aigean Florn. She saw most of her family decimated by Condorian raiders while running a brothel on Taurus Stellar. The allies managed to save two granddaughters. They are being protecting on my home world of Craetoria. She figures she owes us."

Lyra nodded. "If Condorian commanding officers are on the Venus, you must mean to get aboard and take the ship out. If she relocates, you'd still be on the ship and might find a way give her location to our fleet." She paused. "What about the innocents working aboard?"

"If all we wanted to do was blow that particular pleasure ship into infinity, we have a current fix and could do it. The problem is, once they know about the vessel, about a thousand enemy officers located elsewhere would simply move up and take the place of those few we'd manage to kill." He shook his head. "No… destroying the Venus and the Condorian officers on her is only part of the mission—the very last part," he maintained as one hand curled into a fist. "I mean to get aboard, stay alive as long as possible, and collate the information Aigean's people are obtaining concerning enemy battle plans. It's come to her attention that Condorians like to talk when they're full of illegal drugs and liquor and have been sated by whoring." He swallowed some more water before continuing. "The Condorians kept Aigean and her crew alive only to provide high-ranking officers with a luxurious place to quarter and exploit her prostitutes. They do this in virtual secrecy from their own troops. Their minions would turn on them for withholding pleasures in a war zone."

"That's for sure. The average Condorian is nothing but a damned savage! It's long been my opinion that their superiors just point 'em in the right direction and let 'em go. They're like a pack of feral beasts. They don't have any compunction about killing wounded, or consciences when it comes to leaving civilians out of the fray. "

"For the very reason you've just mentioned, the ship's presence isn't widely known among Condorian underlings."

"Yeah. I get it. There are a lot more Condorian fighters than superiors. They're kept in reasonable control by the promise of keeping goods pillaged after battle."

Soldar slowly nodded. "As long as Aigean provides those Condorian supervisors with the pleasure they seek, they let her and her crew survive. But she knows the Venus' days are numbered. She and her crew will eventually become expendable. Especially as enemy officers seek to keep her a secret from their own ground troops," he confirmed. "It's to our advantage that Aigean recruits men and women from all over the known universe. Most have families that've suffered at Condorian hands. According to what was relayed when she last made contact, her employees will readily give us the information gleaned from their nightly liaisons."

"What else, sir?"

He gazed at their surroundings before answering then he turned and moved closer. "Because of Aigean's covert information, we're learning of future battle plans in this sector. She was able to get word of Condorian tactics by leaving microchips that had been secretly recorded on her ship, and then embedded in beacon markers. The beacons were left on planets recently decimated in battle. Our forces found the first one with dead allied bodies. The circumstances surrounding its discovery were odd enough that allied agents opened it and located her message—"

"Of course! Aigean's civilian rescue beacons would be of no concern to the Condorians since they'd transmit exactly like those that are set off by thousands of dying allied fighters…all of whom are slaughtered by the enemy as they lay wounded." She shook her head in amazement. "It's a brilliant plan! Condorians don't bother turning off beacons. The transmissions draw allied medical vessels forward," she confirmed. "That's the reason why most of us won't activate our personal transmitters unless we're damned sure the Condorians have moved on. Nobody wants to get our hospital ships destroyed. We haven't got that many left."

"Precisely! Many injured warriors die for want of a doctor's care. They refuse to turn on their distress units. As Aigean relayed, Condorian officers always order her to land the Venus near a battle, but away from the front lines. They sate themselves while their warriors take out our forces. As she relays, Condorian elite direct battles from her pleasure rooms."

"*Bastards!*"

"I concur. There has never been a more insidious enemy. Condorians are little more than parasites feeding off the rest of us. But their supreme belief in victory has provided a hole in their defenses. Aigean has left word of Condorian battle plans in numerous beacons on a dozen worlds. As you've surmised, their transmissions are the same as thousands coming from a destroyed planet. Hiding her information thus was yielding information we couldn't have gleaned any other way. It was always correct. Her efforts were a huge risk, but they were paying off. Unfortunately, her *last* message was longer. It seems to have been recorded in segments, over a number of days. In it, she advised us that she wouldn't be able to contact us again. What she had to say was highly concerning."

Lyra swallowed hard. "She was about to be caught?"

"No…not *her*. But some of her people were killed when they wouldn't respond to questions Condorian generals put to them. Enemy strategists became suspicious of allied fighters showing up to defend mining outposts like this one." He pointed to the ground to indicate Reisen Four. "Allies were showing up to fight in greater numbers with better armament. The Condorians believed someone—possibly from the Venus—was leaking information."

"So…that's that," Lyra said. "If Condorian officers suspected Aigean's crew, using beacons to communicate isn't an option now. And she and her crew are probably done for."

"Aigean last relayed that Condorians searched for and destroyed any required rescue equipment she had, including transmitters. She barely managed to get a last one off the ship. Obviously, it included information I'm telling you."

She stared at him for a long moment. "I don't understand what your unit could do now. Even if you could disguise yourself, get on Aigean's ship, and slowly gather information about future battle plans, how would you transmit it? Every civilian aboard will be watched. The bridge would be well guarded."

"There is one more chance. It's a plan Aigean previously suggested in the event we had no options. We're at that point." He pushed his hair back and wiped sweat from his eyes.

"This is gonna suck, isn't it?"

"It's the last chance to get aboard the Venus," he said.

Lyra sighed. "Okay…let's hear it."

"Once the Condorians overran her ship, it was obviously impossible for Aigean to contact Allied HQ via her own bridge. She hasn't any encryption codes that would validate her transmission and, as you say, the bridge is constantly watched."

"May I speak freely, sir?"

"Please do."

"The Condorians would have enacted their own locking codes into the Venus' com system."

He tilted his head in acknowledgement. "*Very good!* You know your enemy's battle tactics, Sergeant. But this is the part where I delineate the last chance I spoke of."

"You actually think you can unlock those codes and transmit battle plans after the captain of the vessel or some of her crew was suspected of leaking information?" Lyra rolled her eyes in contempt. "*Sir*...if the Condorians were watching her and staff before they suspected anything was wrong, what the hell do you think they'll do to secure their battle plans now? You have a better chance of slipping in and out of hell than getting on that bridge! In fact, any stranger who gets near the Venus will probably be killed." She lifted one hand in supplication. "As you've said, the only rational reason Aigean and her crew are still alive is that they're still servicing the Condorian officers. Can't you see that the Condorians might take out that crew today, tomorrow, or any time they choose? How long do you think you'd have?" Her entreaty was met with silence. Lyra noted his steady gaze and that his expression remained undaunted. She tried once more. "Sir, *please*...there are about a hundred reasons why this won't work. I may be some lowly Sergeant, but I've got sense enough to see that trying to get on the Venus is suicide! We can ill afford the useless loss of another spec-op boss."

"I have my orders, Sergeant. I'm to get on the Venus and deliver to the allies what information I can, by whatever means and for as long as possible. Had I failed, one of my team was to pursue the same plan. Fortunately, the enemy didn't know who my men were or what they were up to when we took a barrage of laser fire while trying to land. We were just another group of allied soldiers for slaughter." He leaned forward. "But since they are dead...I now have *you*," he finished while pointedly staring at her.

"I'll try again," she insisted. "Your mission doesn't make any sense. Listen to reason!"

"You speak, I'll listen. But I will never be convinced to quit."

"Colonel...you said yourself that your supplies were all destroyed. I assume that included some kind of disguise to get you aboard. How is a Craetorian—a man from a known allied planet—supposed to get on a pleasure vessel where Condorian officers are fucking themselves crazy? You'll be killed on sight. Even if you *could* pass yourself off as someone from a different race, you'd be another male vying for the attention of the sex servants. The Condorians wouldn't stand for that. Hell, I'm surprised that someone didn't suggest cosmetic surgery to make you and your team look like Condorians. On an operation like this, that would be necessary! You should have been better briefed, given fake credentials, and assigned fake names and backgrounds that would make sense if checked against some database."

He slowly smiled. "You don't know everything, Sergeant. There are a few mysteries in this universe that even you Earthlings haven't unraveled."

"I don't understand."

"If Aigean didn't think this would work, she wouldn't have suggested a plan that would get her and her people slaughtered immediately. What would be the point?"

"That's exactly what I'm asking, sir."

He continued his argument. "According to her, the Condorian admiral on her vessel has developed a taste for men. Even those from allied planets are tolerated as long as they assert their neutrality and will make themselves available to any kind of pleasuring. They're useful for a time, even if eventually expendable."

"Th-that's insane," Lyra declared.

"It's true enough. Men from numerous brothels have been recruited to have sex with enemy officers. Condorians find having intercourse with these so-called *neutrals* is not only exotic, but highly enticing."

"If you don't mind me asking, Colonel…*why*?" Lyra choked out.

He raised his brows. "Why does one man want to bed another? Or why do the Condorians want to bed men from allied planets?"

She let out an exasperated gasp. "I *meant*…why would a Condorian tolerate anyone from an allied planet? They don't believe in neutrality. Unless they want to take over a pleasure vessel to screw some doomed whores!"

Soldar suppressed a grin. "Don't you see, Sergeant? What one can't have is always more appealing than what comes easily. Not only that, but this particular admiral takes pleasure out of using men from worlds he believes he'll one day conquer. For him, it's like collecting trophies. It's like rubbing salt into a wound, as you Earthers say."

She simply shook her head in disbelief.

"For this plan…I was to be the new, willing entertainment. As I've told you, another of my team would have taken my place if I'd failed. It would have appeared as though they'd also been recruited as male whores," Soldar continued. "We were to go after enemy battle plans as long as the Venus remained on this planet's surface. Any of us would only have issued a strike command on the vessel when we could no longer obtain information."

"Sir—"

"Aigean has a constant flow of incoming, unusual sexual delights," he insisted. "She offers her sex servants obscene amounts of money and attractive benefits to work on her vessel. Many professional prostitutes can't or won't ignore such lures when their families are starving or their homes have been destroyed by war. Her other employees remain out of loyalty to her and fear for their compatriots should they be caught escaping."

"I-I was wondering how she kept her vessel staffed under such conditions," Lyra mused.

"It seems that many of her employees have no place left to go," he explained. "The Venus is their home. Aigean takes care of them. Her staff is willing to endure the Condorian presence, their sexual proclivities, and threat of death. Many of them want the chance to get their hands around a Condorian's thick neck.

They wait for some way to avenge a dead loved one or their entire families."

"So she says. But—"

"Her information has never been wrong. As to her people, Aigean keeps them in check. She's been ordering them to bide their time. She's playing with the enemy and knows it's a dangerous game. As I've said, patronizing and catering in a war zone are the reasons why she's survived." He momentarily lowered his head. "It was unfortunate that she lost some of her crew when they wouldn't admit to any covert operation. But those lives weren't sacrificed in vain."

Lyra chewed on her lower lip and stared into his eyes. "Did she say how her people were discovered? And do you trust her when she says that the Condorians still don't know who was sending us information? This could be a trap."

"That's occurred to me, Sergeant. But the Condorians would gain very little by luring a few of us into some snare. Such a scheme would hardly be worth the trouble. Especially since my men and I took pains to remain ignorant of current tactics in this area. We simply knew nothing in the way of upcoming battle strategy that could be tortured out of us," he admitted. "To address the rest of your concerns…Aigean was insistent that her employees' deaths be avenged. She relayed that they were caught hiding distress beacons in their quarters though none of the devices contained covert messages. Six were questioned and tortured. They gave up no information, and were slaughtered in front of the rest of the ship's crew as an example." He lifted his hands in a convincing gesture. "To clarify Aigean's purpose, she clearly stated that she'd have 'blood for blood.' It was she who came up with this new plan." He then held up one fist as a show of solidarity. "I believe her. She hasn't betrayed us yet."

"So there's no way to talk you out of this crazy scheme?"

"None. And to specifically address your concern, Aigean told us the origin of her prostitutes has never been an issue with the Condorians. All of the men with me were from different races. It was left for her to explain my presence, or the appearances of those men on my team who followed. She led us to believe that this would be no problem since the current Condorian admiral wants…virile men. As stated, he has a predilection for those from hostile worlds." He shrugged. "I guess I'll do."

Lyra gasped in frustration. "Sir…are you okay with this? Really? I mean…how can you live with the idea of doing such a thing? I can't imagine a worse assignment. Not even if you dropped me onto some planet full of flesh-eating parasites. And what if this plan is somehow exposed? Aigean Florn and all her employees will certainly be slaughtered as spies, right along with you. They won't be given their shot at vengeance. They'll just die when you get caught. So we're right back to where we started."

"You don't give up, do you?" he declared as he shook his head in exasperation. "We were willing to take the chance. We were ready to engage in any sexual fantasy to get the information we need. The Condorians are so sure they'll eventually annihilate us that they cannot imagine we'd go this far," he insisted. "They believe us too weak and frightened to even contemplate such a ruse. And that's exactly why it might work. We're playing to their egos," he attested. "Where secreting battle plans in distress beacons was more efficient, we're now forced to engage more dangerous tactics. We simply must, Sergeant. We're running out of time and people. The Condorians are eradicating us, one planet and one race at a time. We've no choice left!"

"But—"

"Don't go sanctimonious on me, Sergeant! Spies like me have used sexual allure for a very long time. I'm not the first nor shall I be the last. We have men and women in brothels from here to the Antares Alignment who are doing this same thing, under circumstances that are far less comfortable than the amenities provided on a class-five pleasure vessel. I can do it because using sex to get information has always been a ploy, throughout known history, and even on your world if I recall my studies." He snorted. "I remind myself the information I get might just save lives. Up to and including the lives of my family. And besides, while I have my orders I'd have volunteered for this had the opportunity been given. I know exactly what I'm in for. So get over it! It won't be the first time I've been aboard a prostitution vessel, having sex with some man. In fact, I find a certain amount of smug pleasure in bedding an enemy who thinks me too inferior to play mind games. For me it's the ultimate test of my abilities. So…if it makes you feel any better…let's just say I'm a bit sick that way and be done with it," he smilingly finished.

She wasn't so sure he was telling the truth, but it *was* his choice. "All right. So you're into this. But what's my part?"

A very long moment of silence followed.

"I think you already know what you'd have to do," he eventually uttered. "After having explained my place in this charade, there should be no doubt. You'll now replace my team and will come in after me if I should fail."

"I'd actually have to let a Condorian…even one of their slightly more controllable officers…screw me?"

He simply raised one brow in confirmation.

She stood up, stalked away, and put her hands on her hips. After cursing to the sand beneath her feet, she angrily returned and knelt by his side.

"Sir, how do you know…I-I mean…w-what I'm trying to ask is—"

"Just spit it out, Sergeant."

"Sir…thanks again for saving my life. I don't assume that I'd have lived much longer, but every day I do is a blessing." She took a deep breath. "What you're asking is too much." She licked her suddenly dry lips and tried to continue. "We are being eradicated. There's no doubt about that. But I couldn't let one of those sons-of-bitches near me. I-I couldn't!"

"Aigean's people do it every day. We'll be pretending to be just two more of her employees."

"I know, sir. But I have other…personal concerns."

"Explain," he urged.

Lyra swiped her hand across her forehead and tried to continue. "Those of us from Earth take our birth control meds and are inoculated with STD vaccines. None of us is allowed into battle if we aren't one hundred percent clean. The rules are standard in all Earth units. No one can afford to be on the front lines if they're sick. All our remaining medical supplies are being syphoned for those who're fighting. We don't have meds for soldiers irresponsible enough to put their pleasure ahead of our survival." She shuddered and tried to keep going. "There are some incurable strains of VD in existence. There's a rumor out there about some crap a few Condorians have. It's some sickness that's supposed to be so virulent that shots won't help."

"Should we sit back and hope they die of it? Is that what you're suggesting, Sergeant? Because that rumor you've just expounded is the same damnable one I heard two years ago. And even if it's true, I can assure you that there are multi-trillions of Condorians who will wipe us all out while we pray to some higher deity for their demise. In short…we don't have time for a rumor to work!"

"That's not what I'm…" Her words drifted away before she sighed heavily and tried again. She held out her hands in a supplicating gesture. "Sir…you couldn't possibly believe these Condorian animals would accept using a prophylactic. They're nasty, filthy lechers. It's just one more reason why female fighters keep spare rounds in their weapons…if you get my meaning and I think you do. Rot is rot and I can't let some bastard touch me if he's been infected."

He simply stared.

"It would be better if I died in battle."

Soldar put one hand on her shoulder and lowered his voice. "Listen to me, Sergeant…if the Condorians aren't stopped, all our deaths are certain," he firmly promised. "I'm willing to die on this mission. You must use your wits and think—"

"Of what, sir? The only thing fighting women can think about is their dignity and what will happen to our children when those vermin get to Earth. You're dismissing my concerns over the issue because it's a moot point. But it isn't."

"Creator's blood! You have children? And you agreed to fight—"

"No, sir. I don't have kids but I would have liked to someday. In fact, I don't have any family left, thanks to the Condorians. But there are little kids on Earth I don't want those vermin near. That's why some Earth women are here, trying to stop them now. But I've gotta tell you…there are ways to die and then there are ways to go out in pain, agony, and with less dignity than a warrior deserves. I always knew dying was probable. I took that into account when I signed up. All Earth women do. We know we have to fight. There's no choice. But I don't put myself in a position to ask for what you're suggesting. If it comes down to dying, I've made up my mind to meet my maker like the men in my unit. I accept no less."

"I acknowledge your fear," he softly argued. "But what if we succeed in saving other lives, Sergeant? Isn't that why you joined Earth Force to begin with?"

"Yes, sir. It is," she woodenly agreed.

He let out a long, slow breath. "The best we can do is live long enough to get information back to the allies. We'll die when we're caught. That truth negates your anxiety over your future health," he sadly reiterated. "It's our oath to save as many of our people as we can before leaving this life. I'll do that by any means necessary. We must fight until the last breath leaves our bodies. The only difference that this mission will make is in the numbers we might be saving. We might warn thousands of innocent people to escape, even if it means certain death on some future battlefield." He lifted one hand and put his palm against her cheek. "The longer allies last, the greater the chance for all our races to survive. We have to consider the majority and put aside personal concerns. Others are suffering, so we must take comfort in the fact that, for however short a time, we outwitted the enemy. Keep thinking about that and nothing else. You signed up to fight. This is just one more way to do your duty."

She finally lifted her chin, and stared at him for a very long, poignant moment. "Is this an order?"

"I'd rather you came willingly."

She pinched the bridge of her nose between her thumb and forefinger then pointed to the barrens in the distance. "If I run right now, will you use one of your last rounds to shoot me? I'd be refusing a direct order. You'd be well within your rights. Nobody'd question anything since my superiors already think I'm dead. Besides, you won't live through this irresponsible mission long enough to damage my record!"

"If you run, I'll chase you, tackle you to the ground, and bring you right back here," he told her as he pointed toward the dirt at his feet. "You're alive against all reason. You must make use of this chance."

She opened her mouth to argue again, but solemnly closed it and stared into the distance.

"Aigean and her crew are willing to risk everything," he said, pressing his point yet again. "They've been trying to entertain the Condorian officers on their ship though their hatred is equal to ours. We'll be with brave souls. We won't be alone."

"And if nothing comes of this idiotic stunt?" she asked.

"Your insolence isn't appropriate. Neither is your candor, Sergeant. Would you like to rephrase the question?" he angrily asked as he squared his shoulders and glared at her.

She put her hands on her hips and glared back. "If I piss you off enough, maybe you'll kill me."

"Creator's blood! You're unbelievable."

His angry stare continued for what seemed like eternity. But she didn't look away. Anger was all she had left.

"Sergeant Markham…*I* survived bombardment when my men didn't. *You* survived being chased down by a pack of monsters when, by all the odds, you shouldn't have. I'll say it until the mighty mountains of my planet crumble." He pulled her close. "We've both endured for some purpose. Let's take our courage in hand and use this opportunity."

"No matter what you say, sir, the Condorians will kill you on sight. It's impossible to believe that, after they suspected someone aboard that ship for spying, they'd still allow a Craetorian anywhere near it. Even if everyone associated with Aigean Florn swears you're neutral." She drew herself up for one last comment. "And finally…even if I did this, I could at least pass myself off as being from any one of a hundred humanoid worlds the enemy hasn't invaded yet. But that birthmark on your face is clear evidence of your heritage. Why didn't you have it removed before attempting something so crazy? What was Allied Command thinking?"

He touched the black lightning bolt on his left cheek and stared straight into her eyes. "The Condorians *will* accept my presence as a new prostitute. In fact, there's no doubt in my mind."

Lyra wasn't convinced and had the sudden feeling he was hiding something. His gaze never wavered, but she had intuition on her side. That inner warning system had never let her down.

She kept gazing at him and something in his silver-colored eyes remained veiled. Even in the dust of the hazy evening, she could see the absolute resolution embedded in his expression.

A lie was a lie no matter who told it. And Colonel Soldar Nar couldn't hide the deception.

"For the last time I'll say it. Then let this discussion be over. This mission is a go. Your orders are clear, Sergeant."

She looked away. It was as though she wasn't there any longer. Her opinion didn't matter. For some reason she should have died today and hadn't. For that brief respite from the hereafter, she was doomed to pay. Death would have its due.

She'd have to go in that ship when he couldn't get information and was killed. She'd be forced to play a willing prostitute to a butchering, savage race of beings who treated their own women with deadly disdain.

Despair threatened to overwhelm her. She had to find a way out of this.

After a long moment of terrible silence, a window opened in her head. An idea exploded in her brain. It was like some higher force just stuck it there in answer to her riveting fear of being touched by any Condorian. The answer was ridiculously simple. "What if we gave the Condorians something they'd rally to see?"

"I said the discussion was over!"

She grabbed his forearm and, even though his body armor was thick, she still felt the strength of mighty muscle contracting beneath her fingers. "Sir…if we're going to die to get war plans out of a few commanding officers, how much more info could we get if *many* of them flocked to the biggest show in this sector of space?"

He tilted his head.

She interpreted his silence as a willingness to finally listen.

"You said the Condorian leaders crave things they can't have. We all know that's why they're invading every world between here and the end of the known universe."

Again, he said nothing.

"What if they could be induced to watch while you and I are having sex? What if Aigean bills us as the biggest sex duo in the history of brothels?"

"Explain."

"You and me, sir. It'd be safer if we stayed together. And we'd have a better chance of getting information to allied command."

He glared at her then began to slowly smile. "What a transformation!"

"Sir?"

"Your expression," he explained. "You just went from a woman who looked as though death was at her shoulder to someone who wants to fight again."

"Please tell me my idea is acceptable," she begged.

"All right…let's consider this." He paused for a long moment. "There's one flaw I can think of right away…how are we supposed to get information if we aren't sleeping with the enemy?"

"We play hard to get for as long as we can, sir. We make ourselves a couple of divas…unapproachable and unattainable. If those perverted Condorian bastards really want what they can't have, let 'em break down doors to see us. Our disinterest to their presence should dispel suspicion." She rallied and explained more fully. "If we're acting like pampered, aloof snobs while attracting as much attention as possible, how could we be spies? As you said, the Condorian ego is a pretty sturdy thing. They wouldn't believe us capable of walking on board and making ourselves so obvious," she maintained. "And listen to this—"

"Do I have an alternative?"

"Colonel, we can't just stroll onto Aigean's bridge. We could get all the information in the universe then have no way to transmit it." She lifted one hand in entreaty. "But we could be *invited* onto the bridge if we acted as though we're special from the start. Even Condorians get star-struck. I've heard they've kidnapped a few prominent actors and singers from worlds they've invaded. It's been reported that their officials force these captive performers to entertain on demand. We could use that to our advantage."

He ran a hand over his chin in contemplation. "Condorian leaders *are* obsessed with anything that's rare." He lifted his brows in consideration. "There's actually some merit in what you say. But you'd really be willing to pass yourself off as my sex partner?"

"Right…like I wouldn't sleep with you and would rather wallow with a Condorian bottom feeder!"

He laughed outright. "I'm fairly certain that was an insult but I'll ignore it. This time."

She looped her arm through his and ignored his shocked glance at the gesture. "Look, Colonel…your original plan isn't working all that well for me. But this is another choice."

"Sergeant, there's no guarantee the Condorians won't demand our services individually. You must know that."

"There's no guarantee that they won't shoot us when we arrive. Hell," she griped, "they'd kill me if I was found out here in the wastelands even assuming you'd let me stay here and you won't!"

"That certainty is inescapable." He rubbed his chin in thought. "But I believe this was what I was trying to convey when I first outlined my original plan. Your sudden change in attitude, when facing the same probable outcome at Condorian hands, is confounding to say the least."

"Look, if they demand me as a single, I can always take myself out. I'll at least have time to find a knife or something. This Aigean person could say I was depressed or mentally unbalanced. And you could still go on to do your thing."

"Why in the universe is discussing your demise…making you so…ecstatic?"

"At any other time, it'd be sick. But look where we are, sir."

He pulled at the collar of his uniform before speaking again. "You simply see a way of doing aboard the Venus what you would have done had I not rescued you back at the cave. You're determined to die. And have it your way."

She shrugged. "I think my idea can work, sir. It's better than me following you in like one of your men would have. I don't know this Aigean woman. She might not trust me. You've at least seen her communication."

"Considering how your optimism has risen since suggesting this, perhaps your plan is prudent. I *do* need you on that vessel. While my original team was better prepared, two of us is all there is." He picked up several rocks and tossed them into a sand dune before pushing his long hair back and shifting his position. "My reason for commanding your presence on this mission was two-fold. First, your death in the wasteland wouldn't serve as high a purpose. Second, if one of us fails the other might succeed. The only problem left is that I'm not sure how Aigean would explain both of us arriving at the same time. Her plan was to have a new male plaything to service the Condorian admiral." He rubbed the back of his neck with one hand. "I suppose we could always say that you came along as a…the Earth word for it suddenly escapes me…"

"Freebie," she supplied as she saw her only way of dealing with the situation taking root. "Let me do this with you, Colonel. Don't leave me out here to come in after you. We can argue until we go hoarse, but we'll always come back to one conclusion."

"And that is?"

"We both believe we're gonna die. I want to go down fighting. I don't want to check out knowing that I'd willingly got in bed with a Condorian." She shuddered. "Christ! If you'd left me to fight out here on my own, I'd have had that option. Since you've ordered me to go to the Venus, I don't."

"I am sorry, Sergeant. Your propensity to keep stating the obvious is wearing thin. I didn't want you in this predicament any more than you wished to be here."

She appealed to his sense of chivalry, assuming he had one. "Orders may be orders. But crazy plots devised by generals sitting in comfortable quarters, on some safe vessel in outer space, are way over my pay grade." She slowly shook her head. "Is there any way in this galaxy that you can convince this Aigean person to change the plans?"

"I don't know."

Lyra remained silent for a long moment then came at him from a different angle. "Do you have anyone back home that you care for, sir?"

He exhaled loudly. "Your blatant attempt at psychology is pointless, Sergeant. I'm not that dull-witted. I know the ploy when I hear it. But, to answer your question, yes…I have a family that I care about. Deeply."

"You must miss your wife."

"No…that wasn't the kind of family I meant. There's been no time for any one woman. I can ill afford the emotional drain that being so far from a mate and children would cause. So I remain without them." He paused before speaking more softly. "I-I had a younger brother…he's been missing-in-action for some time. Aside from him, my loved ones remain safe on Craetoria…at least for the time being. Last I heard the Condorians were only a year from invading my home."

"I'm sorry the enemy is so near your planet," Lyra said honestly. "And *very* sorry that your brother is missing. Maybe you'll see him—"

"I thank you for your concern. You know what missing-in-action means as well as I." He nodded in confirmation. "He is dead and that's an end to this conversation."

Lyra sat and waited for any other option to come to mind. None did. It seemed like the hand of death hovered over them both. Their choices were over.

"You're very good at winding emotions to your end, Sergeant. You're trying to get under my skin so that my duty isn't clear. You want me to see you as a substitute for someone I care for, and give in to your desire to stay out here and fight alone."

"No, sir. I'm not trying to make this all about me. I just wanted you to understand the fear every woman is living with these days. It's not something that can be trained out of you. There's no book a female cadet can read that will make her less terrified of Condorians. But we put on a uniform and we fight anyhow," she proudly told him. "We do it because we believe in freedom and because we have the right to survive." She hesitated then followed with, "I have no family left. My two brothers died early in the war. My parents were botanists who were killed by Condorian pirates." She struggled to keep the rage from her voice. "I-I expect to see them in the afterlife. It's what I believe. So I'm fighting for them. And I know they wouldn't want one of those foul, ugly, lewd, deviant bastards touching me." She stared straight into Soldar's eyes.

He sighed heavily, shook his head, and stared upward before gazing at her again. "I have never met one person so persistent that the senses are completely scrambled. You are the very personification of belligerence. All right, Sergeant," he finally relented while dragging his hands through his hair. "We'll play this your way. Aigean will have to come up with some excuse to get us on that ship. As a duo."

Lyra let out a shaky sigh. "Thank you, Colonel. You won't regret this. It's a better choice. I feel it. And I'm never wrong about these things!"

Soldar reached for his helmet. "For the love of all that's holy… enough talk! From now on, use only first names. If we're to do this, we should know at least that much about each other. Now… let's get to that oasis."

• • •

Soldar slid down the hillside to the murky pond below. Cascading rock and dirt followed him as he skidded to a stop. His new partner followed, but he kept his eyes on the surroundings.

"*This* is somebody's idea of an oasis?" Lyra joked.

He nodded. The place was nothing if not barren. "Don't try to drink this. My people tell me that even a purifying tablet won't work. There are supposed to be supplies, including water, somewhere near. Help me look," he ordered.

Lyra did as she was commanded.

When he later saw that she'd stopped moving and appeared mesmerized by something, he pulled off his helmet, shook his hair back, and approached.

In front of her, on the ground, lay a trunk. It had been shoved underneath an overhanging rock and was so nearly the color of the landscape that it would have been almost impossible to see had she not walked right up on it. He pulled it out from under the overhang, put his gloved palm on the lid, and prayed it wasn't rigged to explode. Condorian officers preferred to kill their enemies where they could witness the carnage from a safe distance. If they were out there somewhere, traps could be set anywhere. Despite his assertion they wouldn't set snares for only two allies, he hadn't survived this long without due caution.

"Here goes," he warned as he watched Lyra back away. Her quick-footed response told him she knew at least as much about the enemy's ground strategy as most officers of his acquaintance. He pulled the lid open with one swift jerk. When nothing happened Lyra moved closer.

What was inside caused them to simultaneously gasp.

Inside the large container lay every kind of delicacy. He was so shocked that he momentarily remained as still as she. Neither of them could have accessed the food in that trunk for years. They weren't available on most allied planets these days.

He reached for a large piece of citrus fruit that lay in a basket. It was at this point that Lyra finally pulled her helmet off. He glanced between the fruit and her face. "How long has it been since you've seen anything but a dried protein pack?"

"I-I don't remember," Lyra replied, almost inaudibly. "Where did all this come from?"

He put his attention on the rest of the trunk's contents. There was a great deal of food that could have only been obtained from looting. In this sector of space, such fare didn't exist for the average fighter or colonist.

Along with the fruit was a wrapped loaf of bread, rashers of what looked like some kind of dried beef, and bottles of clear, cooled water. "The Condorian leaders have made themselves a very generous haven of Aigean Florn's ship. I don't think for a moment that it's to pay her back for her staff's sexual favors. The savages simply don't want to do without. Certainly not as the rest of the galaxy is existing!" he remarked bitterly. When Soldar handed her the piece of citrus, he was shocked to see her back away. "What's wrong?"

"How many people died to grow this and to keep the tree it came from hidden? There has to be child somewhere needing it. My friends would have done *anything* to have had a piece of fresh fruit before they were butchered."

Her poignant, softly spoken words cut right into his heart. Every syllable rang with heartfelt honesty. "Take the fruit, Lyra. Remember what we've come here to do. Remember that the sons-of-bitches who've inflicted us with every kind of horror will pay for what they've wrought. *Our* races may not live to see that day, but it *will* come. And with every bite you take, remind yourself of those you've lost and what they suffered," he insisted. "Stay strong and healthy so we can keep our wits and do the job. We do this for those we left behind."

Shakily, Lyra pulled off her right glove and gently reached out for the fruit.

Tears began to fall down her cheeks unchecked. In that single moment, he wanted to be somewhere else with this strong, loyal woman. Perhaps in some garden on his own world where flowers still grew, birds still sang, and no irradiated clouds filled the skies. It was an overwhelming daydream to have in the middle of a grubby, colorless world. His life and hers weren't their own. Neither of them would see their homes again. But that piece of fruit now represented everything most of the galaxy had lost. He handed her a small knife from the bottom of the trunk. It wasn't big enough to use as a weapon, nor was it very sharp.

"Cut it with this," he gently instructed.

She took the blade, cut the orange, and handed him half. "Please, take some. I-I'm not sure I could stomach all of it after living so long on protein packs."

He took the small knife from her and dropped it back into the trunk as she handed him his share. As they bit into their portions, their eyes met. The woman still didn't realize she was crying. When something salty hit his lips, he realized that *he* was weeping as well.

It was only a piece of fruit. But it meant everything. And in that moment, some connection was forged that would never break. He realized he'd never forget this desert-planet Master Sergeant, assuming they lived long enough to go back to their respective forces. Fate had brought her into that canyon. He was as sure of that as he was about fighting for a lost cause.

He put one hand on her shoulder and pushed her backward until the backs of her legs came up against a table-like outcropping of rock. "Sit down. We don't know what tomorrow will bring. Tonight we rest. You look exhausted."

She finally broke her gaze from his, looked down at her fruit, and continued to eat it in silence.

"Remember," he told her while fighting unexpected emotions, "keep the mission in mind. We don't know what we'll be asked to do. This is for our comrades and countless others who will never know us. Everything we do is for them."

She nodded and ate the rest of the food he offered.

Soldar watched her carefully for the rest of the night. Neither of them slept as they should have. His comrade was a bit too calm. A bit too brooding. And when a slightly brighter dawn broke over the horizon, he reached into the trunk for clothing folded in the bottom, hoping some of it would fit a man his size. They were sure to be far too large for her slender frame.

The garments were meant for the men that should have accompanied him. Aigean had promised that so long as those other comrades were present, she'd try to get more food to whoever was left at the oasis. But those plans were blown apart now. No one would be staying behind. It seemed Lyra *was* ready to die. She just didn't want to do it alone. He could respect that.

"If you'll excuse me, I have to find someplace to do my business," she uttered.

"Wait." He moved toward her while raising the electronic keypad on his left forearm. "I assume your standard-issue ID microchip is located just behind your left ear?"

"Yes, sir. Why?" she asked as she put her hand to her head.

"I've got the technology to disable it, the same way I neutralized mine and my team's before we landed," Soldar explained. "If the enemy has close-range scanning equipment, our covers will be blown. That identifier has to go."

He saw her take a deep breath as he pointed the lights on his electronic wristband toward her microchip. Then he pressed several flashing buttons until they went green, indicating her ID was shorted out. She winced as he completed the task, but that was the least of what she'd suffer if the Condorians discovered who she was. Now the chip containing her name, serial number, rank, and other pertinent information was destroyed. Should she be killed on this mission, no one would know who she really was, even if the remnants of the chip were located.

"Take the clothing I've picked out for you, some bottled water, and some soap. Clean up as best you can," he instructed. "We'll be expected to look reasonably presentable. The idea was that whoever went to the Venus would look as though they'd just arrived on one of Aigean's light speed shuttles. That's going to be difficult since we're exposed to the elements and don't know exactly when Aigean will arrive. But we must not get caught in uniform now."

"For the sake of getting our stories straight, how would our civilian transport have gotten past all the Condorian battle cruisers in this sector? The ones who don't know about the little setup on the Venus? Why wouldn't they have fired on us?" Lyra asked.

"I'm assuming such a transport would be allowed through. The enemy officers aboard Aigean's ship wouldn't want to miss their deliveries of looted food, drugs, or alcohol. Aigean's unwanted *guests* would have gotten it through Condorian lines without so much as being searched or even tracked." He switched topics. Time was passing and they needed to be ready. "Bury your uniform where it can't be found. Take nothing with you that can give your identity away. If I recall your surname correctly, you're now Lyra Markham…*seductress*."

She nodded in acknowledgement of his memory. "Just so you know…I intend to do whatever it takes to see some enemy blood on my hands. My dead friends would have given anything for one decent meal before they died. Those raiding thugs are going to pay…I swear to God!"

He said nothing as she stalked around a stone outcrop to change and relieve herself. It occurred to him that her prudishness in not completing these small tasks in front of him was ridiculous in light of the roles they were engaging. But the last of normalcy would soon be gone from their lives. Let her do what she must and have a bit of privacy, while she had the chance.

Lyra Markham was a warrior and wouldn't appreciate his telling her not to go too far from the oasis, but his protective instincts still emerged. She was so small next to him. How could she have been effective in battle? Still, to achieve her rank she must have done something right. He shook his head and pulled out clothing for himself.

As he relieved himself then washed with copious amounts of bottled water and a bar of his own, old-fashioned soap, he tried to imagine how their so-called intimacy could work. They barely knew each other. What if they couldn't pull this off?

He prayed to the Creator that some good would come from this effort. Either they'd make a huge difference, or they'd die on this gritty world without anyone having known what they'd been up to. The only damned reason the Condorians had chosen this place to attack was because of the ores that could be turned into fuel. From Reisen Four, a number of planets could all be reached within the span of a few days using wormhole technology. And there was the added benefit of being able to land their pleasure vessel in the wasteland far away from their ground fighters.

Few would suspect that members of Condoria's High Command had the Venus hidden on this rock. Enemy ground troops, intentionally deprived of such delicacies as sumptuous food and women, would certainly turn on their leaders. It had happened before. Their officers had been slaughtered in very inventive ways, by their own subordinates. He'd seen the remains.

If it hadn't been for the idea that a man might get aboard and relay a great deal of information back to Allied Command—with the help of Aigean Florn—it would have been more expedient to call in a strike on the Venus and kill everyone. As Lyra suggested, even the innocent aboard her craft would normally be deemed expendable by the powers-that-be.

The very worst scenario for his new partner was obvious.

The Venus could be overrun by Condorian ground troops while she was aboard. And while Aigean's staff would be killed, how much worse would it be for Lyra if one of the employees gave her away as an allied soldier? That could obviously happen even if the enemy officers weren't discovered by their own men.

This was an outcome Lyra must still be considering.

As for him, he'd been prepared for that possibility. Though Aigean had sworn allegiance to the allied cause, and she had been correct with all her information, how much could anyone really trust her? She'd survived a very long time among the enemy. How?

Something in his brain kept warning him, like an alarm. What was it about the proprietor of the Venus that wasn't right, even as he'd been prompted by his superiors to trust her?

Back at the cave he'd promised Lyra a quick, painless end. Whatever happened, he'd see it done before letting those savages get their hands on her. That was the least he could do for having taken away her last round, her only means of a quick, humane end.

• • •

He rolled up the sleeves of his tunic, leaving the front of it untied. The heated breeze was almost cloying now. At least his armor had been insulated for this environment. The dark pants and high boots were attractive, but they protected nothing.

The wind lifted strands of his hair and thrust them into his face. He quickly tied the mass out of his way with a strip of cloth torn from other clothing. The boots he'd been given fit even if the rest of the clothing was skin tight.

He turned when he heard Lyra approach. He opened his mouth to relay another command, but the utterance faded away. The creature now approaching didn't resemble the battle-hardened warrior he'd trudged alongside. She'd neatly belted an oversized, light-colored shirt in such a way that it flowed over her curves in a very closefitting tunic style. She'd chosen to wear the dark male tights he'd thrown at her without any pants. The length of her legs overpowered the size of the shirt so that the effect was very enticing. She was hiding what was underneath, but not so much that any man with a beating heart wouldn't take a second look. Even down to the oversized sandals she seemed perfectly attired, a woman to notice. With her body armor removed, she was trimmer than he'd imagined. The way she moved spoke of a light, athletic, and graceful body.

Once again, he found his body inappropriately responding. This time, the urge to touch her was almost impossible to deny. In fact, he lifted his hand to run it across her drying hair, and then quickly lowered it again. Her tresses looked as though they might be reddish brown in the hazy light. Strands now curled just under her chin, where she'd tucked it behind her ears. A soft fringe of bangs fell sweetly over her forehead. Without the excess dirt, she was as lovely as a Craetorian summer day. He'd have given ten years off his life to have known her before this horrible place. The scent of her fresh skin, so recently cleansed, was heady. It had been so very long since he'd been near anything so feminine. The idea of them becoming lovers now appealed in countless ways.

They may not have long to live, but he'd have a lovely little Earth goddess near him when the Creator delivered his last breath. And oh, what a way to go! If only they'd met before the war. If only…if only …

She gazed at him but whatever her response was, it was inscrutable. He curled his fingers into fists and forced himself to act professionally, not let any of his sudden ardor show.

"Some blankets were in the trunk. I've picked out a protected spot to lie on. We need to get some rest," he gruffly instructed.

"Is that wise, sir? Shouldn't one of us remain on watch?"

"With what? Two volleys of laser fire?" He shook his head in denial. "No. We'll hear the enemy approaching long before they get to this spot. The rock on all sides is too loose for them to sneak up…assuming they know we're here. And all I'd need is a moment to fire on you."

"Thank you for remembering," she softly said.

He simply nodded. "It's best to get some sleep. Aigean said she'd offer the Condorian guards some incentive to stay near the vessel and away from our locale. That should work since they'll be watching for their own ground troops. All we do now is wait for her. If she can't safely pick us up, she'll try to get us more food and water. This was the same thing she'd have done for my men if they'd made it this far."

There were a few moments of silence as they each straightened their clothing and tried to fluff their hair in the breeze to dry it. He stretched his arms above his head and saw her attempting to hide a grin. Her gaze moved over his body and she shook her head.

"Is something wrong, Sergeant?"

"I was just thinking that you wouldn't like that Condorian admiral's attention, sir. I mean…if you'd gone in by yourself and assuming he didn't kill you on site…you'd be his boy-toy, his tool, his mattress monkey, his—"

"I get the point!"

She lifted one hand and shrugged. "Sorry, sir."

"If you're really sorry, then why the continued smirk, Sergeant?"

"To paraphrase something I recently heard…I'm just sick that way, sir."

"Talk about double standards…look…just keep your thoughts to yourself and lie down. I'll let you pick your side of the blanket."

"What happened to using no titles…*sir*?"

"It's habit. And it's one that's hard to break when you keep addressing me by *my* rank…so stop it!"

She suppressed a grin once more. "Yes…Soldar," she quickly responded while plopping on the soft blankets.

The sudden use of his name—yielded from such soft, sweet lips—was unnerving.

Even someone's thoughtfulness in providing them with assorted large blankets didn't make his bed comfortable. Nothing would be comfortable again. Not as long as this beautiful fighter was lying within arm's reach. And not as long as he kept thinking of the so-called act they were supposed to provide aboard a pleasure ship.

He plopped next to Lyra and exhaled noisily. It took everything he had to put his mind on sleeping and off the soft-looking body next to his. The woman was only an arm's length away. Soon, they'd be doing a great deal more than resting together, and that sensual thought had his body, particularly his cock, responding with vigor.

The air needed to be cleared while they had time. He was pretty damned sure this Earther had never heard about a Craetorian male's body since she'd admitted to never having seen his race before. What gossip she may have gleaned might be incorrect. "Uh…Lyra…I think there's something you should know."

She turned her head toward him just as he turned his toward her. "Yes?"

"It's none of my business how…experienced…you may or may not be. But a Craetorian male has sexual organs that are somewhat differently shaped. My people are taught these variations from puberty—"

Lyra suddenly leaned over and put her fingertips over his lips. "Don't. Don't tell me anything. If we're billing ourselves as a couple who likes to perform together, I should already know this."

He gently removed her fingers but kept them in his grasp. "But you don't. That's the point."

"And that's what will help me act spontaneously. I have to behave as though you and I have never been together, and that your making love to me is the most wonderfully, fulfilling experience of my life. That's what will make our performance so appealing. That's our act. It'll be easier if I don't know too much. You get it?"

He briefly closed his eyes and smiled. "I suppose that makes some kind of twisted sense. But you really ought to know that—"

"Shut up! I don't want to know. Not unless our bodies are incompatible. But even if I couldn't get you inside me, I'd still find some way to have intercourse so we could pass ourselves off as a sex act," she insisted. "I won't sleep with a Condorian. I mean it!"

"Lyra…your point has been made."

She sighed heavily. "I sound panic-stricken. I know I do, but I'm not. Don't pay too much attention to me right now. I'm tired."

He tried to lighten their mood. "You know…there's a slight chance, however infinitesimal, that we might be successful, and may have a chance at arresting the Condorian contingent on this ship."

"Keep dreaming, sir…Soldar," she quickly corrected while curling up on her share of the blanket. "And while you're daydreaming, why don't you imagine a fleet of allied war birds appearing and taking out the entire enemy contingent. Then imagine we're offered private rooms with warm, soft beds, hot tubs, massages, and dinners consisting of nice juicy steaks, loaded baked potatoes, and cases of cold beer. Plus three whole months of nothing but sleep!"

Soldar actually grinned at the burst of imagination but he persisted. "Of course, it could go the other way. I could either be killed in an attempt to get to the bridge or I'll succeed…and then be killed. Or I could give bad head and be ripped apart for that—"

"God! Hopefully, you won't have to give anyone 'head.' Besides, you need me for more than just sex. You'll find my technical knowledge might come in handy. Assuming we can get to the bridge at all," she informed him wearily.

"What technical knowledge?" He raised himself up on one elbow.

"Before I joined Earth's ground forces, I worked for a small distribution company. We were always fighting to stay in business against some very large competitors. My brother and I…well…we *might* have figured a way to hack into some of our competitors' systems and take a look at what they were doing. Of course…I'm not admitting to anything and this was all a long time ago—"

"Why didn't you say something about this?" he angrily interrupted. "You might have mentioned it when I detailed Aigean's plan!"

"You didn't ask. I figured you at least had my hacking skills or you wouldn't have been chosen for this mission." She adjusted her position on the blanket to better face him.

He moved his index finger in the air, back and forth between their bodies. "It's called communication, Lyra. It works both ways!"

"Okay…Christ!" she uttered and then paused for a long moment. "Is it that important? I mean…if I'd gotten to the bridge without you and didn't have any knowledge of hacking, what was I supposed to do with any information? I figured that this Aigean person would help transmit."

"She will. All her messages indicated she's trying to get locking codes that the Condorians installed in her systems. The point is… if she can get her ship's computer back, we can send any message to allied vessels. They'll know the information is true because of the authentication I'll add. Obviously, all this is assuming we can get on the bridge in the first place."

"But *I* don't know that authentication."

"*Lyra*…it's the same authentication you'd always use to send a message from one allied vessel to another."

She sat up and stared at him.

He simply shrugged in confirmation.

"*That's it!* That's your 'secret code'?" she asked while making quotation marks in the air with her fingers.

He pinched the bridge of his nose between his thumb and forefinger. "The Condorian excrement never broke it!"

"God! Allied ground forces are being commanded by idiots!"

"No," he said in a patronizing fashion, "it's actually quite brilliant."

"Please…enlighten me."

He frowned at her and used his most condescending tone of voice. "As you know…the standard ship-to-ship, allied authentication system is very simple. It only takes a few keystrokes or negligible hologram manipulation to engage…depending upon how old the com console is. Furthermore, it can be changed immediately if it becomes necessary. And since the message would be coming from Aigean's ship…a woman who's helped us in the past…it doesn't really make any difference if the damned thing is read by a fleet admiral or some probationary cadet," he clarified. "By regulation, the communication still has to be delivered to the recipient…and that will be General Elias Shafter." Soldar moved closer to her. "The 'code,'" he responded with equal sarcasm and by making the same quotation marks in the air with his fingers, "is just fine!"

"And if our fleet doesn't ever get a message, what then?"

"If there's no information coming from the Venus in two weeks, it's to be assumed this mission failed and the strike will take place regardless. At least there'll be a few of those bastards that won't ever fight another day, and Aigean and her crew will finally be free from tyranny, even if it's in the afterlife," he asserted. "Satisfied… Admiral Markham?"

Lyra gasped and shook her head in shock. "You know…I just don't get it. We've got some of the best intelligence people there are. Sad to say that there aren't enough…but we've still got good ones," she told him. "So whose bright idea was it to use a code a monkey could break?" She held up her hand when he would have spoken. "Oh, I realize it's simple. That's why it was designed. It's meant for allied troops to talk to each other from one ship to another and it designates minor chatter."

Soldar turned away. "You don't understand—"

"Explain it to me!"

"Lyra, you and I—"

"We…*what*?"

"I suspect you and I are the only allied survivors on this planet, Lyra."

She was momentarily taken aback. Her brow furrowed and she chewed on her lower lip for a moment. He waited for her response and was suddenly sorry to have even said anything.

"What does that have to do with someone not devising a more elaborate transmission code for this mission?" she asked.

He carefully considered his words, but truth was the best option now. "Lyra…there's no one left!"

She shook her head in confusion. "What exactly does that mean?"

"When did you land on this rock?"

She tucked a stray curl behind her ear before swallowing hard and answering. "Four days ago. My unit was tightly packed until a photon trungeon bomb blew up right in the middle of us. We were scattered after that."

"My team landed three days ago. Rather, we *tried* to land," he solemnly advised. "My superiors told us on the way down to the surface that six of Earth's galaxy-class fighters had been totally destroyed."

"Six…n-no…that c-can't be," Lyra muttered as she shook her head in denial.

"It's true. Five of our own regency dragons-of-prey were taken out."

"But that would mean—"

"That's right," he sadly summed up. "The Craetorians only have three vessels left in this entire sector. Earth has one. The allied fleet here has been decimated. There were just too many Condorian battle cruisers and we hadn't a chance." He ran one hand over his face and tried not to look into her stricken gaze before continuing. "With the exception of the Earth ship, the Craetorian contingent is being manned mostly by a class of cadets and their trainers. We're down to sending children into war," he bitterly told her.

Lyra looked away but not before he saw her shaken expression.

"The remaining craft are badly damaged. There are a few engineers and technicians left alive to make repairs. The message we'd be sending from the bridge of the Venus has to be encoded in a way those cadets understand and can immediately relay. That's why the frequency will be the same we always use between allied vessels. Simplicity is best when life support systems are compromised and injured kids are at the helm." He glanced up at the sky. "There isn't an encryption officer among them. All of those were on flag ships, not the older destroyers that survived at the back of the fleet."

"I understand," Lyra softly acknowledged. "Even with the lowest power available, basic communication and its enabling codes remain functional." She gazed at him and slowly nodded. "I apologize."

"No. I should have told you sooner. I don't know why I didn't except I was waiting to see if we'd even survive our first night on that enemy-infested pleasure ship," he said in a less harsh tone. "Just understand we have two weeks to make first contact with our fleet. Sooner is better than later."

She slowly nodded.

"If either of us can get reliable information and get on the bridge—"

"And assuming Aigean can get control of her com systems—" she interrupted.

"Just transmit what you can to the remaining allied vessels, Lyra. If you think you won't get another chance, order our remaining ships to fire on our location. But in the event our transmissions keep coming regularly, those cadets will relay whatever we send to the closest allied base of operations in this sector. They'll have to remain in deep space to stay away from the Condorian cruisers."

"Soldar, you know we'll only get one shot to transmit before the Condorians are all over us!"

"Others hoped we might have a little longer."

Lyra dragged one hand through her hair. "This is insane. You know that, don't you?"

"The nearest Allied flag ship is in the Degar System. Even though our cadets sent distress calls, it will still take weeks for help to arrive. The Condorian battle cruisers will have moved on, and will have attacked other civilizations. I'd like to think we could avenge our dead before that happens. We could strike a great blow to their pride and offer some measure of honor for our dead." He gently grasped her upper arms and pulled her closer. "If two of us can infiltrate and destroy a group of Condorian officers on their pleasure craft, it could go a long way to boost morale. And our warriors desperately need that now."

Lyra returned the gesture by gripping his biceps. "If General Shafter is still alive then it's his corsair that survived. A star-class Earth corsair is meant to travel fast and maneuver. It's small and carries a crew of eighty-five," she said as she gazed into his eyes. "If there aren't any more surviving allies on the ground, then there're only—"

"Eighty-six Earthers alive in the entire sector. That includes you. Your calculations are correct," Soldar finished.

She continued staring at him as the news sunk in. "Once the Degar vessels arrive here, there's only one fleet between this planet and Earth." She actually began to shake. "Using the latest wormhole charts…Earth is only seven months away." She lifted one hand and wrapped her fingers loosely around her throat.

The astonished expression on her face grew more intense but she said no more.

Once again he found himself wishing they were in some other reality. If she couldn't get her emotions under control, they wouldn't last a single night on the Venus.

But honesty wouldn't allow him to find fault with her response. He was scared too.

Chapter 3

Soldar wasn't sure when Lyra collapsed on the blanket and finally fell asleep. She was exhausted and the events of the day were brutal. Emotion had drained her as it had him. His new partner simply couldn't stay awake any longer. Especially not after having endured a firefight resulting in a chase through the badlands. All while wearing heavy armor.

He fought depression and gazed into the distance wishing he hadn't had to tell her that truth. But she'd insisted on questioning the transmission codes they'd use if they ever got the chance.

Just before she'd slumped to the blanket and fell into deathlike slumber, there'd been a terrible look in her face. If he had to name the expression, it was very like defeat. But he finally stretched out next to her and took the liberty of pulling her close. Something told him she wouldn't mind.

Everything seemed so hopeless. Their struggle now was ludicrously ineffective in light of the facts. Having voiced the allied situation, he needed to be close to someone who was on his side, someone who understood the desperate stands in space like this one.

In her sleep, Lyra responded to his caresses on her shoulder and hip. She scooted backward, toward him. Her slender, tight little body pushed against his frame as if, in her deep slumber, she wanted to meld her form to his. The result of such blending, ever it went unchecked while she was awake, would yield a discharge of energy that could rock the universe. In his gut, he knew that the joining of any other two souls wouldn't be more powerful. They were living their very last days and that enhanced every emotion. Every single feeling whether one of happiness or sorrow was so much more exaggerated. Every touch, every kiss was more powerful.

His blood fired.

Now he felt his body's acceptance for what had to come. With every fiber of his being, he believed it was no coincidence Lyra Markham had run down that canyon, straight into his life.

If their end *was* to be—and there was nothing to offer hope for life—he'd throw everything he had into their final days. He'd use their cover to pleasure her so thoroughly that the energy from their union would last forever. A part of his soul and hers would filter into the universe, as his Creator led him to believe. In that way, they'd never really die. They'd never be apart. Their fusion would go on.

Perhaps the situation was causing him to lose perspective. He'd faced death so many times, but never with such a sense of utter despair. And never with a tempting little enchantress as his partner. He didn't believe in coincidences. Nothing happened by accident. She stirred in his arms so he took that opportunity to pull her closer.

"You're so warm," she murmured against his chest.

"As taxed as you seemed, I'm surprised you're awake," he said as he nuzzled her hair. "The temperature dropped. I can get more blankets."

She barely shook her head, but kept her eyes closed. "No. Don't move. Please don't get up, Sol. I-I'd like to have you near."

"Sol?" he murmured.

"That's what I'm gonna call you," she softly told him. "It means *sun*."

"I know. But I don't get the reason for the reference other than the rather impudent shortening of a superior's first name," he teased.

She reached out, pulled a portion of his hair forward and said, "It's because of this…your hair."

He knew she was blocking their grave circumstance with mindless chatter. He'd engaged that psychological ploy on a number of occasions. "Its color reminds you of a sun?"

"It's bright. Even out here in this half-light. And you remind me of something else," she told him as she stared into his eyes. "You remind me of a hero in an old Earth legend. His name was Thor."

He gently stroked her back while she stretched out against him. "I'm afraid I'm not familiar with Earth myths. As to the length of my hair, it's a tradition. It's not necessary to wear it this long, but I wanted to hang onto as many of my world's customs as I could… *while* I could."

"I understand. If you don't think you'll ever see home again, every detail of your culture seems crucial." She took a deep breath in and let it out slowly. "Maybe this Aigean person won't come."

"And maybe the Condorians will lay down their arms, ask forgiveness, and we can all go home friends?"

"I can dream. Even if it's only for a few more hours."

He wrapped his arms around her protectively, and took the opportunity to stroke her hair since she'd touched his so gently. "You're still very tired."

"Not so much," she advised, and proved it by maneuvering her body on top of his while continuing her steady, deep gaze into his eyes.

Soldar saw the molten look in her stare and knew what she wanted. Apparently, she'd reconsidered her request to delay sexual contact for their "act."

His body responded instantly and he readily opened his mouth for her kiss. This was a custom he knew his race and hers shared. And it had been so very long since he'd felt a tender touch or a woman's lips. She'd be the last he'd touch. He'd be her last lover.

He let his tongue entwine with hers and felt heat drill into his body. That molten sensation hadn't been present in ages. Even his most ardent lovers in the past had never dredged this encompassing, flooding sensation of passion. Blood rushed into his penis. He was rock hard in an instant. But then he'd been ready for an erection since meeting this woman. And when he heard her moan deep in the back part of her throat and felt her hands splay across his shoulders, only the sound of an approaching craft routed him from the embrace.

"Someone's coming," he blurted and was on his feet in an instant. From beneath the blankets, he retrieved the laser weapon and saw Lyra pull a Condorian blade from its hiding place beneath a rock. Her weapon would do little good unless a hand-to-hand confrontation ensued. Still, he admired her courage. Any enemy facing *her* would see the blade as it was clearly marked with Condorian edges and half-moon designs on the handle. They'd know it had been removed from a fallen fighter.

Long years of battle experience forced them simultaneously to their knees, to make smaller targets of themselves. The craft glided over the top of a nearby hill. If its occupants fired on them, he and Lyra were better off close to the ground.

He held off using his laser when the unmarked craft—bearing a very humanoid looking male pilot—put the conveyance in hover mode several yards from where they crouched. As it came closer to the ground, another cloaked figure became visible. This person was seated in the back of the open, elliptical-shaped, silver transport. *This* being, however, didn't bear the fair-colored complexion that he and Lyra shared. In the hazy light, the female he stared at appeared blue or green. Her hair was very pale and cut quite close to her skull.

"Elderian," he blurted when a tall, lanky woman with pointed ears stood.

"An allied world," Lyra responded as she sighed in relief.

Soldar noted how Lyra didn't re-sheath her blade. He understood her caution as he kept his own weapon ready. Whoever this Elderian was, she could easily give them away. Some civilians did that to allied troops when they mistakenly thought Condorians might let them live.

He stood beside Lyra as the hovercraft passenger stepped off her vehicle and walked toward them. Because of the sand and rocks beneath her craft, the lady had to pick up the hem of the long, expensive, whitish gown she wore.

"I'm Aigean Florn," she announced in perfect Earth English. "I see you're wearing clothing my employees mistakenly discarded from my ship." She looked them over. "Who are you?"

Soldar stepped closer to Aigean. "I am Soldar Nar—obviously from Craetoria. In the last message you sent, you welcomed someone of my race to board the Venus." He didn't want to say too much, in case she'd been found out and was being monitored. This woman might want to help the allied cause, but she could just as easily betray them in a desperate bid to keep herself alive a bit longer. His words were meant to sound as innocuous as her greeting, and as though she'd sent some missive for entertainment at a time while she still could.

"I asked for five *men* of different races. Not one man and one woman," Aigean responded as she cast a disdainful gaze toward Lyra. "Some of my most discriminating clients desire men to service them."

He stepped closer to her. "Am I not the perfect, brawny, virile male for the job?" *Perfect, brawny, virile male* were the code words she'd asked to be used. If she didn't respond appropriately, he'd know they were being monitored. If that was the case, Aigean would have to take the lead. He had no other instructions.

Aigean glanced over her shoulder and nodded toward the pilot.

The pilot let out a sigh of relief, and slumped into his seat as if he'd been frightened.

Aigean faced them again and spoke more candidly. "You are safe, Craetorian. All is well but I had to make sure. As I stated, there was no mention of bringing a woman with you."

"I'm sorry to disappoint, but the four men who originally landed with me are dead. A Condorian trench torpedo hit our transport. I was the only one thrown free. This woman is an allied fighter I hooked up with in the badlands. We'll have to suffice."

"How the hell do we know we can trust you?" Lyra asked.

Aigean moved in front of her and boldly looked her over. "What is your name, girl?"

"I'm Lyra Markham…Master Sergeant with Earth Force. First Defense Platoon, Tenth Earth Regiment. I got cut off from the last battle near the Plageian Escarpment. The Colonel and I met when he saved my life."

"*Colonel?*" Aigean blurted.

Soldar nodded. "That is my correct rank. Again…it was *my* unit that was supposed to have served as your new entertainment, Ms. Florn. To keep the mission intact, the sergeant and I have agreed to present ourselves as an erotic duo. This was an alternate plan we hoped you could explain."

Aigean looked them over more carefully. "Am I to understand the *two* of you are basically strangers, and you've agreed to jointly display your sexual prowess…while Condorians watch? Or am I misinterpreting the situation?"

"That's correct," Soldar told her. "As it happens, Lyra is somewhat familiar with hacking into computer systems and *might* be able to use your communications console to intercept messages coming from your ship's private rooms. I realize that your com room is compromised, but our cover might give us access. We'd need your assistance with that."

"All this poses a monumental change in plans," Aigean mused, as she began to pace back and forth in front of them. As she walked she pushed up the sleeves of her long gown. "I have been promising my…*clients*…something unusual. Something that will amaze them," she stated bitterly. "If I don't give them what they want soon…my employees' lives may be forfeit."

"How did you get away from your vessel without being noticed or monitored?" Lyra asked suspiciously. "Why isn't there a contingent of Condorian war guards with you?"

Aigean stopped pacing and stood in front of them. "Everyone who isn't an employee or on guard duty has been imbibing drugs and alcohol for weeks. The enemy wants more and more. And because of their addictions, they stay virtually out of touch with reality. All they know is that I've left with but one employee and one surface transport craft with only enough fuel to traverse a short distance. This hardly poses any concern for them. Besides, they think I'm here to pick up a new male toy for the Condorian admiral…a contemptuous lout who has been quite demanding concerning his needs. I received permission to pick you up from a small convoy of entertainers headed toward another Condorian pleasure haven somewhere in this sector. That is the story concerning your arrival in this area. Fortunately, there seems to be a mutual agreement between Condorian hierarchies to maintain living standards, and keeping quiet about who else in this sector is doing the same." She clasped her hands in front of her. "Condorian officers don't ask when it comes to the transport of spoils of war. The admiral aboard my ship seems to be particularly feared. He gets his choice of booty first."

Lyra's eyes narrowed. "That explains how you got here without guards. It also offers a good cover for how we happen to be on the planet. But it doesn't explain how you manage to keep supplies coming?"

Soldar knew his new partner wasn't convinced of Aigean's claims to help allies. He'd already had a conversation with Lyra concerning how the Condorian elite would make sure their needs were met even before their underlings, but he said nothing. Lyra's interrogation gave him a chance to watch Aigean carefully.

Aigean glared back at Lyra, but answered slowly and in a way that seemed unrehearsed.

"Had the Condorian smugglers not just raided a law enforcement blockade around Korid Prime I'd be running low on all kinds of supplies," she responded. "As I've said, those smugglers made sure the Condorians on my ship got first pick of everything. Thankfully, whether by legal means or not, the problems concerning food, water, supplies, drugs, and alcohol have been addressed. As to you two and whatever meager skill you may possess with communication systems…it might be possible to get one or both of you on the bridge. But only if you are convincing in your behavior and only so long as the admiral thinks he is in complete control. His ego and addictions are such that this poses less of a problem than one might imagine."

"And you're sure your employees aren't going to turn us in to save their hides?" Lyra persisted.

"My employees have been through more than you can possibly imagine, young woman! They do not even have the benefit of escaping through use of drugs or alcohol. They must be clear-headed at all times. Having maintained such sobriety is how information began to flow from drunken barbarians to us, and to the allied fleet. In my guest's current *celebratory* state, my movements are barely scrutinized. The enemy knows I would not run from my ship, my crew, and my friends." She suddenly stepped closer to Lyra and began a closer inspection. "Let me look at you, girl."

Lyra glanced between the Elderian woman and Soldar. "*What?*"

"Oh, for the love of Beydor's Moons, turn around and let me get a good look at you!"

Lyra hesitantly did as she was asked.

"With some work, you might do," Aigean advised, then turned her attention on Soldar. "And you, Craetorian. Let me get a look at *you* as well."

Unused to being perused in such a way, Soldar was about to balk, but the bluish woman stood her ground and glared at him until he complied. After he turned for her perusal, their new hostess slowly nodded.

"I have something in mind," she said as she tapped one cheek with her long, red-tipped index finger. Unfortunately, you'll have to leave the weapons behind. The Condorians have installed equipment on my ship that will detect laser devices. Even members of their own units don't patrol my vessel while armed. Their commanding officer feels that doing so might give battle-weary veterans an excuse to discharge arms when intoxicated," she confirmed. "Their admiral came here for peace and quiet. He wants no headaches that an ensuing fight among his own men might cause."

"Too bad," Lyra muttered. "I'd pay to see them kill each other."

"You must realize something about the man who now runs my ship," Aigean countered. "He is crafty. Do not underestimate his intelligence. He has many warrior friends aboard the Venus. They are his eyes and ears." The older woman paced a bit more before speaking again. "It's to our advantage that his contingent believes my people incapable of such audacity as planting spies aboard his current haven. I have bartered an uneasy truce with him even when he killed several of my employees he perceived as spies. For this reason I've ordered my crew to cater to his every whim. His total complacency and delight in his latest victory makes our situation easier," she instructed, "but you'll still be watched. The boarding guards could search you for contraband. They'll most certainly take any personal belongings. Nothing you carry or your bodies can be considered private unless you capture the enemy admiral's particular interest and protection. Do you understand?"

Soldar glanced at Lyra. His new partner frowned. The implication was that they were sexually expendable, just as he'd surmised.

But something in him had changed since meeting her. Some protective instinct deeply embedded in his core was integrating Lyra's fears.

He knew, with every cell in his body, that he'd never let anyone rape her. She personified all he held dear—all he'd never see or love again. She was courageous, spirited, and lovely. And even if his emotions were amplified by the situation, the truth was that he could never see a woman—any woman—hurt. It wasn't in him.

He'd asked her to come along while denying feelings in this regard. He'd tried to see her as just another soldier. But she was and always had been a woman before being a soldier.

He now realized his mistake in not leaving her in that cave. She might have starved or died of thirst. But she'd have died as an allied fighter. Now Aigean and one of her employees knew of Lyra's existence. If tortured for any reason, they'd talk about her presence to save themselves. No one could withstand Condorian interrogation for long. And Lyra's presence was a gambit that could be used to delay agony or even death.

"You'll need to know where the enemy stores their weapons," Aigean continued. "Their lasers are located in the ship's lowest storage bay. I'm not allowed in that area any longer, and my people tell me the passageways are guarded in shifts. That compartment is only unlocked when the Condorians leave to rejoin their units and their personal arms are released back to them."

She glanced at them both for a long moment. "If you two can get over your militaristic bearing and act as if you're who and what you purport to be, we may have a covert operation that could garner information. Indeed…before you transmit the location of the Venus and…Creator willing…eliminate the parasites who've taken over my ship…you could gain access to highly classified Condorian strategy."

She took a deep breath and briefly clasped her hands in front of her. "Before the Allies are finally defeated, we may yet strike a critical blow for our cause. We must make the attempt. We must never give up!" she vehemently asserted as she curled her fingers into fists. "We might succeed if you follow my instructions."

Soldar gazed at Lyra. Her face was a mask. He couldn't tell what her real thoughts were at that exact moment, but it didn't matter. He'd put her into this. Now he must see her through it. "Let's do this," he responded.

Aigean nodded and glanced behind her. "Though a female wasn't expected, I believe we can contrive a plausible story for the change." She looked them over once more. "I have working knowledge of where the enemy has traversed and what neutral, English-speaking world where *you* might have originated," she added as she glanced at Lyra. "There's obviously no hiding the race from which Soldar hails. As to the language you may use, many of my own people speak English fluently. Maintaining that tongue is of no consequence. In fact, my staff notes that some of the enemy prefers having sexual relations with anyone from outlying Earth colonies."

Soldar snorted. "They like to gloat. If it's during sex with prostitutes from conquered planets, all the better. It's typical of Condorian enmity."

"Indeed!" Aigean nodded. "This is why having a Craetorian aboard will cause no particular problem. In fact, your presence will greatly peak the admiral's libido."

"No offence," Lyra blurted in obvious irritation, "but I just don't see how Soldar won't be tortured, then beheaded. I'm not sure whose bright idea it was to send someone from his world, and without even trying to alter his features. Language may not be the problem, but his planet of origin sure as hell is!" She faced Soldar and glared up at him. "I'm going to say what I've thought all along, whether you like it or not, sir."

Soldar opened his mouth to defend Aigean's claim, but Lyra was actually angry now. She even reverted back to his title as evidence of her outrage and disbelief concerning this entire plan.

"Colonel…you've got allied warrior written all over you. I've heard it said that Condorians would peel the skins off Craetorians killed on the front lines. It's rumored they've even taken body parts as trophies. Every allied soldier knows that Craetorians seem to be heavily targeted by the enemy. We haven't figured out why except for the ferocity with which your people are known to fight—"

"That's enough, Sergeant!" he commanded sternly. "I don't need to justify my presence. The explanation you were given is sufficient and all you need to know." He stared pointedly at Aigean so *she* wouldn't inadvertently say more. Elderians were among the few races that knew a dark secret he wasn't obliged to share. Lyra was speaking out of fear. But her instincts were uncanny. If she lived much longer, she might find out exactly how and why his presence aboard the Venus was necessary.

Aigean lifted one brow and slightly tilted her head in Soldar's direction.

In that moment he knew the older woman had understood his desire to keep certain subjects closed.

Aigean then faced Lyra squarely. "I can assure you, girl… the Condorians will accept Soldar and you aboard the Venus if your acting is credible. After all, my entire crew hails from all allied worlds. The enemy knows my contacts for hiring new prostitutes would be the same contacts I've always used. Had the Condorian admiral not believed I'd deliver entertainment, from any source, he'd have blown the Venus out of the sky when he first encountered her. But that's not what he intended for us. At least, not yet. Unfortunately, we are all alive at his whim."

"Why do I not believe you?" Lyra muttered.

Aigean merely looked away.

"Sir…something's wrong! I don't like this," Lyra continued.

"In case you hadn't noticed, none of us likes it!" he responded. "And quit using my rank to address me. We won't last five minutes if you can't get your mouth under control."

Lyra glared at him but finally shut up. His insult was unintended. A battle-seasoned warrior shouldn't be spoken to in such a way, but he had to get her mind on the ruse they were to play and off his being Craetorian.

Aigean sighed heavily and continued. "At least some luck is with you. There are no listening devices on the Venus. The admiral takes a dim view of his sexual liaisons being monitored. Political rivals on his home world would use such recordings to ruin him. Indeed, many aboard the Venus are keeping the spoils of war for themselves, and not paying off old debts back home. As always, if Condorians aren't fighting everyone else, they still fight among themselves." She straightened her sleeves and cast her gaze toward the surrounding area. "Should they decide to install any kind of surveillance equipment or change their behavior in any way, my crew will inform you."

"Your crew knows about this plan? All of them?" Soldar asked in amazement.

"They must. Their job is to protect you as a means of helping defeat the enemy among us...an enemy who has already killed their families and friends. Had any wanted to betray you, the deed would have already been done. You may live to see your worlds again...for however long they exist...if you guard your actions and mind my words."

Soldar and Lyra moved closer to her and listened intently for the next hour.

• • •

As the Venus came into view, Lyra took the Elderian woman's last warning to heart and tried to paste on a bored expression. She'd memorized her part of the cover story Aigean quickly formed. As their new comrade had explained, the gargantuan vessel that housed over a thousand pleasure seekers and five-hundred employees—including sexual attendants—had been designed in an elliptical, flattened shape for a reason. The outer hull of the ship wasn't

69

meant for speed or looks, but for what its interior could house. This one, painted what the light reflected as flat, battleship gray, appeared as innocuous as any vessel could be. But it was still many times larger than any pleasure ship Lyra had visited on shore leave.

This particular enterprise, as their new host clarified, produced a vast amount of wealth for Aigean and her staff—or at least it had before the Condorians arrived. Lyra still had a difficult time believing any Condorian, leader or otherwise, wouldn't kill Aigean's people on contact. Perhaps the only real thing holding them in check was the fact that they'd get no sex at all, except with each other, if the ship didn't exist. But it was a very weak compromise Aigean must have maneuvered. It couldn't hold forever.

As the hovercraft entered into one of the docking bays, it took everything she had to keep from gawking like a tourist. Even the entry area was resplendent with houseplants and hanging tapestries. Impeccably uniformed men and women scurried about with professional bearing that reminded her of a colony of ants. All seemed to accomplish their tasks with efficiency. There were no overseers barking commands or shouts or yelling of any kind. Everyone went about their chores silently. Doing so would presumably draw attention no one wanted with Condorians on board.

One bright spot in the craziness of the operation was that there was color everywhere. This particular ship, like all of them in its class, was equipped with full spectrum lighting. The lights were dim, but still displayed true hues. For the first time since landing on Reisen Four, Lyra saw the rich, royal shades of artwork, and the various robed uniforms she surmised were to denote each employee's rank or specific occupation. She could even feel the cool, re-circulation of fresh air.

In her wildest dreams, she could never have afforded even one night on such a luxurious craft. Its outward appearance didn't do it justice, just as Aigean claimed. She stepped off the hovercraft and onto the red carpet of another world. Her less-than-perfect appearance made her edgy, but there was nothing to be done about it. Aigean hadn't known when she could slip away from the ship to find them in the barrens. Providing them with clothing that was too much like what was already being sported by other employees was suspicious. They were supposed to be brand new employees who'd just arrived.

The best she and Soldar could hope for was to get to their room before too many Condorian *patrons* saw them and trouble started.

Some of the staff covertly nodded then quickly looked the other way as she and Soldar walked by with their mistress. Certainly Aigean wouldn't have personally brought every new client or employee aboard. Not when her presence would be necessary to manage such a large enterprise. Lyra knew talk amongst the employees would spread—she and the Craetorian were the expected spies. All the Condorians had been told was that a new sexual plaything was aboard. That was to have been Soldar. The news would now have to be extended to include her.

Unfortunately, Aigean hadn't had time to design—and circulate—plans around a male-female voyeur act *and* come up with cover stories all in the same half hour it had taken to get to the ship. Everything considered, there'd be a lot of dramatization she and Soldar would have to engage. She just prayed that some Condorian didn't suspect them.

• • •

As they rounded an interior corner of a red, silk-lined passageway, Soldar felt his senses fully engage. He heard voices coming from the other direction and knew, before he caught sight of them, that a group of Condorians was near. The smell gave them away.

A foul, unclean race, the louts apparently hadn't availed themselves of the showers or bathing areas on the ship. Hope that he and Lyra could get to their rooms before being seen was gone. He saw Aigean stop and hesitate in the passageway. From the anxious expression on her face, the Elderian was at an impasse as to how to explain what was to be her newest sex act's lackluster, unannounced, grimy appearance. If she provided the best entertainment, how was she to explain their dinginess? He, too, was at a loss for words. But they'd have to pass the Condorians, one way or the other. The next few moments could be their last.

He put himself in front of the women, thinking to protect them however he could. The average Condorian warrior outweighed Lyra and Aigean many times over and *they* had no weapons. But the quick-thinking little fireball-of-an-Earther by his side came to their rescue. She put *her* body in front of *his*, faced him, and slapped him as hard as she could. His shock kept him silent as she began a tirade that was awesome in its heat. All of this occurred exactly at the same time a pack of Condorian officers turned a corner.

Lyra began a ranting, diva-driven tirade that would be sure to cause attention and an immense amount of gossip.

"I'll never let you handle our transportation again, you fool! *Look at me.* I'm forced to enter an elite pleasure craft in clothing the servants wouldn't be caught dead burning. All because you don't know how to hire a pilot," she bellowed. "You overbearing bastard! We ended up walking through a wasteland to get here. If not for Aigean finding us, I'd be out there dying of thirst, facing who knows what kind of vermin."

To her credit, Aigean reacted magnificently and put one arm around Lyra's shoulders in mock consolation.

"This is the second time some idiot shuttle pilot crash-landed us right in the middle of nowhere," Lyra bawled. "His crew ruined my costumes. And what's worse…just *look* at my hair! How am I supposed to perform after this kind of horrendous experience? I'm an *artist*." She stomped her left foot hard and flung one arm up in mock despair. "How can you be so careless, Sol? I was frightened to death!"

Impressed by her acting, Soldar could do nothing to add to the scene. He simply stared down at her. But Aigean swiftly carried on. Again he found himself mesmerized and impressed by the quick-thinking females in his company.

"There, there dear," Aigean gushingly placated. "I'm sure your lover would have done anything to have kept your craft from breaking down. You surely don't think he'd make you walk miles through the barrens or risk having you injured if he'd had a choice? It wasn't as if he planned it," she placated. "Your pilot was able to keep out of the war zone. Be thankful you were nowhere near the fighting when your craft was disabled. And you won't have to ever see that silly pilot again. His shuttle is repaired now and he's long gone. Isn't this true, Soldar?"

He finally got the idea.

Out of the corner of his eye, he saw the Condorian men watching them carefully. That little part about him being an "overbearing bastard" gave him the impetus to respond. "Let her bitch! It was *her* idea to take this job. She let our agent sign the contract against my better judgment." He crossed his arms over his chest in a recalcitrant if infantile gesture. "Let her throw all the tantrums she likes. You've said it once, Aigean, but I'll say it again. We're in a war zone! But she didn't listen and never does. Why should I care if she broke a damned nail? She should learn to listen!"

Lyra rallied to his lead with a little more gusto than necessary.

"You hear how he treats me, Aigean? Do you see what I have to put up with? This blond asshole thinks he can talk to me like I'm someone he can just *order around?*" she shouted, then buried her head against the Elderian woman's shoulder and pretended to cry.

Aigean patted her back in a motherly fashion. "There now, darling...we'll get you to your room and you can have a nice, leisurely bubble bath. I'll send up some wine and you can relax. I'll have my people get you something to wear from our costumer."

"The clothing won't be *miiiiine*," Lyra loudly whined in a pitch that almost had the Condorians wilting.

Except for that jab about being someone who could "order her around," Soldar might have actually grinned. But he tamped the urge, shook his hair back, and stared right into the tattooed faces of his Condorian enemies. "Do you see what a man has to put up with?" He began a soft cursing tirade, pacing back and forth as if his patience was at an end.

The Condorians strode by them, looking *him* over as if he was something that ought to be scraped from the bottom of a boot. His masculinity took a huge hit. He wanted to bury his fists in those murdering savages' faces, but the three of them were finally alone in the passageway again. The charade Lyra had started with her ridiculous, spoiled diva act would circulate throughout the ship, giving them a brilliant excuse for why the new sex act didn't look more presentable.

When the Condorians were gone, Lyra raised her head from Aigean's shoulder and let out a long breath. "God…that left a bad taste in my mouth!"

Aigean was beside herself with glee. She quietly murmured, "My girl…if you keep acting like that, I have no doubt about your success. That pretense was dazzling! Half of what I was at a loss to explain has just been clarified."

Lyra turned to Soldar and stared up at him meekly. "Sorry for the slap. If it makes you feel any better, my hand really hurts." She rubbed it to make her point.

He likewise rubbed that part of his jaw her hand had contacted. "I'll let it pass…this time." He smiled down at her and they continued to walk where Aigean led.

Ten minutes later, they found themselves ensconced in quarters he could only describe as sinfully luxuriant.

As he looked it over, guilt washed through him. His exuberance over Lyra's fine acting didn't mitigate his sudden, emotional distress. They stood in the middle of the finest extravagance in five sectors of space while others were suffering horrifically.

He saw Lyra's torn expression and knew she was thinking the exact same thing. He crossed the room and stood very close to her. "Remember why we're doing this."

His gentle reminder didn't help and he knew it.

Aigean moved toward them and spoke softly. "You must think me a monster to have all this while so many go hungry and bed on blood-stained dust." She took one of their hands in each of her own. "My dears, you must understand…if it weren't for the Condorians, I'd send this enemy-plundered splendor to any world who asked for it. All my food, all my medical supplies, and everything else I've ever earned. But it would only last a few days when distributed. And what I intend to do is to stop a great many Condorians once and for all. One time long ago…I tried to convince myself that I could remain neutral. That I could go to some peaceful part of the universe and ignore what's happening," she bitterly mused as tears filled her eyes. "But it took the deaths of my own loved ones to make me see the light. I was blinded by greed and the need to survive at all costs. But no more!" She tightened her grip on their hands. "I paid for my lack of care. I have only two granddaughters to love now. And I thank the great Creator that those children are on *your* home world, Soldar. I realize their safety will be short-lived but we have a chance to make a difference. And I've also come to know that I have it within my power to right some wrongs. I will do this if it costs my life." She let their hands go. "Now, do not dwell on guilt. You are not to blame for having survived. You're here for a reason."

Soldar leaned forward and gently kissed Aigean on her cheek. "Your words are filled with wisdom. We'll do our best."

Aigean nodded. "I'll come to you later with a schedule. Rest while you can. My people will arrive shortly with more clothing and food."

"Thank you," Lyra offered.

"Keep up the act you displayed in the passageway," Aigean encouraged. "Make yourselves above being abused. The Condorians are nothing but cowards. With your battle experience, you should know this," she affirmed then fell silent for a moment as if in thought. Then she turned to Lyra. "You may escape their sexual demands if you act as though there'll be severe repercussions for molesting you. Ingratiate yourselves to the admiral. He's arrogantly possessive of my ship and crew. He's taken ownership by right of superior rank. Indeed…I think he'd actually kill one of his own underlings than lose the only luxury in many sectors."

"And you're sure he doesn't suspect anything?" Soldar asked.

"If he did you'd most certainly be dead by now." She lifted one hand carelessly and let it drop. "He believes I'm nothing more than a stupid woman. That greed and hope of survival rule my actions. To keep the worst of their repugnant ranks out, I charge exorbitantly. Their vile leader would suspect my motives were I not so insistent about my compensation. He revels in his superior exclusivity. So I let the swine think what he wants. His complacency serves our purpose."

They watched Aigean march out of their quarters.

Soldar locked the electric hatch mechanism behind her. He turned to scan his surroundings, as any good soldier would. Lyra did the same.

Their quarters were decorated for the express purpose of sexual arousal. Tasteful nude statues were displayed on small columns that reminded him of otherworldly, amorous deities. The entire area was roughly the size of most small homes on most allied worlds. Rooms in homes on most planets were divided by curtains which could be pulled to more or less block the view of others sharing the space. But curtains for that same purpose here were gauzy, sparkling, and ineffective for any real privacy. Indeed, they invited others sharing the space to watch sexual liaisons.

In each curtained area within their quarters, he saw a table where beverage bottles were artfully displayed. Beds were no more than huge pillows with jewel-toned, small cushions piled upon them. The entire color scheme reflected the deep and sparkling hues of rare gems of many worlds. Blue, gold, silver, green, and red were placed to excite or conversely sooth any occupants' demeanor. It looked exactly like some ancient harem he'd seen in historical references. Even the floors and walls were covered by more warm tapestries to keep one from being reminded that the bulkhead of a vessel stood on the other side.

He shook his head, unable to imagine the expense of such design or where the goods had originated. Even the royal rooms on his home world couldn't compare with this magnificence.

Raiding Condorians may have provided these luxuries if only to accommodate their taste. The bastards were driven by having the best while showing the rest of the universe they deserved nothing but death.

The one real jewel to covet in this room was the brave woman who'd accompanied him from the wastelands. He kept wishing he'd left her there. It was likely the last bad mistake he'd ever make.

•••

Lyra slowly turned to see her superior's reaction, but he wasn't looking at the sinfully opulent décor. He was staring at her. His silvery gaze was more poignant than before. It suddenly occurred to her that she was seeing him—really seeing what he looked like—for the very first time. And he wasn't as pale as she'd assumed. He wasn't pale at all. What the half-light and sepia tones hid, the lights of the Venus now revealed.

His skin was bronzed like the room's Grecian-like effigies. And his hair was a pure, spun gold color. In truth, staring at him was like looking at a sun god. Muscle bulged from the open vee of his pale-colored tunic. She saw massive curves of defined body strain within his tight clothing.

Such an inspection was only occurring now, when she was at least a bit easier as to safety. Before, when they'd first entered the docking bay, she'd had her full attention on her location, where her room was positioned, and how to get to the nearest exit. Then there'd been that roll-playing scenario in the passageway, enacted for the benefit of their suspicious enemies. Now that was over she was faced with the actual appearance of the man whose ultimate mission was hers. The same huge man she'd be making love to in front of total strangers.

• • •

Soldar couldn't take his eyes off her. In regular light, she was so much lovelier. He realized she was seeing him in a new way too. That was why she stared as intently as he.

Her eyes weren't blue as he'd thought. They were really an unusual shade of blue-green. They were so brilliant that the difference from what he'd seen outside the ship was stunning. He couldn't have stopped his next words if his life and hers depended on it.

"I looked but didn't see," he softly told her. "You really are the loveliest thing I've ever beheld." He slowly walked forward, put his hand on her left cheek and drew her closer. He folded her into his embrace even as he lowered his head over her upturned, goddess-like face. He allowed himself the luxury of gliding his lips against hers. They weren't a Master Sergeant and a Colonel. For this moment, they were just a man and a woman. They were lonely, frightened, and close to death. He'd seen the desire in her gaze and meant to answer that unspoken call.

His body burned.

It seared and drove into him in a way he could never forget. The kiss deepened. It went on and on until time and their present circumstances were lost. Nothing mattered but the moment. Nothing mattered but holding her close, caressing her slender body, and sharing that blazing, rapturous instant.

He finally broke the contact though the blood in his veins cried out to continue. He dropped his hands, aching to continue his caresses. "Under normal circumstances I'd be thrown in the brig for two months for touching any subordinate like that."

"Breaking the rules is our mission now," she responded. "We're only buying a little time for our people even if this works."

He shook his head to clear it and get his mind back on matters at hand, then backed off and turned to gaze at the room. For a long moment neither of them spoke. He finally found a subject that would keep his mind off sex. "How many poor bastards lost their lives when the Condorians stole these luxuries? I've no doubt half of what we've seen was due to their killing. It's been a long war. Aigean couldn't have maintained this level of quality without their thievery."

"I-I was just wondering the same thing," she admitted. "I'm not sure I can sleep on one of these beds. I'm used to transport cots friends and I shared in shifts."

"Indeed," he responded while trying to breathe normally. Even as he'd made another attempt to capture his professional bearing, he knew there'd come a time very soon when they'd have to engage in sex. It was their cover. Still, he found himself unbelievably elated at the prospect. He should exhibit a blasé attitude to fool the enemy. But how did one do that when he so desperately wanted her?

His need was driven by going so long without a woman. He'd had men—friends who'd shared each other for the sake of dimming the lonely hours. But he simply preferred women, their warmth and femininity. And this one was all the things he craved, right down to the long, lean-looking, and shapely legs and the soft—*so ultra-soft*—fully kissable lips.

"I-I need a cold shower," he blurted. "Maybe you could scrounge up something to eat. We have to keep focused," he suggested, more to remind himself of duty. "See what you can do."

• • •

Lyra watched him walk away.

It was obvious he was as shaken as she. She ran her hands through her hair and prowled the room and the scrumptious delights there. It wasn't long before she had two plates filled with appetizers that more than made a decent meal.

There was no shortage of fruit, cheeses, wine, and other beverages. What must the actual main courses be like aboard the Venus? How many were starving for want of one piece of molding bread, never mind the crispy crackers and snack rolls? With all this, Aigean needn't have ordered them a full meal.

But where the food would sate hunger and the luxury would repair parts of her tired body, nothing but his touch would stop the burning he'd started. And touching, simply caressing and kissing, wouldn't be good enough. She was aware of his mutual desire. It had been evident in his unwavering gaze.

She couldn't guess what he really thought about her, other than he believed her to be physically attractive. In this situation, any woman would probably have driven him insane with desire. As for her feelings on the matter, Soldar Nar was the embodiment of every hero she'd ever wanted. And if they were going to die, she'd have him and not give a damn who watched or whether those voyeurs were entertained or not. If these were her last days, and they got caught getting information back to Allied Command, then she was going into the hereafter with the taste of him on her lips and the feel of him deep within her body.

Chapter 4

It only took Soldar a few moments to find the luxurious shower space and quickly unclothe. He stood within a vault-like compartment two sizes larger than the entire sleeping area on any transport ship.

Within the black marble stall, water sluiced over his tired, dirty body from every conceivable direction. It was hot and there were even colored lights emanating from the same water jets that directed the spray. Scented soap provided an aromatic experience that was both pleasing and soothing. He hadn't such a luxurious experience in years.

Once more, he tasted the bitterness of guilt. How could he stand there soaping himself and relishing the feel hot, fresh water and the smell of cleanliness? His comrades were fighting and dying.

He quickly put a bar of hand-milled, herbal soap back in its holder and was determined to end the shower and the remorse it caused. He'd only stay long enough to wash off the rest of the suds and return to the main area or their quarters. But thoughts of the woman in the other room kept taking precedence. He was glad she'd run down that dead-end canyon, toward him. He was thankful to have her company while conversely wishing her safely back in that cave. But the truth was simple: there simply *wasn't* any safe place any longer. His world and hers would be attacked eventually. Whatever remained of their cultures would be destroyed by the Condorians. And realizing that, he let his guard down and simply gave way to emotions a leader shouldn't harbor. Not in these circumstances. He should keep his mind on business, and his penis in check until it was time to use it.

Even as he tried to keep their mission before anything else, his body was still aching for her touch.

His left hand slid down his wet body while his right began to finger his nipples. The need to release couldn't be contained. He imagined himself making slow love to Lyra, on some planet away from war, strife, or any conflict.

He spread his legs and began to stroke his thick rod. It and its accompanying *flange* were fully erect and when he gazed down he saw the telltale red glow of his testicles. He'd been in need for a long time. Lyra's presence just augmented that desire by a hundredfold.

For just a few moments, he'd give in to desire. Get it out of his system and he'd be able to return to the room more equipped to think.

His hips began to automatically thrust forward as he stroked his shaft from the very base out to the tip. Occasionally, he'd tweak the flange on top as it vibrated in response to his stroking. His bullock-like testicles swung forward from their dropped position between his lower thighs. Their subtle glow grew brighter as he neared ejaculation.

"Lyra," he whispered, "I want to take you hard! Creator…help me. I want to be deep in you…somewhere far away."

With the words said, he closed his eyes and stroked himself faster and with his hand more tightly closed around his shaft. He swung his balls harder. The act of tweaking his nipples, the swinging of his testicles, and the stroking of his penis finally gave him the full barrage of sensations his body required. He released his seed against the shower wall hard and long. It took all his control to keep from shouting out while thick semen spattered onto that surface and washed down the drain.

The wonderful climax took him to another reality where only pleasure existed. The entire time, he conjured a vivid, nude image of Lyra sucking him off, pulling his balls with one hand

and fingering his flange with the other. And when he was done, and stood there dragging air into his lungs, he actually felt better, more in control. Perhaps the release was needed to clear his brain. His body had been trying to tell him this since meeting the little Earther.

Now, he believed he could go back in the main area of their quarters, and let her go to one bed while he rested in another. The woman must be dead tired. She *must* rest. And that meant sleeping, not screwing him when it wasn't necessary for their cover.

He desperately needed sleep as well. Who knew when Aigean would come for them and they'd have to fuck at length for an audience. Shaking his head slowly, he recognized impulses that were centuries old rising in his heart and mind.

Harboring Craetorian instincts to protect his would-be lover, his conscience was at war over how to guard her and entertain a roomful of spectators. That this entire situation was a farce made no difference to thousands of years of breeding. He was already projecting mating overtures on Lyra.

As to the *performances* they'd have to provide, he needed to again broach the subject of his genitalia as he was certain she'd never seen anything like it given her admitted ignorance of his race. The woman should realize what she'd be taking inside her slender, tight little body. Her preference for "spontaneity" for the audience's sake, and in order to make their cover of an exciting sex duo more plausible, might not be a good idea if she actually didn't know how to accept his cock. Then again, if he ended up showing her his package, he'd want her. That brought him right back to the subject of needing adequate sleep. By this time tomorrow night, he'd be a walking zombie if he didn't rest. And she wouldn't be able to function at all if he gave in to his needs.

With calm deliberation, he got out of the shower and dried his body. Then, he shrugged into a thick black robe, tamed his drying hair with a complementary brush, and walked back into the main room. Lyra was pouring them each a glass of water. A bottle of wine was also sitting nearby, but the water was a healthier choice given their tired status.

• • •

Lyra glanced up when *her* bronzed, godly superior came striding back in the room. The moisture in his hair caused its blond hue to turn a few shades darker. "Uh, if you don't mind, I'd like to grab a shower myself. I don't want to eat while I'm so filthy. Not if I don't have to."

"Of course," he readily agreed while drinking a tall glass of clean, iced water.

She entered the spacious bathing area, took a look at the black and silver grandiosity, and smothered the desire to spit on everything. What right did she have to be so coddled, even on a mission of this importance? Her friends were dead and here she was, living in the lap of luxury. Her life expectancy might be even less than what she'd endure outside in the wastelands, but the comfort dead heroes would never have ate at her conscience.

She took a deep breath, shed her clothing, and threw it in the auto-wash service bin. Then she stepped into the still-steamy shower that Sol had exited. She turned on the water and was inundated with warm, soothing spray from all directions and accompanying optic lights that set the mood for her next actions.

The feeling of being unsoiled almost made her drop to her knees in thanks. It had been such a long time since so much water had been offered. Her body cried out for the need to be clean, for as long as possible. And then she remembered the man who'd just left the same space. She could almost feel his body heat on the thick marble walls.

As she stood there considering the immediate future, a strange thing happened. Tranquility encompassed her. It floated around her like the hazy mist of water. An image of the Colonel standing there took her fear and rage away when nothing else could have.

Her right hand slid between her thighs. Her left hand reached for the old-fashioned bar of scented soap that had been new but was now used as her superior's choice for bathing accoutrement.

There were soap dispensers for the more squeamish bedroom sharers, but she wanted to have the same bar skimming over her flesh that he'd put next to his. It would bring her closer to the orgasm she craved.

Hate would come again. She had enough of that in her heart. For now, she could do what she hadn't been able to without others watching on a transport vessel. Now she could have a little time to herself.

Death was there, just around the corner. But there was also the feel of warm, wonderful-smelling soap that a god-like, soon-to-be sex partner had just used.

Afterward, eating, sleeping, and thinking of the mission would be easier. She just had to touch herself first. She had to. Everything suddenly seemed so desperate; this was one thing she owned.

Her fingers separated her labia as she rubbed the bar of soap over her face, breasts, and stomach.

What would it be like to have him washing her and filling her pussy at the same time? She softly moaned as an image of him kneeling behind her came to mind.

She'd always preferred to be entered, vaginally, from the rear. Sometimes being on top was great, but a man could more easily play with her clit if he knelt behind her. And since fantasy was an outlet for her pent-up emotions, she indulged herself like the doomed woman she was.

She thrust her middle finger into her pussy, rotated her hips forward, and rubbed her body harder with the bar of soap. In her mind, it wasn't her finger inside her body, it was Sol's cock. Using her imagination, she pretended her finger was large, thick, and throbbing.

She'd heard stories about the men of his race and assumed those rumors weren't entirely accurate. How could they be? The exaggerations were preposterous.

But as she both manipulated her labia and thrust her fingers deeper, the scene she envisioned was much better than any story. Something told her he'd be better than any man she'd ever had. She'd make it so. Time was so short now. And if he would be her last lover, then God couldn't have sent her anything more fantastic.

She fantasized about how it would be. Even in the middle of an enemy-controlled vessel, she could still imagine. No one could take that away from her.

She and the big man in the other room wouldn't just be playing a sex duo, traveling the stars for the purpose of showcasing their abilities. No. They'd be making memories for the short time they'd have together.

Lyra dropped the bar of soap and began to pull her nipples. Wet and soapy as they were, the sensation was fantastic. She took several steps forward so that her nipples barely grazed the black marble wall. This, too, was an added sensation that had her licking her lips in expectation.

She'd hoped for a longer round of play, but being tired and horny had the effect of rousing her body more fiercely and quickly than usual. She felt a tightening in the back of her pussy. It squeezed forward toward her clit, where her fingers played. Her body undulated with the coming orgasm, while her breasts were flattened against the shower wall. She rode out the climax with her fingers still embedded deeply within her body. When it was over, she stood there panting, then finally placed the palms of both hands on the black marble wall in front of her. She fancied she could still feel heat there that wasn't associated with the warm water.

The entire scenario hadn't lasted five minutes, but the wonderful experience was now over. Her mind could center on business again and not on seven feet of make-believe Norse mythological male in another part of their quarters.

After drying her body, she marched back into the main room wearing a copy of the robe Soldar donned. But needy feelings quickly rose to the surface again as she studied the massive pectoral muscle jutting from the open vee of his bathrobe.

So much for thinking a quickie would work.

She focused on eating. Sustenance was necessary or her energy would give out. Despite what they'd consumed in the desert, her body actually craved better fare than the protein pack most of the Allied Forces were issued. She shoved aside her guilt and decided to eat well. Maybe filling up would lend extra energy to kill a few Condorians—when the time came.

•••

Soldar momentarily closed his eyes in frustration.

The beauty who shared his quarters was still enticing him. He wanted to run his hands through her drying hair as it curled around the nape of her neck, and under her sweet chin and shell-like ears. He wanted to pick her up, carry her to one of the sumptuous-looking oversized pillows that served as beds, and make love to the woman until the next day. But not knowing when Aigean would come or what she'd have planned, it behooved them to keep their professional wits and not act like hormone-driven adolescents. He'd have her sooner or later.

"Drink plenty of water," he advised, "and eat lots of fruit."

She half-smiled and nodded. Her fingers closed around a piece of pink and orange striped gactor fruit from the planet Cygnus.

That particular choice was one of his favorite treats when it had been available on Craetoria. Seeing how hungry she was and how hard she was trying not to show it, Sol handed her pieces of bread and cheese. She smiled at his friendly gesture, but ate without comment.

He picked up the last of his water, swallowed it, and then stood. "I suggest we get some sleep."

Lyra stood, tightened her belt around her waist, and offered up concerns for the day's encounters. "Sol, Aigean doesn't really know what to do with us, does she? I'm not even sure she knew what to do with just you, had you arrived alone…just as you and your men planned. The woman barely knew how to get us on her ship. This leads me to believe she's desperate."

Accepting the shortened version of his name without comment, he nodded. "I agree. But being watched as she is, it's courageous of her and her crew to continue. Most people in her position wouldn't be willing to risk so much."

"But this spontaneous mess makes me reconsider that tantrum I threw in the passageway. I brought a lot of attention to us. What I did might not have been so smart. Maybe what we looked like wouldn't have been all that noticeable to a bunch of drunken, drug-induced thugs."

He shook his head in denial of that censure. "Your ingenuity was brilliant. Had the Condorians wanted to know who we were, you dispersed any suspicions. Now, don't think on it any more, Lyra. Go find a bed and get some sleep. Something tells me tomorrow will be a very long day. As an old Earth saying goes, we're playing this by the seats of our pants. That could be to our advantage."

"How?"

"If we don't know what we're going to do next, the enemy surely won't!" When she simply nodded and began to clear away the remains of their meal, he put one hand on her forearm to stop her. "Leave it for the servants to clear. In the event all of them aren't so loyal to Aigean, one who services this room might think it odd if we clean up after ourselves."

"Of course. You're right," she said as she put their plates back down.

The nearest bedding area was to her left, so she climbed onto the pillow and didn't bother removing her robe. Sleep and a full stomach seemed to overcome her. She didn't move for several moments after she plopped down. He found a pillow-bed nearby and stretched out.

Above him, sparkling decorator lights shimmered like stars on a warm Craetorian night. But even that lovely vision didn't take his mind off the woman sleeping nearby.

How long was he capable of remaining the professional commanding officer? And if he couldn't, how could they complete this mission?

He *craved* her.

Even though he'd tried to cast out all such longings in the shower, he still recalled every nuance of her face and lips. As he now was, he daren't even kiss her for luck. His need wouldn't allow such innocent contact and leave it there. *This* is what a warrior from his world suffered when he'd been too long without feminine company and desired it above all else. This is what happened when a female Earther ran down a narrow canyon and into his life.

He turned on his left side, struck the pillow several times with his right fist, and buried his head into the indentation. Even though his body ached for hers, the comforts of a plush bed coupled with absolute exhaustion eventually quieted his brittle nerves.

The soft sheets and luxurious bed cover felt like a warm breeze against his skin. His eyelids drooped but he quickly jerked them open again as he would have had he been in battle too long, without rest. But sleep finally came.

• • •

Soldar awoke to what he thought was the next morning. He slid out of his pillow bed, tightened the belt on his robe, and checked the time on the holo-com work station. "Corona's balls!" He passed his hand through the holographic image as if by doing so might change the time. It was many hours past morning. Too many. He hadn't expected to sleep for so long.

There were no messages on the computer system. That meant nothing was amiss; Aigean was calm enough with the situation to let them rest. It was conversely bad if their hostess actually couldn't warn them.

Perhaps they'd slept too long and the woman couldn't get to a holo-com because she was being watched. But no alarms had sounded. Surely they would have been activated by the Condorians themselves, if they perceived a threat.

His left hand automatically dredged through his hair and he decided to awaken Lyra. Since she hadn't done him that favor, he assumed she was still asleep.

Indeed, he found her snugly tucked beneath a blanket, resting like a soft little bird. His hand moved forward to gently nudge her shoulder, but he hesitated and pulled it back. All he'd have to do was sidle into her bed, stretch out next to her, and pull her into his embrace. Some instinct told him she'd turn into his body and cuddle against it as if she belonged there.

The first kiss they'd shared at the oasis vividly came to mind. It would be so easy and warm to awaken her with another but he couldn't yet find it in his heart to break her soft slumber.

Asleep, she was the most captivatingly sweet sight he'd seen in a very long time. She lay on her right side with her hands tucked beneath her cheek. Her palms were pressed together. It was as if she was praying.

He'd once witnessed her Earth brethren praying before going into battle. During that instance—where these brave fighters had stopped to ask forgiveness before their priests—Soldar had stopped to observe and learn. He'd asked questions about their deity. An Earth cleric had explained creationism philosophy that was eerily similar to his planet's beliefs. Sadly, he'd later learned that most of those praying warriors, and the priest who went with them to serve as their battlefield minister, had been slaughtered.

That memory forcefully brought his senses back to the mission. No one was safe. No one was spared. And they might be set upon at any minute if Aigean's people faltered and one of them gave this mission away.

Such things happened when people panicked. They could trust no one but themselves until proof of loyalty was presented. There was no question where his partner's allegiance lay. Lyra ran upon his location while turning to fight an enemy she thought would kill her. She'd die before giving up this mission. Everyone *else* must prove they could be trusted. As for him, he'd never give up the encrypted codes that Allied Forces used to identify messages as authentic. To that end, they had to make some quick plans that wouldn't include Aigean's bridge crew.

He slowly sat on the bed so as not to alarm her, then leaned over and pushed the fringe of soft silky bangs off her forehead. "Lyra…it's time to get up," he whispered.

She took a deep breath, turned onto her back, and slowly opened her eyes. "W-what time is it?"

"By Reisen Four time, it's evening of the next day. We slept for many hours."

He dropped his gaze when she sat up. The front of her robe had fallen open and the full swell of her breasts was quite visible. She quickly pulled the right side of the garment over the left and retied her belt. As he saw it, the gesture was a bit pointless seeing as how she'd originated the idea of their being a traveling sex team. But they weren't putting on an act for anyone right now. Both of them needed to keep perspective.

"Was there any communication from Aigean?" she quickly asked.

He shook off the pleasurable sight of her round, cream-colored breasts, stood, and turned away. "No, and that worries me. She should have left some kind of message."

"Let's not borrow trouble," Lyra reasoned as she scooted off the bed and stood. "I was hoping someone might show up with clothes. If we put on the same things we arrived in, we'll look even worse than when we just came in off the badlands. I'm sure everyone except the Condorians must be dressed impeccably."

Soldar was about to concur with that point when the buzzer to their quarters sounded loud and long. He held up his hand, motioning for her to stay put, and went to the hatch that served as their door. The security monitor allowed him to see Aigean and half a dozen of her crewmembers standing in the passageway, all bearing crates, cases, and bundles of goods. "It's all right," he confirmed and saw Lyra let out a sigh in relief.

They stood in the middle of the room after he let in their hostess and her minions. It was a shock to see Aigean breeze into their quarters smiling, as if the universe had no problems too big to handle.

Crewmembers with her were wearing dark blue robes. Their hoods were pulled up to designate them as servants, not sex givers. These silent vassals flooded in behind the blue-green Elderian and began to unpack sundries.

Soldar glanced at Lyra and shared a confused shrug with her while the people worked. He noted that some of them were Elderian like Aigean. Others were from various worlds where every skin hue was represented, along with a spare arm or two.

"What's all this stuff?" Lyra asked, gesturing toward the boxes, crates, and parcels.

Aigean gazed around her before explaining. "We told the Condorian guards that these were the crates of goods and other paraphernalia necessary for your act." She moved closer. "You still intend to pass yourselves off as a traveling sex duo, do you not?"

Soldar and Lyra simultaneously nodded.

"You may speak in front of any of my employees on this vessel," she assured them. "I know this is difficult to understand, given what you two have probably experienced, but you can trust them with your lives."

When Soldar glanced at the faces of the crew, they concurrently nodded. This *we can be trusted* signal was appreciated but he was still of the opinion that confidence needed to be earned. Apparently Lyra thought the same thing.

He held up his hand and gestured toward the sleeping area he'd used the night before, silently asking both Lyra and Aigean to follow.

When they were in his bed area, Soldar spoke softly. "Aigean…I appreciate the danger you're in, but we have no plans at all. I came here depending on you to have the details worked out as to my movements. If one of your crew is ever accosted or threatened by a Condorian, they could easily sell us out."

"They wouldn't," Aigean argued. "Not in this life or the next."

"Others we thought were allies *have*," he insisted. "We need to know what's going on and right now. Why didn't you contact us or leave a message? Why were we allowed to sleep so long?"

Aigean raised one brow. "First, as I've already told you, every one of my people has lost family to the Condorians. They'd as soon die rather than cater to them, but do so on this ship to glean vital information. They find it repugnant to even have them near. I'll warrant my employees' experiences are as horrific as anything you may have seen while fighting," she vehemently insisted. "It was information my people gleaned that kept me from contacting you these last hours. But we'll get to that in a moment." She arranged her long, tunic-style gown around her figure before continuing. "Second, I don't know if either of you were aware of how desperately exhausted you looked. I could see it in your eyes, and knew you'd never make it through events I've contrived if you didn't get some much needed rest. My information has the same importance attached now as when I received it. It will be the same tonight, so that's when you'll get it to Allied HQ."

"Explain," Lyra responded.

"The midnight shift period will be the best time approach the bridge, and use your authentication codes to send a message. But only Lyra will be able to actually gain access to that area."

Lyra held up her hands in confusion. "Okay, back up. Could you explain everything you just said? We're moving pretty fast here. Why tonight?"

Aigean took a deep breath before continuing. "Some of my sex servants were attending the Condorians at a private party in Admiral Kardis D'uhr's quarters. The Condorian contingent was quite drunk and full of Ambrosiaq…a terrible substance I would never allow on board if I had a choice. Infuriatingly, the bastards insisted on bringing that foul, hallucinogenic sexual stimulant on my ship." She pursed her lips in apparent contempt. "At any rate, the Condorians' tongues were sufficiently loosened that the servants heard a plan concerning the mining colony of Taurean Seti-Seven. The Condorians intend to loot it for Lorbidrium. I'm sure you know they use it to fuel their ships."

"My God! Now I remember where I heard that name. Admiral Kardis D'uhr is the new leader of all the Condorian attack forces in this entire sector," Lyra blurted. "Information has it that he took over suddenly. Nobody seems to know why."

"He took over when the old admiral mysteriously died in his sleep. Or so our captors say," Aigean confirmed. "But D'uhr is nothing if not tenacious. He's attacking hard and early in his new position. He means to wash this entire sector in the blood of every last ally. So if you can get a message to Allied Command that the Lorbidrium on that world is about to be looted, and that the miners and their families will be attacked, our side may have time to evacuate or at least hide the citizens. Certainly, the Allies will be able to destroy the fuel depots. That, of course, will leave some of the older allied vessels without a fuel source, but I understand that the Condorians are hard pressed to provide energy for their thousands of ships. I believe they can ill afford to run low, whereas the allies are having a difficult time finding enough troopers to even staff their vessels. Never mind fuel them."

"Fuel is one of the reasons Condorians declared war," Soldar mused. "Their race claims they haven't enough of it, or enough provisions to provide for all their people. So instead of making diplomatic offers, the vermin attacked and took what they wanted. Losing part of their population hardly bothers them when there are so many. They have many more colonies around their home world than all the allies combined…something I'm sure all your employees are aware of."

Aigean nodded in agreement. "I believe they won't launch the attack until Kardis can send word to do so from my bridge. He hesitates only to allow his fleet to gather for the strike…that and he's so sated with sex, wine, and Ambrosiaq that he can't function properly most days. The bastard certainly doesn't want to return to his own vessel. I do my best to make sure that, if he's here, he stays satiated," she informed them. "I waited until my people could glean every detail they could before coming to you now. This is one reason why I let you sleep…besides the fact that you both desperately needed it, as I've said."

"But why would I have a better chance to get on the bridge?" Lyra asked.

"No Condorian will allow Soldar access. Even *if* they believe he's neutral where his planet's politics are concerned, he wouldn't have any reason to be there so soon after arriving. But *you* could do it," she insisted.

Lyra shrugged in confusion.

"You can disguise yourself in one of my servant's robes," Aigean explained. "We'll alter your appearance to look like someone else.

You're of a similar size and stature as many of my women. But Soldar's size makes disguising him impossible even if we could cover his facial mark. He's simply too conspicuous."

Soldar shook his head in objection. "Lyra doesn't know the authentication codes. They're long. Even if she could memorize them in such a short time, she hasn't time to enter them into the computer *and* enter a message to HQ from the bridge. It would take several minutes for her to do this, assuming she got everything correct," he argued. "Her actions would surely be noticed. Furthermore, those codes change every seventy-two hours. I'm the only member of my team left alive who knows the sequencing alterations."

Aigean lifted her hands in frustration. "How did you intend to get any information back to the allies, then?"

Soldar walked to the wall computer in their quarters and put one hand on the monitor. "All ship spaces have computers like these. They're solely for internal communications."

"Go on," Aigean prompted.

"It's dangerous, but I was going to store the codes in one of these work stations and get someone I felt I could trust onto the bridge. Once there that spy could enter brief messages to HQ. Then I'd have shown that same person how to attach the stored authentication codes from the work station and onto the message sent from your bridge transmitter. In fact, I was relying on you for this part of the mission," Soldar outlined. "I had a hunch I could never get on the bridge and I couldn't just hand over the codes to one of your people."

"That was your plan?" Lyra asked in wide-eyed amazement.

He stared at her for a moment before responding. "It was the best I could come up with on such short notice. I wasn't even assigned to this mission until HQ learned I was in the area. My previous orders were to head to Canis Tor to rescue a diplomat. Turns out he's dead anyhow."

"What Sol's saying can certainly be done," Lyra agreed as she stroked her chin in thought. "I know how. I can quickly move what I've transmitted into a disguised file and out of the main indexes. Still, unless my actions are overwritten, or I delete everything on your entire computer system, someone searching could eventually find what I've done. If we pass on too many messages to Allied Command, someone on this vessel will eventually fall under suspicion."

"That will be *you*, Aigean," Soldar confirmed. "If the Condorians begin to suspect their battle plans are being leaked from this ship, you and your people will suffer first. And they *will* find Lyra's transmissions. One of the first things they'll do is to go the bridge and search your entire hard drive. Lyra can hardly delete it without further causing suspicion as to why all the ships' systems are offline. She certainly can't do that every single time she transmits…assuming we don't get caught during this first attempt."

Aigean sighed heavily. "So, if you enter the message authentication codes in your room's computer and Lyra accesses them from the bridge, will the codes in your room's work station be found?"

"That depends," Lyra advised. "I can delete the index file from the room computer the same way I delete the index file from the bridge transmitter. Again the problem is the codes will *still* be in this computer here, until overwritten or I delete the entire hard drive. But if it comes down to it, getting rid of everything on the room work station will be much easier than trying to hide what we've transmitted from the bridge." She shrugged and tucked a strand of hair behind her ear. "Hell, if I have to, I'll pull the damned thing out of the bulkhead and smash it. I can always pretend I was throwing a tantrum the way I did out in the passageway. Unfortunately, I can't do that same thing to the bridge transmitter."

Aigean paced for a moment before turning to them again. "We mustn't ever leave your room computer unguarded then. This is just in case some Condorian should find his way into the room, and attempt to order food. Or use the wall work station for some other petty task. If such a thing happened, he could accidentally stumble across the authentication codes. Even if they're changed every few hours on allied vessels, the very existence of them…in these quarters…will still give you both away."

Lyra crossed her arms over her chest and frowned. "Why would any Condorian be in this room unless invited?"

Aigean held out her hands in an anxious gesture of explanation. "I've already told you. Nothing on this ship is private, including your quarters."

"But if the enemy is as inebriated as you say, perhaps they won't want to be here," Soldar suggested. "There are many more pleasurable places."

"We can hope," Lyra chimed in.

"Right now, we must focus on the task at hand." Aigean told them. "Before you can get to the bridge transmitter at midnight, or even send the information about the Taurean Seti-Seven attack, you both have a rendezvous with some very highly placed Condorians…including Admiral D'uhr."

Soldar glanced at Lyra and found her staring back at him in fear.

Aigean briefly hung her head. "I'm sorry. I wish you'd had more time. But the admiral's guards were the ones in the passageway when you arrived. Because you were with me and because of Lyra's outburst, they've assumed what you wanted them to. That you're the new sex act I promised. That being the case, D'uhr wants to meet you tonight."

Soldar lifted one brow in concern. "That's what we wanted them to believe. And it seems to be working. So why the anxious expression, Aigean?"

Aigean briefly clasped her hands. "I fixed Lyra's background as originating from Gratis Major, which is a neutral planet. As long as she remembers that, no one will suspect she's from Earth. The denizens from both worlds look exactly alike. But before Lyra made an appearance and I had to quickly concoct *that* tale, I told the Condorians that the new sex servants would be men. Perhaps several of them. So when you showed up with a woman, Soldar, I told the Condorians that the men I'd hired had broken their contracts. I told them I'd taken great pains and had gone to massive expense to engage a new act that was extraordinary. If I'm correct and you *do* succeed with your cover, the both of you will be very popular. There's a possibility that the one or both of you will find sex partners accompanying you to this room or some other quarters for the night. *This* night!"

Lyra balked. "Wait just a minute! I came up with that story because I didn't mind—for the sake of duty—making love to an allied fighter. But I'm not about to let any Condorian touch me. Not if frost forms at the outermost regions of hell! I'd rather have a laser blast tear through my skull."

Aigean sighed. "I'm afraid that's exactly what might happen, my girl. A woman who looks like you simply doesn't book a job on a pleasure vessel without *desiring* such attention. Even though you're passing yourself off as a sex couple…emphasis on the couple…I couldn't promise that you'd never be confronted with offers to pleasure men or women separately. That's why you may find someone in this room. Someone who might accidentally run across the authentication codes hidden in the work station."

"So, we went to all this trouble for nothing?" Lyra asked.

"Lyra…we discussed this at the oasis," Soldar quietly reminded her while feeling his own anxiety rise in proportion to hers. It was quite possible she'd take her own life rather than face the consequences their hostess just described. He put his hands on her shoulders to sooth her distress, then saw her gazing up at him oddly.

"Y-your eyes are glowing," she remarked.

"That happens sometimes. When people of my race are under duress," he lied. Fortunately for him, Aigean knew the truth of his race and quickly intervened with a total change of subject.

"If the discussion about what will be done on the bridge is over, I'll need you both to undress," she commanded.

"*What?*" Soldar and Lyra asked in unison as they snapped her heads in her direction.

"I want you both to undress and let me watch you. We have a few hours before your first performance, and I need to see this so-called act so I can offer any suggestions that might lend credence to your ruse. My staff may as well watch," she stipulated as she lifted a hand to encompass the crew she'd brought into the room. "You'll be more comfortable in front of an audience if you've practiced it here. I assume neither of you has done anything like this before?"

"Not in *this* life," Lyra quipped.

Soldar sighed heavily and began to untie his robe. That was when he remembered Lyra didn't know about genitalia differences specific to the men from his planet.

While he'd been told by physicians that internal organs of Earthers and Craetorians were extraordinarily similar, the men of his world had outer extras that were vastly different for some evolutionary reason. His own take on the matter was that males from his planet had evolved sexual stimulating genitalia to better service their women. Craetorian women's sexual organs were exactly like those of Earth women. At least that's what he'd been *told*. Never having been with anyone from Earth, he couldn't be sure.

Either way, Lyra wasn't expecting what she was about to get. If she couldn't take his penis in her body, what other act could they possibly put together at this late hour?

Her explanation for holding back at the oasis was for the sake of *spontaneity* during their live performance. But he could see the absolute downside to that idea. She simply had to know about his anatomy now! Any inhibition onstage could be disastrous for all concerned.

Some drilled-in code of ethics tried to keep all this on a professional, staid level. But his body was already responding to the situation. Lyra had her back to him, but was also untying her robe slowly, hesitantly.

He saw Aigean and her minions take up seats on a nearby pillow lounges.

When Lyra turned to him and dropped her only garment to the floor he swore then and there and by all the deities that had ever lived in any universe that no one would *ever* have her but him. At least not while they were on this mission. He shrugged out of his robe, saw the shock on her face, and walked toward her.

Chapter 5

Lyra couldn't help gawking. Before her stood a true god. Almost seven feet of male hewn body stretch upward. Every muscle, sinew, ligament, and tendon cried out to be touched as it all blended in perfect harmony. From his massive shoulders to his highly developed quads, Soldar Nar was everything any woman could have ever wanted. His hard-packed, pillowed abs stood out in such bas relief that they made her want to lick his midsection. His boldly trained, healthy body was devoid of any hair save the perfect triangle of golden curls between his thighs and the thick, long pelt on his head.

Like many sentient beings from some worlds these days, his race may have developed the blessing of not needing to shave. She couldn't imagine he'd allow any artificial enhancers such as permanent laser treatments for body hair removal. Aside from leaving a bit of pubic hair and that which grew on her head, she'd availed herself of hair removal procedures before leaving Earth. It simply made sense when one didn't know how long it'd be before accessing a very small transport shower. But if laser treatments were the reason for the smoothness of his skin sans hair, he'd surely have opted to have numerous scars removed from his flesh during the procedure. Instead, old healed wounds were there as evidence to his warrior status and the battles he'd survived. The total effect was that his body gleamed like polished bronze. Even the scars seemed perfectly right. He was hard, megalithic, and awesome.

She daren't look into his eyes. Their unholy, silvery gaze was fixed on her. She felt the intense heat of it as she could have felt any blazing sun. But all her attention now was drawn to the genitalia hanging thick, long, and prominent between his thighs.

The man's penis was long with a bulbous, thick head that made her mouth water to taste it. On top of it, but at the base of his thick shaft, was another appendage that jutted up about four inches and was divided at the top. This lesser head looked like a small set of rabbit ears. That was the only frame of reference she had for this secondary sexual organ.

And most striking sight of all was the long, bullish testicles that hung very low, down between his gargantuan, muscular thighs. Within their globular depths a red glow began. That was when she finally lifted her gaze to his.

•••

Soldar couldn't help his response to her perfect, divine proportions. Lyra's full, pert breasts were made to be suckled and massaged. Her narrow, flat waist and tightly defined abdomen spoke of many hours of hard work and more time spent fighting. Even her legs and arms were toned and well-shaped. They weren't emaciated or weakly thin, as so many women of his acquaintance imagined to be attractive. The pretty thatch of brown curls between her slender thighs begged to be stroked. He could imagine spreading her legs, diving between them, and hearing her cry out his name in release over and over. Her body was like a Craetorian woman's except she was so much smaller. The expression in her gaze was electrifying. She wanted him. There was no denying her desire. And his body responded to that silent call with vigor. His penis jerked in response as blood flood to the organ.

Aigean clapped her hands loudly.

"I-I'm sorry," Soldar muttered, his gaze still on Lyra. "Did you say something?"

"Not that either of you was listening to a word I said…but I told you both to *lie down*! And do it now," Aigean commanded. "We only have a few hours to get your act together and it's going to take every moment since the two of you seem to have lost your wits."

Soldar did as the Elderian woman asked. As he stretched out on the pillowed bed he'd slept in the night before, his cock remained upright as testament to his unbridled arousal.

• • •

Aigean turned to Lyra. "Now…you get on top of him and—"

"I know what to do. Just get out my way," Lyra interrupted as she gently pushed the other woman to one side.

Aigean smirked. "Don't rush on stage. The audience will expect a prolonged act. Remember, you're supposed to be performing for *them*. There's no harm in enjoying yourself."

Lyra swallowed hard as she looked over Soldar's perfect, immense body. Strangely, it was only *then* that she noticed what was on his arms.

Wrapped around each of his twenty-inch plus biceps were two golden armbands. Each of these bands was about four inches wide. There was some kind of silver dragon embellishment on them. She hadn't seen them before because he'd been wearing long sleeves. The robe he'd just dropped and his tunic earlier hadn't hinted of such jewelry.

She took the moment to breathe deeper and slow her pounding heart. She kept her eyes on the arm ornamentation. Being intimate as they were about to be, she could ponder the beautiful bands at length. The small diversion could hold her attention and steady her nerves as she mounted him. For more than just the mission, doing this exactly right became very important.

She began by slowly crawling up from the foot of the rounded, pillow bed.

"You know, Earthlings have stories about the same kind of dragons depicted on your armbands," she softly told him. Then she traced the outline of his gargantuan quadriceps before moving forward. "We have myths of them from many centuries ago."

His only response was to stare straight into her eyes.

"If it's true we really come from shared ancestors, I guess this is where I get to explore how much we have in common. Myths, men, and women," she whispered.

Soldar lifted his body so his weight was on his elbows, his body still reclining back.

Lyra felt her nipples graze his flesh as she maneuvered over him.

He licked his lips, as if he anticipated tasting her.

She stopped crawling forward when her face was directly above his genitalia. Before she moved one more inch, that part of his anatomy deserved her full, undivided attention.

She gently lifted his testicles in each of her palms. The two four-inch orbs filled her hands with warmth and the red glow brightened to a molten color. Glancing upward, she saw his eyes begin to glow as well. There was a reflective quality in them that reminded her of an animal being caught in the headlights of a hovercraft. Some instinct told her she was on the right path to pleasuring him. In doing so, she was sure to be equally satisfied.

As it had since the war began, her mind grasped at the shortness of life. This experience with her comrade had to mean something so that if they should fail, some good would come from this mission. Even if it was only the last pleasure they'd share.

"Does this happen only when you're aroused?" she softly asked, referring to how the round part of his balls were glowing intensely.

"Yes. I like having them stroked and pulled. From the base all the way down," he instructed in an equally hushed tone. "The extra appendage on my penis is called a *flange*." He smiled slowly. "I pity the women of your race."

Lyra smiled too. Part of her brain told her that passing themselves off as a professional pair of love-makers was critical to their mission. The other part, where her needs as a woman resided, simply wanted to see him writhing in ecstasy. There was something very empowering about being on top of this impressive warrior and taking total control of the situation. Especially with the enemy outside their quarters and death so close. The situation was the ultimate aphrodisiac.

• • •

Soldar momentarily dropped his head back and closed his eyes when she lowered her head and began to lick his glowing balls. At the same time, she massaged them and then alternately pulled each of them toward her. He heard a strange, feral moan and realized the sound was coming from him. In that instant, he knew the woman owned him. She could do whatever she wanted, ask for anything. He'd tear out his heart to give what she wanted. Some other new emotion, one he hadn't anticipated, also welled within him.

"Mmmm, I like the way you taste," she whispered. "But then, I knew I would."

Soldar dragged air back into his lungs so he could speak. "Show me what *else* you like!"

She gently lowered his testicles after bestowing a few more kisses and licks in such a way that he thrust his hips in expectation of the next contact. Then she turned her gentle attention to his penis and its flange. He watched as she considered their size. She shook her head as if shrugging off any entry problems.

She'd probably had to do worse things in her life than slide down a differently shaped penis. And for now, that was what he most craved. He needed the feeling of luxurious heat blanketing his shaft.

The time she was taking taxed his wits. He'd go crazy with desire soon. She seemed intent on having a slow, deliberate inspection of his goods.

He couldn't touch her yet. If he put his hands on her now, he'd be thrusting inside her in haste. With all the willpower he owned, he gripped the bedclothes on either side of his body and simply stared downward, between their two bodies. His expression must speak for him because he could not utter another word. Not right now.

She ran her hands over the tops of his thighs, his abdomen, and his chest. His skin tingled with the need to have her touch his cock and balls again, but she teased and used her palms and fingers to come close to them.

He concentrated on the muscles of her inner thighs and how they strained to straddle his much larger body.

But oh, the flesh beneath her palms!

It heated more and more with each passing stroke. He actually began to tremble with need. Still, he didn't speak. His chest moved in and out as he dragged breath into his lungs. And his gut tightened when her fingers eventually circled his penis again. She slowly slid them from the tip, all the way to the base. Her lingering touch was so soft. So encouraging.

He briefly closed his eyes. But he quickly opened them again when she crooked her left index finger over his flange. She'd correctly assumed this was a clitoral stimulation organ. Because she'd so effectively aroused it, it began to vibrate as it would when inside or against her body.

As she closed her index finger and thumb around it in a lengthy, massaging caress, he thought he'd lose his mind. He gripped the bedclothes even harder, trying to hold off taking her quickly. He needed her in a way that addicts needed drugs.

He saw the light of uncontrolled, desperate passion in her eyes and knew the entire Condorian army could have pounded the hatch down and it wouldn't matter. He'd still have her.

For Soldar, no words could do his feelings justice. How could he utter what it felt like to have her inner thighs grazing his outer hips? How could a man ever explain the beguiling nature of her gentle caresses?

There was no planet called Reisen Four, no existence at all beyond the blue-green depths of her lovely eyes and the intense passion he saw in them. Then, she lowered her head and began to lick everything all at once. She did it slowly, with the tip of her soft, warm tongue.

His hips moved in time with her tonguing. She stopped and a desperate, feral growl echoed through the room. Could it have come from his throat?

She maneuvered her slender hips over his penis. She had to actually put the palms of her hands on his abdomen in order to life her hips high enough. But his lover was quickly positioned in such a way that the opening of her wet pussy met the very top of his cock.

He saw her take a deep breath and lower herself, inch by inch. And the heat that encircled him was many times more powerful than anything he'd ever encountered. Now he knew a difference in their bodies no one had gossiped about.

What lay between her thighs was hotter, tighter, more pliable than anything he'd experienced. Her body molded around his. No glove could have fit a hand any better.

He hadn't been prepared for the difference an Earth woman could bring to lovemaking. In truth, it was love. It wasn't just sex and never could be. There was an expression of warmth and trust deep within her sparkling eyes.

And as she slid ever lower, she grew even tighter. Women he'd slept with simply hadn't the capacity to squeeze as she did. He heard another animal-like groan. This time, there was no doubt it had been wrenched from his lungs. It was yet one more time she'd been able to make him respond so wholly automatic. So loudly.

He felt her slide all the way to the base of his penis. His flange found and separated her nether lips. The smaller organ's erect, ear-like protuberances circled and massaged her clit. He could feel the heat radiating from his balls. Then he concentrated.

The head of his cock began to rotate within her body.

"*Sol!*" she cried out as she fell forward.

He immediately sat up, wrapped his arms around her soft, warm body, and held on tight.

Now that he had her in his arms, he drew in air and spoke softly, commandingly. "Ride it, little Earthling. Just let it happen. Enjoy it," he encouraged and continued to speak tenderly and slowly. "You feel so good! Creator's blood, I can't describe how good this is." He finished on a low moan of ecstasy as she gripped his shoulders and slanted her mouth against his.

The kiss—like their entire interaction—was wild and unpredictable. As her body began to gyrate, reacting to an oncoming orgasm of great strength, he kissed her more deeply and broke the contact only to mouth more words of encouragement.

"I…can't…stand…it," she uttered after moving her mouth a breath's distance from his.

"Yes, you can. You can take me deeper. "Try it. Just try."

Lyra rotated her hips forward and Soldar felt his circling penis massaging the insides of her pussy. The action was so thorough that an intense, earth-shattering orgasm began deep within her body and wound its way out to her clitoris. He knew it was her time to release because his flange sensed it and jerked faster around her clit in response.

Her much smaller body began to almost spasm with the intensity of her orgasm.

No matter how hard she tried to evade his flange, he knew it would massage and push against her clit, urging the orgasm to go on. It existed for that very reason.

That, added to his size and the ability to circle the tip of his penis within her body, made her cries come in shrill, broken bursts.

She dropped her head back and let out one long, final scream. The rest of her body dropped backwards, toward his legs.

He took that open opportunity to wrap his palms around her soft back, support her weight in them, and ravage her nipples with sucking kisses.

His flange did its job well.

He felt another orgasm deep within her body as it pulsed and convulsed on his cock.

His climax followed with unexpected force. His cries matched hers as his extended seed flow gushed into her pussy.

But it seemed she wasn't done. Lyra plunged her hands into his hair and twisted it around her wrists. A third orgasm swept through her, quicker and harder. She squealed now and bucked against his body, eager for more.

Her desire was answered.

One more tightly centered, hard climax gripped her, right at her clit. His flange actually transmitted the exact spot through his body. His need to release every last drop of seed kept their bodies clenched. He shook with its outward flow and felt the force as it exited his cock.

Finally, he thrust his hips forward several more times as the last of the fluid left his body. He held her as she collapsed into his embrace. But he didn't withdraw from her deep, hot pussy. He needed to feel her heat and the shuddering little convulsions that were still emanating from deep within her slender, taxed frame. Finally, he shifted his weight and pulled her on top of his chest.

They were now disconnected in body only. Nothing, as he saw it, would ever sever the experience. Nothing.

She pressed her lips to his and they shared another kiss that was soft, intimate, and passionate. This time, the kiss wasn't born of desire, but some profound sense of togetherness. He felt her fingertips drag through his scalp, then wander over the skin of his shoulders and his biceps. He caressed her back and butt in long, slow, circular movements meant to comfort and encourage rest. Then, she kissed the black, jagged mark on his left cheek. This served as the birthright of every Craetorian who still existed in the war-torn galaxy.

"Lyra...look at me," he whispered. He waited to speak until she raised her head and gazed down at him. What he saw in her eyes shocked and moved him in a way he'd never expected. In her expression, he saw deep loneliness, need, and trust. It was all mingled together in her blue-green gaze.

She hadn't just been displaying their sexual abilities for onlookers any more than he had. This was for real. Neither one of them would say it. But it was impossible to feel emotions so deeply if some powerful force hadn't meant it to be.

They could die at any moment. Everything they'd experienced together hadn't been for Aigean's approval...but for them.

Aigean smiled slowly. "I don't think I've *ever* seen anything quite so dramatic. And here I was, about to instruct the two of you on how to have sex!" She took a deep breath. "I daresay you could teach my most talented prostitutes a thing or two."

• • •

Lyra blinked, quickly rolled off Soldar, got up, and retrieved her robe. Before she could put it on he moved faster, picked up his own robe, threw it over one shoulder, and approached her from behind. With gentle care, he turned her around to face him.

"Aigean...could you give us a couple of minutes, please?" he quietly asked.

The older woman stood to leave. "Cleanse your bodies quickly, then meet me in your dining area. I'll have food ready for you as well as your instructions for the night's performance. And don't forget that Lyra must still get back to this room before midnight so my people can dress her as one of the bridge servants. That message to Allied Command must be sent tonight."

Lyra watched the woman saunter away with her servants and almost wanted to call them back. She wasn't sure she wanted to hear whatever Sol was about to say. He knew as well as she that the war was right outside their quarters. There wasn't time for—nor was the situation appropriate to—developing any relationship. Not when they were likely to be killed. Still, she couldn't deny what they'd just experienced. It was richer and more profound than anything she'd ever known.

But whatever he'd say in the loneliness after Aigean and her crew left would be too personal. She wasn't sure she could handle such emotional intimacy along with the demands of the mission.

He brushed back her hair and gazed down into her eyes.

She didn't move.

Slowly, as if there was some precious meaning to the act, he reached for the golden armband on his right bicep. After pushing a locking mechanism the four-inch-wide piece of metal sprung open.

She swallowed hard as he carefully and reverently put it around her left bicep and closed it. His gentleness while completing the task was one of the sweetest moments she'd ever shared with anyone. His demeanor was that of a prayerful penitent.

After it was around the upper part of her arm, she gazed down at the elaborate, golden ornament and was about to tell him the band was far too large. His hand was still holding it in place. It would never stay where he'd put it. And given its expense and intrinsic worth, it was appropriate to give it back. For as long as the Condorians would let him keep it and wouldn't steal it from him—perhaps taking his arms off to get the pair—he should be the one to keep such treasure. Her lips parted to tell him so, but a strange thing happened.

As he held it in place the armband quickly molded around her upper arm. It seemed to attach itself to her bicep as it had to his. In fact, the device was so light that she barely felt its presence. Nor could she tell where the newly closed ends met. When she passed her right palm over it, the band actually felt as if it was part of her body.

"What are you doing?" she asked and tried to push the object off.

"You can't remove it. I alone know the locking sequence on the dragon design," he told her. "I chose it when the bands were placed on me, during the celebration of my thirteenth year. The alloy is the most precious of its kind in the universe. In your language it's called *fusion gold*. It naturally conforms to your body like a second skin. The silver dragon on the band is pure Aladium." He briefly put his hand over the band still remaining on his left bicep. "This marks you as a member of the *Nar* household."

"I...I don't understand."

"Some Craetorians wear these to mark their lineage. If we were to survive, you'd never see another pair just like them. Not unless that other individual was part of my family."

She swallowed hard. "Why would you gift me with something so precious? Why would you even risk bringing them into a war zone? You know what Condorian scum do to get anything they value."

He smiled. "Let's just call them good luck charms, shall we? As for my wearing them into a fight...I don't. They'd usually be left with my personal belongings, to be sent back to my family if anything happened to me. But when I got word of this mission, I put them on. It would be expected that any man or woman from Craetoria owning such ornaments would wear them. Especially if they *weren't* going into battle. The Condorians know the custom. By donning them, they'll assume I mean no hostility." He gazed down at the band on her arm. "I know they'll be taken if this mission goes badly, and that's a deep regret. But in the long run, if some miracle doesn't happen to save us all, the Condorians would get them anyway. And many more just like them."

"So wearing them marks you as neutral? You're demonstrating that you won't fight and therefore don't expect them to be taken?" she asked.

Soldar nodded once in confirmation. "It probably won't work, but every signal I can send indicating I'm not hostile is worth the chance."

Lyra gazed up at the brightness of his perfect smile and realized what she hadn't a moment before. This was the first time she'd ever seen that beautiful expression on his face and wondered at the way it made him look rather boyish. For that instant he was not the stern officer she'd first encountered. She felt herself smiling back at him. "I don't understand its significance on *me*."

"As I said, the bands are supposed to bring great fortune."

She kept gazing up at him with suspicion. "You're trying to somehow show a connection so the Condorians think twice about approaching me...aren't you?" She shook her head in denial. "That's crazy. They wouldn't think twice about killing you if they wanted me and you stood in the way."

He simply shrugged. "If you'd save a laser volley so the enemy couldn't take you alive, why turn down a lovely piece of jewelry that might keep you safe? As I've said, the ploy isn't likely to work," he admitted. "Condorians don't value a man's claim on a woman. But these are officers. They tout themselves as being above the common rabble they command." He touched her armband again. "If there's any chance this can make a difference to your safety... any chance at all...then I want you to wear it."

Now she was annoyed. "I'm a fighter, just like you. I don't want special treatment because I'm a woman. All I ever asked for was to die without being raped if it came down to it. I can take care of myself, *sir*."

He ran one hand through her hair then cupped her cheeks between his palms. "Do you know why I hesitated to communicate in that cave?"

"I thought there was something wrong with your translation device, that you didn't understand Earth English."

He shook his head. "I was shocked into silence. The men of my world don't allow our women to fight, though I'm fully aware other allied planets do. My first inclination, on learning there was a woman under all that armor, was that I'd have moved mountains to keep you safe…if you were mine. You'd have never been allowed into battle."

"I'd heard your women don't fight. Don't they want to?" she asked. "Don't they have as much to lose?"

"Our women are among the fiercest warriors in the known universe. I once saw my mother throw a spear and hit a target no one else could see until it was struck. And she accomplished that while mounted on a running unicorn."

"Then I don't understand—"

"On Craetoria, there are roughly five men to every woman. By our Creator's will it's always been that way. It's for this reason that we can't risk them. And for the same reason they agree to stay home, safe for the time being. If our race is to continue, they know we have to preserve the givers of life," he explained.

There was a long pause between them. She finally broke it.

"In the badlands, you mentioned your family back home. Are there any women of fighting age?" she asked.

"No," he told her with a slow shake of his head. "My family is large. I have been exceedingly blessed. My parents and grandparents still live. I have three younger sisters and many male cousins. But most of my kin are too young to fight. Eventually they all *will* and they will all die. In you, I see their heart and spirit. I see what's left of our future." He looked away for a moment before turning his gaze back to lock with hers. "All of this is why I put the band of Nar on your arm. I'd have done this for any woman who was working with me, had such a mixed-gender team been conceived. You and I *are* that team. And here we shall do our best to hold off the inevitable. We must fight for as long as we can and pray for a miracle."

"If we don't get it, we're all dead. Everyone who stood against the Condorians will be decimated. The neutral worlds won't last much longer."

"I agree. But if it's any consolation where we're concerned, Condorian men know one thing about the males of my planet."

"What's that?"

He pulled her into his embrace. "When they see that band on your arm, they'll know we're not just a sex act. They will assume you're my mate, and that to harm you is to insult me. If this should ever happen, they know I'll find the offending party and kill him!"

"Sir, you might have asked or explained before attaching this thing to my arm."

"Consider the wearing of it a battlefield order. I locked it on suspecting you'd disagree. So the choice has been made for you, Lyra."

She glanced down at the lovely gift once more. The man was insistent that while any chance for safety existed, he meant for her to take it. "It is exquisite. I guess I've been asked to do worse things than wear jewelry." She slowly smiled and tilted her head into the palm of his large, warm hand.

"The odds are against us. But if we get out of this, you can give it back. Do we have a deal?"

She considered that. "All right, sir…it's a deal." She held out her hand to seal the bargain.

Soldar looked down at the extended palm. "First…quit calling me *sir*. Second…a handshake is a bit platonic considering what we've just shared. I think this is more in keeping with the moment." He pulled her into his embrace, slid his lips against hers, and kissed her passionately. At the same time, he ran his hands over her body and moved his chest against her breasts.

Someone cleared their throat, indicating they weren't alone. Lyra broke the embrace to find Aigean watching. "Lyra, I *suggest* you shower. My women will help you prepare before dining."

Soldar stood there glaring at Aigean. His jaw visibly tightened and his eyes narrowed.

"I'd never get either of you to stage tonight if I left you alone," Aigean defended. "Besides, there's news I must share with you, Soldar. We can talk while Lyra gets ready. Then you may take your turn cleansing. Remember, you must perform tonight. You must look refreshed and ready."

• • •

Aigean waited until Lyra was on her way to the bathing area, accompanied by several servants. Then she spoke hurriedly. "Some of my people were ordered to help the Condorians loot the remains of dead allied soldiers today. These would be the same freedom fighters that died in the battle at Plageian Escarpment. It's some distance from here so I've just received word from my employees that—"

"Who gave the command to disturb the dead?" he demanded, outraged by the act of desecration. It wasn't as if enemy looting didn't happen after every battle, but this time he could at least get a name. Perhaps there'd be a way to punish the responsible party.

"It was Admiral D'uhr who gave the command; we could hardly refuse."

"Did the Admiral's butchers find survivors? I can imagine what he had done to them," Soldar muttered.

A slow smile spread across Aigean's face.

He stared down at her, barely able to believe what she might confirm.

"There *are* survivors," she told him, "but D'uhr doesn't know about them, and never will if we don't want to be marched into the badlands and murdered."

Soldar stepped toward her "Tell me your news!"

Aigean anxiously clasped her hands. "When I heard my employees were being ordered to scrounge for D'uhr again, I did what I normally do…I had the only remaining crates in my inventory loaded on our transport craft. These crates look like any other large shipping containers, but they're not. I once used them to avoid tariffs on wine and silks. They have false bottoms that are quite large. My crew knows about them though the Condorians don't. I suspect their size and weight make them too much of an encumbrance for the enemy to inspect. If they had, they'd have found the hidden compartments."

"Go on."

"For obvious reasons, my people didn't communicate with this ship when they found fifteen allied soldiers alive. The fighters were unconscious, lying near each other, and hidden behind a shattered bulkhead. Apparently, they were casualties of a concussion device. At any rate…when my people on the ground found they were breathing, they coordinated efforts. Several of my pilots landed their cargo craft in such a way as to block the Condorians' shuttle and a clear view from their transport bridge."

"You brought them to the Venus!" Even now, in the middle of this desolate sector of space, miracles happened. Ordinary people still fought by working together, using their wits, and honoring the dictates of their consciences.

"Their maneuver wasn't all that difficult," Aigean told him. "Daylight was dwindling, narrowing visibility to a very short distance. And, as is usually the case when D'uhr orders these expeditions, the idiotic Condorian guards planted themselves on their shuttle and let my employees do all the work. They were drunk, under the influence of numerous drugs, and anxious to get back to the luxuries on this ship." She carelessly shrugged. "They simply never investigated what was going on. But then they've always underestimated the capabilities of my people."

"How, by the Lords of Craetoria, did your crew get the survivors on the ship? How were you able to hide them without the Condorians finding out?"

"The injured are now in my servants' quarters and several other places. Since our living quarters have been ransacked and are practically barren, our captors see no reason to regularly visit them. They prefer to stay in the most luxurious surroundings on the upper levels. Knowing the admiral's and the guards' routines as they do, my people quietly spread the word among the rest of the crew. Laundry bins full of old linens were brought to the landing bay. This is nothing out of the ordinary since we always take refuse through that part of the ship. Our incinerators are beyond, in the aft."

"Those fools left the landing bay unguarded?"

"No, but the crates were carefully off-loaded very near the far bulkhead, right where my crewmembers always direct the hover bins to the incinerators. They were actually going about the business of saving the injured while hiding *between* the crates and the bulkhead itself. The injured were removed very quietly and quickly. Then they were hovered off to various rooms for hiding."

He blinked and dragged his hands through his hair. "If D'uhr ever finds out—"

"He won't. At least not any time soon. Even the fighters' body armor was removed in those same hover bins then covered with more torn linen. By now, the incinerators must have destroyed every trace of allied survivors."

"Aigean...I-I don't know what to say. I have misjudged you in many ways!"

She shrugged nonchalantly. "What's done is done. We can thank the Condorians for thinking so little of us. And as to what happens next, I can disguise the survivors as crewmembers. Assuming the more seriously injured recover."

"And how will you accomplish that? The enemy must know exactly how many people you have," he reasoned.

"They do. But I'll use the same ruse Lyra will employ to enter the bridge."

"I don't follow." Clearly the woman's plotting sprinted far ahead of his. But then she'd probably honed that skill swiftly. Her crew had survived because of her intellect. Apparently, they'd paid attention and learned some of her tricks.

"As you may have noticed," she softly explained, "the servants accompanying me earlier all wore dark blue robes and kept their hoods raised. Indeed, almost all my workers dress in this attire. The only exception to this rule is my prostitutes."

He nodded. "In anonymity they find a measure of protection. Even among the Condorians."

"Usually...if they make no trouble and do their jobs. The Condorians crave their comfort. They wish to be served. Our enslavement makes them feel superior. But one cannot be served by the dead, can they?"

"That logic will only go so far."

She slowly nodded. "I know. Sooner or later, the admiral will demand another inspection of our personal quarters. But I can schedule everyone to be in various parts of the ship, allowing fifteen servants extra rest periods. I'm hoping the added bodies, scattered from bow to stern, won't ever be noticed."

"And that's how Lyra might have a chance?"

"Only six servants bring food and beverages to the bridge. Six will enter tonight. Lyra will simply take the place of one who will be elsewhere," Aigean confirmed.

"And what about the immediate needs of those injured fighters? Do you have any medical staff?"

Aigean nodded. "I have a very good medical technician. She's seeing to the wounded, even as we speak. The problem is, while she has sufficient surgical equipment D'uhr impounded all the drugs from sick bay. He has them in his quarters. We believe he keeps them for personal use."

"He's ill?"

"Creator willing!" she viciously blurted. "But whether he is or not, he's never contacted my med-tech for treatment. Some of his minions have, but the morphine isn't available for use on any soldier. Not even his. It's thought he covets the drug for recreational purposes or to sell at high prices on his home world."

"Is there any way one of the staff could get to the meds?"

Sadness and anger were pasted on her countenance as she slowly shook her head. "D'uhr keeps them in a locked safe. It would be easy enough to break into, but the whole ship would suffer for the act. He'd go searching for what he assumes is his, room-to-room."

Soldar heartily agreed with that eventuality.

"If it makes any difference, my crew will keep me constantly informed of those with dire needs. We'll do whatever we can for them," she promised. "My people are ready to approach certain Condorian quarters and use sex as a bribe. But this would only get us a small amount of recreational drugs."

Soldar stared into space before speaking again. "Say nothing to Lyra. She's to know none of this."

* * *

Lyra hadn't yet entered the main area. She'd just finished her quick shower, and her makeup and dressing session with Aigean's women. They were still in the bathing area, preparing it for Soldar's cleansing. The sound of hushed voices prompted her to stop behind several layers of gauzy curtains. Some impulse made her eavesdrop on her superior, the man she'd so recently trusted with her life.

It served her well to have hurried through her bathing routine. Sol would never have said a word about the survivors. He knew she'd argue for helping them, but wanted her to keep to their original plan—sending messages from the bridge.

As she saw it, *both* needs could be met. She wasn't sure how, but if he didn't trust her with all the information Aigean provided, then his desire to keep her in the dark was about to backfire. So long as she pretended not to know there were wounded fighters present, she had the same power he reserved. He couldn't stop her if he didn't know she had information.

When it came time—and there'd soon be a chance—she was going to get to those drugs. Her own brothers might have needed them before they died. In rooms around this ship, other brothers, sisters, fathers, or mothers suffered. But the Craetorian Colonel was more concerned about messages he could get to HQ. She sadly considered he might even covet tributes for having completed this task, even if he was able to send just a few messages before being caught and killed. While his world survived, they'd mark him a hero if his actions saved lives. Especially since he was in command.

Angry, but tamping the emotion down so he wouldn't see it, she made sufficient noise and entered the main room. Sol turned and, from the rapt expression on his face, she knew the outfit Aigean's women had chosen captured his full attention. The strange glow in his eyes might have been worth the trouble, but again she thought of the wounded lying so near. They'd been suffering while she was uninjured, eating wonderful food, and bathing in luxurious facilities.

Soldar Nar had no right keeping such information from her. But she forced a smile on her face and posed for him, taking his mind off what he hadn't told her and putting it squarely on her figure.

If she could tempt a megalithic Craetorian warrior, how hard would it be to get close to a Condorian admiral? She'd bet the last breath that she could get somebody to give up medicine. Her only concern was how to go about this without actually letting the bastard touch her.

She planted images of those injured in her brain. Her rage at being kept in the dark fueled her intent. *I've got a new mission, Colonel Nar. And nothing's keeping me from it.*

Chapter 6

Soldar felt as if every cell in his body had been torched.

Lyra stood in radiant glory, like a star shimmering in a midnight sky. Her already lovely features were now accented via some cosmetic expert's hand. The sparkling blue-green eyes staring back at him were now shadowed with a smoky hue that made her appear exotic. To add to the breathtaking image, her skin had been dusted with some substance that shimmered in the dim light; her lips glowed with shiny red gloss that only accentuated their fullness. The shiny hair that normally curled just under her chin had been tucked behind each shell-like ear and her bangs softly fell just over her left eye. But it was the clothing she barely wore that almost made him drop to his knees.

She'd donned a silver cropped halter top that was tied just behind her neck. The tall goddesses' slender, defined abdomen and midriff were bare. A matching silver skirt rode very low on her hips. But it only fell to her mid-thigh area. Around her waist was a crystal encrusted silver chain. It draped to one side. The loose end of the belt bore a blue stone that exactly matched the color of her eyes. Long, beautiful legs—the kind a man would kill to have wrapped around him—remained bare. Her tiny feet were shod with high, strappy sandals. A sweet, sparkling ankle bracelet made him want to lick the skin where it rested.

"She's exquisite, isn't she?" Aigean asked as she circled Lyra.

Rather than reply, Soldar simply turned away, intent on getting to the shower. There were no words that could do such beauty justice. And the thought of any Condorian actually seeing her in that outfit, much less nude, filled him with protective zeal and fear. Somehow, he had to guard her. Part of his brain reminded him she was a soldier. But the other part was on full, shielding alert.

Before he'd even left the room, he heard the women speak as if he was no longer within hearing range. He couldn't help but note the droll tone in Lyra's voice though it shouldn't be there.

"I think he liked it," Lyra blurted.

Aigean blithely responded with, "I think he's already hard."

On entering the room where the servants were laying out his clothes, Soldar briefly acknowledged them before sending them away. The clothing he was meant to wear hung near the bathing area. He'd need no help dressing in just the black leather-like pants and tall black boots. Since no shirt was provided, he assumed his chest was to remain bare so as to titillate any of the men or women in the audience. Obviously, whatever he put on now would have to come off during the performance. But he wasn't worried for himself. The very thought of having intercourse with Lyra—in front of the enemy—was abhorrent. Even though fear tore into his conscience and heart, his testicles glowed with red-hot intensity. Confusion overwhelmed him. Either he wanted this, or he didn't. Which was it?

No, it was the fact that Condorians were in the audience and would see that precious flesh exposed and would most certainly crave it. That made him even more afraid for Lyra's safety.

All that angst notwithstanding, he was still quite ready to masturbate in the shower, just so he could rid himself of the lust clouding his every thought. No armband was going to stop any man from approaching his Earth counterpart for very long.

As he stood under the water and thought of her body, he pulled his testicles downward with one hand and stroked his cock with the other. It wasn't long before semen shot forward but without the benefit of a warm, soft cavity to capture it. And as he watched his seed flow down the drain, and the climax ebbed, an idea came to him.

There might be one other way to keep so much of Lyra's sweet, sensual body from scrutiny. Aigean might not like it, and the plan was feeble at best. But it was all he had.

It might be possible to shield her from view, using his own body as a sort of wall.

After finishing his shower, he dried his body and brushed out his hair. Donning the clothing took very little time. He placed the palms of his hands on the bathing area vanity, stared in the mirror at his reflection, and waited until the telltale glow in his eyes cooled. For some odd reason, a wash of homesickness hit him hard. The war had gone on too long. He missed his family and balmy, beautiful nights beneath safe, starry skies. If he tried, he could almost smell the flowers in his mother's garden and hear his father arguing with his grandsire over some ridiculous move made while playing a board game. The laughter of his younger cousins and the faces of smiling servants were only memories. His family might not even recognize the man he'd become after so many years, and only intermittent radio or visual communications sent when his troop vessel was close to Craetoria.

All he wanted to do was walk in the woods during the evening hours, to be able to eat a meal or drink a clean, cool goblet of wine without feeling guilt over those whose homes had been decimated. The weight of everything he'd seen and all the death he'd delivered pressed on him. Now, he was responsible for yet one more life. And that soft, lovely, feminine image wouldn't be driven from his mind.

"Creator, kill me or let me see home again. Please do one or the other soon. I can't take much more of this."

With those words softly uttered, he literally threw the brush he'd been using against the bath area wall. It was the only infantile gesture allowed him when his every move and word had to be guarded.

He was a soldier and a ranking officer. Others depended upon his calm demeanor for support and for the confidence to do their jobs. But his patience and his will to keep going were almost at an end. Before the night was over, he was surely going to put at least one fist through the face of any Condorian he could. His hatred of them knew no bounds. Because of them, the best part of his life was being lost to war, far away from home.

When he re-entered the main area where the dining table was located, he saw Lyra and Aigean seated. They were conversing while sipping from wine goblets. It was all so cozy and amicable except they were in the middle of a war zone and men in other rooms lay dying. He couldn't even help those poor injured souls, from whatever allied planets they originated, without risking his mission. His impotence concerning this matter didn't help his chaotic disposition.

He knew Lyra watched him closely as his movements became short and jerky, driven by supreme frustration. But the mission had to go forward and he hated it more with every passing moment.

Rather than question him, his new partner turned to Aigean and queried *her* about the evening's proceedings.

Lyra somberly faced Aigean and laid out her plans for after their show was over. "When we're finished, we'll head back to this room and Sol can enter the authentication codes into the room's computer. I'll do my thing on the bridge and we'll see what hits the fan afterward. We'll take one moment at a time."

Aigean nodded, then leaned forward and outlined the actual show.

• • •

Ten minutes before they were to perform, Soldar stood at the hatch to their quarters. Lyra, in all her seductive brilliance, stood beside him. He didn't dare touch her, but simply waited for Aigean to unlock the hatch and lead them down the passageway and to the ship's entertainment section. His loathing for the war and those who'd caused it only grew.

"Remember," Aigean instructed, "simply do what comes natural. From what I witnessed, the two of you should have no problem amusing the crowd. Afterward, you'll leave the stage by the same means I'll show you now. I'll make excuses to anyone wishing to meet you. I'll say you won't accept visitors or invitations until well after midnight," she assured them. "This will be in accordance to the contract we agreed upon. But rest assured, you will both be summoned. I suggest you don't anger the Condorian leaders. If you won't heed their beckoning, they'll come looking for you. And remember that you do not want them anywhere near this room's computer workstation, where the codes will be imbedded."

Lyra nodded, took a deep breath, and raised her chin. "Okay, let's do this."

Soldar took one look at the courageous expression on Lyra's exquisitely designed face and hated himself for ordering her aboard. At least she'd have died with her much-protected dignity, in battle like a warrior. Here, she'd be nothing but a whore, served up for some man's amusement.

"Remember your promise?" she asked softly. "You said you'd take me out before letting one of them have me."

"I've forgotten nothing."

Aigean broke into the conversation. "Need I remind you that the goal is to stay alive for as long as possible? My employees have learned to put up with great sorrows. Surviving is everything! Quit dwelling on what you can't accomplish, but what you must endure to help others live. This situation has made whores of us all, in one way or another. Live to fight another day. Survive to see the enemy suffer!"

Lyra shook her head. "There are some things worse than death. Lying with a Condorian is about the most despicable act I can imagine."

Aigean drew herself up in anger. "Use your wits, girl! I assume you have them to have survived this long. There are ways out of any situation if you only think. Dying does nothing but help the enemy. Death will come to us all one day, perhaps sooner than we'd like. But while you live, fight. Never give up. Never surrender."

Soldar held up his hand to stop any ensuing argument. There was no time left for exchange of philosophies. "There's nothing we can do except continue this pretense. But I can tell you this, Aigean…it should be the man or woman's decision as to when and where to share their bodies. Your people made the decision that was acceptable for them, I'd have made the decision to be here if given the choice. But if Lyra has made *her* choice then so be it. I'll defend it with my last breath. I'd no more see her taken against her will than I'd see one of my kinswomen ravaged. She's a fighter, not a prostitute. The lives of those in each occupation are vastly different. I cast no judgment of your business or those employed by you, but surviving has to include a quantum of self-respect. Without it, what are we fighting for?" He turned to his Earth companion. "Whatever it takes, I'll honor the promise I made, Lyra. Pray to the Creator I don't have to." In response, Lyra stared up at him with sheer gratitude painted on her features.

"You'll never know how much hearing those words means to me." She took his hand in hers.

"So be it," Aigean groused. "But I believe there's an old Earth expression about having more than one way to skin a cat. *This* is mine." With that said, she led them toward the ship's theatre.

• • •

Together, they strode through the passageways where various customers mingled. Soldar's gaze moved from one individual they passed to another, always watching and waiting for any sign of aggression. He noted how Lyra kept her gaze straight ahead.

"Relax, girl," Aigean softly comforted, "you're with your man now. All you must do is please him in front of an audience then go back to your quarters. You won't be able to see those who watch you. The lights will be too bright."

Lyra said nothing but gripped his hand more tightly. He reckoned the truth was just hitting home. There was a huge difference in having suggested this farce and actually being inflicted with it.

He saw her chew on her lower lip and moved closer. Approaching sounds of revelry signaled a crowd.

They'd yet to see a Condorian except for the guards they'd initially encountered after leaving the oasis. These were the same men they'd play-acted for.

In every passageway and hatch, there were men and women sharing bodies. He recognized beings from virtually every known neutral world in the galaxy. There were also a few creatures present he hadn't ever heard of.

As it was, this vessel seemed to be filled with sex servants who were in the group having had enough of Condorian rule. As Soldar walked by them, there seemed to be a telltale spark of rage in their eyes. They'd glance at him as if they knew exactly what he was up to. But they kept working, as if nothing was amiss.

Tall red men openly felt-up green women. Those with multiple appendages were making good use of them by embracing and fondling each other. But even their various sexual behaviors and states of dress—or *un*dress—hadn't diverted him from the task ahead.

Though he detected covert nods in appreciation of his presence, he tried to appear blasé. But he wasn't sure the ruse would ultimately work the first time he contacted the occupying admiral. Despite claims of wanting to outwit the enemy and wanting to engage this mission to make that attempt, it'd take everything he had to keep from strangling the bastard.

Finally, their walk ended. Aigean stopped in front of a hatch that was larger than any they'd passed. She lowered her voice and instructed them for what was likely the last time.

"This entrance leads directly to the stage. You've both been told what's expected. When you're finished, I'll meet you back here or most certainly in your quarters." She raised her hands with her palms facing them. "May the Creator of all things be with you."

Feeling the woman beside him shudder, Soldar turned to her. "It's only me and you out there. No one else. Just as Aigean said. Think of only *me*, Lyra."

When he cupped her cheeks with both hands, she simply nodded and watched as he pressed the hatch button to open it.

Before them, bright lights almost blinded their entrance onto a white stage. The place they entered was surprisingly clean. As Soldar's vision adjusted, he saw several of Aigean's employees beckon them forward and onto the dais that would serve as their *performance* area.

One of the assistants took his hand. Apparently he was to stand between two columns, as indicated by his assistant's quick gestures. The pillars reminded him of supports decorating great halls of learning back on Craetoria. Why such a trivial thing would enter his mind at a time like this, he couldn't fathom.

The women helped him out of his black pants and boots. He now understood these had only been donned to get them to the stage without sexual offers slowing their progress. He also reasoned that if they were the main entertainment, they would hardly appear as professionals by walking nude through the passageways, freely displaying that which others paid to watch.

His body reveled at the thought of seeing Lyra nude again. There was no denying what she could do to him. But the sensation wasn't enough to forego his sense of duty. As for Lyra, when he glanced at her now he saw a woman almost paralyzed by fear.

Where charging through a barren wasteland and fighting had been no issue, what she faced now seemed to unravel her nerve at its deepest source. Before he'd speak to her again, he'd wait for Aigean's women to complete their work. It was up to them to actually pull her clothing from her body. She simply wasn't responding to their hurried encouragement.

Aigean's instructions stated: if they got through this performance without any problems, their garments would be waiting for them in the passageway. The only clothing Lyra *wouldn't* discard was the sparkling, silver chain around her waist. As she moved, the dangling end bearing the blue stone swung from side to side, striking her left hip.

Soldar stood there, silently gazing at her luscious body. And then his gaze rose to catch the utter terror in her eyes. There was no doubt in his mind that she'd give her left arm for a laser pistol and a chance for a fair fight—a procedure with which she was *infinitely* more familiar.

As Aigean's assistants loosely tied his wrists to the columns, he vaguely noticed a round, white-covered bed being mechanically hoisted onto the dais. As with everything in this make-believe fantasy, the décor was startlingly bright. He assumed this was to make their bodies more visible.

As he'd been told, once the thick white curtains surrounding them were raised, their voyeurs would surround them from all sides, hence the circular shape of the stage. But that bed was where they were eventually supposed to end up. Their rendezvous there was to occur after Lyra had her way with him.

In another time and place, or in another reality where no war existed, the scenario would have exited him no end. But Lyra's fear drove such protective instincts into his core that all he cared about was calming her. Only years of training and fighting held her together. She was faced with performing a very intimate act in front of enemies who'd shadow her every movement. They'd want her and would ultimately stalk her. They both knew it.

"Lyra…look at me," Soldar commanded softly.

She did so automatically. Apparently his command sunk in where nothing else might have.

"Remember what I told you," he whispered. "It's just us. No one else exists. No one." He kept repeating this mantra over and over.

Finally, she lifted her chin and moved toward him. In that small act, Soldar knew he'd seen something very rare.

In her almost paralyzing fear, the woman showed fortitude no general on any battlefield had ever displayed in his presence. When she stood only a few inches in front of him, the curtains slowly lifted. Aigean's employees hadn't given her time to cut and run. But then, she wouldn't have taken that course. He witnessed a determination in her gaze, however fearful it might be. And this completely overwhelmed him. The woman had pushed her alarm deep down, into some dark place. She suddenly became the dauntless warrior-goddess he'd seen in that canyon. He kept whispering to her, sure that no one in the audience could hear him above the applause and banging of hands and mugs on tabletops.

Some part of his brain recognized the introduction of sultry music.

"I'm right here, baby, right here," he crooned. "What do you want from me? I'm here for you to take. It's all yours. Whatever you want."

• • •

She felt his warm breath on her cheek, heard the soft words, and knew them for the comfort they were meant to be. But a very unusual dose of courage suddenly rose, brought on by his soothing verses.

She placed the palms of her hands against his chest and moved them over his nipples.

"That's it. Just do it. Just have me. Think of how good we were. Remember that? Remember how it felt together?" he murmured.

Lyra didn't respond. She just kept listening and actually felt her hips begin to sway to the slow, sexy music. His fresh, clean scent surrounded her. It was like a protective blanket, enfolding her within some barrier no one else could penetrate. And, as she actually brushed the tops of her thighs against his, Sol's eyes began to glow. In their heated depths she found motivation and more. She found her passion.

She witnessed his response to her slight but suggestive movements. That body-graze, while it was whisper soft, did more to engorge him than any caress from her hands. Though his wrists were only loosely tied to the columns and he could have shaken off the bindings at any time, he gripped and pulled against the restraints as though they were the strongest chains. It was as if he'd been bound for only one reason—to please the mistress she was meant to portray.

"You have me right where you want me, Lyra. And I need you. Feel how much I need you?"

She did. His swelling penis rose between their bodies and brushed the skin between her thighs as it did. Despite where they were and the hushed silence that overcame the crowd, her body responded to his. Suddenly, there *was* no audience. There was nothing but the man, the moment, and her. She glanced down and saw his testicles begin to glow. Though it might have been a trick of the light, there seemed to be a droplet of lubrication dripping on the tip of his penis. She gazed up at him and licked her lips.

"Take over…love. I'm yours. Do with me what you like," he continued to whisper.

Lyra teased his nipples again. Then she twisted them, which brought forth a low moan from deep within her huge, god-like partner's throat.

She daren't speak. There were no words but his. What he uttered energized and charged her to do more. Because of his soft entreaties, her fear all but fled. If she died now, she'd go having him. There were thousands of worse ways to perish. His was a physique women fought to own.

And there he was, all hers to enjoy. What harm would there be in taking this, perhaps her last night of life, to extremes.

Soldar rotated his hips forward when she ran her fingertips down the outside of his ribcage to his lower hips. Then, she dragged her fingertips toward his abdomen and firmly grasped the fully engorged cock before her. Without thinking of any consequence her actions might have on the audience, she knelt before him suddenly and took his cock in her mouth, all the way to the back of her throat. A loud moan of sheer, animal-like pleasure tore from his lungs. The sound of it echoed throughout the room. Then she simultaneously began to pull his balls straight down, stretching them to the max as she did so. He spread his thighs in response.

"Suck my balls," he begged.

She accommodated him while continuing to stroke his penis with her fingertips, lightly and gently. They flew over the organ as if they were butterflies searching for much needed nectar. The bondage illusion was something she'd never tried and wished now she had. But then the man she was with made all the difference when it came to doing something so out of her comfort zone.

• • •

Minutes passed as he enjoyed the most luxurious sucking, kneading, and massaging of his entire life. Lyra must have sensed his approaching orgasm because she suddenly stood, using his body as a ladder to pull herself upward. His *pretend* lover had to stand on her toes to kiss him, but she did so with all the intensity of a sun going nova. Her tongue entwined with is in a heated duel of passionate thrusting. And then she broke the contact to jump up and wrap her arms around his shoulders. From there, his passionate war-woman untied one hand and then the other by using the loose and dangling ends of his wrist restraints.

He wasted no time putting his hand underneath her tight, perfect butt. He immediately hoisted her up and then drove her back down onto his cock. Her moan of utter satisfaction was rendered softly, for his ears only. Lyra actually bit into his shoulder to keep from making any further noise or shouting out as she might have done if no one had been present.

She clung tightly to him as he walked with her to the bed. Once there, he laid her back onto the soft, white silken material and proceeded to plunge deeply into her tight little pussy over and over. He was in ecstasy once more, savoring the heat of her body against his penis, flange, and testicles.

"No one touches you but me, Lyra. No one!" he softly promised as he thrust even harder and alternately tasted her sweet, erect nipples.

"Deeper…go deeper!" she pleaded as she spread her legs wide and felt his hands move to the inside of her knees to help her. And to take him more fully, she rolled slightly backward. The action placed her more on her shoulders than her back.

Soldar was now plunging into her from an almost vertical position while holding her legs at the ankles and in a very wide position.

"Mine," he growled and continued to test the limits of her heated depths. "You're mine, Lyra!"

He saw her grab the luxuriously soft cloth on either side of her. She closed her eyes and her head lolled from side to side. His flange pulled and played with her clit so there was no escaping the small, caressing attack.

Just three more deeply powered thrusts, and his flange allowed him to feel a massive orgasm beginning at the very back of her vaginal wall. It worked its way forward, into her clit. Only then did she cry out loudly in release.

But he kept going. Her cries drew from him an amazingly full orgasm of such intensity that he almost lost his vision. Only rarely had he heard of Craetorian men experiencing such a momentary loss. It could only occur if their mate's orgasm was very intense. His own experience was raw, pure, strong, and ongoing. His climax dragged seed from him for a full minute and then some seconds longer. He finally collapsed over her, panting and pulling her into his embrace at the same time. It was some moments more before he realized the curtains were closing around them to thundering applause.

He could feel Lyra shaking and clinging to him. Her fingertips were still clawing at his back, an automatic response to their lovemaking. After a few minutes, he separated his body from hers by only a few inches. Then he gazed down at her face. The expression in those glittering blue-green eyes was glorious. In their depths he saw a promise of the future that could be theirs if they could survive. His fingers went to her soft hair and involuntarily pushed the bangs off her forehead. "It's over, baby. Night one is all over."

She swallowed hard, nodded, and hugged him hard once more. Tears came to her eyes and he nuzzled his cheek against hers. The warrior in her might hate the weakness she was showing after sex, but the woman needed the release tears provided. Sol understood and rocked her back and forth, murmuring sweet endearments. But their soft fantasy was quickly broken when a blue-robed servant approached.

"Please, mistress and master, you must don your clothing quickly. Lady Aigean can't make it back here. She had pressing matters to attend elsewhere."

Soldar nodded and caressed Lyra's hip once more.

"One warning," the girl quickly continued, "there are Condorian officers in the back hallway leading to the stage. Admiral D'uhr is among them. I believe it is his intention to seek a private audience with you. We tried to explain that you would need rest, but he would not be stalled. Be assured that we will not leave you alone. I and my companions will stay until you are safely in your quarters."

Soldar pulled away from the warm safety of his lover's body. He held his hand out to help her up. "I'll assist Lyra with her clothing. Keep the Condorians diverted for a few moments."

Lyra swiftly stood beside him. He watched her take deep, cleansing breaths. Then he waited while she ran her long fingers through her chin-length hair; the curls seemed to find their exact right place beneath her lovely chin and around her soft, tiny ears.

"Okay?" he asked.

"U-huh," she breathlessly responded. "Get me dressed fast. I don't want any Condorian near me without my clothes on."

He pressed a gentle kiss into her forehead, grabbed her clothing, and proceeded to see to her dressing first. His own pants and boots were in place several minutes later and luckily so. A gruff, loud voice sounded outside the stage hatch. The hatch slid open and a Condorian of massive proportions pushed his way past several serving women and toward the stage where he and Lyra stood.

Protective instincts Soldar couldn't control surfaced. He pushed Lyra behind him and stood ready to fight off a legion for her sake. Behind him, he could feel her body tense as if she was also going into battle. It occurred to him that she might not have ever been this close to the enemy without running, firing her weapon, or ducking other armament. The hulking creature before them was horribly impressive, but Soldar understood size was how the Condorian race chose their superiors. The biggest and largest of the men, and the most aggressive of the women, were always the top cast. Everyone else was expendable and easily sent to die on their behalf.

• • •

Lyra dug into herself and found the power to paste on an almost bored expression. Still reeling from Sol's lovemaking, this was no easy task. She somehow felt stronger and more able to cope with this confrontation than she'd have ever believed possible. Briefly touching the armband he'd attached to her left bicep, she stepped from behind her Craetorian protector to help him face this most monstrous of all the Condorian leaders. This particular creature had a reputation for mistreating everyone around him, including his own officers. It was said they all yielded to his whims, or they faced torture. It was this same, single-minded brutality that kept him feared.

Admiral Kardis D'uhr was about six feet, six inches in height, but he'd had to turn his broad shoulders to get through the hatch. Like all Condorians, his head was devoid of hair. Black, tattooed tribal markings had been etched all over his bald pate as well as his face, arms and that part of his chest she could see through the vee of his leather vest. The rest of his body likely bore similar artistic renderings. His pants and tall boots thankfully covered them.

There'd been dead Condorians on the battlefield. Of those whose clothing had been blown away, she'd seen numerous tattoos. His eyes were similarly dark to those deceased; his broad face and thick neck were frighteningly fierce in appearance. Like all his people, he looked more like a raging berserker than a true warrior. Every muscle on his body was as well-defined as Sol's except there was no lion-like grace in his movements.

D'uhr was arguing with the servants, who insisted on trying to protect the *entertainers*. His bare, meaty arm rose to strike the girl who'd tried to keep him outside the stage hatch. That was when Soldar moved forward. Had her warrior-lover not done so at that exact moment, Lyra was sure the blow from the admiral's hefty Condorian hand would have broken the slender girl's neck. D'uhr, like all his people, had no patience. But what could she have expected from a leather-clad, giant bully? From his thick, socialistic black boots to his nasty grin, the man was evil incarnate. His malevolence was palpable. Thousands had died by his command.

* * *

Once more, Soldar moved slightly ahead of Lyra so that she stood just behind his right shoulder. Her bravery was awesome, but he didn't want it tested. Not now.

He interrupted D'uhr's attempt to strike the serving girl with a very assertive comment. "Was there something you wanted?" he loudly asked in Earth English.

D'uhr stilled his hand then slowly turned and presented a smile as he looked over the only Craetorian in the room. Straightening his shoulders, he moved onto the stage. "I…am Admiral Kardis D'uhr. It's obvious what planet you hail from," he stated in broken English as he puffed out his chest and gazed back with suspicion. "Do you not seek to fight my race alongside your brethren?" he suspiciously asked. "What brings a man like you to a place like this? What could a Craetorian possibly want so far away from his own world, and why do you not speak in your native Craetorian tongue?"

Soldar pasted on a vapid expression. "I speak English for my partner's benefit. And as to why I'm here…I side with whomever can offer me the most remuneration. In this case, that would be Aigean Florn."

"Ah, that makes you a neutral?" D'uhr questioned cagily.

Again, Soldar bowed his head slightly in confirmation. "I see no point in fighting for a lost cause. The sight of blood…well, it sickens me." He lifted a hand in greeting. The offer went ignored so he dropped it by his side again. "I'm called Soldar, big fellow. At least that's the stage name I'm using for this gig. As performers, we go where the contracts are to our advantage. I'm sure a man of your status can understand making the best business deal." He looked the Condorian over with what he hoped was his best, come-hither expression. D'uhr had to want *him*, not Lyra. If the admiral's tastes now ran to men as Aigean claimed, then she might be safe for a while longer.

Kardis stared back at Soldar. "You have scars on your body that mock your words." He stepped closer. "If I believed there was a spy among the crew, I would take everyone off this ship and have them beheaded for harboring such an agent." He put his hand to Soldar's throat and squeezed a bit for effect. "I would then take that spy below deck and allow my men the luxury of a long and entertaining torture."

"What? These little cuts?" Soldar girlishly responded in reference to the scars. He also raised one hand and sensually stroked the fingers now closing about his larynx. "Law enforcement authorities incarcerated me for six months on Signus Mondi," he lied. "The constables took exception to an escape attempt I bungled. I've been meaning to make an appointment to have these unsightly marks removed, but some of my clients actually find them attractive. It's been said they enhance my masculinity."

D'uhr stood straighter when the name Signus Mondi was mentioned. The admiral's eyes narrowed and he fixed his gaze on Soldar as if the mention of that world was the most important thing he'd ever heard. "And what was your crime? Were any incarcerated with you?"

"Prostitution was the infraction listed on the books. And yes… there were others with me but I prefer not to talk about it right now," he insisted as he slyly shifted his gaze in Lyra's direction.

Kardis nodded covertly then turned an impassive countenance toward Lyra. "And who is this creature?"

"Just call me Lyra," she swiftly answered without offering her hand in greeting. "I speak several languages if English bothers you. It just happens to be the most universally accepted on these pleasure ships."

"You obviously hail from some world other than Craetoria, woman. You have no face marking as one of that race, but you are banded with this man," he stated as he suspiciously looked her and her armband over.

"I'm from Gratis Major," she easily responded. "We speak English there, but you must surely know that." She lifted the palm of her right hand and covered her armband with it. "As to this old thing…don't take it to heart. Sol and I paired for business reasons. It's a mixed-race arrangement that makes getting work easier. As a twosome, we're more in demand." She glanced downward at the admiral's hand.

Soldar saw her quickly avert her gaze. To see what had so alarmed her, he also glanced down at D'uhr's hands. He understood why Lyra hadn't offered a handshake.

The back of the admiral's hands were covered with strange red blotches, ringed by darker red circles. There were other such markings on the man's neck. D'uhr had apparently tried to hide it by wearing his collar higher. When the huge Condorian saw where *his* attention lingered, the brute's gaze took on a hostile gleam and he pulled at the fabric of his clothing in an apparent attempt to conceal his ailment.

"Since learning new entertainment was hired, I insisted on meeting you," D'uhr stated as he stuck his hand behind his back. "I have ample provisions in my quarters…only my most trusted officers are ever present. But Aigean tells me you'll only be available in the early hours of the morning." He glared at Soldar before stepping closer to him. "What possible reason could there be for my demand being dismissed?"

Soldar simply shrugged. "Our contracts allow us time to cleanse ourselves and have massages after performances. Regrouping for the next show takes time."

Lyra chimed in. "And I'd certainly have to pick out some appropriate clothing at any rate. An extra half hour or so with the masseuse would be delightful."

D'uhr studied them for a long moment. "If preening will make you more amenable to my…*hospitality*…then I'll expect you at the ringing of this ship's two bells. Do not be late!" He turned and took several steps away then stopped and glanced backward as if one other detail needed clarification. "Signus Mondi, you said?"

Soldar stepped closer to him before murmuring, "We can discuss whatever's on your mind later."

For a moment, D'uhr froze in place. Then he gathered himself, shook his head as if to clear it, and stalked away.

When the enemy was out of earshot, Lyra let out a long breath and ran both her hands through her hair. "Slimy, scum-sucking son-of-a-bitch!"

"For half a Craetorian coin I'd break that bastard's neck and incinerate him on a pile of refuse!" Soldar bitterly agreed.

The servant girl who'd almost been struck approached them. She'd hovered in the background, waiting for her chance to speak freely. "I-I thank you for not letting him strike me, Craetorian. It would not be the first time he's done so. However, it might be better in future if you allowed him to vent. It would seem too honorable to keep him from hitting me again," she cautioned. "Now, please, we must get you to your quarters. Aigean will meet us there. She must make apologies to others who are queuing to entertain you. It would be impossible for you to accept *all* the incoming invitations."

With a sense of purpose, Soldar took Lyra's hand and followed the servant girl back to their quarters. The sex scene he thought would be one of the most arduous tasks for his partner was just the beginning. Lyra still had to get on the bridge and deliver the warning about the Taurean Seti-Seven attack. Then they had to act as if they were flattered to be entertained by a Condorian murderer.

If the Creator saw fit to gift him with a fully loaded laser pistol, he'd have used it on D'uhr without question, forgoing a mission that was likely to fail. Nothing could undo the fact that all the Allied Forces were outnumbered and would eventually fall. Walking through D'uhr's hatch later in the night, and firing on him and then his cohorts would be well worth his life. But committing such a foolhardy act was not worth the lives of innocents on this vessel who protected him. Nor was it worth having the surviving allied warriors discovered where they lay, secreted within servants' spaces.

Finally, such a foolhardy act would never be worth Lyra's life. No, he couldn't indulge his desires to go off mission. There were hundreds of officers at Allied Command awaiting any message pertaining to future attacks. His selfish, impulsive instincts had to be put aside. Of the factors that kept him from plunging his fist into Kardis D'uhr's face and breaking his neck, Lyra's safety outweighed them all.

More and more he was finding himself connected to the Earther. She induced desires no other being ever had. He quickly tried to sort his feelings and put them into perspective. Perhaps the peril of this situation was endowing her with more importance than would have otherwise existed. A place deep in his heart told him differently.

As they strode toward their quarters, he glanced at her.

Lyra walked on his left side. Apparently ignorant to the meaning, this was the position any Craetorian bride would take while walking with her man.

The left side of the body was closer to the heart, and the woman who stood on that side possessed the unconditional love of her mate. Coincidentally, a small lift of her chin made her appear even more Craetorian than Earther. The fear she'd displayed before their performance seemed buried. Her lovely eyes blazed with spirit and there was a feisty, determined expression on her face. For however long this mission lasted, he knew she was his. Raising his right hand, he briefly touched the armband on his left bicep. The gesture was a reminder that they were, indeed, connected. Surprisingly, he felt her grip his left hand tightly. Then she lowered her right cheek to that band on his bicep and silently nuzzled it. It was as if she knew what he was thinking.

He quickened their pace. Every moment they had was precious. If all they had was tonight, he'd take memories to the afterlife, memories of her magnificent bravery and intelligent companionship.

Soon they stood in front of their quarters. He opened the hatch for them to enter. After Lyra, the servant girl, and he were inside and the hatch closed behind him, he pulled Lyra into his embrace and kissed her passionately, knowing tomorrow might not come. She responded to his gesture with wild fervor. Only the servant girl speaking to them in urgent tones eventually broke the contact.

"Please, mistress and master, Lyra must don the costume she will wear on the bridge. And the authentication codes must be entered into the room's computer so she might access them later. Aigean will be here soon, but we must hurry," she begged.

Lyra backed away from Sol and nodded. Then she turned away and let the servant lead her to the bathing area.

He stood there and offered up a whispered prayer. "Creator, keep her safe. I'll give you anything you want. Just protect her."

Chapter 7

Less than five minutes after Lyra left to don her disguise, the hatch buzzer sounded. Soldar carefully checked the security monitor and let Aigean and six servants into the space. She hurried forward, glanced around, and motioned her minions closer.

"Where is Lyra?" she anxiously asked.

He closed the hatch before responding.

"She's changing. I'll wait until the last possible moment to enter the authentication codes," he said as he gestured toward the bulkhead computer.

His hostess turned to her staff and motioned one of them forward. This person pushed the hood of her robe back, fully revealing her features. "This is Gentis," Aigean introduced. "Lyra will be replacing her. She's offered to bring up schematics for you to find your way around. This is a normal function for new employees so the search request on your computer system shouldn't be suspected."

"I'll reiterate what's about to happen," Soldar announced for all those present. "If Lyra's successful, she'll be connecting the computer in these quarters with the one on the bridge. Her actions will be hidden unless someone gets suspicious. The weakest link will be at this end, on the computer in this space," he said as he pointed toward the bulkhead.

Aigean nodded, as did the servants. It was she who answered for them.

"We understand. We won't allow your quarters to remain empty for any reason. Since someone can access deeper files…until they're erased or overwritten…we'll take no chances. One of my servants will lock the hatch behind you when you leave. "However…it's been decided that if the admiral *insists* on entrance and lives may be lost if the command isn't obeyed…we will comply."

He opened his mouth and stepped forward to seriously protest this change in plans, but she lifted a hand to silence him.

"My employees maintain that to argue for your privacy would only increase the Condorians' suspicions. Their activities in others' spaces are normally limited to pilfering personal belongings, not to searching for what you've been up to on your private computer. It's for this reason we will plant trinkets and theft-worthy articles within your suite, so as to give them something to take. If they act as they usually do, they'll ignore everything else," Aigean explained.

Soldar glanced at each of the servants before staring at Aigean again. It seemed there'd been concern over the matter, hence this new tactic.

"Without any reason to dig deeper," Aigean insisted, "the computer will only reveal the food you've ordered or the conversations you've engaged with other passengers."

"I suppose I see your point," he slowly relented.

"Quite so. And being accustomed to patronizing performers, my servants will explain there are more employees assigned here because you are my best act, brought here at considerable expense and in need of constant, self-centered attention," she told him. "In this way, there will still be friends here to watch your computer and divert attention from it."

"I assume this is the best we can expect, but I hope we'll at least have some privacy."

"Unfortunately, privacy depends on D'uhr's good will. Please him and you'll likely be left alone."

"Until he tires of us or the real reason for our presence is known," Soldar wearily declared.

Aigean ducked her chin in acknowledgement of that fact.

Swiping one hand across his face, Soldar finally turned his attention the servant introduced as Gentis. Her midnight blue skin and white-blonde hair denoted her as a citizen of *Cloton*

Damatris. He considered her for some time then rolled his eyes in frustration. "Would someone please explain how Lyra is supposed to pass herself off as a Cloton?"

"The transformation will be dramatic," Aigean explained, "but there's a reason for this particular choice."

"And this is where I hear about it," he muttered.

"Soldar…the Condorians wouldn't remotely suspect that the Cloton woman who's serviced them since the bridge was overrun is now the female who performed on stage tonight. When hiding something, putting it in plain sight is the best course of action. This is how I smuggled goods by the authorities for years."

He shook his head in denial of this ploy. Passing herself off as a Cloton woman would mean Lyra's change would take time. That might be time they didn't have on some evening. There would be other messages to send if they survived long enough.

Soldar slowly paced back and forth. He half expected the Condorians to see through his ruse, never mind Lyra's, and pounce at any moment. Aigean poured a goblet of wine and stood in his path. The act forced him to stop moving around the room and stare directly at her.

"Drink this, sit down, and relax," she suggested. "I think you and the Earth woman have been fighting far, far too long. While this mission is certainly dangerous, you're even more paranoid than I."

Soldar shook his head at her offering of wine. "I need to keep my wits about me."

"Then I'll order my people to serve you only sparkling water or some other non-alcoholic beverage when you're outside this room. It's easier done than you think if the containers from which you drink are opaque." Aigean lifted one index finger and smiled conspiratorially. "In fact, I can give you some of the herbal sleeping powder that my med-tech makes from plants we have on board. While the greenery in our passageways is lovely in appearance and certainly adds to the ambience of the ship's interior, each species was chosen for its properties in this regard."

He put his hands on his hips and raised one brow.

Aigean smiled. "One never knows when a general sleeping potion will be needed. Before the Venus was overrun, we used it on customers who were a bit rowdy and needed soothing. Nowadays, if any of my employees find themselves in trouble and they have the time to do so, they simply slip the stuff into the offending party's food or beverage." She shrugged. "Of course, these additives take time to work…normally a half hour or thereabouts."

"And all your people have access to this potion?"

"Yes."

"And you're just now telling me about it?" he asked angrily.

She sighed and shook her in frustration. "If one of you is about to be raped, it wouldn't make any difference. There'd be no time for it to take effect. And we can't get back to the allied planet where the plants grow, so we have a limited supply. Besides," she reasoned, "there have been occasions when the stuff doesn't work at all, so it was pointless to relay such minor details."

"No, you'd rather we slept with those vermin!"

"You *are* here in the guise of prostitutes. And it *is* in the throes of vigorous sex that my people get their best information. Drugged, the enemy says nothing at all. And we never know when we might get that one vital bit of information that could save lives. So…you see the dilemma."

Unfortunately, he did. "The Condorians don't know you have such a potion?"

"We'd be dead if they did." A wicked gleam entered her eyes. "I've often imagined using a slow-acting, horrible poison on them all."

He snorted. "That's worth imagining."

"I know," she admitted, "and if it wasn't for the information we get from them, I'd do it. I'd kill D'uhr and all his parasites as easily as I take my next breath!"

"The Condorian contingent would hunt you into infinity," Soldar murmured. "I've heard rumors that many have family assigned to vessels in the same sectors."

"What you've heard is quite true," she agreed. "D'uhr's own brother is a commander on a support craft. His son, from one of those forced breeding programs to which Condorian women are subjected, is one of the new bridge crew. Though D'uhr favors men since the whelp was born, the boy is still his pride and joy; brought here to keep him from harm and to see him well pleasured." Aigean frowned in apparent distaste. "As you say, even if I actually did take my revenge someday I'd be overrun again."

"Still, the fact you have that kind of sleeping medication might be useful," Soldar confirmed as he mentally filed the information away. Then he realized what she'd been doing.

The banter of the last few minutes had been purposely engaged. As he stared at Aigean, a sense of amused suspicion now took the place of angst.

"You've been trying to take my mind off Lyra."

She shrugged and patted him on the shoulder. "I thought I was being crafty. But if it means anything, I'll be at D'uhr's party tonight. There'll also be some other guests attending, all citizens from neutral planets, of course. Unfortunately, they were aboard when the enemy overtook us."

He ran one hand across his face in a weary gesture. Some of the women with Aigean had gone to the bathing area, probably to help Lyra get her audacious disguise ready. The others were busy cleaning and refreshing fruit containers and water.

Now he understood some of Lyra's torment when she first stepped onto the stage tonight. For hours, she'd been inflicted with waiting for that scenario to take place. Now, he was forced to do the waiting and it didn't sit well. He wouldn't know how she fared on the bridge until her assignment of the night was over or she was caught.

Action was best. Fighting the enemy in the field was easy compared to plotting and scheming while moving among foes. Aigean could do it because she'd made it her life's profession to outwit authority. For his part, he'd never been on the wrong side of the law in his entire life.

He was beginning to hate everything to do with undercover work. This mission was making him painfully aware of the nastier side of allied defenses. It was necessary. He knew it. But it left him feeling as though the ends justified the means. He'd only been ordered into this place because his physical appearance fit the specifications of a male prostitute. He'd been eager to do the job because of his inner need to best a superior force using only his wits.

On previous assignments his team had remained in uniform at all times while employing stealth to achieve results. None of them had ever been asked, until *this* mission, to actually take off their allied armor and pretend to be anything other than what they were. So far, he'd patted himself on the back and had been greatly encouraged by Lyra's innovative acting and sincerity. Sooner or later, however, their real warrior personae would show. Being anywhere near D'uhr was obnoxious. The admiral's very presence would exacerbate their disgust. The Condorian would eventually glean his identity and Lyra's if for no other reason than mutual hatred of each other's races.

He didn't know how much longer he paced or how many times Aigean tried to calm him down. Only Lyra's sudden appearance from the bathing area stopped his wearing a hole in the luxurious, exotic carpets. He moved toward her and was shocked by the transformation.

"If my family was still alive, even they wouldn't know me," she sadly uttered while turning for his inspection.

Soldar couldn't help staring with his mouth open. Her face, neck, and hands were now a perfect dark blue. Her hair was white-blonde. Indeed, Lyra could have been Gentis' twin. He preferred her as she really was. But her disguise was so well done that if he'd walked by her on any city thoroughfare, he'd have never known her.

"How was this accomplished?" he asked as he turned to Aigean.

"The magic of makeup, dear heart. I've had actors on this vessel before. Knowledge of their art comes in handy from time to time." Then she put her attention on Lyra. "Lyra, this is Gentis. She can show you the map of the bridge and where it's located. She'll also apprise you of all the duties you'll perform in her stead. Once you walk out of this room, Soldar will enter the authentication codes then study the same map for his own edification. I'd have had you both do this earlier, but neither of you was in any mental state to memorize a vessel's blueprints." Then she motioned Gentis forward.

The servant girl who was to be replaced on the bridge handed Aigean two vials of white powder. These were only about an inch in length.

"This is the same sleeping potion my crew carries," Aigean explained. "You should have been told about this concoction while you were changing, Lyra?"

Lyra nodded. She took the vials from Gentis and tucked them within the sleeve of her robe. "It makes me wonder what other little tricks you've got tucked away. Conveniently!"

Aigean ignored the sarcastic comment and reiterated the plans. "Get to the bulkhead computer over there, and start memorizing your route," she commanded as she pointed toward the other end of the living space where the computer was situated. "The walk from here to the bridge is quite simple. You'll meet other employees bringing food and beverages to the bridge, simply blend in with them. If something should go wrong, and you cannot hack the Condorian security codes, stop what you're doing and run. But not back to this space," she insisted. "Remember, for all intents and purposes, you're a Cloton woman. If the Condorians suspect you and you return here, Soldar will be immediately taken into custody as a conspirator. There are other places where you can hide. Places where Lyra Markham will not be connected to any Cloton servant from the bridge. If you can stay hidden until you can discard the costume and the makeup, you might still survive. Understand?"

"Yes. The servants listed a few places to run," Lyra confirmed as she arranged her robe around her. "Everything hinges on my being able to hack the security encryption the Condorians placed on your bridge console in the first place. And if I can get past that without an alarm going off, then all I have to do is link the allied authentication codes hidden in the bulkhead computer here, attach them to the message concerning the next Condorian attack, and then send the whole flaming mess through space… praying like hell it gets to the remaining allies close enough to receive the message." She paused and glanced around. "What the hell could go wrong? It's a frickin' piece of cake."

"*You* will not be associated with whatever happens on the bridge," Aigean contended. "The Condorians will be looking for a Cloton if anything goes wrong. Hence the disguise."

"Which brings up the million dollar question," Lyra shot back. "What happens to the Clotons on this ship if one is suspected of spying?"

Gentis took the opportunity to speak. "I am the only one of my race on board, Lyra. And I am prepared to accept the consequences."

Soldar had stood silently by up to that point. But now he had to speak up. The plans had never included implicating an innocent woman. "Aigean, you'd be sacrificing this girl. You've set this up on purpose!" He shook his head in frustration. "I can understand Lyra's anger. Parts of this mission are moving too fast, and you aren't communicating with us as well as you should."

Aigean sighed heavily and faced them. "If I don't tell you everything I've planned, then I have good reason. The less you know in some instances, the better. Gentis is prepared to be blamed so that your covers remain intact," she stated. "It still may not work if D'uhr discovers our ruse. In that event, we'll all be dead anyway. Besides all this…the circumstances being discussed will be moot if you *don't* get caught, Lyra. Do your jobs correctly and everyone remains safe."

Soldar gestured toward their bulkhead computer, indicating the need to access the ship's schematics. His Earth comrade pursed her lips, but strode to the far end of their living space without further comment. Gentis followed her, apparently to help bring up the schematics.

He then turned his narrowed gaze back on Aigean. Something wasn't right. The owner of the Venus was altering plans without consulting them. He and Lyra were simply expected to accept the arrangements.

But for now, he and Lyra simply had no other choice but to proceed.

• • •

It was ten minutes before midnight when Lyra stepped out of their quarters and into the passageway. As she did so, Sol simultaneously entered the long authentication code into the bulkhead computer in their quarters. That code was the only thing Allied Command would use to verify messages as being real. Everything—including Gentis' life—depended on acting as if she was who she was pretending to be. She drew herself up and made a determined decision.

No matter what happens, I won't fail. I won't.

With thoughts of one young girl's life hanging in the balance, she became less and less frightened.

As she blended in with other servants who were moving toward the bridge, they silently nodded in acceptance of her disguise. They knew who she was, seemingly agreeable to the plans of the evening.

Together, she and five others finally stood outside the bridge hatch and entered as a group. Each of them silently went about distributing food. The fare had been sent up from the galley via small service lifts within the bulkheads.

Once this chore was done, they proceeded to take away the remains of the Condorians' previous meal, clean the area, and bring the bridge officers anything not accessible from the galley, including drugs and alcohol.

Broken bottles and half-eaten food was strewn everywhere. That the bridge officers felt so comfortable carousing on the main command post said much about their arrogance and complacency.

Lyra forced herself to ignore everything except the mission. All she had to do was get as close as she could to a transmission terminal. More than a dozen were located throughout the ballroom-sized space. Her heart began to beat faster as she actually recognized the electronics in the consoles.

Like many allied vessels nowadays, Aigean had apparently salvaged her equipment from old, class three transport vessels just like those *she'd* seen on numerous barges. These barges had served as shuttles for her division as they'd made their way to the outermost part of the galaxy and into battle zones. Watching the repairmen fix those electronics had kept her mind off the coming fights. She'd learned enough to even help repair them when flying time became too tedious.

This is almost too easy.

When one of her hooded male comrades dropped his serving tray then looked up at her covertly, she knew she was being given her diversion. The Condorians near her clumsy friend cursed his getting in their way. Their attention was briefly focused on ensuing subservient and loud apologies.

She maneuvered a cart full of alcohol close to one terminal, used her wide robe as a shield, then acted as though she was distributing the drinks on a flat panel directly over and behind it.

It took only a moment to locate a translator switch at the top of the console. It was on as it should be, but the entire computer section was set to operate in Condorian.

Covertly scanning as she poured drinks, she quickly located a button bearing three overlapping circles. This control universally represented Earth English. She pressed it then began.

While pretending to rearrange glasses, bottles, and other paraphernalia with her left hand, she entered her message on the old-fashioned touch pad with her right one. The sleeve of her long robe hid her movements as her fingers flew over the surface of the pad.

Condorian attack eminent. Taurean Seti-Seven.

Then she easily accessed the authentication codes from Sol's location.

The message was composed; the codes to authenticate it were attached. The entire task only took her just a couple of minutes. The only impediment was getting by any security lock set up by the Condorians.

By ordering the computer to sequence and re-sequence every digit and symbol on the pad, it should only take a few moments to break through any locking ciphers. But knowing she'd gotten so far without mishap didn't make her feel any easier—if she set off an alarm, the bridge hatch would likely close to contain her, all the servants, and the Condorians.

Suddenly a green light appeared at the top of the console. This signaled the system was ready to send the message she'd composed.

It can't be this simple.

She swallowed hard when reality smacked her in the face. The security key to allow messaging was the hull number on the ship. Aigean's original bridge crew—now known to her as the servants who'd helped her put on her disguise—had told her the old unlocking numbers. They hadn't assumed the Condorians had left them intact but had mentioned them as a reference, a place to begin hacking.

Out of fear and the desire to move as fast as possible, she'd subconsciously entered the numbers they'd given her. That was why the keys on the pad looked so worn.

Oddly, the Condorians had never replaced Aigean's security pass with some locking ID of their own. As she stood there staring down at the console in shock, the reason suddenly became obvious.

Why should they change it?

This particular enemy nest was deep behind enemy lines, just where D'uhr had ordered it. His arrogance was such that he believed no one on the Venus would ever attempt what she just had. In fact, he probably thought Aigean's people were too frightened, subservient, or unintelligent to make this attempt.

Without considering her luck one more second, her thumb hit the send button and she glanced down to make sure the red transmit light was operational. It took a few seconds more before that red light turned green again then went out.

This sequence indicated the task had been successfully completed.

For a long moment thereafter, her mouth went dry and her hands shook. As the others around her hurried through their work, she helped and mimicked their motions to clean and haul away old debris for the incinerator.

Almost an hour later, she walked back into the passageway with the others, barely believing the scheme had worked. Her conspirators glanced at her questioningly as they walked. She covertly nodded, but said nothing. The answering look in their gazes was worth every risk she'd just endured.

Then reality set in.

This little escapade would only last until D'uhr figured out the nearby sector attacks had been thwarted. He'd be embarrassed among his peers, which was no small thing for a Condorian leader of his ilk. She'd heard competitive high-ranking officials used failure as an excuse to remove others from powerful positions.

Assuming this was true, D'uhr would go seeking answers. Failing any other reason for the allies to have evacuated Taurean Seti-Seven, he'd go straight to Aigean. And if he searched her ship's files deeply enough and her transmission wasn't overwritten, all hell would break loose. The entire ship's compliment would be lined up as spies. And that quick end she'd prayed for would be replaced by a round of arduous tortures. Still, innocent lives had been saved. For this moment in time, D'uhr was being outwitted. And that stood for something.

• • •

Soldar paced the length of his quarters. "She should be back by now."

"If the alarm hasn't sounded, then she completed her task," Aigean soothed. "Have you no faith in her abilities?"

"I'd have more if we'd been better briefed," he curtly replied. But he quickly turned when the hatch buzzer sounded. One of Aigean's servants checked the monitor, opened the hatch, and let Lyra in. Without thinking of how his actions would be perceived, he moved quickly toward her, swept her into his embrace, and held on tightly.

"It went just as planned," she murmured against his shoulder and hugged him back with equal fervor. "The damned access encryption is still the hull number. The idiots never changed it."

"That actually makes sense. There's no need to," Soldar agreed.

"Of course not!" Aigean chimed in as she lifted her hands in surprise. "The bastard's son is aboard. I'll bet my last breath that D'uhr is using *him* to transmit every battle plan from another enemy vessel. Some ship out in orbit. D'uhr wants nothing known about his occupying the Venus. He wouldn't take a chance on transmitting vital information from this bridge if there was any way it could be traced back here."

"He'd have every Condorian who didn't know about this little oasis calling for his blood," Lyra remarked as she pulled herself from Soldar's embrace. "If it wasn't for the fact that we'd all be slaughtered, I'd like to transmit a little memo to the rest of his stinking fleet!"

"We mustn't pat ourselves on the back prematurely," Aigean reminded them. "The evening's activities aren't done. We must tread carefully. D'uhr still wants to see the new sex act in his quarters." She clapped her hands for servants in the other areas of their quarters to come forward. "Lyra, get out of that wig and makeup," she commanded. "My women will help you. We have no time to lose. D'uhr wants to be impressed. You must look nothing less than splendid. And remember…behave as though you're above everyone in his quarters. You and Soldar have established yourselves as celebrities and you must act the part."

•••

Lyra stood beside Sol and tried very hard not to stare at his muscular frame. The skin tight black pants he wore with matching leather belt and tall black boots did nothing to hide every bulge. His shirt consisted of nothing but a white sleeveless tunic that was open in front. It made his bronzed, healthy skin look more appealing. She was in tight black pants and high boots as well, and her bustier pushed parts of her breasts up and forward to the point that she might as well not have any top on at all. She now sported what could only be referred to as *shelf cleavage*. Sol kept staring down at her, shaking his head as if he didn't approve of the clothing. But what could he really say to change the need of it? She'd already made love to him in front of hundreds of thuggish Condorians. It was expected that her clothing would be a bit revealing without offering free visible access of the goods.

"Remember," Aigean instructed for the hundredth time, "I'll join you in D'uhr's quarters soon. It wouldn't do for me to walk in on your heels. I'm supposed to be attending to other business as usual. I know you've studied the ship's blueprints so you won't miss your destination. Good luck to you both."

Without another word, Lyra took Soldar's hand as he walked out of their quarters. She felt his strong grasp around her palm and could almost smell his anger. He was like a walking time bomb; he was a man who was used to being in command. But on this ship and during this mission, Aigean was making sure her agenda came first.

The smell and the rowdy sounds coming from Condorian quarters told Lyra she was in the right passageway. Sol stopped and stared down at her for a moment.

"Are you all right?" he whispered. "I can feel you shaking."

"Sorry, I didn't realize. I'll be fine."

He put one hand on her left cheek. "Don't forget. That armband marks you as my mate. Even if I'm acting as though I prefer men, it'll be expected that I react violently to any contact on your person. It's a pride thing," he explained. "That reaction would be expected from any Craetorian. Understand?"

"If you do that you could get yourself killed."

He shrugged. "Maybe the odd luck we've had will hold and these bastards will be so full of booze and drugs they won't notice us. Now stay close."

She took a deep breath and gripped his hand even harder. To her surprise, he lifted it and kissed the back of her palm only seconds before they walked into the sickening, stench-filled den the enemy had made of their quarters.

Everywhere Lyra looked, Condorian men were lying on pillow beds with male and female sex givers. Some were in the process of feeding each other fresh fruit, and others, more secreted in other gauzy parts of the large space, were moaning. She heard soft entreaties for partners to continue with whatever they were doing.

Pasting on a jaded expression was the hardest thing she'd ever done. Her brief experience on a pleasure ship was nothing like this. On other such ships spaces had been kept separate, like hotel rooms. But her limited experience in that regard seemed like a hundred years ago, when she was less exposed to the cruelties of life.

She strode into the darkened room, where only artificial candlelight illuminated small tables near a bar. Couples not ensconced in darkened recesses talked, kissed, or felt each other up as a preamble to sexual interludes. Since they'd got this far without much notice, Lyra kept her mouth shut and her eyes peeled for anyone approaching.

• • •

Soldar took a seat at the end of the bar, with his back to a bulkhead. He pulled a stool very close to him and held Lyra's hand as she mounted the cushioned chair next to him. The blue-robed crewman behind the bar nodded surreptitiously toward them both.

"I think you'll find our ale to your liking," the barman suggested.

Sol nodded and held up two fingers indicating that they'd both have the same thing. When two silver goblets were placed in front of them, however, the beverage he sipped was nothing more powerful than amber-colored fruit nectar. He glanced over the top of his drink at Lyra. She acknowledged her non-alcoholic beverage with a covert drop of her chin. It seemed that—while the brothel participants stirred around them, and were fueled by too much wine, hallucinogens, and aphrodisiacs—they'd likely remain the only sober revelers besides Aigean's crew.

After a few moments of sitting in silence and blissfully being left alone, their luck ran out. From some sordid, smelly hole Soldar glumly noted the approach of their host.

Kardis D'uhr stumbled toward him, their nemesis' eyes latched onto *his* presence…not Lyra's.

The nasty bastard was tightening his belt as he half-wobbled forward, leaving any sober person to assume the man had just exited a bed. Had Lyra not suggested their pairing as a sex act, he would have arrived on the Venus as a prostitute, and might have just shared that same seedy den with D'uhr.

"Welcome, Soldar Nar and Lyra Markham." D'uhr punctuated the greeting by pushing a nearby guest off his stool so there'd be a chair for his own use.

Soldar sipped his fruit juice, pretending to be unconcerned over the rude act. His first words to D'uhr were, even to him, dripping in condescension.

"I want to thank you for inviting us, Admiral. Forgive our late appearance but Lyra and I needed time to ourselves before venturing out of our quarters. We've both barely recovered from our shuttle mishap."

D'uhr looked him over slowly. "And where did your shuttle break down again? My men haven't been able to find any sign of a forced landing."

Soldar lifted one shoulder in dismissal. "The last time we saw it, it was being serviced by that sorry excuse of a pilot. He seemed intent on getting it fixed. The bastard actually cursed us for his bad luck and insisted on more payment."

"Perhaps he will return?" D'uhr quizzed.

"I don't know and couldn't care less. He was an idiot. We'll need to find better transportation to get to our next gig. I don't want another near-death landing." He paused and made himself stare wantonly into D'uhr's dark eyes. "It's no longer an issue. I'm here now, ready to…*perform*," he suggestively added.

Kardis slowly smiled and moved closer to him. "I don't think you'll need to worry about your next transportation. You'll have plenty of entertaining to do on *this* ship. You aren't going anywhere!"

"You mean to keep us?" Sol responded as he gushingly affected concern. "Our agent will have our butts if we don't show up."

"Your self-centered complaining means nothing to me. You will stay or leave by my wishes. And I command you to stay!" He put one hand on Soldar's shoulder and ran it down his back.

"I love a strong-willed warrior," Soldar murmured as he sipped more fruit juice and stared into D'uhr's eyes.

D'uhr chuckled then turned his blood-shot gaze toward Lyra.

Soldar tensed. His partner's ruby-tinted lips and smoky, blue eye shadow seemed even more alluring in the dim light. Unfortunately, that sultry look caught D'uhr's attention.

"You and I can come to some beneficial arrangement," D'uhr stated.

Lyra rolled her eyes before responding. "I'll tell you what I told the last three men who asked. If I give it away, I can't negotiate contracts like the one I've signed with Aigean. I'm quite sure you don't mean to pay me for my time."

Kardis leaned forward. "You're right. I *won't* pay you. But I wasn't talking about bedding you, whore! I was talking about your man!" He loudly laughed and tapped the armband on her left bicep. "You are his mate, but I will see you have other entertainment while he shares my bed."

"Oh…*that's* the arrangement you meant," Lyra said as she rolled her eyes.

"I'll suffer no jealous histrionics from you," D'uhr declared. "Is that understood?"

She opened her mouth but Soldar quickly spoke first.

"If a man of the admiral's influence wants to bed me, then I don't see the harm. It isn't as if I'd be servicing everyone on the ship. Aigean could hardly make a contractual fuss over the matter," he offered. "You and I will still perform for the other passengers. And maybe the good admiral can help us find transportation to our next pleasure ship…if I cooperate. Isn't that right, Admiral?" Soldar said as he looped one arm around D'uhr's shoulders.

The inebriated, glassy-eyed Condorian smiled broadly in response.

To push his point, Soldar continued with the distasteful flirting. "It's so much more pleasant if I just take up the offer…*Kardis*. You don't mind me using your first name, do you? I mean…if we're to be intimate I assume that would be appropriate."

D'uhr nodded and stroked the black lighting mark on the Soldar's left cheek. "Yes…it's more than appropriate, you magnificently delicious man-lover. You may call me anything you please. Service me well, and I'll see you want for nothing," He licked his lips as he gazed up and down Soldar's frame.

Sol noted Lyra's alarmed gaze. She'd correctly assumed *he* was doing his best to keep her out of a Condorian bed. She also knew the danger involved if he didn't please D'uhr, whatever that entailed.

She finally spoke, though it was through barely clenched teeth. "What you're suggesting isn't in our contract, *darling*. Aigean won't like it. Besides, our agreement stipulates that I must perform with you, but without the use of any prophylactics. The admiral is a warrior who's taking risks a man of his…passions…would take. I can't afford to come down with some disease that can't be cured."

"Unfortunately, *sweetness*, it was your idea to have our agent book this gig," Soldar shot back. "You knew it was in the middle of nowhere. It's a sector's distance away from any hospitals or doctors."

Lyra suddenly relented with a careless lift of one shoulder. "If a man as powerful as the admiral could locate medicine…like antibiotics I could use to fight off infections…then I might be amenable to the arrangement. Obviously, I can't perform if I'm not in the peak of condition."

Soldar stared at her in shock though he did his best to hide it from D'uhr. The admiral seemed oblivious of this little exchange. The man was busy fondling *his* cock, through the thick leather pants he wore.

Something about the way she emphasized the words *antibiotics* and *infections* made him suspicious.

Then it hit him.

The crafty little Earthling had overheard his and Aigean's conversation concerning the medicine needed for the hidden allied fighters. Lyra had manipulated the situation in a hardly tactful attempt to get antibiotics while shoving his duplicity down his throat.

But if she wasn't very, very careful, her intentions could backfire. He tried to dispel any suspicions her request might have nurtured.

"I'm sure what you're asking imposes on the admiral's good will. In fact, you might be asking for too much. I'm sure the man has need of his medication."

Lyra simply glared at him and narrowed her eyes in response.

Kardis swallowed a drink the barman provided and entered the conversation at last. "Woman…are you implying that I may carry a venereal disease?"

She snorted loudly then poured on the denial. "I would *never* remotely suggest such a thing. But some of the men and women you've been with might not be as healthy as Aigean claims. Of course, they're supposed to have checkups, but one can never be too careful."

"Perhaps you mean to avail yourself of some pleasure while your man is with me? Is that it?" Kardis laughingly asked, apparently wanting to drive a wedge between Lyra and his new male love-interest. "Maybe your claim that I might give Soldar something—then give it to you—is to cover the fact that you're already infected...is that it?"

Soldar took up that idea and ran with it. If others on the ship got wind that she was infected with VD, they might keep their distance. "Yes, my dear mate, what have you to say to that?" he assertively pursued as he glared at her. "I haven't seen your medical profile since we last visited your home world. I assumed you were keeping yourself clean, but I could certainly be wrong!"

Lyra coyly ducked her head, making it seem as if she might, indeed, have been infected. "Please...Admiral...this discussion is in the poorest taste. If you could just give me some antibiotics, I know everything would be fine."

Soldar ran his hand lightly over D'uhr's thigh and gazed deeply into his enemy's eyes. It sickened him, but the ploy seemed to work.

"If my new plaything wishes you to have something to cure your ailment, then I might be receptive. It's clear you want it badly and have learned there is no such curative aboard this vessel unless you come through me. So whether it's to satiate an addiction, or to hide an infection, it's of no concern at all." He leaned close to Soldar and nibbled his left earlobe.

Soldar pasted on what he hoped was an expression of pure lust.

"So long as this pretty Craetorian pleases me, and as long as you don't pester him when he enjoys my company, I'll give you something to take care of your needs. But if I hear any whining out of you, then I'll have my men take you into the badlands and lop off your head off! Do you understand?" D'uhr told her.

She nodded. "You've made your point abundantly clear. I won't interfere with your uh…*arrangement*."

The admiral snapped his fingers toward one of his entourage. When that soldier came closer, he issued a stern commanded. "Bring the woman antibiotics from my private supply."

The minion rushed to do as he'd been ordered.

Lyra pretended to look away as if embarrassed by the subject, and Sol wanted to thank the Creator for having put such an intelligent woman in that canyon, if anyone had to be there at all.

"Where did you say you were from?" Kardis demanded of Lyra.

"Gratis Major."

"Hmmmm…they're due to be invaded soon." He quickly shook his head as if that knowledge shouldn't have been shared.

Lyra glanced at Soldar then pursued the slip-up. "Admiral, Gratis Major is a neutral planet. My home world has given you everything you've asked for."

Too late, Soldar saw D'uhr's eyes narrow, and quickly spoke up to cover her dangerous opinion. "Don't listen to her, Admiral. She's a stupid woman." For his attempt to mask her anger, he received one of the most fiery, unforgiving stares a woman had ever cast in his direction. Irrationally, her response made him want her even more. But his subterfuge apparently worked. The big Condorian quickly turned to *him*.

"And what of your world, Craetorian?"

Picking up his drink and sipping it before responding, Soldar gave the best response he could, though it left a very bitter taste in his mouth. "I say let you Condorians have it. We'll be under one rule and the fighting will be over." He gently rubbed D'uhr's bald, tattooed head. "But think on this, my big tattooed warrior, who'll serve you if we're all dead? I mean, someone has to do the dirty work."

Kardis snorted in disdain. "And you'd be satisfied with that?"

"If it's serve or die…I'll serve. But we can discuss matters of a political nature when we're alone. Can we not?" Soldar responded while attempting to paste a poignant expression on his face. He then lifted his hand, slid it into the admiral's vest, and stroked his left nipple. "We have more important matters to discuss, I can assure you."

"We'll see, Craetorian. Indeed…we shall see." He suddenly lifted one hand to Soldar's face. Soldar sat perfectly still and stared into his enemy's dark eyes. "You know, Craetorian…you are very like someone I once knew. Long ago," Kardis softly said.

There was a very appropriate response, but Soldar never got to utter it. At that exact moment, a Condorian guard arrived with a glass vial in his hand. Kardis snatched it and tossed the bottle at Lyra.

She deftly caught it before it hit the floor and shattered.

"Take that and get out of my sight before I let my men have you. The only reason I don't sic them on you now is because you wear Soldar's emblem. By his traditions, that makes you important to him, though I cannot imagine what he sees in you." He curled his lip and looked her up and down in disdain. "I don't care what you do or where you go, but I strongly recommend keeping your mouth shut! If you don't, no amount of sex Soldar provides will be enough to save your pointless life."

"Please *do* go," Soldar echoed in a simpering tone. "I have some affection for you, sweetness. We've been together a long time and make a good act, but I need more than you can provide. Off stage, a warrior like Kardis can service me better. After all, a man knows what another man needs." He waved a hand in the direction of the hatch. "Run back to our quarters and primp for our next performance. I want to dedicate it to my new lover." He gazed deeply into his enemy's eyes and simultaneously tamped down yet another desire to tear D'uhr's head off.

• • •

The last thing Lyra saw before leaving was the way the two men longingly gazed at each other. She was both amazed and horrified by how easily Soldar had orchestrated the entire scenario. Had she not know the man, she'd swear he was a damned traitor.

She was well on her way back to their quarters, safe for the moment and so long as Sol adequately serviced D'uhr. Still, if she needed backup, her Craetorian partner was stuck in his current situation, and there was no way she or Aigean could extract him. Something told her he'd be furious if anyone tried.

Her one consolation to being left alone among the enemy was in having obtained the medicine.

She concentrated on getting the medicine to the ship's med-tech and silently prayed for a man who was either the bravest warrior she'd ever met or the craziest.

Soldar was probably sleeping with that filthy bastard even now, but he'd intended to do that all along. That had been his primary mission. His actions tonight, however objectionable they might seem, could save allied lives. As he'd said, this *was* his choice.

"Christ, it'd better be worth it!" she muttered to herself.

Her fingers closed around the vial, and she forced herself to not think about what D'uhr might do to Soldar. She had to get the bottle to the wounded, and she picked up her pace to make short work of this important task.

Chapter 8

Lyra couldn't dispel the feeling that some greater power was watching over her every action. Even now a friendly figure stood in the passageway ahead of her. Gentis was working around a hover cart bearing clean linens, and there were no Condorians in sight.

She kept her voice low and made short work of stating her purpose.

"Gentis, can you direct me to the med-tech? I have some stuff she might need." Lyra lifted the vial for the other woman to see.

"I believe she's sleeping, mistress. But if you've obtained what I think you have, the last thing she'd care to do is rest." She leaned closer. "Go down the second passageway to the right, turn left at your first opportunity. You'll eventually come to a dead end. The med-tech will be in the space at the very end, right in front of you. Knock twice, pause, and then knock twice again. The more severely injured are in that room."

Lyra quickly made her way to that space. Her knocks on the hatch were answered by one of Aigean's blue-robed minions. He quickly let her inside and she pulled the vial from where she'd tucked it into her belt. "I conned this stuff from Kardis D'uhr. He says it's an antibiotic. It needs to go straight to the med-tech, but I'd consider testing it first. The bastard hates my guts so it might just as easily be poison."

The blue-robed man nodded energetically and quickly retreated to a darker interior of the large space.

Lyra assumed he was fetching the med-tech and that she was to wait. There seemed no harm in doing so since the admiral had clearly told her he didn't care where she went or what she did. Still, she didn't want to linger longer than necessary.

Gazing around, she noted that the space décor was much less ornate than her quarters, but much cleaner than D'uhr's. The curtained areas where large pillow beds were located seemed to be illuminated by the same, dull red lighting. She could barely make out bodies lying within the bedclothes. The lack of luxury here would leave this part of the ship virtually abandoned by passengers. That meant this had to be servants' quarters.

A rustling of fabric alerted her to someone's presence. She stiffened and hadn't realized she'd taken up a fighting stance when another blue-robed figure appeared. But when this person dropped the hood of their garment, Lyra gazed into the face of a beautiful woman who was humanoid and near her own age. This stranger's short blonde curls were almost the same chin-length as her own.

When the female held out her hand in greeting and approached, the words she spoke almost brought Lyra to her knees.

"I'm Myranda Chase…Earth Corps Medical Unit, Division 1602B. Aigean told me there were allied undercover operatives aboard. But I didn't think one would end up in this part of the ship," she gushed.

"My God…you're with Allied Forces…*Earth*?"

"I've been the med-tech for months."

"But how the hell—"

"My hospital transport was attacked. Our engines were damaged and we crash landed on a minor moon near Alpha Regina. The others on my ship didn't make it, but I wasn't banged up too badly," Myranda explained. "I survived by hiding in the hillsides until the enemy headed into deep space. Shortly after that, Aigean moved her vessel into that system to look for survivors. That's when her people found me. She had no Condorians aboard back then."

"And you've been here ever since," Lyra stated as she nodded in understanding.

"It was my luck to be rescued and Aigean's to find me. She needed a med-tech so I took over until I could hook back up with an allied ship. Unfortunately, Kardis D'uhr raided first and I got stuck here. I'm *supposed* to be from Atnar System Ten." She shrugged. "Olde Los Angeles is my real home."

"Olde Chicago," Lyra muttered by way of introduction, and then laughed when she realized she hadn't actually introduced herself. "I'm Lyra Markham…Master Sergeant, Tenth Earth Regiment. And I can't tell you how glad I am to see you!"

Ignoring the differences in their ranks, the two women exchanged a heartfelt hug before Lyra brought the subject back to their current dilemma.

"The antibiotic…will it help the survivors?"

"I was just testing that vial. The label is gone, but it looks like the stock that was in the ship's dispensary before D'uhr took it," Myranda stated. "The men need it badly, Lyra. They were hit hard with shrapnel."

"I've been down that road a couple of times," Lyra commiserated. "I know the pain."

"Dirt and metal fragments did their job. We have a lot who're suffering. The important thing is the most injured here have a chance…thanks to you. The contents of that vial were concentrated so I think there'll be enough to go around. How did you get your hands on it, anyway?" Myranda asked. "I assumed someone stole it from D'uhr. But that's not likely, is it?"

"No." Lyra quickly explained her and Soldar's sex duo charade. "D'uhr was so impressed by our act that he invited us to his quarters. He's absolutely besotted with my partner and didn't even take much notice of me."

"I know he didn't give that vial out of the kindness of his heart," Myranda quipped.

Lyra winced and made a face. "I…*implied*…I had a nasty case of VD that was causing me discomfort. I hoped he'd tell his men and they'd stay clear of me." She lifted one hand in resignation. "It's not as though a Condorian would care, but it was the only thing I could think of at the time."

"Talk about luck," Myranda muttered as her eyes grew wide in shock.

"Not really. D'uhr did it as a favor to my partner. Like I said, the admiral took one look at the guy and drooled all over himself. That vial was a sort of a bribe to leave the two of them alone."

Myranda stood there with a stupefied look on her face, then blinked and finally closed her gaping mouth. "You need to warn your friend, Lyra. Haven't either of you seen the unusual markings on the Condorians? I understand you haven't been here long, but surely you've seen what I'm talking about."

"Markings?"

"There's some kind of disease spreading through the Condorian ranks. So far, it hasn't affected the prostitutes but that doesn't mean it won't, sooner or later."

"And the good news just keeps coming," Lyra uttered as she put her hands on her hips in disgust.

"Some weeks ago, several of D'uhr's officers came to me, begging me to help them. And then D'uhr got a case of this strange disease, or so I've been told by Aigean's staff." Myranda snorted in derision.

"I couldn't wish whatever it on a more deserving race," Lyra shot back.

"Yeah, I know what you mean. The stuff seems to have been brought aboard by new officers who're sleeping with one another. Aigean provides protection but the damned Condorians won't use it."

Lyra snapped her fingers. "Wait a minute. I did see something. The light in D'uhr's quarters was frickin' low, but there was this kind of red spot on the back of his hand. It had dark rings around it. Is that what you're talking about?"

Myranda nodded. "What you've described are the same symptoms all the Condorians are displaying. I hear D'uhr won't be seen outside the ship or his quarters because it's spreading."

"I hate to bring this up but…the Condorians haven't tried anything with you, have they?" Lyra carefully asked.

"Not yet. I'm the only med-tech they've got since D'uhr's was killed in battle. And though I've made it clear that they won't get help if I'm molested, that small threat won't last if they really want to kick in the hatch and do what they please. I think Aigean keeps feeding the Condorians booze and pills so they'll be inclined to just lie around a lot and leave at least *some* of her people alone. So far, it's working." Myranda paused. "I won't ever admit it to D'uhr, but I know very little about Condorian physiology. It may be that this crud is making him and his men intolerant to light. Other symptoms include fever and loss of mental acuity. But then that's hard to quantify since they're drinking, taking hallucinogens, and were never that sharp to begin with."

"But it's still not circulating among Aigean's people…right?" Lyra asked.

"No," Myranda reiterated. "But D'uhr can confiscate all the antibiotics he can get his thieving hands on. Though he's convinced himself otherwise, it's not going to do him any good."

Lyra couldn't help the sinister smile that spread across her face. "It's that bad? Could the bastard die?"

Myranda snickered. "Don't get your hopes up. It's possible for it to disappear as quickly as it appeared. I only mentioned it in case you guys wanted to be careful. Assuming being careful is even possible when talking about Condorians."

Lyra was torn between going back to warn Sol, or let the situation stand. If she showed up in D'uhr's quarters again, the admiral would have her head cut off.

It didn't make her final decision easier knowing she'd be required to have sex with a man who was sleeping with an infected

Condorian. But she had to acknowledge that her concerns over any such issue really *were* moot. She figured their survival came down to a matter of hours or even minutes. D'uhr would soon discover what they'd done, if he hadn't already.

After sending that message and having the surviving allied fighters smuggled aboard, everyone would be butchered. D'uhr would be so enraged that the Venus would be expendable. Aigean's manipulating wouldn't change anything.

For that reason, and because Soldar had made up his mind long before she'd run into that canyon, Lyra decided she couldn't help him. But she might be able to comfort the injured before they were discovered and slaughtered. For the time they had left, the hidden wounded could at least have fresh water and food.

"Would it be possible to see the survivors?" she asked. "Maybe I could help. I'm sure you've been run off your feet."

"And your partner? Won't he worry about you?"

"He was prepared to die to get information." She shook her head. "My partner made his bed, no pun intended. All we can do is act in the moment."

Myranda lifted one hand and gestured for Lyra to follow. "Come with me. If you ever want to slip in and check on the wounded, I'll find some excuse for you to be in this part of the ship. Just in case D'uhr's men see you wandering. But pick times very late at night. When they've been partying and are in beds with their sex toys."

"I'll be careful," Lyra promised. "The man I came in here with can do his thing. I'll do mine."

She followed Myranda into the recesses of the large space. Several men lay on pillow beds. Though they were a breath away from being discovered, it still felt good to know those soft mattresses were occupied by soldiers who deserved them.

As she walked behind Myranda and listened to her recite lists of their injuries, she noted that all of the fighters looked like they were from Earth. They'd probably been in her same division, now whittled down to almost nothing.

The injured here seemed very well cared for. Their bedclothes and bandages were clean even if they were remnants of sheets or old clothing. At least their bodies were free of the incessant red dust from outside.

When they got to the very back of the room, Myranda's posture stiffened. She passed her hand over the illuminating wall unit and the lights came up if only just a little. She turned and concern was etched into her features. "I hid this man as far as I could from the hatch. Come closer and look at his face," Myranda instructed.

When the med-tech moved aside, Lyra scooted closer to the bed. That's when she saw what concerned her new friend so much.

As she looked down at this large, unconscious fighter, she saw the elongated, black lightning-like mark of a Craetorian warrior. It trailed down this man's left cheek, just as Soldar's did. His long, golden mane spread out over the bedding like a fan.

"The mark can be removed with a laser scalpel," Myranda whispered, "but not until he's better and I have time to do the job. It's a precision-intensive process because it goes deep into his tissue." Myranda bent to arrange the sheets around her patient's shoulders.

"What about makeup?"

"Gentis tried it but it just didn't look right. He'd have to walk around with it on all day, and have someone help him put it on. And then there's his size, his bronze-colored skin, and musculature to consider. So you see…the mark is only part of the problem. I don't know what race we could call him and still hide where he's really from."

Lyra stood there staring down at the injured man. Suspicion cemented her to the spot.

Something was wrong. She could feel it down to the soles of her feet. She recalled Soldar saying something about not having had the time to have his cheek mark removed. He'd said he'd been picked for the mission on very short notice, insisting the Condorians would accept him as is. But why would anyone at HQ choose an undercover operative whose facial markings, size, and coloring would put the mission at risk? As low as the allies were on fighters and if the mission could be deemed worthy at all, then Allied Command should have made time to bring in a covert agent who could pass himself off as a neutral citizen—exactly as she and Myranda were pretending to be.

Even Myranda realized this injured man's appearance would get him killed. That was why the med-tech was considering options to disguise him.

Lyra fully believed the rumors she'd heard. The same ones she'd never mentioned to Soldar.

Craetorian neutrals don't exist.

For years, Earth citizens had heard about Craetorians being the first to charge the enemy. In fact, it was widely known that Soldar's people demanded key positions in every attack. There'd been verified instances of their warriors throwing themselves on compound grenades to save fighters not even in their ranks. The more she thought about all the stories that even her own officers corroborated, the more suspicious she became.

Soldar had argued so convincingly. Surely, there must be neutrals among his people. But Myranda's confirmation of the entire allied opinion was enough to cause great disquiet.

For starters, how could the Condorians know with such certainty Soldar was among those neutral ranks? She and Sol had walked onto the Venus with such ease. The guards let them pass with almost no concern. Even Aigean's plotting should not have gained them such informal access. They should have been hauled before D'uhr in an instant. And when they'd finally met the enemy admiral, D'uhr only vaguely questioned their backgrounds.

Lyra shook her head and raised one brow in anger. She'd been so grateful for her safety that she hadn't fully questioned the details. Now, however, things were beginning to sink in. Somebody was lying about something. Where were these so-called neutral Craetorians that no one but the enemy had ever heard of?

"I think it's best to laser the mark off whether he likes it or not," Myranda confirmed with a nod of her head.

"He still looks exactly like what he is. Aigean won't be able to explain another Craetorian aboard," Lyra softly muttered.

"*Another one?*"

"I'm speaking of the man who's undercover with me...*the Colonel.*" Lyra said.

Myranda blinked. "I-I don't understand."

Lyra faced the other woman squarely. "The man who's undercover with me is a Craetorian. He didn't hide his race at all."

"Lyra, that can't be."

"Don't tell me...no one told you about it, right?"

"I was just told there were two agents aboard. I assumed they were Earth special ops, posing as neutrals from worlds the Condorians haven't enslaved." Myranda shrugged. "Nobody told me differently."

"So you and I both agree that a neutral Craetorian is about as likely as ocean-front property in Olde Arizona?"

"Honey...there's no such thing as *a neutral Craetorian.*"

"According to the man who picked me up in the desert and recruited me for this mission, there are. In fact, that's his cover."

"Or so he says!" Myranda shot back as she gripped Lyra's shoulders. "Lyra...you need to be very, very careful. Whoever this man is, he may have some connection to the Condorians you don't know about. I'm not saying he's with them. But something's not kosher."

"I'm beginning to get that picture," Lyra heatedly remarked. "Though the man I came in here with knows about the injured, I don't think he needs to find out one of them is Craetorian. How could he or anyone else explain *two* on this ship?"

They both gazed down at the Craetorian on the bed. A beeping noise sounded in another part of the huge space, making them both jump.

"God…that'll be the test sample I'm processing," Myranda breathlessly explained. "If the stuff in your vial is still good, I'll give the first dose to this Craetorian. The sooner he's better, the sooner I can get that mark off his face and try to hide his big bronze ass. Assuming that's possible."

Lyra watched the other woman leave, but stayed by the bed in this dim area of what was probably old servants' quarters. Minutes went by and she considered not only the unconscious Craetorian but Soldar and the odd game he and D'uhr were playing.

A low moan prompted her to sit on the side of the downed Craetorian's bed and lean closer. In that split second, before she could utter a single word, his right arm shot from underneath the covers and clenched around her throat. Both her hands came up in an automatic gesture of defense. She ineffectively pulled at his massive wrist.

Her attacker wrestled himself into a sitting position despite the bandaging covering a laser-sealed, raw wound to his abdomen. Jagged parts of that seal were visible at the edges of the white gauze around his mid-section.

As badly injured as he was, the man's strong grip kept her from crying out. His silvery gaze wandered over her features, then to the armband on her left bicep. He shook her and snarled.

For some odd reason, she thought of Soldar. This stranger's long blond hair sifted loose and now lay around his shoulders. Just as her so-called partner's often did.

"I wasn't sure if I dreamed Earth English," he angrily asserted as he used that dialect. "Do you understand me?"

She barely managed a nod as she tried to pull his hands free.

"Where did you get that armband, woman? There're only two ways its owner would give it up. The first is if you're a Craetorian's mate. The second is if the original owner died in battle and had it cut from his corpse." He leaned closer to her. "If that latter of those options is the case, I promise I'll kill the Condorian responsible. And I'll see fit punishment comes to *you* for accepting looted property, taken from a dead hero. Now…which is it?" He finally let her throat go, but grabbed the front of her garment so she couldn't run.

Lyra took a moment to catch her breath and rub her injured neck. "What's it to you?" she countered as she watched him stare back with harsh, suspicious anger in his gaze.

"That armband belongs to the royal house of Ky'Nar. It would not be gifted to a common whore. And while I recognize I'd be dead were you not sympathetic, I know this is a pleasure vessel that must be behind enemy lines." He glanced around him while his eyes took on a wild, glazed expression. "The look of such places is not beyond my experience, but no injured soldier would be brought to such an abode if there was no emergency." He grabbed her again by her forearms. "Start talking, or nothing you've done to save my life will save yours. Not if you took that band from a Condorian as payment for favors."

She tossed her head and glanced down at the band. "Do you really think a Condorian would give this away? It would be considered a trophy, wouldn't it?"

"Tell me, woman!"

At that moment, something Soldar said filtered into Lyra's heavily tested brain. She gazed at his face for a long time and understood why everything about him was so familiar. "Christ almighty! You're his *brother*…the one who's supposed to be missing. And what the hell do you mean by 'the Royal House of Ky'Nar'?"

Silence permeated the space.

Finally, the man spoke quickly, but never stopped to even breathe. "It seems I must trust you. In case I am mistaken, I know nothing you can use to your advantage. Torture would do no good."

"You're being hidden from the Condorians who control this vessel. You'd be wise to keep your voice down."

He considered her for a long moment. She assumed he believed her as he finally responded more calmly.

"My name is Cordis Nar. I was separated from my Craetorian brethren months ago during a fight on Rimbor Alta. I took up fighting with an Earth unit since orders to maintain communication silence stranded me with them," he explained. "We've been fighting on a star-class vessel, deep in enemy territory. Our last orders were to engage the enemy on the surface of an old refueling station."

"Yeah. That'd be Reisen Four which is where this ship has landed." Lyra ran her hands through her hair and tried to comprehend this coincidence. "God, he thinks you're dead!"

Cordis gazed at her armband, then back at her face. "I fear I've made a grave mistake. Is the person you speak of my brother? Is *he* the one who thinks I'm dead?"

She slowly nodded.

"Then he *is* alive," Cordis responded as he smiled. "And you are no whore."

"I've probably been called worse," she somberly joked. "Soldar put this band on me. He's on this vessel pretending to be a male prostitute. I'm his partner."

"And you did say the Condorians control this ship?" he asked.

She nodded. "You need to stay hidden. A lot of lives depend upon you not being found. Do you understand?"

"I will cooperate."

"Good. My name is Lyra Markham, Master Sergeant from Earth…"

The stress amassed over the last few days was taking its toll. She shut her mouth and tried to gather her thoughts. This mission was one surprise after another. She heartily wished for a battle where she knew who the enemy really was. This subterfuge would kill her long before the enemy did.

"You're his mate!" Cordis suddenly blurted.

"Our arrangement is for the duration of this mission. He thinks he's protecting me—"

"If he put that band on your arm, it was not just for protection." He wearily plopped back down against the pillows.

Beads of perspiration scattered across his forehead. She swiped at them with her hand then arranged his covers.

What words could she say to give hope? Common sense told her there was none. But he was injured and it seemed cruel to offer anything else. "The med-tech has something to make you feel better. Remember, you need to stay quiet."

"If it's t-true that Soldar is as near as the enemy, then do not b-bring him here," he haltingly insisted. "Do not tell him I'm present."

"I think he'd want to—"

"He will try to save me!" Cordis glared at her as his hands clenched into fists. "In the absence of any Earth officer, regulations give me the right to command you, Sergeant. I outrank you. And on this issue I remain adamant."

She sighed and rolled her eyes. "All right...okay! Whatever it takes to shut you up."

The similarity of the brothers' thinking wasn't lost on her. She was on the Venus because Soldar quoted the same regulation Cordis just had.

"I-I'm sorry if I hurt you," he apologized.

"No worries. Just rest easy. You'll be better soon."

Luckily, Myranda arrived only a few moments later, carrying a small injection gun. Lyra gladly vacated her spot so the other woman could do her job.

"Glad to see you're awake," Myranda softly said as she gazed at Cordis. "I'm going to administer a general antibiotic. It'll work on just about anything you might have picked up outside the ship." She put the injector gun to the side of her patient's neck. "I'm also shooting you up with something to make you sleep."

Cordis winced when the trigger was pulled, but he had time to reiterate his command. "Do not tell him about m-me. He must continue h-his mission…"

Lyra watched the man drift off to sleep and saw Myranda glance at her questioningly.

"What's going on?" the med-tech asked.

"Strange and maybe not so coincidental shit! If you have a couple of minutes I'll explain," Lyra said as she ran a hand over her forehead.

• • •

Half an hour later, Lyra finally walked out of Myranda's makeshift infirmary with the profound sense of having too much weighing on her soul. It wasn't enough that she and her partner were about to die. Everyone would when the Condorians eventually discovered the hidden allies. But the occurrences of the night were so twisted and irregular as to confound anyone.

She was deep in thought, trying to make sense of the night's discoveries, but jumped and automatically assumed a fighting stance when a body rounded the corner. She was equally quick to relax when Aigean stood in her path. "Where were you tonight?" Lyra demanded. "Sol and I were expecting to find you in D'uhr's quarters."

"There was some business requiring my personal attention," Aigean quickly explained. "I just left the admiral's quarters, and came searching because Gentis told me she'd seen you in this area. She tells me you got your hands on some medicine."

"I did." Lyra stepped closer to the Elderian woman. "Why didn't you tell me your med-tech is from Earth or that the Condorians are carrying some disease?"

"Don't presume to question me," Aigean furiously responded. "What difference does any of that make? We needed Myranda's skills. She needs to make herself as inconspicuous as possible. As to the ailment afflicting the enemy, there's enough fight left in them to kill everyone on every allied world. Their maladies don't concern me."

"And what about that Craetorian warrior brought aboard with the other injured?" Lyra further quizzed. "Did you know he's Soldar's brother and that Soldar thinks he's dead?"

Aigean simply stared back with a passive look on her face.

Lyra's fingers curled into fists. "You *did* know!"

"I have two reasons for seeking you out," Aigean said, ignoring Lyra's suspicions. "The first was to see if you had safely delivered the medicine to Myranda. The second was to impart news of an urgent nature."

"What news?"

"Listen carefully. I haven't time to be interrogated." Aigean glanced around before beginning. "My servants inform me there was some kind of confrontation in D'uhr's quarters. I arrived too late to see it, but I've been told the situation was serious."

"What about Sol—"

"I'm informed his anger was such that he actually struck a support beam and bent it." Aigean clasped her hand and sighed. "He's back in his quarters. Servants say he's still angry enough to kill someone."

"What about D'uhr?"

"Leave him to me and my people. Get back to your quarters and be careful. A Craetorian's rage can be very…" She stopped and briefly closed her eyes before continuing with her warning. "Just get back to your quarters and don't anger him further!"

Lyra looked into Aigean's eyes and knew things were falling apart. There was nothing left to say so she strode past the Elderian and silently prayed *somebody* would end this crazy mission soon.

Chapter 9

As with Lyra's trip to the hidden infirmary, there were no guards in the passageways. The lax security told her D'uhr's minions had either been called elsewhere, or their level of sobriety was so precarious that duties were no longer a priority.

That situation changed when she walked down the final stretch to her quarters.

From many yards away, she saw Condorian guards standing on either side of the hatch to her space. The glares on their faces indicated what they'd like to do, but they said nothing. She noted the telltale red marks and red rings around their throats and faces. It looked like their sickness was progressing.

It took everything she had to paste on an unconcerned look, open the hatch slowly, and leisurely stroll in. Until she knew who was inside, she'd play the witless sex diva to the last.

Thankfully, she was met by servants. They'd faithfully remained to divert any thieving guards away from the bulkhead computer. These silent, blue-robed allies said nothing, but kept their heads down or averted.

A sound made her turn her head to the left.

Soldar stood by a refreshment station pouring Alturian whisky into a glass. There was no mistaking the shape of the bottle or its contents. His insistence on keeping a clear head was to his credit. But something had made him reconsider that rule.

"Are we entertaining…guests?" she quietly asked.

One of the servants finally lifted his head and shook it in denial. She let out a long sigh of relief and moved closer to Sol.

Her Craetorian partner hadn't even acknowledged her presence when she entered, but promptly turned his back on her now. When he remained silent for almost five minutes more, she tried again.

"I overheard you and Aigean talking about the survivors," she admitted. When he didn't respond, she pursued the subject. "I took the vial D'uhr chucked at me to the med-tech. As it turns out, she's from Earth. Aigean rescued her from a crash site before the Condorians overran the ship."

There was still no response, so she dug in like a Preatorian Fever Tick.

"You knew I'd try to get my hands on medicine. That's why you didn't want me knowing about the injured. Am I right?"

Whatever had happened in D'uhr's quarters, he wasn't opening up. She took heed of Aigean's warning but they had to communicate. Soldar couldn't stand there forever, silently drinking himself into a stupor.

"Look…I'm sorry I eavesdropped. It wasn't like I planned it," she softly apologized. "And I had no idea that you'd revert to your original plan…pretending to be a private sex toy, I mean." She moved closer, trying to get him to look at her. "You know, your acting skills are amazing. You had me believing you wanted D'uhr. He's obsessed with you. I could see it in his eyes."

To get his attention, she almost blurted out the news of his brother's survival. But years of following orders made her close her mouth. Cordis was right. Sol would try to get to his brother. And while the injured soldiers would be discovered soon enough, there was no sense getting Myranda killed for harboring spies. D'uhr might need a med-tech, but there was a limit to what the enemy would tolerate. In Myranda's case, she'd be lucky to die quickly.

• • •

Soldar stared down into his drink.

He should have known his silence wouldn't drive her off. He listened to her ramble on for some time but couldn't respond.

When she eventually asked the servants to complete their chores in some other part of their quarters, he knew the woman wasn't going to simply take a shower and go to bed.

Her eavesdropping on his conversation with Aigean should have been a serious matter. He should be lecturing her about the need to come to him with misunderstandings. But the occurrences in D'uhr's quarters were so bizarre that he couldn't get his head wrapped around them. His shock was as deep as any of the Condorians who'd witnessed the event. In fact, they'd backed away from him when it had happened.

Aigean or one of her people had obviously told Lyra about the confrontation. It was equally clear they were leaving specifics for *him* to explain. But how could he? He had no answers for the thing that had arisen from deep within him and had gone away just as quickly.

In the deepest part of Craetorian history, the ability he'd displayed was archived. It had a name no one on his planet took seriously since it was more legend than fact.

The darkening.

How was he going to tell Lyra he'd shape shifted right in front of everyone and for no other apparent reason than he'd had enough of the Condorians?

He threw back the contents of another glass, put it down, and slowly turned to her.

"Soldar…what happened tonight?" she slowly asked.

The question was put to him quietly and with an almost reverent care. There was a deep, concerned look in her blue-green eyes that made him want to scream he'd never hurt her. But how did he know that? He kept seeing the faces of those Condorians when they'd backed away. It was the first time he'd ever witnessed their version of paralyzing fear.

He should tell her. He should.

But what did one say when the sudden ability to shape shift—along with the comprehension of was happening—suddenly manifested? Worse, he felt he'd done it before. And *that* was scaring the hell out of him.

He took a deep breath and tried to speak normally.

"I…I accepted this mission to get close to D'uhr. Doing so might have left me feeling somewhat…degraded," he softly told her. "But I'm dealing with it."

"Tell me," she prompted as she moved closer.

"The fight you heard about had nothing to do with D'uhr. He was drunk and full of drugs. He'll sleep for some time. Obviously, our covers are still intact or we'd be dead."

"You look like someone did something—"

"I'm all right," he reiterated as he lifted his chin and injected what he hoped was a note of dignity into his voice.

She reached up, gently cupped his cheek, and stared at him. Then she lowered her hand and swallowed hard before speaking. Her attempts to be gentle would have been sweetly comical had the night not played out in a way no one could have imaged. He finally had to say something if for no other reason than to ease the fear she was displaying. And all of it was on his behalf, not her own.

"One of the servants told me about the disease that seems unique to the enemy," he said. "It's said there's no treatment though it hasn't led to any deaths." His change of subject wasn't working. He saw how desperate she was to know about the situation in D'uhr's quarters, but he just couldn't speak of it. Not yet.

Her next words were a tactful ploy. Her discretion originated from what she thought was his lurid sexual encounter with D'uhr. Little did she know.

"Um…like I said…the med-tech is from Earth. Her name is Myranda Chase and she knows about us," Lyra advised. "It's a long story, but she got trapped on the Venus and is claiming neutrality like us. I…I wasn't sure if you'd been told any of this."

A long interval followed. It was clear she didn't know what to say, and was probably convinced he'd been raped when he hadn't been. There simply was no way to describe the sudden manifestation of a shape shifting ability that *shouldn't* exist.

"Sol, I've gotta ask again. Will you please tell me what they did to you?"

He stared straight into her eyes and said the only thing he could. "It's done. There's no sense speaking of it."

"I don't like that answer, but…I'll be here to listen if you change your mind."

In that moment he wanted to take her hand, head for the nearest exit, and take their chances in the badlands of Reisen Four. They'd never live out another day. He knew it. D'uhr would be told what he'd done and would have them both killed. He was now far too dangerous to be kept alive.

"Lyra…I need to give you the entire authentication sequence in case something happens to me."

"Only officers with security clearances have it. I…I don't—"

He gently took her by the shoulders and more firmly put forth his case. "Be quiet and listen to me!"

She dropped her gaze to the middle of his chest but did as he ordered.

"I have a bad feeling about what's coming next," he told her. "This is why I'm ordering you to accept this information. If something happens, you might be able to continue the mission."

"Sol, I could be tortured. If they got the sequence out of me, they could send any message and trap the allied fleet. Eventually HQ would figure out the breach, but they'd be transmitting information for days before that happened."

"The Condorians don't know our frequencies," he lamely offered.

"If they get the damned sequencing, how much longer would it take to figure out we're using normal frequencies because our cadets…which are what's left of our crews…can't process anything complicated!" She lifted her hands in supplication. "Why are we standing here arguing the obvious? If you die, so will I."

"Not necessarily." He lifted one hand to run it over her hair, but quickly dropped it. He didn't yet trust himself near her. Not so soon after experiencing what he had in D'uhr's quarters. He briefly closed his eyes then opened them to continue what might be his last command. "I know having that kind of information frightens you, but you'll be in charge when I die. I have faith in you, you won't be alone. Aigean will make sure nothing can be tortured out of you," he said with finality.

"You're saying all this as if you'll be checking out soon," she whispered.

He simply lowered his head but was heartened to hear her next words.

"All right. I'll do it and I won't let you down."

He put his mind on the equations and nothing else. Time was so short. Ironically, he wanted to live more than ever. He wanted to know why he'd shifted, what the hell had caused it, and why the Condorians so feared what they'd seen. But everything was coming to an end. He could literally feel it, the way he felt her warm presence standing so near.

"The sequencing is based on mathematics," he began. "The first one you used was a rather simple equation for escape velocity. The next authentication code will be that same formula, adding one for perigee radius Rp. Subsequently—"

"The next code would be the first, the second, and then add on a calculation for eccentricity of orbit. This is all rocket science."

Her words made him smile when nothing else could have. "So…the computer hacker knows a bit more than she lets on, eh?"

"I'm not as stupid as I look. Vector squared equals vector parameter. And radius times one, times radius squared," she recited.

"I believed I held all the cards in this game. But I should have known better," he admitted while smiling more broadly. "Since we met, you've outshone me in every way."

His reservations about touching her fled. He suddenly understood he'd never harm her. He couldn't. And with that realization, he granted himself permission to do as his heart bid. He gently pulled her into his embrace.

"Just remember, Lyra, the sequencing changes every seventy-two hours."

"I know what to do," she confirmed as she blinked back tears.

"I wish…"

"What? What do you wish?" she softly asked when he hesitated.

Soldar brushed her cheek with the knuckles of his left hand and stroked her armband with the other. "I wish we could have met somewhere else, under other circumstances."

"This is all we have. This is it."

"I know. We don't know what will happen when D'uhr awakens. If he shows up here and forces himself into our quarters, he should find you in one bed and me in another. He needs to think my favor rests with him and that you mean no more to me than part of a show. We need sleep…but there are things I need to say."

"I'm listening," she insisted as she gazed up at him.

"Lyra…I hope you and the Creator of all things will forgive me for my selfishness. My mind should be on the consequences of what happened in D'uhr's quarters. But it isn't. All I can think about is what might have been."

"Don't look at it that way," she tearfully begged. "We've still got a little time."

"Only a little," he agreed as he tried to memorize every nuance of her features.

Suddenly, duty didn't matter. They'd been riding the wings of chance. Plans had changed on a whim and he was no longer putting duty before desire. They'd be killed no matter what lies were told.

He quickly lowered his head, pressed his lips to hers, and greedily accepted her tongue in his mouth.

Their contact was slow, deliberate, and full of passion. He felt his body respond with energy he'd never known. Weariness fled and he felt renewed.

These last hours together were precious and he meant to take every recollection into the next life. He no longer even feared for Lyra's safety. Aigean and her people would see his Earthling painlessly dead before the Condorians could touch her. That scenario had never been verbalized by anyone, but he knew that was exactly what would happen.

The entire crew of the Venus would follow them into the afterlife. Aigean would know how to make it happen.

Even as thoughts of death flailed through his brain, he kept kissing Lyra. Her softness pushed the ugliness of war away. In her arms, there was no battle for supremacy. No regret or pain. Fear fled. And he understood one truth nothing could ever destroy.

He loved her.

In the short time they'd known each other, she'd become everything.

With that deep acknowledgement, peace pervaded every cell in his body. Nothing and no one could take that solace away. And when circumstances separated them in this life, he'd seek her in the next. There was no other woman he'd ever loved so passionately. The clarity of these emotions was simple. It was right. It was the best thing that had ever happened to him.

He eventually, breathlessly broke their contact and ran the palm of his hands over her shimmering hair. He desperately gazed down into eyes that glittered with light from a thousand stars. There was nothing they needed to say.

She took his hand, backed away, and turned. He followed.

She led him toward the shower stall, and he knew they'd share this time in love. Not a pretense but the real thing.

Fears for the future and regrets of not having one faded. They lived in the here-and-now. They were mates. D'uhr and his ugly, obsessive passions couldn't change reality.

After undressing and caressing each other, Lyra activated the water in the stall and smoothed luxuriant cleanser all over her palms. As they stood near the falling water—just close enough to feel the spray and enjoy sensations caused by the mist—she took her time soaping every part of his body, including his burgeoning cock. He circled his hips, loving the wonderful feel of her fingertips on his most sensitive flesh. Then she stood on her toes to plant a sweet kiss in the center of his chest, protectiveness filled him. He slid his hands down her back and to the top of her butt. The softness of her skin was like a summer breeze back home. He dearly wished she could see the seasons on Craetoria, but knew it would never happen.

He hated the Condorians more with every pulse of his heart. They'd started this war. They'd killed billions. Now she would be among that number and her lovely body would never know a quiet resting place. No one would be able to mourn her. He parted his lips to speak, but she covered them with her fingers. Then she slowly shook her head.

He took that hand in his and kissed the back of it. "If I gave you one final command, would you obey?"

"This isn't something I'm gonna like or you wouldn't be asking."

He took a deep breath and expelled it slowly before continuing. "If you have one infinitesimal chance of getting off this vessel, I want you to take it. I want you to get back to the oasis, take the laser I left there, and try to locate an allied unit."

"There's no one left alive. That battle is over and I'm not leaving you."

"You could use your helmet transmitter to send a distress call—"

"Which the Condorians would likely intercept," she quickly countered. "Minus confusing battle transmissions, it'd be like sending up a flare. Besides, our fleet can't afford to rescue one loan fighter."

"So you'll disobey?"

She nuzzled her cheek against his armband. "I won't leave you, so shut up."

He sadly smiled. "Under other circumstances I'd have you in irons."

"I prefer leather, but iron will do."

The nonsensical response in this situation was so like her. He felt her bravery infuse him with energy. He slowly walked her backward, into the direct spray of their steamy shower. His gaze never wavered from hers.

His senses fixated on her and nothing else. He began to imagine.

In his mind now, there were no bulkheads surrounding them. He imagined they were in some forest on his home world. A place of their own where no one could ever bother them again.

Lyra planted small kisses on his chest and swirled her tongue over his left nipple before saying, "You wouldn't ask me to go if I was a man."

"You're not just an allied soldier. You're my mate. When I banded you everything in me said it was right," he whispered. "My instinct tells me to protect you. Do you understand, Lyra?" He planted kisses along her cheek and down her neck. She pressed her breasts against his body in response.

"Show me what being a Craetorians mate means…while there's still time," she pleaded. "For just a few minutes I want to be yours. I want to have you."

He pulled her into his embrace. "Then you accept?"

"Yes. I love you, Sol. God help me…I do! And that's never going to change."

"Then know this…my love for you is unending, Lyra Markham. Whatever deity put us here will forever find favor in my heart. We were never strangers. We were two souls meant to find each other."

She lowered her head and began to softly sob.

"Don't cry, my love." He held her in his arms and kissed the top of her head. "Find me in the next life. I will likely die first so you must search in the ethereal world. Don't give up on me. Promise me this!"

•••

"I promise. I'll look for you."

She parted her lips and immediately felt his tongue spar with hers. Heat rose in her body the way coronas rise from suns. Any suspicions concerning his real agenda on the Venus were shoved aside in favor of this magnificent wave of passion. She needed him now, in ways she couldn't articulate.

Even the mist from the shower stall—as balmy and inviting as it was—couldn't mimic the warmth and security of his muscular body. His sweet breath made her skin tingle. She spread her hands over his massive biceps and felt the golden metal of his armband. It was warm and glowed beneath the water, just like his skin and long, golden mane.

When had she fallen so helplessly in love with him?

Soldar had embedded himself deeply within her heart. It'd come so easily. She'd accepted him so readily, almost as if she'd been looking for him forever. As he'd said, they were two souls meant to be together. She believed they would see each other again. And in that belief, her sorrow turned to happiness. His kiss went on and on and she cherished the sweetness of it.

When he finally broke that contact and slid his lips across her shoulder, she whispered his name over and over. The sound of it seemed to empower him.

His rotated his hips against her body. His erection pressed into the flesh of her midriff.

"This is for us," he murmured.

"I'll find you," she repeated over and over.

The promise he extracted must be entrenched in her brain. It was the last order he'd ever give, the last command she'd gratefully fulfill.

They were at the end a mission and in the darkest part of a war they'd surely lose. Time wasn't on their side. Fate was taking them from shared intimacies and toward death. She treasured every single caress his strong, gentle hands delivered. But he must remember her touch as well.

She slid her palms down his wet arms, to his wrists. With a gentle tug, she lured him to his knees and began to soap his body with the fragrant body wash likely to have been brought aboard from looted allied worlds.

Part of her heart asked forgiveness for the use of the product. If lives were lost in the taking of it, perhaps those souls would understand if she used it to cleanse her lover's skin. At least one brave allied fighter aboard the Venus might have use of the luxury long enough to avenge lives lost during Condorian raids.

She tilted his Sol's head forward and began to wash his thick, golden mane. The mass of long hair streamed over his chest and shoulders like sunlight. Even in the dim illumination of the shower, she gloried in the light color of it. Touching it made her happy, as did massaging the scalp and the shoulders of the big man kneeling before her. She allowed herself the luxury of running the strands through her fingers and gently rinsing them. Even if they lived just a little longer, this was the last time such intimacy could be shared without a lecherous audience gawking at their every move. When his intense, silvery gaze was no longer boring into hers she finally let the tears come in earnest. The misty water on her face hid them. She withheld sobs so he wouldn't concern himself as he had before.

He had to believe she could go on without him. He had to think she'd tell D'uhr whatever their barbaric captor wanted to hear, if only to get one more message off, or to get close enough to put a knife from the galley into his thick, ugly neck.

She lifted her face to the water so the tears could wash away. But there was one thing the recirculated and purified water could never do—it could never cleanse the bitterness from her heart.

She'd found a man to rival all others. A strong man who was brave and who'd give anything to mitigate the suffering of others. Magnificent in stature, glorious to behold, and with the heart of a lion, Soldar was everything she'd been looking for. And she'd found him among the rubble of human tragedy. She'd located him in the last possible place, at a time when she should have died.

Her fingers and palms moved over his body, memorizing every curve and scar. She washed away all traces of any Condorian presence. It took everything she had to shove away images of Soldar being touched by D'uhr. But he'd done what he had to get information. He'd gone willingly and that was a measure of devotion those of allied worlds should understand. If his actions gave some a little more time to live, then he deemed his mission worthy. So she would have to accept his belief in this assignment and come to terms with the consequences.

To make him believe she was good with his choices, she offered him the only tangible thing that was hers to give.

"I want to feel you inside me," she told him. "Love me, Sol. *Please?*"

He immediately stood, put his arms around her waist, and lifted her up. He held her close as his kiss deepened and their tongues met.

She took a deep breath after he ended the kiss. And with strength only a man of his build could muster, he lifted her higher and gently pressed her back against the shower wall. The feral cry coming from her throat seemed foreign. He plunged into her body with all the ardor of a doomed man. She accepted his shaft with all the passion she could.

His penis was deep, deep inside her. He found a way to thrust deeper. The flange on the top of his penis teased her clitoris in an unending dance of pleasure. It seemed right to lift her legs and wrap them around his strong body. She craved him the way the enemy desired drugs. He was an addiction she'd never get over, even if she'd been given the rest of her life to live.

Her fingertips dug into his shoulders. The heat from his glowing balls warmed the skin between her legs. His bull-like testes swung between her thighs and struck her body over and over. The feel of them was intoxicating. The thud made by their bodies thrusting was a wonderful sound. The only sound she loved more was his voice whispering her name and encouraging her.

"You're mine. Never forget that. *Never!*" he commanded.

A rush of pressure circled at the back of her vagina and swelled forward. She knew he sensed it. His flange began to circle her clit faster and faster. That extra organ seemed out of control and alternately poked and pulled at her labia. His huge body began to shake and he buried his face into her wet hair. Her orgasm was the strongest she'd ever experienced. She gripped his muscle and then curled her fingers into fists as the climax spread ever outward.

"Take it all, baby. Take it," he coached as he lifted her higher in the air. "Take my head deep in you. Feel it drive into your body."

When her second orgasm burst on top of the first one, she actually bit into his shoulder.

"I love you," he murmured over and over. Then he cried out as his seed shot forth. His penis throbbed and his flange pounded against the soft flesh of her nether lips. He shuddered and gripped her body in a massive hug as he thrust up and into her. Sol's body convulsed as his seed came in wave after wave. Unlike any human male, he had more of it to give her. His stamina was magnificent. And she would have so loved to have had this experience as a normal couple, and not as two soldiers about to die.

He panted and dragged air into his lungs. Eventually, he seemed to drift back to her. It was over, but he still held her and it almost broke her heart to feel the way he trembled.

Finally, he lifted her up and off his penis and gently lowered her until her feet touched the floor.

"Y-your eyes are still glowing," she said as she cupped his cheeks between her hands.

"That's the power you have over me."

He slid one palm into the small over her back and drew her forward until her breasts pressed against his torso. His hug was warm, safe, and strong. He held her as though she might break, and his caresses were gentle and comforting.

The last thing she wanted to do was remind him of D'uhr. But he intended to sleep in some other part of their quarters in the event the brute broke in on them. The extra few moments of life they might gain with that subterfuge wasn't worth it. She nuzzled her cheek against his chest.

"I don't care if D'uhr comes in and finds us together. Let him rage," Lyra told him. "You're mine. I don't care about him anymore."

"Perhaps you're right," he responded. "Aside from being together, the jealous look on his face would be worth death."

When the heat from the shower began to dissipate, she shivered.

"Let's get you dry and in bed," he suggested. "It's got to be past dawn."

He kissed her once again then turned on the auto-blowers to gently dry their skin and hair. At least they could stand there for enough time to keep from getting into bed wringing wet.

Soon, he led her from the shower and they walked over discarded clothing to one of the sumptuous, burgundy-colored pillow beds.

Soldar stretched out on the bed first then opened his arms to accept her into his embrace.

The feel of his body was so right. She craved him on levels that couldn't be expressed. His ability to chase away fear was a gift.

Whatever had happened in D'uhr's quarters, he was either over it or had pushed it so far away as to make it inconsequential.

She rested within his embrace and felt him smooth her hair back with one hand. For some odd reason, his command for her to escape the Venus floated to the top of her thoughts.

If one of them could live on for a while, it must be Soldar. There was nothing back on Earth for her. She'd only fought as hard as she had so someone else might not have to die. Someone with a family.

He had a home and a family. One of them was lying on the other side of this massive pleasure ship. Guilt about keeping the fact from him silenced her as much as anything else. But she believed Cordis' insistent prophecy.

Sol would tear the ship apart to find his brother. She recalled the sorrow-filled gaze he'd displayed when he'd spoken of a sibling he thought was dead.

Soldar turned his head and pulled her closer. "Lyra, I want you to listen to me."

"Please, no talk about wars or missions. Not now, Sol."

He kissed her temple and pulled her closer. "What I want to say isn't about the here-and-now. It has to do with a place far away. Will you hear me before we sleep? It will be a memory of better places. I promise."

She gracefully moved on top of him, gazed down into his eyes, and planted a brief kiss on his full, luscious lips. "What places?"

"I want to tell you of a world so beautiful that the very sight of it will capture your heart."

She smiled and felt his arms close around her. They were safe and warm for the moment. The war and everything to do with it was temporarily shut out. She'd keep it at bay for as long as she could lie with this man and hear the deep sound of his beloved voice.

Just for these last few hours.

Chapter 10

Soldar closed his eyes as he spoke.

He described the world of Craetoria, the gardens with colorful flowers, forests with trees so tall they dwarfed buildings, and creatures that dwelled in meadows, on mountainsides, and near brooks. All of these would be destroyed when the Condorians overran his home. But he didn't dwell on their demise, just on their existence and how magnificent they were.

He spoke of dragons that actually lived in caves. These were the magnificent beasts his family had chosen for their crests some centuries ago. This was how their image had come to be melded onto their armbands.

He spoke of his father, mother, and sisters, but declined to mention his beloved brother. Words concerning his sibling wouldn't come. It was so much easier to imagine Cordis still alive.

His father had charged him with one duty where his brother was concerned. He and Cordis had been much younger when the order was issued. But he'd never forgotten it.

"Take care of him, Soldar. He loves you with all his heart. See he comes to no harm."

Soldar fought tears of sorrow. There would never come a time when he could speak of Cordis objectively. He could never talk about their boyhood days.

In contrast, Lyra bravely recounted how her family had been killed. Even in memories of family, her courage was steadfast. Though her voice wavered, she made it through her descriptions of them and was able to finally smile.

Not so with him. It was as if he was harboring some dark barricade in his brain and it wouldn't let him recall certain things.

Perhaps that was better. Most fighters didn't have Lyra's strength of will and her resiliency. Most were more like him. For the majority of allied defenders he'd seen, too many hours recalling the past had been devastating. Thoughts of home and loss had driven many hardened combatants insane. He'd watched it happen gradually. Some went mad more quickly. He'd seen the shattered looks on their faces and knew he'd become one of them without that strange mental obstruction that kept grief away.

No, not many were like Lyra. He feared the tragedy she kept locked in the back of her mind would catch up with her sooner or later. But then, she'd never have enough time alone with her losses. She wouldn't live much longer. The Condorians would see to that.

Lyra would be among those who died and flew easily to the afterlife. She would be rewarded. Those left behind were the ones who needed prayers. These would wish themselves dead when the Condorians finally won.

There was one thing all allies shared besides their fear of the enemy. In this they found common ground.

In this war, no innocent was left unscathed. Everyone had lost someone.

He turned his head to gaze at her.

As she'd spoken to him and her voice finally softened, he'd let her slide into blissful sleep. For him, rest seemed impossible. His mind was drained and his body spent. But some demon-like, unreachable shred of memory kept him awake.

The conflict keeping him from slumber had to do with D'uhr.

Lyra hadn't asked about the incident in his quarters again. What could he say that would make sense? The darkening was a power rarely spoken of. Up until tonight, it had been considered a physical impossibility, a legend to tell children on his home world.

Only hours before, legend became reality. He'd accomplished the incredible. He'd seen the way his body transformed and felt how his frame had strained at his clothing. When it happened he'd lost the ability to speak. But if he'd tried, he believed he'd have roared like some wild beast. He'd become less a man, more a canine-like ravaging hunter with all the raw energy of a feral animal. In that moment he knew he could easily rip out a man's throat. He'd seen the long talons on hands that'd become paw-like. The sight of them reminded him of images of Earth wolves he'd seen as a child. Still, he was more man than some roaming forest predator. Sinew had bulged on his forearms. It'd felt as though an electrical impulse surged through his body. He'd felt an awesome strengthening sensation across his chest, and in his abdomen and legs, and even through his penis and balls. In those moments his eyesight was greatly enhanced. He'd gazed into every darkened corner and had seen the terror in the enemy's eyes. A hush had fallen over the crowd. They'd stared at him and he'd changed back as easily as he breathed air. Instinct told him his recovery was due to his shock at having changed at all.

Something was dreadfully wrong. He could be losing his mind.

In the time he'd rejoined Lyra, thoughts of darkness soon fled. She helped him put the fantastic into perspective. Now that she was asleep and he no longer had the comfort of her dulcet voice, fear filled him again.

His shock over the incident had been tamped down for Lyra's sake.

What the enemy feared, she must never witness. There was just so much even a woman of such courage could take.

The strangest thing of all was the recurring feeling he'd shape shifted on other occasions. Bits and pieces of odd dreams and strange scenes meandered in his brain. None of it made any sense.

He snuggled closer to her and buried his face in her soft, clean hair.

What was happening to him? Would he be able to help her if he couldn't control himself?

Shadows began to close around him. Even with his eyes shut he could feel the darkness as if it was a living entity. Part of his tired mind wanted to believe he'd actually imagined his transformation. But the more practical side couldn't shut out the Condorians' faces.

How could it be real?

He almost woke Lyra just to hear her speak again. Whatever subject she chose would be welcome if only to chase away this impending sense of doom.

The darkness kept coming. He knew it covered his body but he dared not open his eyes to greet it. If he did, it would take him. He must stay awake and keep what was left of his mind intact.

With all his will, he focused on her warmth and softness. The sound of her breathing was the only thing keeping him steady. Without her presence, he was sure his sanity would wither.

•••

"Soldar? Lyra?" Aigean called out.

"We're here," Soldar replied while staring down at Lyra. His mate—for they had accepted each other in all ways—stirred in his arms.

Aigean walked into the dim space they shared. When she did, Lyra finally awoke and sat up.

Soldar hugged her once again. Her warmth was like water to a thirsty man. He wanted to drink her in for as long as he possibly could. He turned his attention to Aigean and his heart fell when he saw the dire expression on her face.

"You should be aware of what has occurred," Aigean urgently as she stared down at them. "I knew we would eventually be caught. But it appears our discovery has come much sooner than anticipated."

"What happened?" Lyra asked.

Soldar held his breath, waiting for news he'd expected.

Aigean briefly dropped her gaze. After a moment, she bravely stared into his eyes again. "D'uhr has ordered his son, Fornax, to search the Venus' computer," she informed them. "To keep their activities aboard the Venus a secret, Fornax makes regularly scheduled trips outside this planet's atmosphere using a long-distance shuttle. D'uhr's command vessel is located in deep space, but close enough to Reisen Four so as to maintain control of his crew there. Fornax used that ship's transmitters to contact other Condorian attack cruisers. It should come as no surprise that he discovered Taurean Seti-Seven had been warned. Its citizens were evacuated and all the fuel the enemy sought was missing."

Lyra regarded Soldar before saying, "This is where it hits the fan!"

"Indeed," Aigean concurred. "My people informed me that Fornax arrived back on the Venus in a rage. He was shouting threats concerning *you*, Soldar. But Lyra will also be suspected as she is your mate."

Soldar jumped out of bed and searched for clothing. He kept his attention on Aigean but was aware of Lyra following his example. There was an instinctual need to be dressed. It wouldn't make any difference to their situation, but the desire to be covered drove them.

"Has any connection been made to a transmission from your bridge?" he asked.

"There will be," Aigean warned. "My people could not find a way to wipe the records from the bridge computers."

"Being caught in that attempt would have got them killed," Soldar stated. "When Fornax orders a computer check, he *might* miss what Lyra did. It could take some time to locate her transmission, or tie it to the work station in our bulkhead," he said as he gestured toward the computer in their quarters. "D'uhr won't see his pleasure ship or its crew destroyed until there's an answer.

He's too hedonistic. For that same reason, he won't even ask for the master computer on his ship to link into the Venus' console for a faster file analysis. He won't want his ship's subordinates to know he'd been depriving them of the Venus' pleasures."

"I agree," Lyra added. "His people would mutiny."

"I don't think either of you fully understands the situation," Aigean said as she raised her hands in concern. "Soldar's relationship with D'uhr has Fornax incensed. From what I've witnessed, Fornax sees his father's lovers as impediments to his own significance. His jealousy knows no bounds."

"Great! A Condorian with daddy issues," Lyra mumbled as she finally located clothing and began pulling it on.

"This has been a long-standing issue with Fornax," Aigean reiterated. "My people have heard him and D'uhr arguing over the matter. To D'uhr, Fornax's mother was a breeder who was contracted to get an heir and nothing more. D'uhr has always craved men. Specifically Craetorian males. Fornax will do whatever he must to make sure blame falls on Soldar. Even if Soldar was never on the bridge and D'uhr knows it."

Lyra angrily turned on them. "At the risk of repeating myself, Fornax's hatred of Craetorian men, is another reason why Sol shouldn't have been able to pass himself off as a plaything, or even get on this ship. I don't understand how he claimed neutrality—"

"Hush girl! We can discuss that later," Aigean rebuked as she paced a few steps and clasped her hands together. "Of all the Condorians on my ship, Fornax is the most dangerous. He seeks to gain notoriety among his people. And while D'uhr and his son may argue bitterly over the subjugation of some Condorian woman, D'uhr still shows affection for his son. You might even say D'uhr loves him, if such a thing is remotely possible among Condorians."

"I'd give anything to have those weapons we left at the oasis," Lyra muttered, ignoring Aigean's censure. "There were only a couple of rounds left, but I could see myself putting one in D'uhr's head, the other in Fornax's.

"Those weapons would be the only ones available to us," Aigean said. "With Fornax's suspicions of spying more-or-less confirmed, he doubled the guards on the Venus' makeshift armory. Now…I must think of my people. I must keep them alive for as long as possible. There may be a chance they can glean information and get it to the allies. The occupiers may let them live a while longer to serve this ship, even after the three of us are dead for whatever defiance D'uhr suspects. As long as my crew might live, I cannot order them to rush an armory where they'd all be cut down in an instant."

Lyra opened her mouth to comment.

"If I thought that would have worked, I'd have commanded that action long ago," Aigean said, quickly cutting off the obvious response.

Soldar silently agreed with Aigean. The foundation of the entire mission was to stay alive and send information to allied HQ at all costs. Even if more weapons were out there, getting to the oasis wasn't feasible. With Fornax's suspicions, no one would get off the Venus again. Not for any reason. Lyra knew that, but she was throwing out suggestions because she'd been trained to consider every option. Even as she emotionally accepted their situation, part of her warrior spirit didn't want to give the enemy the satisfaction of having exposed her as a spy. As he saw it, Lyra realized Aigean's assertions were the exact reason why the Elderian hadn't brought the weapons aboard already. To be caught with such minimal firepower wasn't worth having everyone murdered. Especially since there'd be nothing to show for such an impotent gesture.

Most importantly, Lyra wanted a quick, clean death. He hadn't forgotten what he'd promised her. He'd assured her that no

Condorian would get his hands on her. That was the real reason why she considered getting to the oasis.

While they both knew his promise was ludicrous and that sooner or later the Condorian officers would take her, she'd still asked for death by his hands and he'd still agreed. Only the fact that the enemy was sated with prostitutes, drugs, and alcohol had kept her safe.

"So what's the plan?" Lyra asked. "Do we sit tight and wait for them to bang on the hatch demanding entry?

"We aren't entirely without options," Soldar instructed. "We do have one advantage D'uhr and his son know nothing about. We just need to stall for time."

He took her hands in his, stared into her eyes, and saw strength there that no battlefield general had ever displayed. Her courage was all the more touching because of the fears she'd expressed before they boarded the Venus.

He was aware of Aigean considering them meticulously. Why she'd care about their newly cemented relationship, he couldn't imagine, but it was nothing she could alter. It wasn't her business.

The universe and eternity waited for him and his mate. He simply didn't want Lyra entering the afterlife while experiencing more terror from this one.

She took a deep breath, sighed, and actually smiled up at him.

With that gesture, he could outline a plan that would make no difference to their survival. Discussing an option was better than waiting for D'uhr or his son, Fornax, to come for them.

• • •

Lyra didn't want *the show to go on* as if nothing had happened. If they were to allay suspicions this Fornax person aimed at Soldar, then D'uhr had to be convinced his son was only trying to get in the middle of his relationship with a Craetorian.

Added to her angst was her growing suspicion of the woman who'd brought them aboard the ship. Still, the Condorians were acting predictably. They were what they'd always been. Aigean didn't seem to be giving them information to save her own skin. To contradict her own misgivings, she realized she'd only been left alone because of Aigean's sex givers. Those brave men and women were keeping the officers on the Venus from paying too much attention to anyone. Using the enemy officers' sloth against them, the prostitutes were accomplishing what endless battles and covert surveillance hadn't. Still, instinct told her the Elderian woman was hiding something. Her staff did as she bid and more. But Aigean was playing them all. There was nothing Lyra could do to shake that gut-level feeling.

Her suspicions were amplified because the Elderian didn't want to discuss exactly how a race never known to be neutral was suddenly accepted amongst the enemy. D'uhr may want a Craetorian lover, but the biggest question had been left pointedly unexplained.

Why?

Why was D'uhr so fixated on a man from an enemy world? If any part of Aigean's statement was true, even Fornax seemed disbelieving of his father's obsession.

Pieces still weren't fitting.

Against all common sense, Sol believed he'd get on this ship without any problem. Lyra came to the immutable conclusion there simply was no guile on his part. She'd looked into his eyes and seen the depth of a man willing to do the right thing, and give his life for what he believed. Unyielding honesty was etched into his features; it resonated with every syllable he spoke.

Everything was on Aigean Florn. The woman had secrets that were very dark and disturbing. No matter how the wind blew, there was another truth being left untold.

On the other hand, if the woman wanted to offer them up to D'uhr as a means to appease his wrath or barter for her crews' continued existence she'd have done it by now.

So what was she up to?

Lyra took a moment to watch the woman. Was there any sign of duplicity in her manner or gestures? Was *she* endowing Aigean with more power than the woman possessed? Were her suspicions paranoid?

Aigean called her servants into the space where she and Soldar slept. The minions were to help her and Soldar dress for the next performance. A glance in Sol's direction assured Lyra he was oblivious of any treachery.

Conversely, *she* hadn't survived by following blindly. She was a team player and took orders, but only an idiot didn't ask questions of someone in charge. She'd seen a lot of officers get allied ground troops killed because they didn't have experience or didn't know the layout of the battlefield. They hadn't wanted to be seen as incompetent so they'd recklessly thrown around commands. She wasn't about to lower her guard and simply accept everything the Elderian stated as truth. Not anymore.

Somehow, Aigean seemed to sense the distrust she felt. The Elderian immediately stopped what she was doing, slowly turned her attention from her minions, and stared straight into Lyra's eyes.

For a very long moment Lyra saw the animosity in this once-trusted comrade's gaze. It was almost as if the older woman was trying to warn her off. Lyra picked up on that warning immediately.

Then Aigean blinked, turned away, and that intensity was gone. The older woman rushed forward and began to pick out clothing, disapproving of any attire Lyra had previously chosen.

"You need to look as though you aren't afraid to show your body," Aigean said. "Put these on. And will someone please apply makeup," she ordered as she gestured toward a nearby minion.

The powerful moment was lost. Aigean moved to help Soldar don his attire.

Lyra said nothing to Sol. In that moment, her opinion of the Elderian woman changed. And not for the better.

• • •

Lyra dressed in the black clothing Aigean chose. It was shamefully revealing. The outfit was a tight-fitting halter top over skin-blending pants and tall black boots. She may as well have nothing on at all.

Once they were dressed, plans were quickly relayed.

She was to play the sex diva once more; undress for the so-called performance, then put the same clothing back on. There'd be no shared showers with Soldar afterward, no soft talks of his lovely world while lying in his strong arms. They'd have no time for anything remotely civilized.

Even with her wariness of Aigean, a strange sense of peace washed over her. It was fueled by Soldar's continued consideration, bolstered by her own resolve.

He repeatedly glanced in her direction. One corner of his mouth lifted and he gazed at her with love and conviction in his eyes. He was what he'd always appeared to be—a soldier sent to get information.

Because of his attentiveness and the knowledge that death only comes once, she simply wasn't afraid anymore. She'd still find a way to deprive the Condorians of her body while killing a few in the process. As she'd once told her lover, there was always a weapon somewhere. A broken bottle, a chair, a bit of cord used to tie bed curtains, or any heavy object like a statue.

She watched as Sol finished dressing. The clothing Aigean chose for him was as skimpy as hers. His outfit consisted of nothing more than brown leather pants, matching tall boots, and his ever-present gold armband. In an attempt to exploit D'uhr's lust, his chest would remain bare.

She touched the armband he'd given her knowing he'd never remove it. He saw her gesture and touched his own armband. They, like the lives of their wearers, would be forfeited to the enemy.

Sol's quiet conversation with both Aigean and the gentle servant, Gentis, came to an end. The other servants and cleaning staff that'd serviced their quarters were dismissed. There was no longer any need to guard the bulkhead computer where the authentication codes were stored. D'uhr would acquire those from the bridge soon enough. He wouldn't have the modifications to those codes, but that wouldn't matter. He'd know what they'd done. From here on, they were playing a game to see how long they could stay alive. They were going to pit a father against a son and see what trouble they could cause for as long as possible.

There were only four in the quarters now. Gentis, Aigean, Soldar, and Lyra stared at one another.

Soldar took a deep, cleansing breath then let it out slowly. "We're at an end, my friends. I'd like to think a few hundred people on Taurean Seti-Seven will live to fight another day. Maybe one of their progeny will turn out to be a great leader who will vanquish the Condorians back to their home world forever."

Lyra smiled at that bit of wishful thinking.

"Well…we can hope," he smilingly continued. "I state the obvious when I say there's no possibility of getting Lyra back on the bridge. But we made a difference, if only a small one. We knew our ends would come. We always have. Whatever happens tonight and tomorrow, we can't control. What we can do is die with dignity. We can show more honor than any Condorian will ever possess. In that way, we defeat them. They'll remember what we did. It will leave a bitter taste in their mouths forever."

"Well spoken," Aigean whispered. "My servants will spread the word to others within the ship. We're all prepared, as we have been for a very long time. I regret the enemy will now have the codes to contact allied headquarters. It couldn't be helped."

"Don't forget that the sequencing changes will make them ineffectual," Soldar reminded her. "If D'uhr tried to use them to set up an ambush, he'd still need the fuel. They didn't get it off Taurean Seti-Seven. General Shafter will be thankful for the time we bought." He stopped and seemed to consider his words before speaking again. "Look to the stars, ladies. Tonight or by tomorrow, we'll be among them. We'll sail into infinity and dance in their light.

• • •

They walked through the passageways in silence and strode purposely toward the entertainment center of the vessel.

Aigean finally broke their somber contemplation.

"If it means anything, fewer Condorians will be viewing your performance tonight," she said. "Their affliction has grown worse and spread quickly. Many of them have fallen too ill to move."

"This is so," Gentis confirmed, then lowered her voice. "This illness may provide the hidden allied fighters a way to at least die with honor. They have been told of the situation aboard the Venus. Many can barely move but they will still try to fight if they're discovered."

"And they're now in one place," Aigean added. "With the passageways empty it seemed prudent to move the few we had hidden in servant areas to Myranda's quarters. It was the largest space the Condorians previously searched. They found the rust and peeling paint much less comfortable than the lounges and first class accommodation. They haven't been back to that part of the ship since they arrived."

Soldar considered this news. Those injured survivors were the one element D'uhr and none of his minions knew about. It was their presence he'd spoken about earlier, when he'd mentioned the one advantage they had. Now, their willingness to go into a new battle, if they had to be propped up to do it, was one more tribute to allied courage and loyalty.

"If we can take a few of these bastards with us, we will," he stated, "but wait until the situation is right. If it comes to a fight, those injured survivors will be engaging the enemy without weapons. Even if the armory isn't well-guarded now, the Condorians will have it heavily locked. It'd take more time than we'll have to break into it."

"There's other news concerning this strange affliction," Aigean continued. "The Condorians have been leaving their pilfered drugs where they lost consciousness. The cooks even found unlabeled bottles of pills in the galley where the guards eat. I don't know what these pills are, but Myranda may."

All conversation stopped when a very pale, coughing group of five Condorians rounded the corner. They were leaning on several lovely, almost nude prostitutes.

When the women walked by Soldar's group and covertly nodded, any doubts as to the crews' solidarity were abolished.

"Those Condorians are being taken to some space where the last of our sleeping potion will be used on them," Aigean revealed when the sick officers were out of earshot. "When so many became ill overnight, my sex givers no longer felt obliged to give their bodies to the parasites. They can't be beaten now for withholding their charms."

"How much of that potion do you have?" Soldar asked.

"Very little. Only enough to immobilize a few dozen."

Soldar realized these small acts of rebellion were playing out all over the ship. This strange malady was giving the crew a means to fight back. But there were still Condorians not so afflicted.

And *they* could obtain weapons from the armory—assuming they hadn't disobeyed D'uhr and hidden them in their quarters.

The injured survivors, Aigean's employees, and the small group with him were all making their last stands simultaneously. He had no intention of ordering a halt. Fornax may find the message Lyra sent at any moment. That discovery would lead the enemy to the authentication codes in their quarters. He could only pray someone put a dent in the enemy before they all died. Everyone who wasn't Condorian must take what action they deemed appropriate. This might be their last opportunity.

Finally, they reached the closed stage, with its long white curtains. Soldar took Lyra's hand and opened his mouth to speak. She quickly stood on her toes and covered his lips with her fingertips.

"I was the one who suggested this, remember?" she told him.

"Still…I'd wish for a quieter place to spend our last moments." He moved closer to her. "No matter what happens, remember your promise to find me in the next life."

"I will," she whispered.

Aigean issued her last words.

"I will not tell you how to perform this night. I'm not the mistress of this ship any longer, but will assume the position of one more soul dying with you." She placed a hand on Soldar's cheek. "My remaining time belongs to my crew. I have one employee who will part the curtains before he joins the rest of us. When the music starts this time, you will be alone and your performance will signal my people to cease their duties. No further commands given by the enemy aboard my vessel will be honored. I'll make sure that single command is circulated. At long last…my people are free. May the Creator of all things go with you!"

With those words spoken, she looped her arm through Gentis' and the two women strode away.

Soldar faced Lyra again.

The expression in her blue-green eyes was inscrutable. He knew the curtains would be parted when they were ready, so he took time to absorb her smell, warmth, and strength.

No more words could be spoken. With the deepest regret of having found a woman to love, only to order her to her death, he turned away and began to undress. As before, what they'd worn was more for the benefit of anyone still walking in the passageways. Their attire was removed now just to save time on stage. What difference did it make now how or when it came off?

Lyra removed her garb and he watched each graceful move she made, savoring everything he could before this final show.

His conscience was heavy. There were so many things he'd needed to say to his family and never would. He regretted never telling his younger brother that he loved him. Men on Craetoria weren't so open with their feelings when they'd left to go to war, hence his father's admonition to look after his younger sibling. He fancied there'd be a change in attitudes for those who got to see home again, for as long as homes existed.

And then there was the lie he'd told about the confrontation in D'uhr's quarters.

There wasn't enough time.

Words came by the hundreds. They flooded his mind along with images of home, but he couldn't give them the voice they deserved. So he remained silent and prayed his touch would speak on his behalf.

•••

Lyra finally turned to him. They were both nude.

She watched a myriad of emotions pass over his face. It was clear he felt as she did. They were confused and torn. The battle was done and they were being asked to play out this charade before the enemy. It was more of a diversion, to give the crew time to find their respective positions to make a stand. It'd give Aigean's people a chance to entrench themselves somewhere. And maybe this show would give the wounded, including Soldar's brother, time to gather for one last confrontation.

I should tell him his brother is here. I should tell him.

Once those words were uttered he'd hate her for not saying something sooner. She'd be dishonoring her promise to Cordis, and crushing the experience of having her love one last time.

Cordis was with brethren. Soldar was with *her* and she selfishly wanted these last few moments, even if it was playing a sex duo for those Condorians still well enough to watch.

She moved into his embrace, stretched upward, and looped her arms around his neck. Then she began to kiss him slowly and deeply, and with as much passion as she could.

She wasn't aware when the curtains opened. Only a feeling of cold eyes staring told her they were being watched. That chill filtered around her body like a death shroud, but Soldar was there. His presence pushed the iciness away.

Their tongues entwined and his soft caresses enflamed her. Perhaps the desperate situation fueled his desire. Or maybe her newly acknowledged love, and her newfound assertiveness because of it, drove his need to new heights.

For whatever reason, their ardor was generating enough heat and passion assuring their love would follow them into the next life. She felt it as if it was a living entity.

He ran his hands over her body. She knew he was trying to memorize every line, curve, and detail. She followed his example. His soft moans were the sweetest sound she'd ever heard. And in a life quickly coming to an end, the deep sounds were manna from heaven.

His cock was hard and pressed against the inside of her thighs. He was urging her to lie on the nearby bed. There was no audience, no enemy now. It was just them and the growing heat.

She didn't resist as he pressed against her, moving her backward as he stepped forward. When the backs of her thighs touched the bed, he lowered her down into its softness. But then he backed away and slowly circled her the way a predator might before finally taking its prey.

He gazed down at her, his chest visibly rising and falling as he dragged air into his lungs. His eyes began to glow with that ethereal light indicating desire. And with sudden speed and a display of great strength, his slid his hands around her waist, lifted her entire body high above his head, and nudged her thighs apart with his face.

She parted her legs and he tilted his head backward. Their movements put her clit over his mouth.

He tongued her clit as she placed the palms of her hands on his shoulders. She closed her eyes and spread her legs further. The feel of the warm, repetitive teasing was delicious. The throbbing of her clit caused her to squirm and cry out.

Just as she thought she could stand no more, he lowered her to the bed again then rolled her onto her stomach. As before, he circled her but pulled at his cock and his testicles as he did so. She stretched out one hand to touch him but he quickly moved to the end of the bed, where her feet rested. Then he grabbed her ankles.

This time, he lifted her straight up until he made a wide vee of her legs. He tongued her clit again, as she was literally hanging upside down and facing him. The acrobatic pose put her face right in front of his cock and red-glowing, bullish testicles.

As he held her aloft, she anchored herself to his body by grabbing his hips. She sucked his cock and balls with greedy lust.

Some animal was loose in both of them and she didn't care.

With his face down and his lips teasing her clit, she used her tongue as a licking weapon and tasted every inch of his genitalia.

The resulting moan he issued made her crazy with desire. She wanted him and meant to take all she could. There was no sense of time. She experienced no dizziness. Maybe her need to touch, caress, and slide her tongue over his cock, and the feeling of his licking her, overran any discomfort. It was as if she could stay that way forever.

His thighs were hard and the muscle bulged as he held her aloft. The smell of his skin was clean and fresh. He opened his legs wider and he circled his hips slowly as she licked.

She almost knew to the moment when he was about to ejaculate. His balls glowed fiery red just as her body responded to his sliding tongue. Her pelvis began to jerk automatically and he quickly lowered her back to the bed.

He was on top of her in seconds. She spread her thighs wide and waited for his bronzed, warm flesh to come closer before wrapping her legs around his back. With the speed of a feral cat, he thrust deeply and pulled her into his embrace.

She plunged her hands into his hair and planted soft kisses across his shoulder. With barely enough air in her lungs, she whispered one more time, so he would know and never forget.

"I love you. I'll always love you."

She repeated the oath over and over. He kicked his feet. The action pressed him further into her body.

Like a warm spring rain, she felt his seed flow into her body. It was hot and thick. He shuddered and she held him as her own orgasm tore from the back of her vagina and raced forward like a wave meeting a shore.

He held her to him as if he'd never be torn free. She heard him dragging air into his lungs. A fine sheen of sweat covered them both. Still, his scent was so enticing. It was as if she'd run through a storm and ended her race by lying next to a god. His scent was a blend of spice, wood, and clean air. She nuzzled her face against his chest and breathed him in. He lifted one hand and smoothed her own tresses back, kissing her forehead and temple sweetly and almost reverently.

"Never forget us. Never," he whispered into her ear as he kissed it and ran his tongue down her neck to her chest.

The air around them grew warmer. Whiteness surrounded them.

"The curtain is closed," she told him as she ran her hands over his biceps and gripped them hard.

His response was to press his lips to hers and to end the encounter where they began. With a deep, earth-shattering kiss.

When he broke it to gaze down at her, she saw the eyes of a man who could never be defeated. The love reflected there was so pure and enduring no one could ever come between them. His long hair fell against his cheeks and their ends teased her nipples. She lifted one hand and gently closed her fingers around a long, soft section of his golden mane.

They may have only known each other for a few days, but some people spent a lifetime together without feeling this profound, abiding love.

"We haven't got much time, Lyra. I want to lie here with you like this until it ends. But this is where those foul sons-of-bitches get their last look. They've had their show. They'll get no more!"

She hugged him hard. He wrapped his hands around her back and slid them along her spine as if he could blend their bodies together and make one being of them.

Only then did she turn her head to hear the applause outside the curtains. The moment was lost. She wanted to weep for having shown so many savages something that should have been a secret between her and her mate.

When they heard movement nearby, she pulled herself free and grabbed for her clothing.

Once she was dressed, Soldar put his hands on her shoulders and kissed the tip of her nose. The silvery afterglow in his eyes was mesmerizing. There was simply no time left to enjoy the wonders of his Craetorian body.

She'd soon be cold, alone in a grave without him.

But training came to her aid. It lent her the strength to tamp down emotions threatening to choke off air. The sadness was too much. Everything she loved was dead or about to die.

He dropped his hands from her shoulders and slightly lifted his chin. That posturing was sweetly familiar. He was about to say something she wouldn't like.

"Turn around and don't look at me," he softly commanded.

She hesitated. Soldar's expression was a mixture of sadness and tortured rage. The order was given in a voice that was half-growled, half-broken. It was as if he was in horrific agony.

When Lyra turned her back to him, he stretched his arms around her, put one hand on her chin and the other at the base of her skull. "Forgive me, my heart. Please…please…forgive me. *I love you.*"

She heard the pain in that heartfelt entreaty and knew he was about to break her neck. In that instant, she smiled and tried to help.

"There's nothing to forgive. I love you, too, Soldar Nar. And nothing you can do will ever change that. You're keeping your word. And I'll see you on the other side. Just don't keep me waiting."

Though it was the hardest thing she'd ever done, Lyra kept her voice calm and encouraging. He'd be in his own hell for the last hours of his life. She must help the only way she could.

• • •

His resolve broke. Tears filled his eyes, but he had to keep the promise. "Creator…give me strength!" he pleaded.

"Do it, baby. Just do it," she whispered.

Sol lowered his lips to her hair, placed a gentle kiss against it, and breathed in the clean scent of her short, red-brown tresses. Whatever he might have done thereafter was lost to time. Condorian guards swarmed onto the stage, each holding their laser pistols and aiming them at him and Lyra. A very large example of the balding, tattooed vermin sauntered toward him and spoke in a loud, vicious voice.

"Take your hands off the woman," the Condorian commanded. "If it was your intention to save her, you have failed, Craetorian. We know your purpose. Aigean has sold you out and my father will watch you receive justice."

Soldar inwardly cursed. Three more seconds and Lyra would have been free. His hesitation and weakness would result in her rape and torture. She would beg to die before they were through with her. His promise was broken.

"I am Fornax," their captor bragged as he stuck out his chest in an immature gesture of bravado. "I will be pleased to kill you and the woman very slowly, by whatever method my father wishes."

In defiance of Fornax's orders, he held Lyra tightly against his body. He glared at the savage before him, hoping he could anger the boy enough to fire on them and be done with everything. "Justice?" he blurted. "What justice would any Condorian understand? You're nothing but parasites, feeding on the entire galaxy. You are savages and nothing will ever change that!"

"Don't waste your breath. He's too ignorant to understand," Lyra chimed in as she pressed her back into her lover's solid frame.

Fornax strode toward them, keeping his weapon leveled on Soldar. "If I am ignorant, at least I am constant in my devotion to my people, woman. What you know of your Craetorian lover is a lie. His outrage for your cause has been manufactured and drilled into his brain by Aigean Florn."

"Just shoot us and get it over with," Lyra demanded. "Do we have to be bored to death?"

"Die you will," Fornax admitted with a malicious smirk on his face. "But you await my father's will. He alone will decide what is to be done. In the meantime, I find it amusing to enlighten you, woman. You should know that the man you have loved in such an explicitly public manner was not worth your trust. I would see the truth of my words destroy your arrogance before you die."

Soldar frowned. More and more, bits of old memories began to swim in his brain like fish in a small pond. He felt his gut twist when old truths began to unfold. He didn't want Lyra to hear Fornax's words. It was as if he knew what the Condorian was about to say.

"Did you really believe the man who banded you is a Craetorian officer?" Fornax laughed cruelly. "He is not even a Craetorian any longer. He lost his people when he betrayed them with others of his kind, fled his world, and was imprisoned on Signus Mondi for his crimes. He was among others who wanted to reconnect their ancestry with that of *my* people."

"What are you talking about?" Lyra murmured.

"His race and mine were once joined. Do you not realize that his kind still bears the mark of that link," Fornax said as he pointed toward the black lightning bolt mark on Soldar's left cheek. "That mutual history is what sexually draws my father to men of Craetorian heritage."

Soldar swallowed hard and cast his gaze downward.

Fornax put one booted foot on the bed where the sex show had just taken place.

Soldar noted how the red dirt form Reisen Four sifted from Fornax's sole and onto the once pristine sheets, fouling the memory of the love displayed there.

"Did you really know Aercos before he died?" Fornax probed as he gazed at Soldar. "My father cannot forget his first Craetorian lover and saw you as a replacement. Even now, I believe it pains him to cause your demise."

"Soldar?" Lyra whispered as she broke free of his embrace and slowly turned to face him. "What is he talking about? Who is Aercos?"

"Tell her, Craetorian. Tell her about *the darkening* and how Aigean meant to use it to kill my father. Tell her this mission of yours had nothing to do with getting messages to allied headquarters at all."

Soldar saw the questioning look in Lyra's eyes. There was no hiding what he was any longer. He took a deep breath and tried to explain. "Lyra, you must understand. His words are only meant to—"

"Tell me!" she commanded.

He took a deep breath and let it out slowly. But he kept his gaze averted as he spoke. "Many millennia ago, the Craetorian race and the Condorians were one. They were known as the Volan and they lived on a world hundreds of light years away from where our races now reside." He tried to take her hands, but she backed away. "Lyra, you must listen. The Volan were dark and evil. As time went on, some of them learned they could not exist without trade and alliances from other worlds. Other sentient races would have nothing to do with them. Their savagery was renowned and none dared trust them."

"Go on, Craetorian. I enjoy her hearing the truth. The woman's growing mistrust is priceless," Fornax goaded.

Soldar now remembered. It was all there, like water flowing into the well of his brain. Bits and pieces of memory settled into their proper places. He was all Fornax claimed. But he needed Lyra to understand. She *must*.

"Part of the Volan began to suppress their darker urges and eventually succeeded," he softly explained. "They fought bitterly with their brethren when the more aggressive members of the population wouldn't accept peaceful coexistence with others. A war between the two sides almost obliterated the entire population."

Lyra began to slowly shake her head. The growing wariness in her expression frightened him far more than anything Fornax could do.

"Lyra, you must listen," he repeated. "For my people to exist, a severe compromise was finally reached…those who believed in the savagery inherent in the Volan race would separate from those who embraced the light. Because their original planet was decimated by fighting, it was left behind by both sides. Eventually, the half intent on ruling all beings became the Condorians. The other half accepting peace and an adoration of all life became the Craetorians. The names of our two peoples are so similar for a single purpose," he explained. "My race…the Craetorians…wished to be forever reminded of that darker origin from which they sprang. They chose a name very near the one the Condorians chose, to remind them they were only one step away from becoming the hideous, savage monsters Fornax and his people have become." He tried to speak faster. Lyra's eyes were turning colder by the moment. "In suppressing that terrible side that still resides within us, a few Craetorian males were thought to experience a strange shape shifting ability. But this was only a myth—"

"Apparently not, Craetorian! You shifted readily enough in my father's quarters. All it took was one of my men suggesting they would fuck your woman to death," Fornax laughingly supplied.

"Lyra, I need you to understand." Soldar tried again even as he ignored Fornax's taunts, "I don't know that I can say much more. We haven't time."

"I should've been told the truth," she whispered.

"How sad, Craetorian. You are losing her affection." Fornax cruelly laughed. "Is there anything more tragic than unrequited love?" He put his hand over his heart and rolled his eyes in a gesture of sarcasm.

Lyra faced Fornax and took several steps toward him. "Why should I believe *you*? Soldar wanted to kill all of you."

"But not for the reasons you think, stupid woman!"

She swallowed hard and turned to Soldar again. "There *has* to be some explanation. I know you and you could never—"

To stop her questions, Fornax viciously shoved the bed where his foot rested. His display of temper was so violent the entire dais moved several feet to the right.

"Let me make it plain, since your Craetorian lover isn't getting to the point," Fornax chided. "Right before the war started, Soldar Nar was one of several Craetorian traitors who were giving us vital information concerning military tactics. They were about to be captured on their home world and put to death for their treachery. They stole a shuttle and headed into space. Aercos, my father's lover, was among them, and was killed when that shuttle was fired upon by the Craetorian High Guard."

"I and several others survived that attack and managed to lose the patrol in the Andromeda sector. Our craft was badly damaged, so we were finally run down by intra-galactic constabularies. We were imprisoned on Signus Mondi," Soldar quietly added as his memory slowly returned. "Those of us still alive were awaiting extradition back to Craetoria. Aigean had connections on Signus and helped us escape. We gave her an enormous fee in exchange for that help." He shook his head. "To escape further detection, we agreed to head our separate ways. I don't know where the others are now, but I've been hiding out—"

"Until quite lately," Fornax interrupted as he continued the explanation. "Aigean kept track of him and found a way to bring Soldar to Reisen Four. She convinced my father that Soldar could take Aercos' place. But to do so, Soldar would need a safe harbor. He'd need my father's promise of protection and *she'd* need a great deal of remuneration in exchange."

"This is all a lie," Lyra whispered. "None of it is true."

"With the lack of intelligence some freedom fighters show, it is a wonder they have survived as long as they have," Fornax complained.

The Condorian guards accompanying him laughed in response, but he angrily continued.

"Aigean isn't on your side, you stupid slut! She's been working with us until quite recently. Her loyalty failed when a fleet of pirate ships attacked her world, and my father would not send aid since her race claimed neutrality." Fornax circled Lyra in a stalking fashion as he spoke. "Father and she quarreled over the matter. So she eventually decided to get revenge. Soldar, with his shape shifting skills and position as Father's new lover made a perfect weapon. So you see, woman, Soldar is little more than a paid assassin. He is a traitor to his kind and a common criminal. Aigean is pulling his strings."

Lyra's fingers curled into fists. She visibly shook.

Soldar moved toward her but she backed away. His heart broke into shards. Tears ran down her face and he could do nothing to comfort her. Everything Fornax said was true. There was no excuse he could offer.

"Aigean had Soldar tucked in a cave until she had thoroughly conditioned him with her mind control tricks. Her talents in that regard are singularly powerful." Fornax paused for effect then continued. "The story he fed you was one of many she implanted, depending on who might locate him before she was ready to bring him aboard. She took a chance that none of the allied fighters resisting on Reisen Four…assuming they encountered him… would know his criminal history. The story he subconsciously chose for *you* was that he was an undercover Craetorian officer who'd lost his team during a crash landing. Since Aigean put him in an unmarked uniform and gave him an allied weapon she picked up on some scavenging foray, you accepted his story." He shrugged. "We knew a new lover, especially meant for my father, was on the way but not what Aigean would put in his head as a means of revenge."

"You needed him to appear just as he is…a Craetorian," Lyra quietly reasoned. "That's what your father wanted."

"Ah! The little cunt is making progress." Fornax laughed again and pointed at Soldar. "This man you so willingly screwed is wanted in twelve sectors. He couldn't walk into a surgical salon and have his features or body altered. Constabularies had distributed his image, and had offered a very substantial reward for his capture. Plus…appearing as nearly like Aercos was vital. As you've surmised, Father craves Craetorian men and had to want him. Aigean had to make sure *this* Craetorian could get very close to him and in some private space aboard this ship."

Lyra dragged her hands through her hair. "But Soldar killed the Condorians chasing me."

"Our fighters are low-breeds. They are little more than sociopaths. Even your own superiors recognize that." He snorted in disdain. "We have billions more where they came from. Our elite classes control them. Are you so new to battle that you do not know this?" He stared at her while his men chuckled yet again.

"W-what was my part in all this?" she softly asked. "Why was I needed? Why didn't Aigean have Soldar leave me in the wilderness?"

"Aigean claims she was shocked when Soldar picked you up in the wilderness of this barren rock and brought you along. For some reason, he would not leave you behind no matter what subtle mind control techniques she tried. She had no time to deal with the matter because Father was insistent. He wanted his Craetorian plaything—the very same man who'd befriended his dearly beloved Aercos. In fact…Father threatened Aigean if she didn't give him his heart's desire." Fornax frowned as he nodded. "The Elderian did the best she could to cater to Father's whims while explaining your presence, woman. *You* were a glitch in Soldar's mental programming that Aigean couldn't solve. And she feared you would interfere with her plans."

"She used me. Soldar gave her a way to do it," Lyra whispered.

Everyone turned to look at the one Craetorian in the room but he remained silent. There was nothing left to say. He was nothing more than a source of ridicule and disgust.

The guard's amusement was apparent. Sickening smiles were plastered over their faces. To them, the evolving story served as an unexpected bit of entertainment, one far more diverting than the sex act they'd probably just witnessed. He didn't dare look at Lyra. Her anger was palpable.

His soul was dead. The man Fornax just described *was* him. And he was worse than any Condorian. How could he have come to this sad, sorry state?

"Aigean didn't want me talking to her crew and telling them that she's not the kindly benefactor they believe her to be," Lyra quietly mused. "I was suspicious of her and she knew it. She made sure I was alone as little as possible. Soldar was almost always with me and I trusted him."

"Now she gets the picture," Fornax laughingly said as he glanced at his men.

They, in turn, nudged one another. Their enjoyment over an allied fighter's betrayal was obvious.

Soldar kept his gaze down. He was no better than the dirt blowing in the wind outside the ship. He wished himself dead a thousand times over as he heard the deep bitterness and resentment in Lyra's voice. He could have endured anything but her hatred.

"You begin to see…don't you, woman?" Fornax persisted in his gloating account of the facts. "Aigean has always had her own scheme. Even her own people trusted her when she promised freedom. But in truth, they're little more than slaves. She's used our occupation of her ship as an excuse not to pay them, feed them well, or even offer medicine when needed. She required their cooperation to achieve her ends. She needed victims she could control."

Lyra shook her head in confusion. "But she helped me get on the bridge—"

"Get it through your head!" he angrily replied. "She cannot control *you*. Her powers do not extend to certain races, one of which is Earthlings. Another is ours. Because of this she had to convince you she was on your side."

"All that covert crap helped confirm Aigean's political beliefs to her crew," Lyra confirmed. "No wonder it was so easy to make that transmission. To find out what she was up to, you *let* me on the bridge. In fact…there was probably no one on Taurean Seti-Seven. Soldar never had any authentication codes." Her eyes opened wide and she took several stumbling steps backward. "I sent a trash message into empty space and attached sequencing Aigean made up for Soldar. She had several chances to be alone with him even after we boarded. She suggested actions to accommodate my needs and my behavior. No matter what I said, she had control over him the entire time."

"Did I not promise you a night to remember, my brothers?" Fornax glanced over his shoulder as he spoke to his minions. "Do you not see why these freedom-loving allied vermin are better off dead?"

A low rumble of acknowledgement resonated from the other Condorians present.

"Even as they tout themselves morally and mentally superior, these so-called allied warriors are so easily outwitted. It takes nothing more than an Elderian witch with mind-control capabilities to utterly destroy their reason. Look at the woman's face. She is confounded."

Fornax's men growled, lifted their weapons, and closed in around Lyra.

Soldar couldn't move. He couldn't save her. He was, in all ways, a coward with no moral fiber. In that instant, part of him wished he could have been that Colonel she claimed to love. But that was not his life and never had been. All he could do was stand there, continuing to exemplify self-serving inconstancy. All he'd done was for money. Now was no different. He could save himself and beg D'uhr's mercy. Nothing was left for Lyra but death. And the more he thought of his predicament, the less important she became. It was as if his mind was starting to turn back. He was losing the vestiges of her heroic vision and reconnecting with his true persona.

"You should have seen our reaction when she told us you would perform so…*explicitly*," Fornax said as he looked her over. "That alone kept us from breaking Soldar's illusion. The whole spy playact provided many hours of amusement. We even took bets on what this insipid Craetorian toad would do next." He chuckled even as he glared at Soldar. "I've never seen Father so entertained. Sadly, he is still enamored of this mind-controlled idiot. Soldar is very like Aercos and my sire still desires him. Even this duplicity and chicanery has not shaken that resolve. In fact, the whole incident seems to have cemented his determination to have a man he can utterly control."

"Your father realizes that Soldar was being used by Aigean. That he wasn't responsible for what she put in his head. Is that it?" Lyra asked.

The smirk finally faded from Fornax's face. "That will not last long. I will see you both dead. But you will go first." He turned to his men. "Take her!"

"Wait…just tell me one more thing," Lyra insisted as she backed away and held up her hands. "You took the time to explain all this just so you could see the look on my face and make fun of me. So there shouldn't be any problem in my asking one more question."

"Ask then. It only serves my purpose for you to know any of this." He moved very close to her and glared down into her face. The maliciousness of his countenance even made his own minions back away. "I want the entire crew to see your expression as you're tortured. If any of them had similar plans of helping another allied conspirator to the bridge, they will quickly change their minds when they see how you die. They will know how Aigean has betrayed you and them. Worse…*you* will know it as the last bit of blood leaves your body. So ask your question."

Lyra lifted her chin. Her gaze never wavered from his. "How did you make Aigean reveal her plans? What did you do to her and when? I've seen no sign that she's been tortured and you've obviously known about her scheme for some time," she blurted.

"As I've already told you, she and my father quarreled incessantly over his failure to help her world. When she became a bit too cooperative of late, I grew suspicious. I had her brought to my quarters. I did to her much worse than I'd do to any common whore on this ship. And I can tell you…she did *not* enjoy it." He cupped his crotch with his right hand. "Aigean Florn is still a woman. And there are things women fear much more than death. Even brutal tactics would not work on her as well as my particular brand of interrogation." He put one finger under Lyra's chin and lifted it higher. "She yielded her plans rather than suffer my company further. She even revealed that she could reach inside the Craetorian's mind and summon forth *the darkening*. It was supposedly a myth. One caused by the suppression of primeval rage."

"It's some result from having turned from their Volan roots," Lyra stated.

"It was only a legend. But then I actually saw it for myself." He stared at Soldar for a long moment. "That's when I knew what kind of weapon the man would make. If he was near Father whenever Aigean decided to unleash his power…by whatever phrase or gesture she'd associated with it…there would be no chance of my sire surviving." He moved to Soldar, grabbed his belt, and pulled him closer. "To her…you were nothing more than an expendable weapon."

Lyra's hate-filled glared turned to Soldar as she confronted him with one more fact. "Soldar…discussing this in front of you seems to have broken Aigean's mind control. So I guess there's a limit to even what an Elderian mystic can do. Obviously, she has no ability to control Condorians or she'd have done it."

Soldar stared at her and offered the only emotion he now felt. All other feelings concerning her were gone. It was as if they'd melted away, into infinity. "I am sorry, girl. You shouldn't have run down the wrong canyon."

Lyra lurched forward. All her anger was directed at him. That he'd been used by Aigean didn't matter. *He* was the one she blamed for this situation. In his guise as an allied colonel, he'd pulled her into a death trap far more heartbreaking than any demise in the badlands of Reisen Four.

She got close enough to spit in his face before the guards pulled her off.

"I've heard enough," she yelled. "Get me outta here and do what you're going to do. If I ever see this bastard again, I'll kill him myself!"

Fornax gestured several of his men forward even as Soldar wiped her spit from *his* face.

The guards quickly hauled her away. She never looked back.

Soldar stared at her retreating figure.

"I will say one thing about that woman," Fornax muttered. "She at least is honest. And I believe she knows you won't last as long as you think you will. Unlike my father, I do not tolerate Craetorians. They turned on their own kind millennia ago. They cannot be trusted."

"That's between D'uhr and me. Not you," Soldar told him. "He must know I had no hand in this or he'd have had me killed by now. That's obviously vexing you no end."

Fornax wrapped the fingers of one hand around Soldar's throat. "Know this, Craetorian…I will see that girl suffers less than you. She is nothing to me but one more allied soldier. You, on the other hand, represent a much greater menace. Like so many, you seek to replace me in my father's affection. But it will not work."

Soldar roughly pulled Fornax's hand away and shoved the Condorian so hard that he landed on his back, ten feet away. He slowly approached until he stood over Fornax's sprawled body. From that vantage point, he had the satisfaction of seeing real fear in his opponent's eyes.

"Don't threaten me, boy! That girl you just hauled away has no weapons. I…*am*…a weapon. Aigean left me with a power you'd do well to respect. Remember that the next time you're in my presence!"

Without one word more, Soldar turned and stalked away.

Chapter 11

Soldar exited the bed he'd shared with D'uhr and slowly walked to a table. He poured himself a large glass of wine and noted how servants went about their work in the space beyond his veiled sleeping area.

As he drank his fill, he tried to expunge the image of that lovely girl going to her death. He didn't know where she'd been taken and wouldn't ask. His own situation was now secure and that was his only concern.

For using *him* in a mind control subterfuge to kill D'uhr, Aigean Florn could go straight to whatever hell she believed in. D'uhr was saving some special torture for the Elderian. It had to be horrific since the order had been given to confine her to her quarters. No one was to touch her but the admiral.

Because of her intrigues, it had taken the better part of the night and the next morning to prove *he* no longer harbored any thoughts of killing anyone. To prove himself, he'd done everything D'uhr had asked. Every sexual act known had played out in these quarters. In the end, D'uhr's suspicion of him seemed to have evaporated. Now his only problem was Fornax and how to deal with that little spewed mistake of nature.

Fornax wouldn't be satisfied until he was dead. D'uhr's offspring had pestered his father to have all threats neutralized. It may be that an untimely accident was called for. Perhaps the little worm might trip into an airlock during a deep space inspection of this ship. That was an image worth smiling over.

A large hand slid around his waist. Soldar covered it with one palm while continuing to drink his wine.

"In every detail imaginable, you are magnificent," D'uhr crooned. "But why is that drink more to your liking than lying with me?"

Soldar turned to face his lover and slowly shook his head in denial. "You're a hard man to satisfy. I find my energy taxed by so much attention. My thirst drove me to the drink, not any desire to be parted from you."

A loud buzzer sounded at the other end of the room. Scurrying footsteps were heard then a loud obnoxious voice followed.

Solder sighed and rolled his eyes in contempt. "Must he keep interrupting us? This is the third time, is it not?"

"Fornax is only trying to protect me," D'uhr said as he stroked his bedmate's back.

"You've been sleeping the last four hours," Soldar said. "Had I wanted to do you in, I had both motive and opportunity. How many times do I have to tell him, or you, that I no longer harbor Aigean's demonic death wishes? My mind is my own again."

Fornax aggressively pushed the curtains to their bed space aside and strode in. "You will be scrutinized for as long as it takes to assure the safety of my father," he groused.

"That's your choice," Soldar angrily replied as he ambled as far away from Fornax as he could. "But I can't perform under these conditions. I'm not only watched, but I've lost the right to have a private conversation with my lover."

D'uhr opened a bottle of brandy and poured amber liquid into two crystal tumblers. He handed one of these to Fornax and sipped from the other before speaking. "Do not provoke Soldar, my son. He is right. I slept in his arms many times in the past hours and he could have slit my throat."

Fornax gestured toward D'uhr's and Soldar's nude bodies and sneered. "Father, would you and your simpering tart please dress?"

"Why?" D'uhr asked. "I happen to love watching Soldar. What need does he have of clothing?"

His son scowled and threw up his hands in anger. "Fine. If you want to watch the executions nude then so be it. But I hardly think it appropriate for a man of your stature." He abruptly turned to leave, but D'uhr put one hand on his forearm to stop him.

"The time got away from me, Fornax. As usual, you have matters well in hand, my brave boy. We'll be there in short order," he promised as he put his glass down and searched for clothing.

Soldar sat on the side of the oversized pillow bed and sipped more wine. "Is it necessary for me to make an appearance? I'd like to shower and sleep."

Fornax strode close to him and glared. "Perhaps watching your little Earthling die leaves you somewhat squeamish. It may be that you're not in as much control of your mind as you think."

"Accuse me of that one more time and we'll see who simpers!" Soldar warned as he stood and towered over the younger clone of D'uhr.

"The girl still wears your armband as a token of your love, does she not?" Fornax accused.

Soldar lifted his hand to his own armband and quickly unfastened it. He held it out as an offering to Fornax. "The meaning of this is overrated and always has been. It's a piece of jewelry and nothing more. Perhaps you'd like it since trivialities seem to amuse you," he taunted. "I understand your ground fighters kill to get them, so I'd warn against wearing it openly," he finished in a sickening, sweet voice.

"Enough, you two! Put your armband back on, Soldar. Fornax was only teasing. That band would look ridiculous on him." He said with a snort. "Somehow, I find the wearing of one more attractive than both. Perhaps there's something about the lack of symmetry that's eye-catching. It's a bit like wearing one golden earring," he mused. "I find the look quite dashing."

Soldar put his armband back on. D'uhr's son appeared somewhat taken aback. Fornax knew that wearing that armband romantically linked him to his own father's lover. The twisted nature of the gest briefly had the younger man silenced. In some ways, it seemed that Fornax was not as morally bankrupt as his sire.

"My son, you should understand that Soldar never wanted the girl. He cares nothing of the band he put on her arm since Aigean seeded the need of her in his mind," D'uhr insisted. "But I agree with him about the triviality of the matter. This issue will soon be moot."

"What do you mean?" Soldar asked as he saw another oily smile affix itself to Fornax's face.

"Despite all the intrigue, I've greatly enjoyed my time on this ship and have been enormously amused…especially by that girl. Hearing about how she snuck on the bridge, and so earnestly attempted to send a message nowhere did my heart good." D'uhr chuckled and smiled broadly. "Had I not been so diverted I'd have had the little Croton bitch, whose identity she assumed, killed."

Fornax snickered when his father did. Apparently their memories of those events were quite comic, but Soldar didn't see it that way. The Earth woman had been trying to save the lives of others even at high risk to her own. Somewhere, a semblance of conscience awoke. He noted bravery in her actions.

"What I meant was," D'uhr slowly continued, "all good things must come to an end. The wine and food were exceptional and the whoring and drugs amused the favorites in my fleet quite well. But it is time to get back to duty."

"A wise decision," Fornax said as he put his hands on his hips and nodded.

"To finish with this subject of the girl…she provided entertainment on stage and off. I greatly enjoyed hearing of her exploits that came to naught. For that reason only, I have decided she will die fast and painlessly. Torture takes time and I'd rather spend it elsewhere." The amused look faded from his face. One of anger replaced all kinder emotion. "If anyone deserves agony it is

Aigean Florn. I whiled away my hours in bed when I should have seen her skin boiled off."

Fornax lifted his chin and shot Soldar a nasty look. "I couldn't agree more, Father!"

"This little wandering respite in space has served its purpose," D'uhr mused. "We need cleaner accommodation now. My officers are still being afflicted with the red ring sickness. It's likely Aigean put something in our food or drink to induce it."

"How can that be?" Soldar asked as he watched D'uhr dress. "The crew eats the same food and drinks the same wine."

D'uhr pulled on a pair of boots. He used one corner of the bed linen to swipe at a small smudge on the leather before responding. "It does seem quite odd that no other races are afflicted. Even you show no signs of the sickness," he finished as he looked Soldar over once again.

"But where will we find another pleasure craft in a war zone?" Soldar complained. "Surely it's reasonable to locate replacement quarters before destroying the Venus."

D'uhr adamantly shook his head. "No. We've been here as long as I dare. If we do not destroy all traces of her, the Venus will be our downfall. Other admirals and their staff are beginning to question my absence from my war cruiser. They're insisting I answer my own communiques instead of hearing from my son. And to keep communication appear normal, Fornax spends a great deal of his time between the surface of this filthy place and my command ship. His humor of late has been souring. I can only attribute it to his hiding this ship's existence and my presence here."

"That is so, Father. Let your will be done," Fornax insisted. "I'll gather this ship's occupants and our warriors outside. Any of our men too ill to walk will be carried."

D'uhr nodded in agreement. "Drain all the fuel from the Venus and fill our shuttles with it. Empty the armory and take what goods we can make use of. We leave before another day dawns on this stinking, colorless rock."

Fornax narrowed his eyes and stared at Soldar. "And what of *him*?"

"Get over his presence in my life, Fornax! You've been given orders. Follow them," D'uhr tersely replied.

• • •

Dressed in a brown tunic, pants, and tall boots, Soldar accompanied Fornax and his men through the passageways. He was to watch the slaughter that would take place outside the ship. Brown was a less somber color than black. He wasn't in mourning after all. He was being more-or-less forced to watch but he couldn't actually find it in himself to lament.

As always, D'uhr controlled everything. So when the admiral had his fill of his sumptuous leisure craft, he deemed its continued existence unnecessary. And without having so much as a thought about where they'd go once they were aboard his command vessel.

Soldar's conscious mind—that part of him yearning for excess, pleasure, and personal reward—had no interest in the death of the crew or the destruction of this ship. But somewhere deep inside his brain and down to that part some might call a soul, he knew what D'uhr was doing was wrong. Still, he tamped down any remorse. What happened to the crew of the Venus was not his concern. He'd been brought here seeking sanctuary but Aigean had turned him into something he wasn't. She'd used him as D'uhr would. At least in the case of the Condorian admiral, there was some remuneration in his favor. He got to keep his life. Sadly, the crew of the Venus would not keep theirs.

Their support of a doomed allied cause had garnered them nothing. They'd helped that Earth girl get to the bridge when they thought they could outwit D'uhr.

So why had they done it? As the saying often went, *what was in it for them?*

He tried to recall those emotions and thoughts of the fictional Craetorian colonel. The same one who had captured the love of a brave girl. But that man no longer existed.

He snorted in derision.

That man had *never* existed. That doomed creature had been a creation of Aigean's mind and based upon the characteristics of some fictional hero. That persona had been created so Aigean's crew would see a chance at survival and put off their attempts to mutiny. She had no control over them any longer and now feared their refusal to obey would get her killed. She already blamed and hated D'uhr for the destruction of her home, so she'd created a myth her employees could believe in, and a way to strike back at a Condorian she hated. Her actions were born of deceit and sedition, not the common good of her crew.

As he saw it, there were no men or women who were heroes. The Condorians were creating the only reality that would last. He'd tried to convince people on Craetoria to reunite their race with the Condorian Empire and make the Volan whole again. But they'd insanely embraced some altruistic future to which only fools aspire. They'd clung like children to a vision called hope when the only hope anyone had was what they could bribe, pander, or blackmail out of someone else. And if he must be the sex-toy dog of a petty tyrant, then so be it. He would survive where others would not. And whatever dreams these so-called allies had of a better future would die with them.

He was a survivor and a realist.

As they progressed through the passageways and finally exited the vessel through the cargo bay, Soldar witnessed hundreds of crewmembers and fully armed Condorian soldiers assimilating outside the Venus. In the blowing red dirt of Reisen Four, the crew was slowly being lined up against the hull of the ship. D'uhr's men were arming their weapons.

The last time he checked, it was well after midnight. The light was so poor that it was difficult to see at first but his eyesight quickly adjusted.

Even the sickest among the Condorians seemed present, regardless of whether they even knew what was transpiring. Just as Fornax ordered, his men had dragged hacking and coughing Condorians out on stretchers or hover platforms. They'd even been tossed on the ground.

If there was any truth to the theory that Aigean or her crew had dosed Condorians with sleeping potion, Fornax's men would assume those Condorians in semi-conscious states were ill, not intentionally drugged.

Soldar said nothing about the matter. Aigean had lied about everything so there probably never was any such sleeping concoction at all. Mentioning it now would only rekindle Fornax's suspicions, and he was tired of fighting them off. Besides, what did the knowledge of such goings on matter? Aside from him, everyone who wasn't a Condorian was about to die.

As he stood there watching the crew cling to one another, he wondered why they had not done as Aigean had once suggested and poisoned the enemy. Perhaps she'd talked them out of it until she could first see D'uhr writhing in agony by her own hands. Or maybe she convinced them such actions would bring catastrophic results.

False belief in her wisdom or fear of Condorian wrath notwithstanding, look where inaction had gotten all these servants. Knowing they would never be allowed to survive and spread tales of D'uhr's hidden sanctuary, they'd have been better off ignoring Aigean's role in their lives and fighting in any way they could.

But then that one, deceptive little concept always surfaced. He surmised the crew had been consumed with *hope*. Perhaps they'd sadly mused over a method for escape, or considered a way for rescue from the Allied Forces.

He shook his head in wonder. As on many occasions, he felt sorry for those who harbored faith. Faith made people wait too long. Faith required people to believe in miracles and accept inaction versus taking charge of a situation. As always, hope got no one anything. Only playing one's cards the right way meant survival.

Pity was the only emotion he could muster on their behalf.

He strode to a nearby rock. The wind picked up and he wanted to block as much of the blowing red dirt as he could.

At least the hull of the Venus provided the doomed with some measure of protection. While he didn't really care, he found no amusement in making them uncomfortable. The Condorian guards and officers still well enough to participate in the upcoming slaughter saw this as a perfect opportunity to belittle the helpless. They faced the ill-fated men and women of the Venus and yelled nasty insults.

For all the groveling the employees of the Venus had done, and all the service offered, the Condorians were showing no compassion except for a quick end. In fact, all the servants' crying, hugging, and heartfelt wishes to meet in the afterlife seemed to only enrage D'uhr's men. If those wretched souls would just shut up and stand still, the guards might leave them alone. They could meet their respective makers that much faster.

He sighed and glanced away. It was all so depressing, really. Life aboard D'uhr's command ship wouldn't be so pleasurable. But he'd be alive and away from Craetorians who'd pursue him into eternity.

A guard walked by him and spit up blood. Soldar backed away so none of it would land on his boots.

There was no denying some illness was eating away at the Condorian contention. Men among the ranks were actually doubled over in pain. Even in the dim light he saw how the mottling on their skin gave way to rotting flesh. D'uhr, Fornax, and many of the others hadn't yet displayed *that* putrid symptom.

Then his mind raced ahead. How was he supposed to entertain his benefactor if such loathsome sores developed? The mottling, red rings on D'uhr's body were bad enough but this new development was disgusting.

Perhaps he'd be relegated to consuming more alcohol or imbibing drugs as some of D'uhr's men did. In his case, he had no symptoms to alleviate but being smashed would be one way to get through the night while a festering egomaniac laid next to him.

He grimaced and shuddered at the thought. What was he to do now? What if the rest of the men on D'uhr's command vessel were in this state? He'd get through this wretched day then consider options. All he had to do was stay healthy. Take one day at a time.

Sounds of weapons being primed dragged his mind back to the present. It seemed more people had been lined up against the hull while he reflected. As he took in the numbers a guard began passing out more ammunition.

It was going to take a lot to kill all those souls. In fact, there seemed to be more of them standing than guards. At that moment, he wondered why the fools didn't rush the Condorians. It was a strange thought since he was more inclined to suggest barter than hostility. He rubbed his temple when a dull throb began to make its way forward, from behind his eyes.

Familiar voices filtered to his location. He saw D'uhr watching Fornax, and caught an exalted look of triumph and pride on the admiral's face. Even in the haze of blowing red dust, that haughty expression couldn't be mistaken.

Creator's blood, they were taking their time! Why didn't they just get on with the massacre? He fully expected the Condorians would scavenge for anything that might be hidden within clothing. Rings, ornaments, and baubles from another life, or a home left far away, would be looted. Even corpses of those suspected of swallowing goods would be opened. No one was going to bury the dead. Bodies would be left to rot. But if they'd just get it over with, they could leave this horrible place.

Again, he came back to the same harsh conclusion. If this was the so-called hope that allied planets of the galaxy bought, with blood as the price, he wanted no part of it.

His attention was suddenly captured by a tall, matronly figure in a black robe. There was no mistaking the Elderian who'd cause so much trouble. Aigean Florn stood in the dusty swirls with her head held high, looking into the distance. Her bearing was inappropriately regal as poor, clueless Gentis clung to the very mistress who would have sold her out for revenge.

He shook his head in disgust. They all might still be inside pleasuring themselves if Aigean hadn't tried to screw with his head and make him shape shift at some opportune moment. He assumed her crew didn't know what she'd done or they wouldn't get near her. He considered telling them just to see if they'd finally gather the courage to fight. But again, they'd waited too late. Their circumstances left them no other options now.

Aigean's appearance reminded him how close to death he'd been. All because she couldn't do her own dirty work.

Oddly, he couldn't remember when she was supposed to have put the order to kill D'uhr in his head. But D'uhr and Fornax assured him that was exactly what happened. The Elderian had admitted to it, or so he was told.

On that night when he believed he was undercover with the girl known as Lyra Markham, he knew he'd shifted then. He'd actually felt it happen. Perhaps *that* was when he was supposed to do the deed, and something had gone wrong. He lifted his gaze and glared at the Elderian. But for his talent in convincing D'uhr he was no assassin, he'd be standing against that hull with all these other poor creatures, or *worse.* To add insult to injury, his sleeping late with D'uhr had kept the woman from being tortured. And while he wouldn't wish this treatment on any of the others, Aigean had earned it.

Some of the fated crew noted his presence and began to watch him. He shifted his gaze from Aigean and stared back at them. This small group of blue-robed servants and nearly nude prostitutes whispered to each other. Even in the haze he caught a very unexpected expression on their faces.

Was it disappointment?

He quickly looked away.

There was nothing he could do or say to change their plight and he heartily wished they wouldn't stare. How dare they even silently offer their shame for *him*?

D'uhr shouted out last minute orders.

Fornax approached and Soldar sighed heavily. Would he never be rid of that little by-blow from a contracted breeder?

"You show little concern over the impending demise of all these people, Soldar. Are you not even the least bit distressed?" Fornax asked as he nodded toward the Venus' crew.

"Why should I be? I'm on this side of the line," he quipped.

Fornax smiled cruelly and nodded at the gest. "There will come a day when my father tires of you. And there will be a time when your resemblance to and association with Aercos slips away," he said as he looked Soldar over with contempt. "When that day comes, you'll be where the crew of the Venus is now. And it will be me on the butt-end of a laser-photon rifle."

Soldar moved very close to the smaller man. "Until that day arrives, I suggest you get on with your duties and quit inflicting me with your presence. You're covered in dust, you smell like the bottom of a sewer, and you're downwind."

Whatever else they might have said filtered away in the dust-filled air.

Both men turned when a group of Condorian guards dragged, rolled, and pushed some crewmembers out a side hatch. These new additions to the doomed had apparently been unaccounted for and only located now, as the ship was thoroughly searched.

Accompanying these newly found crewmembers was a tall, attractive woman with short blonde hair. She knelt down to help those with her as they fell to the ground. It seemed some were ill and Soldar suddenly feared the sickness *had* spread to the rest of the crew. If that was true, he could be infected.

Before he could contemplate the matter, several of D'uhr's guards approached these new employees. They'd obviously been hiding, and the fact they'd done so enraged the guards. He quickly backed up when Condorians began shouting and pointing. The robes of some of these newly located servants were removed.

D'uhr lunged forward and cursed loudly in his native tongue. He raised his fists into the air in a show of absolute rage. Then he opened his hands and placed his palms on his bald head. It was as if he'd momentarily lost reason.

Soldar's attention was drawn to the dusty melee. He saw what had angered the entire Condorian contingent.

These newly located servants weren't sick, they were injured. Their wounds had been bound to stem the flow of blood. The white bandaging around their limbs and torsos almost glowed in the half light and the red dust.

Some of these injured helped others stand. The blonde woman seemed intent on remaining with them. He hadn't recalled ever seeing her before. Surely he'd have remembered such a beauty. It seemed she was no prostitute. She wore the same robes which delineated Aigean's staff from the sex givers.

At that moment, a tall, slender figure sprang toward the injured and tried to ward off the guards who were kicking and beating them.

Lyra.

He automatically took several steps forward but stopped, glancing quickly around to see if anyone noticed his movement.

Seeing that no one paid the slightest attention to him now, he put his attention on the Earth girl once more.

Lyra's face was a mask of bruised and swollen flesh. There was no mistaking the evidence of some guard's brutality. Thankfully, her clothing remained intact. D'uhr might have kept his word about no raping. But there'd never been anything mentioned about no beating.

He noted how she and the blonde woman embraced each other when they met. The two women put their bodies between the guards and those they protected. D'uhr called his men back, and the newly found occupants of the Venus were also pushed against the hull, along with the servants. It seemed Aigean's people wanted to protect these newly discovered comrades every bit as much as Lyra and her blonde friend. This was the first time he'd seen any sign of gumption among the Venus' crew.

At a loss as to what had just happened, he turned to the Condorians. D'uhr approached and his eyes were wild with ire. The irrational glaze in them reminded Soldar of a crazed animal.

"Members of an Earth unit were hidden on the ship in some hole my men never thought to check after we initially boarded!" he angrily rasped. "Can you imagine the extent of cooperation Aigean's staff used to get them aboard this ship?" His chest rose and fell with fury and his hands wrapped around his bald, tattooed head again. "Is there no sense of duty among my own guards?"

"I rather think your guards were led by example. Fornax may have provided them with a bit too much entertainment and not enough discipline," Soldar advised. "It certainly seems they were remiss in their duties."

"This ends here and now!" D'uhr shouted.

All movement and general hubbub ceased once the admiral had everyone's attention.

D'uhr paced and snarled for a moment before he issued his last orders for the men and women lined up against the Venus.

"I will find out when this happened. I demand an accounting of my officers' whereabouts at all times. Anyone on duty when these enemy soldiers were rescued will be skinned alive and their testicles roasted. Am I clear?" he roared.

The Condorians still well enough to stand jerked to attention and remained silent.

"Fornax, I want these insects squashed!" D'uhr shouted as he pointed toward the Venus' victims. "Incinerate them. Behead the fighters who were smuggled aboard and mount their skulls on pikes. Record the images and send them on full broadcast to every known receiver in the galaxy."

"Father, such a broadcast could be traced," Fornax warned.

D'uhr grabbed his son by the front of his leather vest and shook him violently before letting him go. "It matters not. We will not be in this sector when this location is plotted. I want the allied superiors aware of my wrath. Now carry out my orders."

Fornax displayed a vicious smile. "If you will allow me, Father...I ask permission to bring forth one of the crew." He turned his gaze toward Soldar. "This is an opportunity for your Craetorian lover to prove his devotion. He can take one of these maggots' heads and present it to you with his own hands."

D'uhr displayed a snarling smile, nodded, and slowly faced Soldar. "What say you, my bronzed lover? You should be glad for the opportunity to confirm your loyalty."

Soldar opened his mouth to refuse, but Fornax and a burly guard were already dragging one of the doomed crew forward. This soon-to-die victim wore a blue robe. It trailed in the dust as Fornax threw the man down again. The harried figure hesitated for a moment then struggled to kneel at *his* feet. As this individual tried to catch his breath, the guards grabbed his hood and pulled it back. The face that turned upward was one Soldar recognized. He froze as his beloved little brother met his shocked stare. "*Cordis*," he whispered.

"Father," Fornax loudly announced, "your lover is not the only Craetorian aboard. And Soldar even recognizes the man!" He pointed toward Cordis. "I think it's no coincidence that he's here."

D'uhr grabbed a long section of Soldar's hair and pulled it. "Tell me you have nothing to do with this Craetorian. He can be nothing less than a sworn enemy or he would not be in the company of wounded fighters."

Images raced through Soldar's head. He saw himself and Cordis playing in the gardens behind their family's country estate. Then they were laughing and chasing each other through fields of wildflowers. He saw memories of a day when they raced home, and their beautiful mother opened her arms to joyfully embrace them.

Deep raging anger, regret, and protectiveness all surged up from some dark place. He heard D'uhr questioning him. Fornax stood nearby and wore a vindictive expression on his face. Soldar could no longer make out D'uhr's words, but he understood the accusatory inflection in the Condorian's voice.

In that moment, Cordis smiled. *His* little brother put the palm of his right hand over his heart. This was a customary tradition of their ancestors. One he hadn't seen his sibling use before. The gesture was a show of great love.

A long knife was shoved into Soldar's right hand. He didn't know who put it there nor did he care. He had just been ordered to prove his loyalty by taking his brother's head.

And who had made the sickening command? Who was screaming and petulantly waving his arms in the air as if he was a small child in need of discipline? Who would destroy his world and everything good, clean, and decent in the galaxy?

D'uhr!

Soldar began to shake. The need for vengeance mingled with shame and self-loathing.

What have I done?

He sensed the coming change and eagerly embraced it.

Chapter 12

Lyra could barely see out her left eye. But even with impaired vision and the environment working against her, she could still watch the enemy frozen in mid-gesture. All their attention was on one, very large Craetorian.

From her vantage point near Myranda and the injured allied soldiers who lay against the hull of the ship, she saw Soldar's face and body begin to transform. He dropped the long knife that had been shoved into his hand and he stiffened.

His lower jaw began to protrude and very long fangs dropped from his top mandible. The muscle of his body grew until veins seemed dangerously close to popping from beneath the skin. Sharp, animal-like claws extended at least eight inches from his fingertips. The clothing he wore was close to ripping. His hair grew several inches and changed from golden blond to silver or white. Given the lack of light, it was difficult to tell the exact shade, but that was the only part of the shifting she questioned. Everything else stood out in stark relief, despite the haze and dust.

His eyes glowed red and actually expanded back and up, making them several times larger and tilted. His ears elongated into points that pierced through his thick mane.

If she had to describe him now, he was like some cross between a legendary werewolf she'd read about as a schoolchild and some new species of feral lion. Even the color of his skin seemed to grow darker by several hues. It was as if his body was attempting to assume the color of the landscape.

The overall change was simultaneously hideous and fantastic. While she watched, she sensed absolute, utter fear in the Condorians. Those with weapons began to slowly lower the muzzles. Their eyes widened so the whites were clearly visible. It was like they were afraid of attracting the creature's attention.

No one made a sound except for Soldar.

He opened his be-fanged jaws, drew air into his lungs, and roared like a beast declaring its territory and supremacy. The sound of the deep bellow filtered through the landscape and into canyons many yards away.

He curled the lips of his upper jaw, and slowly brought his arms forward in a bunched position similar to the way body builders posed to display massive pecs.

The leather of his high boots split and fell from his legs in long strips. His feet grew and his toenails lengthened just as his fingernails had.

When it appeared the transformation was complete, he swung his lion-wolf head to the left and right. Lyra felt her heart beating so hard that everyone near must surely hear it. Her mouth went dry and sweat broke out on her forehead. But some instinct made her pick up one foot, then the other. Even as others remained immobile, she slowly stumbled forward.

Soldar swung his massive head toward her and lowered his chin. The effect was chilling. His red eyes narrowed and he glared at her menacingly. He lunged forward taking in yards as he did so.

She heard Myranda whispering commands to stop, but those words seemed to come from another reality. A few seconds more and she didn't hear the entreaties at all. Sol still barreled toward her like some rabid beast. His muscular arms pumped as if doing so would generate speed. Then he stopped a few feet from her, in a sliding whirl of dust and rock. With her presence so much closer, he issued another long, warning growl.

His eyes glowed more fiercely as he stared straight at her. As far as she knew, everyone else remained still. He leaned toward her and she felt his hot breath against her cheeks. Their noses almost touched and drool fell from his jaws in thick, foamy strands.

She never lowered her gaze.

What seemed like an eternity later, his growls faded until he made no sound at all. As she stared straight into his eyes, his ears slowly turned forward. It was as if he was listening. For a long moment neither of them shifted their stances.

That was when she knew a heart could actually break.

Tears clouded her vision and fell down her cheeks. Salt in them stung wounds on her face as sadness overwhelmed her.

At first site, she'd assumed he'd tear her apart. Perhaps she'd moved toward him so he would. Her body ached, but repeated blows from a drunken Condorian guard were nothing compared to the pain in her soul.

How could she have fallen in love with this self-serving, devious man?

He could have shape shifted into any horrific creature and it wouldn't have mattered if he'd actually been the hero she'd made of him. Everything she knew about Soldar Nar was a lie and she'd had a lot of time to think on that as she'd been beaten. Her once beloved Craetorian warrior was in the company of murdering savages who would butcher everyone aboard the Venus, including his own brother.

There was no doubt in her heart that Cordis was an ally. D'uhr hadn't yet made the familial connection between the men. When Cordis was dragged forward, the look she'd seen on Soldar's face was worth a million words. The agony of D'uhr's command forced his shifting experience. He'd been unable to control his emotions, and now he stood before her as some manifestation of his own, horrible guilt.

In a cruel twist of fate, he would experience what millions of others had at the enemy's hands. He'd see his sibling die. Worse, he'd see it done by his own hands. And he was sleeping with the man who'd ordered it.

There was nothing she could do to him that God wouldn't. For however long he lived, he'd have his sibling's blood all over him. She could almost pity him. *Almost.*

The beast before her tilted his head one way, then the other.

No language would ever come out of those misshapen jaws. His canine-like tongue couldn't be capable of forming words. But she believed he was aware of everything. Somewhere in that animalistic shell, a man was still alive and he knew what he'd done. His anger had driven him toward her, intending to rip something apart. What was left of any conscience made him stop when she confronted him.

She slowly shook her head, turned away, and prayed he'd rip her back open. With her heart smashed, someone or some*thing* needed to end her suffering. He whined plaintively. She sensed he wanted her to face him again but there was nothing left to see.

He'd made his choice, she'd make hers.

She stumbled back toward Myranda and was quite ready to die with the others.

• • •

Soldar reached out for her, his palms upturned in a supplicating gesture. He knew he'd changed and recognized the unmoving terror on the faces of everyone present. But seeing the pain in Lyra's eyes was devastating.

He dropped his arms and stared at the back she presented. There were things she didn't understand and he could never explain. Even now, at the end of their lives, he still loved her. Nothing would ever stop that.

That man—the one who'd lain with D'uhr—*wasn't* him. Memories bled into one another, but his soul, heart, and conscience all denied that foppish, self-serving coward who'd so readily ingratiated himself with the enemy. He had not betrayed his world and had never been imprisoned on Signus Mondi or any other penal colony.

Something was wrong with the way his past and present were all colliding like some bizarre collage in his brain. He raised his clawed hands toward his head as a stream of images threatened to blind him.

A sudden scuffling sound made him whirl in an instant. His focus immediately returned.

Fornax was now positioned behind Cordis and had cruelly grabbed a section of his hair. With it, the Condorian pulled Cordis' head backward and exposed his neck. In Fornax's right hand was the sword *he'd* been order to use.

Soldar snarled and bunched his muscles to bolt to his brother's defense, but Fornax manifested one of the more evil grins Soldar had ever seen and raised the sword higher.

"If you can shape shift back, you'd better do it!" Fornax warned. "It won't stop me from killing whoever this is, but I can do it slow or quick…you decide."

Soldar felt intense anger and hatred again. Even if he'd wanted to, there was no way to calm himself. Instinct told him that controlling his emotions was the only way to resume his real persona.

D'uhr moved to Fornax's side and pointed toward Cordis.

"Who is he?" D'uhr demanded. "Do as my son says and shift back now."

Soldar looked down at Cordis. His brother knew how to get out of such a compromised position. They'd practiced it as cadets many times. He was either injured or afraid for *his* sake. And that he couldn't stomach.

His animal alter ego wouldn't be quashed. There was no reason to return to his real body as long as he could fight better in this one.

He lowered his gazed to the dirt, and breathed deeply.

Cordis' scent came to him. It was recognizable in its cleanliness and its lack of fear. He closed his eyes for a moment and hunched downward in a subservient position. His acute hearing picked up the most subtle movement indicating the two Condorians had moved closer together. He didn't need to see either of them to know exactly where they were.

From a crouching position, he propelled himself forward with such speed and ferocity that no volley from any weapon would stop his forward momentum, even if the guards had the presence of mind to gather their wits and fire.

With his body in flight, he raised his head and roared. His outstretched, clawed hands hit both Condorians at the same time and sent them sprawling many yards away. D'uhr had time to draw his sidearm, but it went flying to the left. The sword Fornax held to Cordis' neck also took flight and swirled some yards away.

With Cordis' body being forced back to expose his neck, Soldar had taken the chance and launched horizontally over him. He had the satisfaction of smelling blood. D'uhr and Fornax writhed in the sand, some distance from each other. But he knew they'd try to get up no matter what injuries they'd sustained.

Behind him a woman shouted ferociously. Like some avenging goddess, she ordered a charge. He knew the command came from Lyra.

She loudly encouraged the crew to fight for their lives and freedom. He felt a rush of energy he'd never known. So many Condorians were sick that she'd instantly recognized the chance his launching attack provided. With the fight on, he heard the Condorians shouting at one another, and photon rifles began to fire.

The allies in this fight had a small chance to beat back the enemy. There might be a way for a few to escape to the interior of the ship and seal the hatches. But all that hinged on the servants and prostitutes doing as Lyra ordered. They'd have to charge the

Condorians, lose many friends in the initial attack, then hold themselves together long enough to divide the enemy's lines.

But would they have the courage to pick up any dropped weapons and fire them, or close in quick and fight hand-to-hand?

One thing was certain. If they cringed against the hull then everyone died.

Whatever else happened, there were a few allied fighters who could direct that battle. This included Lyra and Cordis, assuming his brother still lived.

Instinct for battle fired every muscle in his body. But he focused on the architects of this disaster. He looked for D'uhr and his son.

The Condorian officers and guards weren't trained to think for themselves. Every decision of their lives was dictated by someone higher on the food chain. If he could take out the leaders, the minions might falter.

D'uhr pushed himself to a sitting position and screamed in agony as the open, clawed incisions across his face bled freely. One of his eyes hung loose from its socket. But if the smell of blood energized a shape shifted Craetorian, it most certainly strengthened a Condorian admiral's inhumanity. Condorians were at their most brutal when severely injured, and Soldar finally understood why.

The rage *his* race had suppressed to keep from becoming so savage was what he'd tapped to shape shift. But the Condorians wore that fury and hatred outwardly, every day of their lives. They need do nothing more than perceive another being as an enemy or feel pain inflicted during a fight.

On D'uhr's face, Soldar saw the glazed expression of a crazed despot who'd been utterly betrayed. He glanced to his left and his lips twisted maniacally. The vision of his son lying in the dirt, bleeding and struggling to get up, was the last nerve Soldar could have tapped. Caring little about those in his charge, D'uhr seemed to focus on what he wanted at that moment. The obsessive need for revenge was etched into his features.

With the cunning of the animal kingdom he represented, Soldar began to circle the admiral. His hearing was so acute that Cordis' voice sounded in the melee, and he took heart in that deep, familiar tone.

D'uhr pointed at him with the index finger of one shaking hand. "You're dead, Craetorian! No one betrays me. No one," he rasped as he struggled to see with one eye.

This wasn't the fight Soldar had envisioned, and some of his ire began to ebb.

With his sidearm gone, no photon rifle or bullying son to do his bidding, D'uhr was little more than a nasty swaggering thug. Under normal circumstances, his size and strength alone made him dangerous. But the man's injuries aside, a slothful lifestyle had taken much out of the once vaunted admiral. He'd been living a hedonistic existence so long that he couldn't even land a punch, certainly not one that would do much good.

D'uhr lunged forward.

Soldar stepped to one side and let him fall in the dust again.

The repeated sound of rifle fire wasn't encouraging, but it strangely began to ebb. Even D'uhr noticed and angrily turned his head toward the Venus to find out why.

Soldar kept his eyes on D'uhr but the shocked and frightened look on the admiral's face finally summoned his attention as well.

Injured, sick, or lifeless bodies lay everywhere. Some were Condorian, others were crewmembers, and a few were the hidden allied fighters smuggled onto the Venus. What riveted D'uhr and apparently everyone else was Aigean. She had grabbed a weapon from somewhere, aimed it shoulder level, and now stood right in front of Fornax. From her current position, she couldn't miss.

The Condorians began to lower their weapons and back away from the melee. They knew what D'uhr would do to them if they got his son killed. The cellular disruptive sidearm stuck in Fornax's face was one of the more feared weapons because no one survived a direct hit.

"This fight is over!" Aigean loudly announced as she turned her head to her left and stared D'uhr down. "Tell your men to throw their arms into a pile by the cargo bay. Have them put their shuttle fuel back into the Venus, return all the food, water, and drugs then back away from the hull."

"There are rules of engagement which must be followed!" D'uhr furiously insisted. "My son needs tending. Look how he bleeds from his face and neck."

"I will give you the same consideration you gave me," she told him. "I was never a combatant, but was inflicted with your putrid presence when you captured my ship. I can assure you…I have no qualms about killing your offspring and then turning this weapon on you."

Soldar felt his heartbeat begin to slow. If the situation remained in the allies' favor, he could soon shift back. His anger would abate, with the need to ready the Venus for departure. It didn't take any mind control techniques to see Aigean's purpose. Even the members of her crew were already picking up weapons from dead or injured Condorians and placing them by the cargo bay hatch. She meant to take off and leave the Condorians stranded on Reisen Four. With no weapons or means for survival, they'd die slowly or kill each other off for what few containers of water they had on their bodies.

He lowered his head and tried to see himself as he normally was. He shifted back almost instantly. He even sensed his control of this new ability was getting stronger. The standoff was still in effect but it wouldn't take much to shift again. All D'uhr had to do was move the wrong way.

A few long moments more and the admiral furiously gave in.

"Do as this filthy hag says!" he loudly commanded. "And be quick about it."

"When my demands have been met, I'll release your son back to you," Aigean promised as Condorians hurried to do as D'uhr ordered.

Soldar was simultaneously elated and fearful.

One move the wrong way or one small misstep by any of D'uhr's men, and the fight would be on again. If that happened, the odds would no longer be in their favor.

Though D'uhr had lost one eye, the cuts on his son's body were deeper and hemorrhaging at an alarming rate. As the younger man walked slowly forward in front of Aigean, his eyes rolled wildly and he was barely able to stay on his feet. It was obvious he'd only remain conscious for a few more moments.

Even as D'uhr backed away so Aigean wouldn't fire, Fornax fell into the dirt. Unfazed, Aigean simply pointed the muzzle of her weapon toward the back of the young Condorian's skull. She shook her head at D'uhr when he would have come to his son's aid.

"You Elderian witch! Let my son go now or I'll—"

"You'll *what?*" she interrupted. "Have your underlings move faster."

"Do as she wants!" he shouted.

Soldar stood his ground for the moment, but fear for Cordis' and Lyra's safety finally made him attract the attention of a robed, female servant. The small figure loped toward him and pushed the hood of her robe back. Gentis breathlessly gazed up at him.

Thankful the girl had come through the fight unscathed, he briefly took the hand she offered and began issuing his own orders. "Can you get on the Condorian shuttles quickly?

"Yes…many items the enemy stole from us have not been loaded," Gentis advised. "For this reason I believe the guards left the shuttles unsecured."

Recalling what he knew about enemy craft that had been shot down or abandoned when they could not be repaired, he put the knowledge to use. "They're only short-range vessels, but they have communication capabilities that are sophisticated—"

Gentis quickly nodded. "I understand your meaning, Soldar. I will make sure they are inoperable as well as any weapon delivery systems. If Admiral D'uhr wants off this planet he will have to wait until someone comes searching for him and his people. I will have every drop of his fuel transferred to the Venus, as Aigean ordered."

"Good. We don't want him to warn the command ship orbiting this planet. It'll be all we can do to get out of here and avoid detection."

When Gentis hurried away to complete her tasks, Soldar finally turned his attention to the bodies scurrying about. Some of Aigean's crew held weapons on the Condorians as they, in turn, handed over their arms. More of the crew was trying to locate the injured among their dead comrades. Several began to weep loudly.

Now came the part where they felt the consequences of their actions. Brave as they were, wars always came with a heavy cost. Because they had finally chosen to fight back, at least some of Aigean's crew had survived and might be free—if they hurried and made no mistakes.

He walked toward Aigean, but stopped far enough away to avoid being a distraction. "I've got to find Cordis and Lyra. Can you watch D'uhr alone?"

"I have been dealing with him alone for a long time," she responded without taking her gaze off D'uhr. "He knows what will happen if he moves."

Soldar nodded then turned away. His duties at that point were clear.

First, he must make sure the crew efficiently went about the tasks Aigean listed. Of particular concern was getting the weapons into the cargo bay so they couldn't be used to fire on the Venus as she took off. Some of the photon rifles could take out a ship even the size of Aigean's, if they were aimed properly.

But he was determined to get everything done *while* searching for his brother and the woman he loved.

Cordis was easy to spot. His brother held a sidearm on Condorians who were offering their weapons to the Venus' crew. Most of the enemy was so ill it appeared they no longer had the stomach for a fight. Sounds of their coughing and vomiting filled the dirty air.

Soldar tentatively moved toward Cordis. He feared he might be dreaming and that his missing brother wasn't among the fighters Aigean had hidden in the bowels of her craft. But then Cordis turned his head and their gazes locked.

When his sibling smiled and tears began falling down his cheeks, Soldar knew their meeting was no dream. He rushed forward to embrace his younger brother. Cordis quickly handed his sidearm to a robed servant so he could return the hug.

"I won't ask how you got here. I don't care," Soldar whispered as he held his brother tightly.

Cordis returned the hearty squeeze then moaned loudly.

"You're hurt," Soldar muttered as he backed away and gazed down at the blood seeping through the front of Cordis' blue robe.

"The wound is days old, my brother. It's nothing incurred during today's skirmish, though it's opened up a little." Cordis waved off the concern with one hand. "The med-tech cared for me well. But so you won't pester me about my appearance in this sector, I came looking for you when you were reported as missing-in-action."

Soldar tilted his head in confusion. "One of us is very confused. *You* were the one missing. No one heard of your whereabouts for months. I received messages to this effect."

"Soldar…it was not I who was reported as missing. It was *you.* I used my influence with General Shafter to attach myself to an

Earth ground division though I told Myranda and your mate that I'd been separated from my comrades and was unable to contact a Craetorian ship. I didn't want anyone knowing I'd used the family name to come searching for you."

Soldar blinked and held out his hands. "I-I don't understand."

"Soldar…Mother and Father have been worried sick. They and our sisters have sent numerous missives asking about your safety or any news of you. I was originally aboard a Craetorian ship about to be sent into deep space, to fight in another sector. But I knew you'd last had contact with the general and that all Earth ships would be ordered to converge on this planet. It only made sense that, if you were still assigned to Shafter, you'd engage the enemy on Reisen Four. I just didn't know it would be aboard a pleasure craft that'd been overrun by Condorians!"

Soldar stood there staring at Cordis for a long moment. Something in his mind made connection to memories. Cordis wouldn't lie about such a thing. There was no reason for his brother to fabricate anything.

"Your mate is a brave fighter, Soldar. You should have seen her leading the Venus' crew into the fray. They would have fought demons from the Ascers Nebulae on her say so! She was magnificent."

"Lyra!" He put his hands on Cordis' shoulders. "Have you seen her? Do you know where she is?"

"The last I saw of her, she fought her way toward the bow. That was where most of the Condorians were fleeing. They were almost ready to give up in the face of healthy, energized combatants rushing them so unexpectedly. Your shape shifting had them stupefied. I only wish I could have joined you but I have never been able to tap into that rage as you do, and Aigean was not nearby to help me."

Cordis' hastily uttered words were confounding but the meaning of them could be sorted later. He had to find Lyra and make sure she was safe.

"Come with me," Soldar ordered as he navigated his way through a sea of robed servants, prostitutes, and sick, dead, or injured combatants.

What he found minutes later made his blood freeze.

Myranda was kneeling on the ground shouting orders for drugs and bandaging. Her patient was a lovely girl, lying still and pale. She was stretched out beside the hull of the ship. Red dirt was filtering over her wounded body as the breeze began to pick up. A long gash, probably delivered by an incendiary pulse pistol, meandered down her left thigh. Bone and muscle was exposed to the filthy air. But the more serious wound was a huge hole in Lyra's lower left side. Myranda had torn away what little her patient wore to expose the wound for treatment. A quickly applied pressure bandage wasn't enough. The hole was large and the gauze originally used to patch it had soaked up all the blood it could.

Soldar fell to his knees.

Myranda looked at him and shook her head. "She's badly hurt. Without any armor, she took the full force of the blast. I haven't the equipment necessary to repair massive organ damage, assuming I can stop the bleeding."

"Please, there has to be something we can do...*anything*," he insisted as he pushed his way to the other side of Lyra's body and clasped her hand.

"I might be able to combine some drugs and induce a coma," Myranda told him. "If I can slow down her body processes enough, without making things worse, it'll give her a few hours. But if we can't get her to a star-class surgical unit..."

As her words trailed away, Soldar closed his eyes and fought for control of his emotions. He could do nothing for Lyra if he couldn't think. After a moment of fighting his fear, a door suddenly opened in his brain and years of experience took over.

"We need to get off the surface of Reisen Four. I can send a coded distress message to Elias Shafter. His command ship has a well-equipped sick bay. But we can't stay *here*. D'uhr's ship is in orbit and Shafter's vessel will come under attack if we attempt a rendezvous on the surface. We need to get into deep space and try to escape detection."

"Give me the sequencing for Shafter's ship, Soldar. I'll get to the bridge and send the message," Cordis said as he automatically assumed command of the evacuation. "Stay with Lyra. I'll coordinate everything. We'll be off this damnable rock in short order. I promise!"

Soldar swallowed hard and repeated the sequencing twice so there'd be no mistake with the transmission. As an officer and ground force captain, Cordis would know how to send a message so D'uhr's orbiting base ship couldn't intercept it. But just before he hurried away, Cordis squeezed his shoulder in support. Soldar smiled at him and bid him to hurry.

Once Cordis was gone, Soldar couldn't move. His entire body shook and he felt his reason leaving. His emotions were almost out of control. All he could do was sit there and stare down at Lyra's beaten face.

The bruises delivered by Condorian brutes threatened to cause another shifting experience. But he fought it with all his might. They couldn't afford such an outburst now. He had to help Myranda. He must concentrate on getting Lyra inside the Venus.

To steady himself, his mind reached out to Myranda's shouted commands. He clung to her professionally delivered orders. And slowly—ever so slowly and with great deliberation—he held onto his real persona.

In the midst of all the chaos, more memories returned. The images in his mind made no sense and some faces in those memories weren't recognizable. But he held on and did exactly as Myranda bid.

• • •

"I've done all I can and there're other wounded to tend," Myranda softly advised. "If we can get to that other ship in time, she has a chance. But I won't lie to you, Soldar. Even Shafter's physicians might not be able save her."

"She's a fighter. She'll hang on…I know she will," he woodenly responded. He sat on the pillow bed next to Lyra's body and carefully arranged the bedclothes around her shoulders and smoothed back her hair. His fingers skimmed over the swollen wounds on her face.

Once again, he held back the shifting demon within him.

Why did Earthlings allow their women into battle? He silently cursed their independent natures. But then, that was the very thing he so loved about Lyra. She was a courageous warrior. She had a right to fight and die for her freedom. If the Condorians reached Earth, she'd fight and die *there* no matter what anyone did. It was better that she was trained and took the battle to the enemy.

In the time he'd known her, she'd never lied about anything. She'd only covered Cordis' presence because of an order. Cordis had explained that he hadn't wanted to interfere with whatever mission was ongoing. He further explained that Aigean couldn't clarify the sudden appearance of another new Craetorian—one who hadn't been previously accounted for among the crew and who looked so much like D'uhr's lover.

Indeed, Cordis' discovery would have led the enemy to the other injured allies.

All this information supported Lyra's decision to keep Cordis' presence a secret. She'd followed a command to the letter. His brother had lived because she'd kept all the survivors' existence hidden. That was all that mattered.

He was aware of Myranda leaving the quiet space they'd chosen for Lyra. The comfort provided by Cordis' presence was indescribable. His brother gave him hope when nothing else could. Though he knew Lyra wanted to live, there were some things a great heart and fighting spirit couldn't endure. She'd lost so much blood and was now in such a deep coma she couldn't possibly know who was present or what was happening.

At least she couldn't feel any pain. That was one reason Myranda had loaded every drug she safely could into Lyra's system. But those same drugs could harm her and bring on her demise. Her body functions could shut down as they tried to save her brain.

All Myranda had done was buy some time so burned organs could eventually be treated and her blood pressure stabilized. It was a small chance.

As Soldar stared down at Lyra's face, a goblet of fresh water was shoved before him.

"Drink this, brother. You won't do her any good if you expire from thirst. It's been two hours since we reached deep space. The Creator is with us. D'uhr's vessel either didn't detect our departure or there are so many sick crewmembers aboard his ship that they didn't care."

Soldar took the goblet his brother offered and sipped his water slowly before speaking. "There are things we need to say to one another, Cordis. You seem to know about a shape shifting ability I never knew I had before boarding the Venus…and you accept it."

Cordis looked away.

"What's going on?" Soldar asked. "What's happening to me?"

"Now isn't the time for revealing secrets. In fact, I should help Myranda and the crew. There are dead comrades in the cargo bay and they should have words said over their remains."

"You're too wounded to move safely. It's a wonder you haven't torn that suture open again," Soldar said as he gestured toward Cordis' healing midsection. "Myranda gave you an order to stay put and rest. In fact, she seemed curiously concerned. More so than a simple med-tech might show toward a patient…if I'm correct in my summation."

"To keep away from the Condorians, she stayed with the hidden wounded that had been moved to an old section of this ship,"

Cordis explained. "It's a huge space that was of no importance to the Condorians since Aigean could no longer maintain it properly. All her crews' time was expended on seeing to the enemy or staying out of their way. There was little time to scrub, paint or—"

"I'm not talking about the space in which you were hidden. I was speaking of the way Myranda looked at you when she told you to stay here and mind your wound," Soldar asserted as he raised his brows.

"She and I had a long time to talk," Cordis remarked. "We became…close."

"How close?" Soldar gently teased.

"What difference does it make? Once we reach General Shafter's ship, she'll be expected to help the injured. And there'll be many more wounded allies aboard that vessel than we have here."

A moment of silence followed as Soldar gazed into his brother's eyes. "My memory seems to fail me," he declared. "I keep seeing things that don't make sense. I know why I'm on the Venus, and why I was sent here. But there are other issues that—"

"Leave it, Soldar. When we're safely aboard Shafter's ship, you'll know more. Right now, there's nothing that can be accomplished by discussing the matter. Besides, you're only trying to keep me here. You'd rather speak of anything than face reality. You're frightened for *her*," he said as he nodded toward Lyra.

"I…don't know how to explain…I banded her…*obviously*," he blathered as he pointed toward the armband on Lyra's left bicep.

"That was nothing to do with the mission, brother. I know wearing the bands in front of the Condorians would denote a peaceful intent. That would be assumed and it would have been a very good ruse to placate D'uhr. But putting your band on her arm had nothing to do with whatever mission you'd been assigned."

"She wasn't on this mission. I'd lost my insertion unit and ordered her here."

"But she wears your band by consent. Does she not? And she didn't leave the Venus. Aigean could have hidden her somewhere if the girl really hadn't wanted to join you." He paused for a moment before continuing. "She did her duty. That much is clear. But the acceptance of your armband is something *else*, outside the purview of your mission or her duty."

"I believed, by wearing it, that the Condorians would leave her alone. They did…at least until her identity was discovered and she was beaten. There was something to do with a man called Aercos." He put his hand to his forehead as a dull ache began there. "That was the real reason D'uhr kept me alive and relented in the matter of Lyra's safety. The beating was bad enough, but she would have received worse treatment if this so-called Aercos hadn't clouded D'uhr's judgment." He blinked his eyes as the pain in his head grew worse. "Fornax uttered garbage that wasn't true. What he said about me didn't remotely approach reality but I believed him…at first. And Lyra believed him. I saw the look on her face as he told his lies."

"As I've said…this can be discussed at another time and when you know Lyra is safe," Cordis insisted.

Soldar leaned forward and lowered his voice. "I'll ask one more time. I want the truth *now*, Cordis. What's happened to me?"

"Keep asking and I'll leave," Cordis threatened but without any real anger in his voice. "I don't have the strength to carry on the discussion, and I don't have all the facts. I can't do the subject justice. Right now, all you need to do is care for your mate. You must be with her as long as you can."

Movement nearby alerted them to another presence. Both men snapped their heads in the direction of a shuffling sound.

"These are things neither of you should discuss," Aigean said as she walked toward them like a wraith from the darkness. "One day, I will reveal all."

"I suspected you'd used mind control techniques. That was one thing I know Fornax wasn't lying about," Soldar said as he placed his palm against Lyra's cheek.

Aigean nodded. "Your suspicions are justified. I had my duty and you had yours. And in reference to obligations and the weight we bear, there is one thing that should be mentioned before we rendezvous with General Shafter's ship. I would not want either of you to assume blame for what I've done," she warned.

"What are you getting at?" Cordis asked suspiciously.

"It's about the Condorians we left behind," she told them as she glanced between the two brothers. "D'uhr and Fornax attempted to rally their minions, even as we were preparing to leave. As I was the last person to board, I saw their actions as a threat and took such action as I deemed necessary."

"Aigean…" Soldar began.

"D'uhr and his son are dead," she blurted. "So are all the Condorians we left on Reisen Four."

Both men remained silent as they stared at her.

"My planting of a wide-range trungeon mine, retrieved from the Condorian's arsenal, came as no surprise. Indeed, their expressions as I set the coded detonator and closed the hatch were rather matter-of-fact." She paused to rearrange her cloak and gather her hood more snuggly around her neck. "I ordered the crew not to reference the large surface explosion as we made for deep space. Trust me when I say that no one outran that blast. Besides, the two of you were otherwise occupied."

"There were wounded and sick enemy fighters among those we left behind," Cordis reminded her.

"As there have been on every unarmed allied or neutral colony the Condorians assaulted," she readily responded. "It may interest you to know that I retrieved every last bit of food, water, and medical supplies for *our* wounded. After all…the Condorians won't need them where they're going."

With that, she turned and strolled away.

•••

Three hours later, Soldar sat in a passageway of the USS Valiant. The rendezvous with the vessel, and the transfer of the wounded had been completed without incident.

Cordis sat beside him but remained unusually silent.

Myranda was in the sick bay, helping with the wounded from other battles. *He'd* been banned from that area when Lyra was taken into surgery. Pestering doctors about her was wearing thin, and they'd threatened to sedate him if he didn't "shut up."

He'd expected General Shafter to make an appearance, accept a report, and debrief them, but it seemed the only supervisor outranking two Craetorian field officers was caught up in some business on the bridge.

Crewmembers scurried about and kept to their duties efficiently. All he could do was wait. The bright, clean passageway was a blessed relief after the darkness of the Venus. Still, the lights and banter of the crew in that area wore on his nerves.

Aigean's uninjured employees remained on the Venus. Aigean was among them. The one-time haven for Condorian elite followed a course paralleling that of the Valiant. He could look out any viewport and see the Venus as she flew. But he couldn't recall officers sorting any particulars out. Events since leaving Reisen Four flew by at light speed. Everything *except* the delivery of news from sick bay.

His head still ached but he ignored the pounding. He impatiently ran his hands through his hair and got up to pace, but Cordis caught his arm and urged him to sit again.

"There's nothing you can do, Soldar. The fact that she's survived this long proves she'll make it. I have no doubt about that outcome," he consoled. "You saw Myranda's expression when they took her away. She seemed quite pleased."

"I'd feel better hearing something from a physician." He clenched one hand into a fist and covered it with the other. "I realize humans don't understand the meaning of the armband Lyra's wearing or my having put it there—"

"I don't see how they could ignore those facts since you reminded them a dozen times."

"Cordis…why are we sitting here waiting for battle news? If the general can't debrief us, another officer should. And what if D'uhr's ship pursues us using trace elements from Venus' teckion engines? The Valiant is a good vessel, but she can't have enough of a crew left to man all stations. Every craft in the combined Allied Forces is shorthanded. There are just not enough of us, and we have so many wounded aboard." He got up to pace again.

"Older brother, all this speculation is pointless. Myranda said she would inform us of any news. So sit down and gather your wits. Or I'll take the doctors up on their threat to shoot you so full of meds that you won't walk for months."

Soldar grimaced, but finally sat down again. He hung his head between his knees and stared at the floor. "I just want to hear her voice again. I don't care what she says. She can hate me until the end of time but I can't stand not knowing."

Cordis put his arm around Soldar's shoulder. "I've never seen you like this."

"She thought I was a traitor. There was no time to explain."

"No. She used your assault on D'uhr and his son to rally the Venus' crew. In the end, she saw where your loyalties lie, I'm sure of it."

"What do you mean by 'in the end'? You were convinced she'd recover," Soldar said as he sat up and stared at Cordis in alarm.

Cordis slowly shook his head. "That's not what I…Soldar, take a deep breath and remember she's safe. So are you. I think it's been so long since you saw the inside of an allied craft that you can't acclimate. With you, there's always the next battle. Clear your mind and think of what you'll say to Lyra when she awakens."

"I'm sorry. I just want to know…*something*."

They remained silent for the next hour. Soldar didn't move again.

Myranda finally rounded the corner of the passageway followed by groups of crewmembers who were babbling excitedly and hurrying to greet their comrades. Apparently, there was some momentous news spreading among the crew. Soldar saw the animation in their faces and knew the update had to be good.

"Lyra's okay. She's gonna make it!" Myranda smilingly announced when she was within several yards of where Soldar sat. "Once they have her in a stasis chamber, you can go see her. But she'll be unconscious for some time."

He stood and hugged the med-tech with so much gusto that Cordis had to break the contact. Soldar felt like the weight of a planet was lifted from his chest.

As long as Lyra was all right, he could explain everything, or at least what he remembered. Surely no one would begrudge him that disclosure since she'd been involved from the start.

But his moment of joy was quickly diverted. Hubbub among the crew grew until it was almost a roar.

"What's going on?" Cordis asked.

"It's the Condorians," Myranda announced as she glanced at both men. "They're sending an open broadcast, asking to cease hostilities."

Soldar shook his head in denial. "It's a trick. They're attempting to locate the coordinates of allied ships."

"I don't think so," Myranda denied. "I was told that General Shafter has authenticated the transmission. The ship's captain is in conference with all the officers. There's a rumor going around that the Condorians are so overcome by disease that they can't fight.

Someone in sick bay said they're dying by the thousands and want medical assistance."

"Shafter can't fall for that! He mustn't," Soldar declared. "They'll get their medicine and come at us with everything they've got."

Myranda put one hand his forearm as she stood between him and Cordis. Crewmembers continued to run by them in increasing numbers. The three of them had to move into an area that served as a lounge. It was the only way to avoid the onslaught of humanity suddenly gathering around them and running in all directions.

"Listen!" Myranda continued once they were able to talk again. "I hear the general has ordered all Condorian vessels to gather in one sector. I don't think he's going to give them anything until they disarm and turn over their battle craft. No medical staff will go onto an armed Condorian ship. It's just not gonna happen. No matter what anybody says!"

"The Condorians won't agree to disarm," Cordis told her as he gazed at Soldar. "Would they?"

Soldar considered the news with gravity. "If they did then… then…"

"Then it's the end," Myranda whispered as they stared at each other in disbelief.

"I need to get to Lyra," Soldar told them as he finally understood why Shafter or no other officers had approached two high-ranking Craetorians in their midst. This news must have been processed by the bridge crew for the past few hours. The crew wouldn't have been privy to such information had someone not confirmed it.

He turned away and loped toward the sick bay. And that was where his brother and Myranda found him several hours later.

The crew was still grouping and gossiping among themselves. Laughter and joking broke out. As for him, he'd only believe the information when his own supervisors confirmed it. His heart wouldn't accept hope until different sources verified the same thing.

Soldar gazed through the viewport of the silver, tank-shaped stasis chamber where Lyra lay. Her color was much better. Only seeing her in person made him actually believe she'd make it.

Myranda and Cordis pressed coffee and food into his hands. He ate automatically because he must.

"I contacted the Venus," Cordis whispered in deference to other injured soldiers who rested in nearby spaces. "Surprisingly, Aigean didn't seem shocked about the news."

"She runs pretty deep," Myranda confirmed. "Who knows what she's really thinking?"

Cordis sipped hot coffee and smiled as he looked through the viewport at Lyra again. "She'll be fine. Why don't we get some rest?"

Soldar protectively wrapped his arms around the chamber. "I can't leave. I just want to stay here."

Footsteps approached their quiet gathering spot and all three of them turned to see a young, male lieutenant standing in the sick bay hatch. He gazed around as if he was searching for someone. When his gaze fell on their small group, he walked toward them and saluted.

Soldar was about to remind him there was no need to acknowledge his rank or Cordis' since they were out of uniform, but circumstances prevented him from making the correction. Besides, what did it matter if the news the lieutenant might impart was good?

"Sir, we've received a message from the Craetorian corsair, Faerlyte. She'll be docking with the Valiant in under an hour, Earth time. She'll take on Craetorian wounded. I was told you'd be here visiting them."

For a moment, Soldar bowed his head in shame. He'd been more interested in his mate than any wounded Craetorians rescued from other battles. Cordis gripped his shoulder in support, but there was no excuse for his having ignored his injured people.

What was worse, Cordis had been worried on *his* behalf and hadn't left his side.

Their mutual lack of concern was a break of compassionate custom if not an outright breach of duty. But the dereliction was his fault and not his brother's. He stood taller and vowed to pull his head together. He needed to act like the officer he was.

The young lieutenant continued. "The captain and General Shafter *did* know you were aboard, Colonel Nar. They send their sincere regrets at not meeting you and informing you of all the news in person. But as you can imagine, they've been quite busy on the bridge. They convey their wishes for a good journey home. You'll be pleased to know we've located new wormholes the enemy knew nothing about. The coordinates will be loaded into the Faerlyte's navigation console," the young man explained. "With any luck, you can be home in a matter of weeks. The captain of the Faerlyte has generously offered to escort the Venus safely to Craetoria. So…until such time as you depart, please accept the ship's full hospitality. Please let us know if there's anything you require, and have a safe journey."

Before Soldar could respond, the lieutenant saluted again, smiled then hurried away.

Soldar stared at Cordis.

They were being dismissed and sent home. It was that simple. General Shafter had important work to do if the Condorians really were surrendering. And he and Cordis would be needed at the nearest Craetorian outpost. In this instance, that station would be the Faerlyte.

He should be filled with joy. But some hollow hole opened within his chest. If anyone had imparted this news a few weeks ago, he'd have been ecstatic. He hadn't seen Craetoria in years and part of his heart felt the pull of his beautiful garden world. But he gazed down through the viewport again and the surreal quality of the situation was more bizarre than victorious. They hadn't won anything. Some illness had defeated the Condorians, not any combined allied efforts.

So where was the ecstatic elation? Where was the sense of justice having been served? Their worlds would be safe. Shouldn't that be cause for unending thankfulness?

"I can't leave her," he whispered. "I can't just walk away."

"I…I guess…we'll all have to go our separate ways now," Myranda murmured as tears filled her eyes. "That doesn't mean we can't stay in contact. Does it?"

"I don't know what to say," Cordis sadly added. "It's not real. It can't be. We've shed blood together. And now we go back to…to what? Are we supposed to just pick up where we left off?"

Soldar registered Cordis' hand grasping Myranda's. They made contact across the space of the stasis chamber. He slowly shook his head as his heart ached. It felt like someone had just punched him in the gut. His brother and the med-tech who'd saved his life felt it too.

Was this how wars ended? Were they simply supposed to put their weapons down and go home? Had all the fighting really ended? Just like that?

The three of them stood by Lyra's chamber and stared at each other in silence. In the distance, songs and revelry of the crew seemed to punctuate their sudden, overwhelming melancholy.

Soldar knew the truth. It would do no good to argue for Lyra's transfer to the Faerlyte. She was not a Craetorian citizen by Earth standards. Their mated union wasn't official and she couldn't speak for herself. He had no legal claim on her.

But none of that would have mattered if he thought she'd understand. He'd have torn this ship apart and tossed aside any impediment—if he thought she still loved him.

But Fornax had uttered the Condorian side of the truth and that ended everything. Even *he'd* believed the stories Aigean had embedded in his brain. These were the same ones meant to make him utterly convincing and incapable of yielding when or if he was ever tortured. Lives had depended on his mind-altered status.

His shape shifting attack on D'uhr and Fornax notwithstanding, Lyra had gazed at him one last time. Pity and revulsion had been written all over her face, and she'd turned her back on him. He suspected that what he'd changed into wasn't nearly as vile as his purported, traitorous acts. In that instant before he'd attacked Kardis D'uhr, Lyra let him go.

For these reasons—and not by any generals' orders—he knew he'd leave her behind. He'd never see her again. She'd have no way of knowing what had really happened. She wouldn't want to find him. In her heart, he was someone undeserving of life. Hadn't she said she wanted to kill him? And wouldn't she see him as a Condorian sympathizer to be abhorred?

At least she was safe. That would have to be enough. He began to shake as tears clouded his vision.

Myranda stretched out her arms and drew him and Cordis into her embrace. As one who'd endured life aboard the Venus, she understood.

He accepted her compassionate offer.

Chapter 13

Two years later
Craetoria
New Earth Embassy

Lyra stood on the balcony of her tenth floor apartment. Everything Myranda said about Craetoria was absolutely true.

As far as the eye could see, flowers, landscaped hills and gardens, tall trees, paths, and wondrous color filled the senses. Strangely colored birds, large butterflies, and sounds of other woodland creatures could be seen or heard at almost any time of the day or night. The air was balmy in the spring and summer, much colder in the winter—or so she'd been told.

Right now, this part of the planet enjoyed the benefits of early springtime. The evenings could be chilly, but the days were bright and beautiful.

She understood why Soldar hadn't wanted the Condorians anywhere near his home. On other planets bearing equally productive landscapes and agricultural bounty, the enemy had destroyed everything, leaving nothing but charred remnants.

Of all the features in the landscape, she found the Ky'Nar castle on the farthest hill most lovely and enchanting. At some point in the distant past, Craetorians had constructed such edifices to match the grandeur of all the beauty. Some ancient ancestor had brought the similar architecture to Earth where many of those features still stood today. But what remained on her planet were mostly relics, museum pieces for tourist fodder. They were lovely to be sure, but they weren't what she now viewed.

The Ky'Nar family estate glistened the way a ray of light shone through leaded crystal. Its gray walls contained bits of mica or quartz that made them appear almost jewel-like when the sun rose or set. She'd been up at both times just to witness the effect.

Even from this distance, the building's size was awesomely impressive. The upward reaching turrets and towers boasted rooms for over four hundred. That, too, was only gossip but she could well believe the information.

By comparison, the new Earth Embassy compound was many times smaller. But the architecture, such like a miniature castle itself, fit with Craetorian standards. And after all, Earth's diplomats—which now included her—were here only by their hosts' good will. The lovely gardens, high walls, and elegantly decorated rooms reflected the high regard with which Craetoria considered its closest allies. And Lyra's quarters were grander than most. The lovely jewel tones of the walls, paintings, curtains, and other fittings were exactly what anyone might have expected if they were to stay in a mighty fortress. But unlike a structure built for defense, the embassy was constructed for ambassadorial comfort. She had a small kitchen if she wished to cook her own meals, but there was a grand dining facility on those nights she might like to eat out with friends or meet other ambassadorial staff for cocktails.

Her life was splendid now. As the new head of security for the entire compound, she was in a choice position. But she'd got the job only through hard work. The Condorians hadn't simply laid down arms at the end of the war. They'd been systematically forced into doing so with a series of blockades, bribes of medical help, and the ultimate deconstruction of their entire fleet. It had taken many, many months to get where they now were. She was aware that no victory had actually been achieved as much as surrender due to medical necessity.

What was now referred to as Condorian Fever was still a threat to that entire race though science and doctors had it somewhat under control. It had decimated the enemy's ranks profoundly but pockets of them had kept fighting on. She and everyone else knew that, but for the strange malady, the war would still endure, with horrific results for the allies. But armistice stood. The war was officially over. And it'd been a microbe saving most of the galaxy. The desperate stands in space had bought time, they had saved lives but at a terrible cost to many families. Hers included.

Her part in the extended fighting and her participation in events on Reisen Four helped put her where she was. And she was grateful for everything—this post, her expanded salary, and official lifestyle, her position of power and new friendships.

All that notwithstanding she'd still asked to be assigned elsewhere. Being so near the man she now knew to be a member of the very ancient, royal household of *Ky'Nar*—the Ky being more formally added as a symbol of hierarchy—was disconcerting. Soldar had never told her about that part of his life, having chosen to simply drop the title in apparent expectation of receiving no special battlefield treatment. But then, there was a *lot* he hadn't told her that instilled resentment. She hadn't voiced those personal concerns to General Shafter, but had simply availed herself of the right to ask for another post. He'd seen fit to refuse the request though she hoped he hadn't been influenced by anyone of local, royal lineage. If he had, he'd never mentioned it.

She had the right to ask for reassignment again in one year. And she would until her superior relented. Her mind couldn't be on her job and old war wounds. She didn't want distractions caused by some desperate, war field love affair that was long dead. What happened on Reisen Four was over. She meant to keep it that way. She'd even gone so far as to refuse a few missives from Soldar, choosing to have an aide respond that she was in deep space, on duty and unable to communicate at the time. It was a prevarication. But one meant to shut him out and let him know where she stood.

She'd never wanted to go aboard the Venus. And when she had, he and Aigean hadn't informed her of the truth of the situation, which was how he'd willingly let the Elderian govern his responses via mind control. She wasn't so sure the woman hadn't been in *her* head. And that, more than anything, scared the crap out of her.

Certain tidbits concerning Aigean's powers were considered top secret. And after all *she'd* been through because of them she was still unable to legally access files or even ask about the extent of them. She'd been told the last time she'd made inquiries that if she didn't want to lose her current position and rank, she should "quit asking and stay the hell out of it" or that she "had no need to know."

That very unfair and infuriating response, especially given her service and proven ability to keep secrets, cemented her resolve.

Though Craetoria wasn't her first choice of assignments, she'd still do some good. She meant to make sure certain factions from the Elderian Embassy couldn't use otherworldly powers to sway minds or alter opinions favoring one political party over another. In short, she meant to make sure that Aigean Florn—a former brothel owner who'd oddly been appointed to an ambassadorial position on this world—didn't use her very rare and powerful mind control techniques to deprive others of free thought and open debate.

That was her first priority.

The second was to impress upon Soldar Ky'Nar the very real desire she had to sever all relations, and have him take back the armband he'd placed on her and which still remained. Options to remove the band were now available, but their use meant destroying Ky'Nar property. While giving the armband back may or may not make any difference to Soldar now, she didn't want the object destroyed and thereby engender bad relations with a powerful family. She not only had her reputation to think about, but the embassy's as well.

Once that task was done, she and Soldar would be free of any societal impressions of being a couple. She'd be free of the constant reminder of that terrible mission.

Because of that damnable band's presence, she'd worn only long-sleeved garments for the past two years. Her current black tunic, black pants, and tall black boots were not only the uniform of her position as Security Chief, but one more way to keep any of the population from exaggerating her connection to the Ky'Nar household.

Lastly, she had a more personal agenda. One that was pleasurable, though it would bring her in contact with Soldar, and in a setting inappropriate for a necessary break with the past.

Eight months ago, Myranda Chase had asked for a position at a major Craetorian medical facility. This was prompted by her need to continue relations with Cordis Ky'Nar.

Recently, Myranda's skills and Earth ancestry had earned her a position in the embassy as Chief Physician. Lyra's arrival only a few days ago coincided with Myranda's announcement of her upcoming nuptials to Cordis.

Lyra was asked to serve as Maid of Honor. Their friendship over the past years had grown to the point that refusal to help with wedding plans was out of the question. And Lyra *did* want to see Myranda happy. After all they'd lost, at least one Earthling deserved something extraordinary.

As they settled into their respective new positions, planned for a wedding, and the official opening of the new embassy, life was a bit hectic. But nothing was going to keep Lyra from accomplishing the immediate goals she'd set.

Her friend's wedding and subtlety aside, she meant to officially end things with Soldar. At this time, two years after Reisen Four and their separation, he could hardly argue against logic. What they'd promised one another was brought on by emotional stress in a battle environment. It shouldn't have happened at all. But it was certainly over.

Her door buzzer sounded and she almost tripped while spinning around. She lunged for the control panel and let out a sigh of relief when the security imaging indicated Myranda Chase's presence. She quickly opened the door to her quarters and let the other woman in.

Myranda whisked by, bearing a broad smile. Her hair, now shoulder length, was pulled into a high ponytail. She carried numerous bags and bundles in her arms. These she summarily plunked on the new living room sofa. The garish wrappings were at odds with the dark green of the sofa fabric.

With her hands now free, Myranda rushed forward and enveloped her in a huge hug. "Ohhhh, I'm so glad you're here!"

Lyra laughingly returned the embrace before putting her hands on Myranda's shoulders and pushing her slightly back. "You hugged me four days ago, when I got here."

"I know, but I'm still glad to see you again," Myranda gushed as she glanced toward her parcels. "Come look at what I've got. I picked up your dress from the seamstress. I have your shoes and tons of new makeup."

"And the royal house of Ky'Nar doesn't mind a good old-fashioned Earth wedding, with all the dancing, drinking, and walking-up-the-aisle...*ing*?" Lyra joked.

"When I described it to Lady Aurel, she absolutely adored the idea. She wants Cordis and me doing the total Earth wedding package and even brought in tons of flowers for me to choose from. She said it was a new era. And it was time to adopt some new family customs."

"Right. Lady Aurel is Cordis' mother. And Lord Rycos is his father."

"You remembered. Good," Myranda praised. "The sisters are Dorin, Nez, and Brean. That's in order of age. Don't forget. But it's okay if you do, really. I'll be there to help and of course, Cordis will be there." She walked to the sofa, sorted a few parcels, then glanced up at Lyra. "Didn't Soldar ever mention their names, honey?"

"No. We spoke about family aboard the…well…you know where we were. But we never got very specific. Family was on our minds but that was because mine were gone and he thought he'd never see his again. I-I wouldn't have remembered even if he did name them."

Myranda's expression grew soft. "Honey, sit down."

Lyra tried to make light of the fact that she'd mentioned a subject she never spoke of unless forced to. Mentioning the Venus at all had been a slip of the tongue. She smiled. "Is this the part where I get the Maid of Honor talk?"

"It's the best friend talk."

"Oh. Serious…huh?" Lyra sat in a large overstuffed chair opposite her friend and kept her smile pasted on her face. Myranda had lost all her family, too. Lyra didn't hold a monopoly on grief. And this was her friend's wedding. Myranda and Cordis were deliriously in love. The light in them brightened all spaces when they were together. She'd immediately seen it on arriving, and when in their company for even the briefest moments.

She had to put aside her own personal concerns and do what was right by a woman who'd stood by her, no matter what, over the last two years. Every bit of news, every encouraging thought and word had come from the woman who now served as the embassy's head doctor.

Lyra put her hands in her lap, folded them, and resolved to listen. She was short on friends and couldn't afford to alienate this one.

"This is none of my business, Lyra. But you should have contacted Soldar by now. He knows you're here."

She shrugged. "Why doesn't he contact—"

"After trying and being ignored for two years?" Myranda blurted. "Honey…this is a man with fierce pride. He's not going to come running after you like a lovesick puppy, nor would you have anything to do with a man who would. He got the message loud and clear. It's up to you to do the talking now."

Lyra swallowed hard and nodded.

"I know what happened. I was there. I saw it…remember?" She sighed heavily. "Lyra, are you still afraid of the shape shifting thing? Because you know Cordis has it too. But he hasn't exhibited any inclination toward using it since the war was over. The ability was only induced from some dark part of his gray matter when Aigean dragged it out of him."

"You're talking about matters of a highly classified—"

"Yeah, I know. It's all hush, hush. Top secret and all that crap!" Myranda interrupted. "But whether anyone wants to admit we know it or not, you and I saw it. And I'm not about to let it stand in the way of having the man I love. You savvy? That creature was dredged up to kill a Condorian officer. It's gone now. It's finished."

Lyra stood up, walked a few steps away, then turned to face her friend again. "It's not the shape shifting. I'll admit that scared the shit out of me at first. When I woke up in that field hospital I had nightmares about it. But that's not it anymore, Myranda. I blame Aigean for that."

"Then what!"

Lyra looked away.

"Don't do that."

"Do what?" Lyra asked.

"Don't paste on that I'm-not-going-to-talk-about-it look and go all spacey on me," she said as she raised her voice. "What's bothering you about Soldar? Why won't you talk to him?"

"You're making more out of this than you should."

"Am I?" Myranda stood and put her hands on her hips. "You're wearing his armband, just like I'm wearing Cordis'," she said as she pointed to her left arm and the band that identically matched the one Lyra still sported. "I'm told the Ky'Nar men don't put these symbols of their household and ancient lineage on someone unless they mean it. *Really* mean it."

"Circumstances were different."

"Lyra…I've told you this before. I'm going to tell you again. And this time you're going to get it through your thick head." She moved closer. "I saw that man's face when you were lying in that sick bay. I saw what it did to him to leave you behind. At that point, we'd had news the war was probably winding down. He wasn't a man looking to amend a wartime whim. He wanted you at any cost."

"Myranda…I can't talk about this…you know I can't."

"I'm not the one who needs to hear from you, sweetie. *He* does." She stepped back. "If you don't love him, I understand. But he still needs to hear it. From you."

Lyra paced for a moment then stood in front of Myranda again. She noted the concern on her friend's face and tried to placate her. This was her friend's moment to be happy. There was no excuse for causing grief. But Myranda was looking to fix something that wasn't fixable. When people were in love, they often thought everyone around them should see the world—whatever world they happened to inhabit at the time—as perfect.

"I'll talk to him, 'Manda," she promised, using as shortened version of her friend's name as a convincing gesture. "I guess…I just don't understand…"

"Tell me," Myranda whispered.

"Why is Aigean here? Why is a pleasure ship owner an ambassador and why do my sources tell me she has full access to the Ky'Nar estate?" She drew herself up. "I don't trust her, 'Manda."

Myranda nodded. "Well…there you have the million dollar question. Cordis refuses to talk about her other than to say she's an old friend of the family. The nearest I ever came to having a real break-up argument with him was over her continued presence in his life."

The two women stared at each other for a very long moment.

"We could get into serious trouble even asking. Worse if we do something," Lyra advised.

"If she's still in Cordis' head for any reason, whether it's to help but especially if it's to hurt, then I think I have a right to know. Until you got here, my options were limited to keeping a close eye on my fiancé."

"If she's a threat to security at this embassy, that makes it *my* business," Lyra somberly told her. "Anyone who can control others like that can be dangerous."

"We could be wrong," Myranda softly said. "We could be looking for all kinds of sinister plots that just aren't there. Unfortunately, I know her better than most. I saw how she hid things on the Venus. Back then I kept my mouth shut and my head down. But now…now she's insinuated herself into the life of somebody I love."

Lyra slowly smiled. "And you don't like it. You want something done."

"Let's just say it's better to beg forgiveness than ask permission. And if Cordis is somehow being manipulated then you know damned well Soldar is. *He's* the one with the real power."

"That's what scares me, Myranda!"

"Then, honey…why the hell did you leave Soldar to her devices? If she *is* up to something I'd have thought you'd want to get him the hell away from her. Convince him to throw her out of his life."

"I don't think I have that power. I don't think I ever did!"

Myranda backed up and nodded. "I think I'm beginning to see the big picture here." She took Lyra's hands and paused before speaking again. "You don't know if things on that ship weren't exactly as Aigean planned? Including everything Soldar did and said to you."

"Christ, 'Manda! I don't know if she didn't even get in my head. That kind of power is…just *think* of the implications."

"S-she isn't supposed to be able to control us…Earthlings, I mean. At least that's what I heard on the Venus."

"'Manda…would she want us knowing everything she could do? Would she want anyone to know?"

"So you don't know if what you're feeling is real or a remnant of something Aigean planted somehow? That's it…isn't it?"

"My heart tells me one thing," Lyra whispered. "My head is saying be damned careful. My head is telling me that it was all too convenient. That what we felt was something induced. Either by the situation or by…someone."

"But what possible motive could Aigean have to use any of us now? The war is over."

"After wars are over, that's where the real power grab comes. Think about it, 'Manda."

Myranda stared into the distance. "I-I can't recall that Cordis was ever alone with her on the Venus. Or me for that matter."

"Soldar was. And I was," Lyra declared. "But I've got a sneaky suspicion that her techniques aren't as strong when people she's controlled in the past have been removed from her control for a long period of time."

Myranda plopped down on the sofa. "We've got to do something. Even if we're wrong, we have to tell someone or…or something."

"Writing a report will only get us thrown in the brig. I've already been warned to layoff." Lyra sighed and gazed out the balcony window toward the castle in the distance. "I've got a plan. I don't know if it'll work and I'll have to let Soldar go to do it. But I want him free. He…he deserves that much."

"So…you do care for him?"

Lyra dragged her hands through her hair. "Like I said, I had very strong feelings for him back then, on the Venus. But there were things he never told me. I don't know if it was because he didn't want to, or because Aigean wouldn't let him. But when the powers-that-be won't tell an Earth Embassy Security Chief about the existence of a potential threat, and they refuse to even discuss it…then there's something very wrong."

"What do we do, Lyra?"

"You get married to the man you love." She took a deep cleansing breath. "This is my job. I've gotta handle it."

Chapter 14

Soldar readily accepted Cordis' and Myranda's wedding plans. If they were happy and there wasn't any misgiving in the family, the Earth ceremony only served to reinforce the fact that the woman would be his new *sister*. She already wore a Ky'Nar armband.

Servants bustled around the estate and castle. Flowers now festooned the grand gallery. Tonight, there was to be a rehearsal of the ceremony and dining into the late hours that followed. Tomorrow night was the big event. Myranda and her entourage would arrive just at dusk then stay several days for the celebrating that was to follow. That meant he'd see Lyra again, after being virtually ignored by her for the last two years.

At first, he'd made excuses on her behalf. She'd been shocked into silence by his shape shifting ability. That was understandable considering even the Condorians aboard the Venus had backed up when they'd seen what he'd become.

Then he couldn't explain the traitorous identity Aigean had implanted in his mind to get him close to a high-ranking officer. He had never explained that the Elderian had found countless men and woman who were to have posed as prostitutes or even willing slaves, just so they could position themselves near an important Condorian official. These allied shifters would then use their frightening transformation powers to overwhelm and kill certain enemy officers when an embedded signal was unleashed or circumstances became exigent. The plan was that if the allies couldn't kill the Condorian hordes, then they might be able to demoralize them by taking out their leaders. Leaders who'd always been a minority among their culture. The mission was suicidal. No one involved was expected to come back. But it was hoped that, with Aigean's help in psychically coaching very powerful shifting volunteers, that they could severely demoralize the Condorian Empire or at least slow them down.

It was a last, desperate plot devised by Allied Command. Lyra, at her lowly rank, would have no need to know of such a thing. He'd excused her behavior on all counts because that general rule still stood. She still didn't know, and didn't need to know, the extent of what had been dubbed Operation Broadsword. Allied powers didn't want their populations perceiving such mind control powers existed, even if they were as rare as to have limited scope. General knowledge of it now could serve no purpose, but might create havoc in war weary populations who were heartily sick of fearing what they couldn't combat. In short, the average allied veteran, save for a very few, simply didn't need to know there were empathic, psychic, and mind control super beings that might be able to sway officials against popular will. The operation was over. Those involved were to move on and forget or be so manipulated that their parts in the plan were dimmed by time.

Unfortunately, he was not one of those slated to let the matter drop. As a commander in Craetoria's High Guard, he was one of a few who would always need to know. There might come a time in the future when his shifting might be necessary. He'd argued that up until current times his emotions caused him to use *the darkening* inappropriately and in anger. He'd gone to great lengths detailing what had happened on the Venus. Still, his part in the operation had been deemed a total success. D'uhr and his son, Fornax, were dead and with minimal casualties. He was ordered to maintain his status and his shape shifting abilities. Aigean was helping him in this regard. Cordis' more limited power, on the other hand, would be excused. That was news he could celebrate.

For those who needed to forget, Aigean heartily insisted she could wipe her crew of their collective memories concerning the event. The surviving allied fighters were told varied stories that jumbled into a maddening collection of disinformation. In short, there was no shape shifting. It never happened at all. This was the edict from various highly placed officials throughout the allied worlds.

As for Lyra…she'd accept nothing but the truth. Since she hadn't got it after making repeated attempts to obtain files, she was angry. General Shafter and others recounted the times they'd had to threaten her into leaving the past alone. The woman just didn't understand that Shafter's call concerning whom to tell or not wasn't *his* choice. As a supervisor and veteran, she should have shown more patience and acceptance of the situation. Displaying fierce tenacity, she'd proven she wouldn't. And he took the blame for what she *didn't* know.

Where he'd understood her fears and frustrations before, they bordered on petty and arrogant now. He was tired of chasing a woman who—if she really loved him as she'd claimed—wouldn't have shut off all communication save general missives sent by a low-ranking flunky.

She was his mate. He was being treated like some conspirator in a vast sinister plot to withhold knowledge from *Her Highness*. And what really galled was the fact that even Cordis and Myranda had found a way to develop, maintain, and cement their loving relationship. Lyra's infantile response to the situation on the Venus was unprofessional and he meant to tell her so. Then he'd demand his armband back and tactfully ignore her for the rest of the weekend.

He wasn't about to disrupt his brother's happy day. But enough was enough. He was no lackey to chase a woman whose heart had obviously turned as cold as ice.

He picked up a crystal whiskey decanter, poured a good measure of amber fluid into a sparkling glass, and strode to the balcony. He awaited dusk and the arrival of Myranda's wedding entourage. Fixated on one result and with no sense of time, he started when the door to the castle study opened and Cordis walked in.

"Sorry…did I disturb?" Cordis asked.

Soldar took a deep breath, shook his head in denial, and put his attention back on the front lawn. No one could approach without his seeing them.

"Myranda sent a message. She and her friends are on their way." Cordis poured himself a drink before joining Soldar in his silent vigil. "Are you all right?"

Soldar glanced at his younger sibling and shrugged. "Why shouldn't I be?"

"I sense a bit of nervousness. It's surprising since I'm the one who should be suffering a bout of anxiety, not the Best Man."

Soldar refused to rise to the bait. He sipped more of his drink and kept his countenance stoic, trying to show as little emotion as possible.

"This is none of my business and you can tell me to go take a flying leap off Dragon Mountain…but since learning of Lyra's appointment to the embassy and her participation in the wedding, you've made yourself notably scarce in regards to family gatherings or any other social events. Father and Mother have commented. The girls too," Cordis told him.

"I have duties. Setting up a new law enforcement agency with officers that are too young and inexperienced is proving difficult. Sadly, that's what's applying for the position these days. Our older, more qualified veterans just want to be with their families. The war took its toll in that regard and they aren't open to shift work or dealing with criminals."

"Father has suggested recruitment off world."

"That takes time. Hence my absence from evenings with the family," Soldar reiterated.

"You've been remiss in other areas. You haven't taken the opportunity to welcome the new Earth Embassy staff. Personally. As the eldest son you have obligations in that regard."

"Most of them are part of Myranda's entourage. Because Father will be officially welcoming them during tonight's festivities, I saw no point. I'll add my greetings to his." Soldar said as he turned from the exquisite view and faced his brother. "Where's this going? You should be in the foyer awaiting our guests. Not standing here finding excuses to chat with me."

Cordis put his glass down on the balcony wall. "All right. I'll get right to the point."

"If this is going to be a lecture concerning—"

"It is, Soldar! You've let this thing with Lyra Markham erode your contentment. It's been two years. The incident on Reisen Four is over. If you don't want her, tell her so and let it be done. There are any number of Craetorian debutantes who'd willingly offer you invitations. All you need do is appear more…available."

"Am I a child that you'd lecture me this way?" Soldar angrily asked. "Would a barely legal girl from a prominent family…a girl who probably never had to fight for anything in her life…have anything in common with me? Is that my future?"

Cordis slowly smiled. "If you're in the mood for someone more mature…someone who knows the value of discipline and honor and who's been strengthened through adversity…why are you being such a dragon's ass concerning Lyra?"

"I'm beginning to picture you on the edge of that mountain you spoke of," Soldar groused.

"That's not an answer."

Soldar sighed heavily and sipped more of his drink before retorting, "Let's just say I tried. Seen that. Done that. Got the rejection!"

"To paraphrase one of Earth's most famous bards…methinks thou doth protest too much."

Soldar frowned and glared at Cordis. "That's quite amusing. You're the household sage now?"

"Older brother…if it helps better understand Lyra's silence, consider what she's lost. Consider the fear she might have of losing anyone else she cares about. The war may be over, but you and she are still in precarious occupations. She was still assigned to General Shafter's battle group, mopping up areas of the galaxy we've never heard of. She did this even as we began putting our lives together back here," Cordis asserted as he pointed toward the ground. "Perhaps she's not sure parts of the war are really over. It may be that she's concerned over certain aspects from the past. Matters you and I consider closed."

Soldar couldn't respond. If that was a scrap of information Myranda shared with Cordis, he was sure Lyra had mentioned it only in confidence. Here at last was a real reason, not just an excuse, for her having dismissed him after Reisen Four. Even his shape shifting in front of her would pale next to that kind of fear. She'd sabotage a relationship, as many veterans did these days, in order to avoid any more pain. After ten years of war, that reaction was all that was left to some. Particularly those who'd lost their entire family.

"Don't think on this too long, Soldar. Others won't hesitate."

"What's that supposed to mean?"

Cordis swallowed the rest of his drink before responding. "Think of her as a piece of prime real estate."

"She's not property!"

Cordis patted Soldar on the shoulder. "I know. But you'd do well to stake a claim before someone else does. Sooner or later, loneliness will have its way. And she might find herself eventually accepting someone into her bed. Someone unworthy of her."

Soldar's gaze bored into Cordis' back as his sibling left the room.

The implication was that Lyra hadn't been with anyone since Reisen Four. As her best friend, Myranda would know this to be true and would know the reasons why. In fact, Myranda might have even mentioned the matter to Cordis.

He wasn't tactless enough to dig into Lyra's personal life once she'd dismissed his efforts to communicate. The idea of probing for information not freely given from the source left a bad, gossip-tinged taste on his tongue. This is why he'd kept silent concerning the specifics of having banded an Earth woman. His family knew about Lyra. They knew he had strong feelings for her only because she wore his token on her left arm. They also knew personal matters between them were strained. But he'd said nothing else, nor had he asked for more information other than to inquire after her safety and health.

Cordis was only saying these things now, because something important had come to light. There was some piece of information his younger brother was tactfully trying to impart and without being overtly indiscreet.

He thought on the matter for a few more minutes then saw the shimmer of silver hover shuttles. Over a dozen were headed toward the castle, and from the direction of the Earth Embassy.

He took a deep breath and let it slowly out.

If there was one chance in the universe that they could still be together, he had to take it. Gone were the derisive condemnations. In Cordis' carefully worded explanation, he'd seen another scenario.

As he stood there with his family intact, he hadn't fully acknowledged the pain she was suffering because of the loss of hers. That might be the reason she kept asking for the truth concerning Aigean's mind control techniques. She'd obsessed over the Elderian's powers so much that mentioning the subject one more time threatened her career. He'd heard this from General Shafter's own lips.

It could be that she feared for his safety and any future with him if she didn't know what hold the Elderian might have. Lyra didn't understand that he was truly free from further mental machinations. Her mistrust was born of being ordered on the Venus against her will, and having little control over anything thereafter. Even he'd mentioned misgivings about the Elderian back then. But that was a different time. They'd had to be flexible and a soldier used to taking orders—a ground fighter like her—might not like the by-your-seat-of-the-pants maneuvering.

Though she was a supervisor now, he seriously doubted Lyra would ever keep secrets from her subordinates unless put to the wall by superiors. She disliked hidden agendas. She saw certain tactful omissions as lies. It could be that field supervisors had lied to her and her friends. The result might have meant death for others, cementing her monumental inclination to get at the truth now.

He suddenly recalled a past occasion when Cordis and Myranda had a very heated argument about Aigean. Though it ended with a truce, he strongly suspected Myranda intensely distrusted the Elderian. Even now, Myranda refused to say more but her choice in this matter appeared to be a conscious avoidance of further conflict.

His heart beat more quickly. Resolve concerning his intended breakup melted. He saw things clearer.

If he wanted a future with meaning—a future with a woman of enduring strength—there was no other mate for him. Who else would ever understand what he'd been through but the very one who, even now, might be trying to protect him the only way she could.

He hurried to his room. The old brown trousers, beat-up boots, and comfortable open shirt he wore weren't appropriate for the occasion. Especially not since he now intended to make the impression of a lifetime.

Ten minutes later he stood on the stairs in the grand foyer. Servants were gathering luggage and bags for those who intended to celebrate the rehearsal dinner tonight, the wedding tomorrow night, and the party on the next day, sending the happy couple off on what the Earthlings referred to as a honeymoon. He saw Cordis merrily push through the crowd and greet Myranda by picking her up and twirling her around ecstatically. The joy on his brother's face was inspiring. He was grateful for their love and the appreciation of it. His parents and sisters were gleefully inciting the embrace to go on. He searched the faces of dozens already within the castle doors and those who were only now entering.

Then he saw her.

Fifteen campaigns on seven planets and he'd never frozen until now. Sadly, now was the most inopportune of times. He had a future to forge.

He couldn't stand there like a callow, embarrassed youth. He would be the master of this estate one day. He had duties to perform. But all that drifted into some mental folder where things just didn't matter. Only her presence did.

She let her hair grow.

Swirls of very loose red-brown curls cascaded down her shoulders, to her sweet, full breasts. The very next thing he noted was how brilliant her blue-green gaze really was and how the happy look on her lovely face lit the entire room.

Fading light outside still shone through stain-glassed windows high above the massively arched wooden doors of the castle. In the myriad patterns of glowing color there was an ethereal glow around her slender body. That radiance lent her a magical quality that made her stand out from everyone else.

The halter-top black gown she'd donned for dining plunged deeply. The garment hugged her figure all the way to the floor. Something on the fabric shimmered as she moved. The effect was extraordinary. More so because it was sleeveless. His golden armband shimmered around her left bicep. Pride filled him. Even though he'd told Cordis she shouldn't be considered property, he still couldn't help the utter elation in having loved such a breathtaking woman.

Other women there might have been similarly dressed but his attention was riveted on her.

What she wore was so much more exquisite than the costumes aboard the Venus. This was how she really looked, in a normal life with friends, co-workers, and joy surrounding her. This was how their life *should* be—surrounded by merriment and bliss as they began their existence together.

He saw her smile brightly as she reached for Cordis. His brother finally let Myranda go to acknowledge the Maid of Honor.

Then the three of them—Cordis, Myranda, and Lyra—group-hugged. That heart-felt, wonderful embrace was a bonding experience he wished to share. But before that could happen, he needed to get his booted feet down the damned stairway.

How could I have ever considered letting her go? She's the most beautiful creature I've ever seen. She's everything I've ever wanted.

Finally, he was able to move one leather-clad foot forward. The other followed, if rather woodenly.

He slowly descended the grand staircase.

• • • •

When Cordis and Myranda finally released her from their hearty hug, they immediately pulled her forward until she stood before a lovely, regal-looking woman with very pale hair. Her coif was intricately braided around her head. In it, green jewels sparkled. These exactly matched her green, long-sleeved gown.

A very tall, stately man stood next to this graceful lady. His chest was massive and his square jaw seemed intimidating on first glance, but the older man's size and strength was offset by the graciousness in his silver-gray eyes. His black tunic, leggings, and boots were the uniform worn by a Craetorian High Councilman.

Having familiarized herself with their data-based images, Lyra knew she was about to be introduced to Lord Rycos and Lady Aurel. Three lovely girls stood to the left of the mother, but several steps to the rear. All of them were flaxen beauties also bearing amiable, open smiles. From left to right, she knew them as Dorin, Brez, and Brean. Their current position indicated their birthright as ladies of the household. Lyra was grateful for the research she'd done concerning protocol. She could hardly serve as Earth Embassy Security Chief without some working knowledge of etiquette. Still, there was one person missing. She kept her attention on the family in front of her, resisting the urge to glance through the crowd.

Cordis began the introduction. "Mother, Father…this is—"

Lyra was gently pulled backward against a very broad chest. The movement stopped Cordis' introduction.

She looked over her left shoulder and saw Soldar's spellbinding, silver gaze. He stared down at her intently, as if he was really seeing her for the first time. If he was happy or furious, she couldn't tell. But his hands were warm on her bare shoulders. His fingers closed gently around her flesh, almost possessively. Her body quickly responded to that gentle caress. The reaction was due to the surprising, unexpected gesture. Nothing more. At least, that's what she told herself.

"If you don't mind, brother…I'll take it from here," Soldar insisted.

Cordis smiled broadly and backed away. "Thought you might be late," he murmured as an apology.

"Mother, Father…this is Lyra Markham. She's not only the new Security Chief at the Earth Embassy but, as you can plainly see, she wears my band."

"Of course we know her," Lady Aurel stated. "And you are most welcome here, my dear. You must think of this as your home."

Lyra smiled, bowed her head courteously, and curtsied. This was all protocol. But as she was introduced to the rest of Soldar's family, the kind words and genial hugs seemed to blend.

She knew that covering the armband with long sleeves would have been construed as rude since she was new in their household, and was reasonably sure everyone there knew she wore it. Myranda and Cordis had already said so. But how was she supposed to really respond? Was she supposed to smile as if she was happy to accept a looming confrontation? Should she adopt a taciturn air?

They were behaving lovely. In response, she tried to smile brightly and answer questions intelligently. But what was her exact position? Hadn't Soldar told them she'd been out of direct communication with him for two years? Didn't they expect her request to remove the band?

"If you don't mind," Soldar eventually announced, "as Lyra and I have been out-of-touch, we'd like a few moments alone."

Lord Rycos moved toward Soldar, put one hand on his shoulder, and nodded, almost imperceptibly. The look the two exchanged was sobering. It was as if the father was trying to silently console the son. Or give him courage to take some previously agreed upon action.

Maybe she'd had it wrong? Maybe he actually wanted the armband back so badly that even his family was pushing for the breakup. It *was* Ky'Nar property after all. And she had treated the eldest son with terrible disdain.

The small gesture between father and son made her feel as if she was in a place she didn't belong. But she'd agreed to stand up with Myranda. If not for that promise, she'd have waited a respectable period of time then asked for a shuttle to take her back to the embassy compound later in the night.

"Lyra, will you come with me?" Soldar softly murmured as he took her arm and looped it through his.

For some stupid reason, she wanted to cry. But as he silently led her through the gray stone hallways bearing lovely, colorful tapestries, the reason came to her. It was always there and always would be.

God help me, I still love him! I don't want to lose him. He's going to take back his armband and it'll be like I never existed.

Chapter 15

She tried to breathe deeply while looking as though she was in utter control of her emotions. It was the hardest thing she'd ever done in her entire life, including that damned mission on Reisen Four.

He was dressed in black like his sire. The expertly altered uniform of a commander in the Craetorian High Guard only made him look that much larger, more muscular and officious. The metals pinned over his heart epitomized his courage. They made a soft clinking sound as he marched.

The only other sound was that of his boot steps. These echoed off the hallways in steady cadence.

She dared do no more than glance at him. What she valued of her self-control would be gone if she did. Had he always been so tall? Had his shoulders been so broad before? And had his blond hair ever shimmered, almost looking like silver in the low light? Or had she pushed this all out of her mind so she could let him go?

His gentle but insistent touch, his stoic bearing, and even his strong stride all indicated a momentous decision had been made. He didn't look at her. He stared straight ahead as he moved. This only reinforced the sad scene to come. She hoped she wouldn't stammer or, God forbid, cry. Tears had no place in a galaxy where she'd been through hell only to face this.

Only years of running fast gave her the strong gait that allowed her to keep up. If he was in such a hurry to get his property back, he could have stopped in any hallway away from the buzzing crowds.

At least he wouldn't do it in front of everyone. He'd never been that cruel. He'd never been a cad, nor did she believe he'd changed in that respect. But why were they moving so far from the main foyer? No one was near now. Not even servants passed them.

Somber, silent moments later they exited the castle. She found herself on a patio overlooking a garden where late afternoon light illuminated brightly colored flowers. The half-glow made the blossoms look as if they were shining on their own. Thousands upon thousands of beds and herb gardens lay there to be explored. Moonlit paths would be enjoyed by many this night. In the distance now, lanterns were being lit for that purpose.

Over distant mountains, dragons flew. She could see their massive silhouettes even from the castle's patio. It was from these noble creatures his family had chosen their emblem. She resisted the urge to glance down at it. Her armband was such a part of her now that its removal was going to feel strange. In his culture, the gesture would be viewed with the same legal ramifications as a divorce.

Still, she maintained her silence even as he kept his.

There'd be a full moon tonight. Planets and stars would glow down on Cordis and Myranda. Maybe the couple would stop and make love in one of the hidden glens. She hoped so. And she prayed she had the strength not to break down during the celebration of their love. She'd wept for her family. She'd cried for lost friends. Cordis and Myranda deserved better than a broken mess-of-a-woman to stand up for them. All she'd have left after tonight was her career, and she'd come to know this wasn't enough.

The balmy air was infused with floral scents. Sadly, Soldar had chosen a place of such awe-inspiring beauty to tell her to go straight to hell. And she had only herself to blame. Now she'd live with the consequences of her choice, and for the rest of her life. She'd be in a position to know when he took a new mate since she couldn't leave for another year. A man like him wouldn't stay alone. He could have his pick of anyone on this planet or any other.

But what else could she have done except let him go? What other choice did she have?

She waited. And when he didn't speak, she finally turned to face him. His profile was every bit as noble as that of the dragons in flight.

Finally, he slowly turned. His face was hidden in shadow. She hoped hers was as well.

This was where that hopeless affair aboard the Venus ended. All the heartsick promises they'd made there were shattered. Those quiet promises had been uttered when they believed they were doomed.

But what had once seemed no more than a wartime love affair, augmented by desperate times, suddenly became the most real thing in her life.

She hadn't wanted to come to Craetoria because she feared this more than anything. She feared loving him with all her heart. She feared knowing she always would.

•••

He took a moment to breathe deeply. The light was leaving the garden so it was hard to see her face or her eyes. But her posture was very straight. Very still. With his next few words, he'd know if she'd be in his life forever or if what they'd forged ended here and now.

He chose his words carefully. Clearly, she wasn't speaking until he did.

"I'll say this without preamble, Lyra. We can deal with details later."

She lifted her chin slightly. A sudden gleam of light from the setting sun illuminated her features. It flashed in her eyes. And he saw fear. She was desperately trying to hide it, probably the way she had for years. Where she'd used it to survive so many battles, and he was thankful for her instincts, that same emotion was his enemy now.

He stepped closer.

"I have a hunch you wanted that removed," he said as he pointed toward her armband. "But my heart bids me leave it where it is. I still love you. We can speak of these past two years later. I want only an answer for the future now." He moved closer still and saw her chest rising and falling in expectation. "I can't take it off. What it means…what it represents…is *everything*. I could no more take it back than I could stop the wind from blowing or that sun from setting." He nodded toward the horizon and the hovering sun which was just moments away from yielding to twilight. "What say you, my heart? The promises I made are forever. I'll never take them back."

She gasped and leapt toward him.

He caught her against his body, put his hands around her waist, and lifted her until her face was level with his. Then he kissed her passionately. All the loneliness of the universe washed away as he did.

"I love you too," she tearfully whispered as she broke the kiss. Even as her lips still rested against his she tried to explain. "I was scared. Everyone I've ever loved is dead and I didn't know how much longer the war would go on. It wasn't your shape shifting. I was just afraid to lose you and not know what you'd be asked to do for the sake of duty. Can you forgive me, Sol? Will you let me tell you what happened?" she asked on a sob, as tears came in earnest. "What if you're still under mind control? What if I am? What if this isn't real at all?"

"Look at me and tell me we're being manipulated in any way? Look at me and listen to what your heart says, Lyra. Listen!" he insisted. "As long as I know I can turn my shifting abilities on or off at will, what use can anyone make of them now? And who'd attempt to use you when I'd tear them apart for trying?"

"But—"

"Listen to your heart!" he repeated. "If you do that we can work everything else out. No one can control how we feel. Not with so much love between us." He slowly rocked her back and forth for a long time. Then, as it seemed she was more in control, he let her slide down his body until her feet touched the solid surface of the patio again. "If, for once, you'll let someone else take charge…stay by my side for the rest of the evening and the days to come. All you have to do is let me help you. You don't have to do everything alone. You don't have to always be the strong one," he told her as he pushed her hair back and smiled down at her upturned face. "It's not you against the galaxy, Lyra. Understand?"

She nodded, swallowed hard, and responded with a lovely smile of her own.

"Now…I'm going to kiss you again. Hard. And I want you to hold me with all your might. Just so you know this is real," he murmured as he pulled her into his embrace once more.

Almost half-an-hour later, a sound made him stop the most exciting embrace of his life. He kept Lyra in his arms but turned to see his father standing in the arched entrance leading to the patio.

His sire smiled and nodded. "I take it things are better now?"

Soldar nodded. "They're very nearly perfect, Father." He gazed down at Lyra and saw her nod as well.

"If it's not too much trouble…both of you are expected to attend the wedding rehearsal, then the dinner after. I wish I could excuse you, but obligations are what they are," he laughingly reminded them.

Soldar took Lyra's hand, kissed the back of it, and took a deep cleansing breath. "Shall we?"

"We'd better," she responded. "Myranda won't forgive me if I'm not there."

Soldar straightened his shoulders and tried not to grin like a child with a new treat. "Let's make the best of the weekend. I won't steal the happy couple's thunder, but I'd like to make an announcement about our own Earth wedding once Cordis and Myranda take off for their honeymoon. I rather like the way Earthers do things. And I want everyone to know about us. Will this be acceptable, Father?"

Rycos burst out laughing. "Son…why are you asking *me*?

Soldar joyfully turned to Lyra and spoke softly. "Will that be all right? Can we celebrate the start of our lives in this way?"

She gently kissed his cheek. "Nothing would make me happier."

Rycos strode forward. "Thank the Creator! He's finally out of his misery, my dear. For the longest time, he's been walking around looking like the bottom of a garbage scow. I was the one who advised him to tell the truth concerning his affections and see where it led," he bragged.

Lyra looped one arm through Rycos', the other through Soldar's. As she stood between them, she smiled up at Soldar once more. "My heart would have broken if he hadn't."

Soldar lifted his free hand to caress her cheek. "No more talk of breaking hearts, the war years, or the pain it caused us. Not tonight. Tonight is a time to celebrate life."

"Indeed!" Rycos shouted as they merrily led Lyra back through the hallways, and to the celebration ahead.

•••

Three months later, Lyra stood in her office reading a classified communiqué that had just been sent. It had been broadcast to embassies all over Craetoria. She couldn't guess how other officials would react.

As for her…matters were well and truly settled. She briefly closed her eyes and sent up a silent prayer in thanks.

First, Aigean had been caught attempting to manipulate a highly placed Craetorian official in matters concerning what was left of the Condorian race.

The illness still plaguing them had diminished their number to almost half. Condorian Fever still raged on their home world though doctors were having a decided advantage in saving the children. It was believed their juvenile immune systems were better able to fight off the symptoms since they hadn't yet been exposed to unhealthy lifestyles inclusive of mixing drugs and abusing other substances.

Not satisfied with the outcome of the strange illness, Aigean had attempted to use her mind control techniques on members of the newly established Allied Council, studying reparations the Condorian race owed.

In short, Aigean openly campaigned for the Condorians to be completely eliminated. She'd argued that as long as they lived the entire galaxy was still threatened. The Combine Allied Council, or CAC as it was known, had decided the threat had long since been mitigated not only by the ravages of illness but because the Condorians had turned over major ammunition dumps, fuel ships, battle craft, and even their ground armament.

While Lyra couldn't bring herself to forgive what they'd done, and knew she was in a vast majority in that regard, the council's edicts had to be followed. If they weren't to become what the enemy had, the allies must show compassion. They had to be better than their attackers.

It was her hope the Condorian children now being helped by medical experts might come to understand the rest of the galaxy was not their enemy. Someone had to start the peace process somewhere.

Still, Aigean's plans may have come to fruition but for one thing.

Soldar had listened to *her* concerns. Aigean had been watched and certain official offices had been bugged in such a way that the Elderian couldn't have suspected. And in those recordings, her techniques were revealed. In three days, she was to vacate her position with the Elderian Embassy and leave the planet's surface. She was ordered to stay away from any allied officer, subordinate, or official.

There was no indication if Aigean knew who'd foiled her plans. Lyra suspected retribution would come once the woman found out. Thankfully, her powers were so rare that she'd even embarrassed officials within her own embassy. They were more than happy to isolate the woman until she could be escorted to the next shuttle leaving this world. Sad for her, the crew of the Venus opted to go their separate ways some months after Aigean's ambassadorial appointment. The ship was being scrapped; its metal was being used to build housing on Craetoria's surface.

For Lyra, it was a final end to the war. The ground fighting had been over for some time. But in her heart, the woman who'd found a way to use Soldar's long quashed powers had always been the last threat. Now, at least, Soldar and Cordis, and perhaps others who'd been mentally cajoled into turning a shape shifting ability into a weapon, were now safe. That was what mattered most to her.

"Chief...your husband is waiting at the main gate. Should I signal him in?" The alerting announcement came over her wall holo-display, via the perimeter guards.

Lyra checked the time on the display and smiled. "No. It's five minutes past quitting time. I'm outta here for the weekend."

"Have a good one, Chief," the gate guard announced.

She grabbed her uniform jacket, shrugged into it, and hurried to meet her new husband.

He stood just outside the gate, beside a touring-class hover shuttle that was sleek and fast. It was not only designed for speed but safety and comfort. This weekend, they were using it to tour the forests and garden districts that covered the entire surface of the planet.

He unbuttoned his uniform tunic when he saw her approach. As it fell open, he presented her with a raised brow and a concerned expression.

"Hi, baby," she greeted. "How was work?"

"You know how it went," he told her. "Every embassy official with a need to know got the communiqué. Aigean finally revealed her true nature."

"It took long enough, but I figured she would sooner or later." She shrugged and sighed heavily. "I wish I couldn't say I told you so but…"

"You have every right!" he admitted. "And no one is ever going to second-guess your instincts again. Least of all me." He pulled her against his body and quickly kissed her. "I didn't want to believe Aigean capable of such deception. I'm sorry I ever defended her. But better we know what she's up to now so we can deal with it."

"No more talk about her, Sol." She ran her fingers down the center of his chest. "I'm done with her. And feeling like you're finally safe has made me horny as hell. I want to be outta here. All I could think about all afternoon was how much I need you. In fact, I want you so deep inside me that I won't be able to walk for three days."

He softly moaned as he moved closer to her and ran his hands over her body. His caress stopped at the curve of her butt. "I've got the shuttle on auto-pilot. There's a hamper full of food in back along with chilled champagne. Let's get out of here and start the weekend." To punctuate his need, he gently swiveled his hip against hers. "I'll make you forget this entire situation. Nothing is going to exist outside the cockpit of our shuttle. Promise, baby."

She felt his erection and the heat of his glowing testicles, even through the thick fabric of his black uniform pants. "I'm so glad I married you…so damned glad!"

Without another word, he whisked her into the shuttle and hit the control button. They slowly glided away into the late spring sunset and the rest of their lives.

About the Author

Candace Sams (aka C.S. Chatterly) graduated from Texas A&M University with a BS in Agriculture, worked as a police officer with the State of Texas, did a brief stint with the Texas Department of Public Safety Undercover Narcotics Task force, and was also with the San Diego Police Department. She taught for the San Diego County Sheriff's Department and worked in law enforcement in Alabama.

She currently trains as the senior woman on the US Kung Fu Team (working on her fourth black belt), and has been awarded the Medal of Putien from China and the Statue of Tao for her work in martial arts. She is the holder of several international martial arts titles. In 2000, she was one of a fifteen-member team, authorized by act of Senate-to represent this country as a martial art's ambassador to mainland China. Experiences in law enforcement, martial arts (Shaolin Kung Fu) are frequently used in her career as an author—she is known for writing fight scenes into her fictional works. As an added note, Ms. Sams is also a master gardener and loves working outdoors.

After publishing more than fifty titles in the fantasy, science fiction, paranormal, and action-adventure genres, she's received more than thirty awards from various organizations, including five National Readers' Choice Awards and a *USA Today* Best Book nomination. Her *Tales of The Order* series, as well as several other works, are now being vetted for movie options.

Hailing from Texas, Candace loves the country life. She and her husband of over twenty-five years, live in a rural area of the U.S. A plethora of dogs and cats have adopted them. She loves to hear from readers and can be contacted through her website at *www.candacesams.com*. Candace also writes erotica as C.S. Chatterly and can be contacted from *www.cschatterly.com*.

"I am so very hungry. Even though he does not want to recognize my presence, and has done all he can to attribute it to waning sanity, he will soon have no strength left to defy my haunting manifestation. As always, I will grow strong from his pain. No one on earth can break my spell."

• • •

"Same as usual, Sarge?"

Cort O'Leary nodded and pulled some bills out of his pants pocket. As sergeant was—by act of law—the highest rank any peace officer in town could reach, most folks used the moniker as a show of respect. The mayor got the same deference. *He* couldn't be *chief*, when the head of the local fire department already held that honor. The allocation of specific titles made things easier on town folk. Everybody knew who was being spoken about when there was any kind of emergency. But what the heads of various civil institutions were called mattered little to Cort. He just did his job.

As he paid for his meal, Millie, the girl who worked behind the counter of Haskell's café, shot him a come-hither look. Although pretty and hot, Cort wasn't interested in her. Luck always passed him by in matters of love. Better to leave amorous thoughts to the small town Lotharios who vied for Millie's attention. She'd be better off and so would he. The only hot thing he wanted from the café was his damned chili. He worked out hard every week just to enjoy this one meal.

After making his purchase, Cort went outside and leaned against the side of his patrol vehicle. The DEA-seized sports car was a perk the town had offered him to come and work in an out-of-the-way burg like Maple Corners. It was his to use as he saw fit, but the small interior wasn't suitable for hauling prisoners. As it happened, he'd seldom had to arrest anyone. As bad as New York had been, his current address was the exact opposite.

He carefully set his coffee cup on the hood, opened the carton containing his chili, and prepared to raise a spoon of the greasy, thick stuff to his lips. The next thing he knew, he was on the ground with hot coffee pouring over the inside of one thigh and thick chili oozing down his clean, light-blue uniform shirt.

"*What the hell!*" Cort swiped at the mess on his shirt. A figure bent over him and swayed.

"So very s-sorry, old chap…must have l-lost m'balance a bit. Terribly clumsy of me."

"Mister, you just lost more than your balance." Cort grimaced at the hiccupping, burping man standing over him. *A drunk.* If the older man's difficulty in speaking hadn't given him away, the smell of whiskey on his breath and his staggering certainly did.

Cort jumped to his booted feet and winced as his uniform pants brushed the coffee burn on the inside of his thigh. "You picked the wrong guy to piss off, mister!"

The drunkard held one hand over his mouth as he burped yet again. "M-my sincere apologies, dear fellow. I'm afraid I'm in me cups."

He glowered at the English-accented boozer, put his hands on his hips, and glanced back down the street. It was late in the day and Flaherty's Tavern had been open for several hours. Apparently the stranger in town had found a way to quench his thirst, and the staff at Flaherty's hadn't cared if the old guy got behind the wheel of a car or staggered out into traffic.

"What's your name?" Cort demanded as he pulled off his service cap and set it on the hood of his patrol car.

"P-pardon?" The man asked and swayed dangerously close to the curb. "I'm afraid my hearing isn't what it should be."

Cort grabbed him by his coat sleeves and hauled him to a safer spot on the sidewalk, away from the street. "What is your name?" He repeated, and enunciated each word clearly so the man could better understand.

"Morbius…Morbius Nightshade at your service." He bowed and almost stumbled again. "Always willing to oblige an officer of the law. A rather large officer, I must say."

"Morbius Nightshade? Yeah, right." Cort snorted in disbelief. Even drunks could make up names. He'd heard a thousand of them and every alias he'd ever come across had been better than this one. "Do you have some identification, Mr. *Nightshade?*"

"'Course I do, my good man. S-somewhere…let me see…"

When Nightshade began to fumble in his pockets, Cort's guard went up. His right hand crept toward his weapon, and he silently unsnapped the holster. Even in Maple Corners, it was possible for bad things to happen.

As the older man drew out a wallet and it fell to the ground, a six-inch knife also fell out and landed at Cort's feet. He gripped the butt of his semi-automatic and quickly withdrew it from his holster. "All right, mister. Don't put your hands in your pockets again. Keep 'em where I can see 'em." He aimed his weapon at the guy and had the satisfaction of seeing Nightshade's face go completely white.

Cort pushed the fellow against a building. Then he restrained the older man's hands with one of his own, holstered his weapon, and cuffed the guy. He then conducted a thorough pat-down of his suspect which didn't reveal any other ready weapons. Nightshade didn't resist.

"Please, my dear boy, I wouldn't h-hurt a soul. The knife is just…just an old heirloom."

"Yeah, tell it to the judge. You're under arrest for public intoxication." He then proceeded to recite his rights, although uncertain if Nightshade was sober enough to hear or understand what was being said.

Once he finished telling the man he had the right to remain silent, he pulled Nightshade toward the knife, and held him upright with one hand while carefully retrieving the weapon *and* the guy's wallet from the sidewalk. "What kind of knife is this anyhow?"

"Very old. Very rare." Nightshade said as he nodded toward the object. "I have to take it to…to…oh my stars! I've forgotten."

Cort examined the weapon in the setting sun. It looked like the smooth blade might be made of pure silver. Indeed, he found a hallmark that confirmed just that. The blade was straight but a careful edge-pass with his thumb revealed it was very dull. There were nuggets of either glass or semi-precious stones embedded within the black, wooden handle. "This doesn't look like the kind of thing a person picks up just anywhere."

"Very astute, m'boy. It's special." Morbius hiccupped again. "Very ceremonial and of great importance."

"You said you were taking it to someone. It isn't yours?"

Morbius didn't respond. He just hung his head in shame.

Cort sighed heavily, flipped the wallet open, and found some money and a driver's license. What he didn't find were credit cards, pictures, or the other wallet paraphernalia people usually carried. Surprisingly, the license indicated that his prisoner's name *was* Morbius Nightshade.

"All right, sir…we're going to the station. I want to run a check on you and this knife. If it's stolen, things will go a lot easier if you just speak up now," Cort warned. "Will I find out you're wanted for anything?" He wanted to give the older man a chance to come clean.

"Oh, no…of course not. I obey the law, my good fellow." He wobbled toward Cort again, who caught the man before he could fall.

"Odd, but I sense that you really aren't angry with me," Morbius noted. "You seem to have a rather s-stern desire to do your job, but your hands aren't those of an uneducated ruffian who abuses his powers. In fact, I'm sensing a g-great deal of patience; especially after seeing a knife come flying out of my coat pocket so…u-unexpectedly." Morbius hiccupped. "In another place, officers of the law might not be so soft-spoken," he finished.

Cort just shook his head. This was the first time a drunk had ever *complimented* him.

He raised one hand to his microphone. With it clipped to his epaulet, it made the job of calling for a patrol car easy. He need not reach to his side to remove his radio from his belt.

It would only take a couple of minutes for the evening shift officer to drive from his current position at the station, only three blocks away.

Cort hadn't made that many busts in the three years he'd worked in Maple Corners. But because of all those he *had* completed while in New York, dealing with drunks now wasn't any big deal. On the other hand, it was a great big *flaming* deal to the people who'd grown up in these parts.

Incidents like coming across a knife-wielding, smashed, British guy weren't normal for the town's citizenry. The event had drawn a crowd on both sides of the street with a few of the spectators pointing at the stranger. He could only guess about the gossiping comments. This was more action than the town had seen since the Farquar twins had got in a fight over Magdalena Knothill at the local Fourth of July sociable. Cort had had to break up that fight, and the locals commented for weeks on how big-city cops handled things so efficiently.

If his life weren't so pathetic, the town's interest in him and this ridiculous encounter would almost be funny.

To add to the town's rumor-fodder, Bucky Porter, the evening shift officer, drove around the corner with his car's overhead lights on and the siren blaring. Cort assumed it was Bucky's one chance that year to make a showing for himself—hence the noisy, theatrical entrance.

He shook his head in frustration. All they had was a drunk. Bucky would make a federal case out of the entire thing. Still, Cort couldn't fault his fellow officer's dedication to his work. Everything was a matter of perspective. To Bucky and the people of Maple Corners, they might have a *real live criminal* on their hands. To Cort, the entire episode was just a load of paperwork that would have to go before the town council, the mayor, and everyone else who thought they had a right to know.

The town's people were lucky not to have experienced a real dirt-bag first hand, or to know any of the truly evil people who walked the face of the earth. But Cort would keep those stories bottled up. More to the point, he just didn't want to get close enough to talk to anyone about the meaner side of life.

• • •

"Look, Bucky, just go home. I'll take care of the paperwork."

"Are you sure, Cort? Don't you think you'll need some help with this guy?" Bucky glared at Morbius.

Cort wasn't sure the drunk would be safe with Bucky. It wasn't that the younger cop would hurt anyone so much as Nightshade's blood-alcohol level indicated he was probably on a real bender. If that was the case, the man might need medical treatment later. Since *he'd* made the arrest, it was his responsibility to see to the prisoner.

"Why don't you go tell the mayor what happened?" Cort tactfully recommended. "This is just mundane work that I can get cleared up in no time. But you know politicians around here. They're gonna want an official report. You're the best person for the job, Bucky." The response to that suggestion was a huge smile.

"Right, Sarge. You've got it." Bucky saluted and strode out of the station.

Cort almost grinned. Bucky wasn't a bad kid but he did need to lay off the TV cop melodramas.

Like most of the world, Bucky just wanted to be needed. Cort recalled having that same desire…once. Sadly, he couldn't summon the will to care anymore.

"You have that young man's respect. You know how to handle people, don't you?" Morbius asked from inside the jail cell. "You certainly could have treated *me* with less dignity."

Cort glanced up from his paperwork, but said nothing.

"Indeed, you've been very accommodating," Morbius continued. "Why, this cell has a soft bed and a barred window that lets in plenty of fresh air." He shrugged. "Of course, I dislike being incarcerated, but it's entirely my own fault."

Once more, Cort ignored Morbius's comments and looked over all the documentation he had so far. When he spoke again, it was strictly about business—he wasn't in the mood to be sociable. "According to the state and the feds, you aren't wanted for anything, Mr. Morbius. You've got no outstanding traffic fines or an arrest record. Oddly, I can't find out anything about this knife," Cort mused. He turned the weapon over in his hands and studied it. "Are these real stones or do you know?"

"Oh, they're *quite* real. They're garnets, moldavite, citrine, and amethyst," Morbius supplied. "Each stone represents a specific quality."

"What do you mean?"

"Well…the garnets promote purpose and commitment. Moldavite is formed by meteors and is best used to serve humanity. And citrine…well it's a stone that disperses negative energy. The last stone on the handle is amethyst. It aids in spirituality and peace. They're very powerful minerals." Morbius paused before saying more. "That object has been in my family for generations. I can't believe I've allowed it to come to this."

Cort noticed how his prisoner sounded almost sober. Still, what he was saying made no sense. It might be a good idea to monitor him just to make sure he'd be okay. "If the knife is *yours*, can you produce any paperwork?" Cort asked. "There're no identifying marks on it."

"No. I have no papers, but I have family members who can vouch for me," Morbius insisted. "I *am* allowed a phone call am I not, my good man?"

"You can have any *reasonable amount of time* on a phone," Cort relented. "Just don't waste my time or the taxpayers' money."

"Upon my word as a gentleman, sir, I shall do neither."

Against his better judgment, Cort kind of liked the guy. Even half-sober Nightshade had a certain class and dignity. He took the time to look the older man over and sum him up.

Nightshade was dressed in a quality business suit that looked tailor-made. He had blue eyes, dark brown hair, and would have been rather stately in other circumstances. Overall, Nightshade reminded Cort of English lords he'd seen in old movies from the thirties. More to the point, there were no bad vibes coming from the man. For some odd reason, he didn't think his prisoner was capable of lying and getting away with it. But he quickly tamped down the idea of giving the older gent a break. His cop's cynicism wouldn't let him go that far.

Shrugging off feelings of empathy, he studied the man further. When Morbius was cleaned up, he would probably be considered a very handsome individual. And at the age of fifty-five—according to the birthdate on his driver's license—the man wasn't all that old. So how on earth did this quiet-spoken, intellectual type end up in a place as dull as Maple Corners—drinking his ass off?

Despite his skepticism, Cort finally relented to his instincts, picked up the keys to the cell, and let Morbius out.

"The law says you have a right to be on the phone *alone*," Cort advised. "It's on the desk. I'll step outside and will trust you not to run."

Morbius straightened his tie, pulled at his shirtsleeves to remove the wrinkles, and raised one brow. "My good fellow, I'll do no such thing. I am a Nightshade. We do not…r-r-r-r-run!"

As he walked out the front doors, Cort found himself chuckling at how the arrogant British gent rolled his r's. Clearly the guy wanted to appear above such dastardly, ignoble acts as trying to high-tail-it out of town.

He gave his prisoner about fifteen minutes. But before he could reenter the station, Morbius stepped out on the front stoop.

"Well, did you get a hold of an attorney?" Cort asked amiably.

"Hardly, Sergeant. My niece will be here in the morning. She can explain everything. I don't think a solicitor will be necessary. My rights haven't been violated, and I'm not guilty of anything except a minor indiscretion. That hardly defines me as a hardened criminal."

"Sorry. But unless your niece has papers proving who that knife belongs to, I have to thoroughly check it out." He continued to explain his reasoning. "Look…a little over a year ago there was a massively distributed report asking law enforcement agencies to be on the lookout for stolen artifacts. Most of the stuff was rifled from shipments on loan to museums across North America. The curators only found out about the missing property when a lot of it didn't show up when and where it was supposed to. I want to make very sure this knife isn't part of that haul. It certainly looks like it could fit the bill."

Morbius stared. "But I've told you it belongs to my family."

Cort took a deep breath. Apparently, being questioned about his honesty wasn't something Morbius Nightshade was used to or liked.

"All right…why are you carrying it? Why are you in Maple Corners? Why were you drunk in public and where are you employed? There's practically nothing about you on any computer except records saying you have a driver's license," Cort said. "Since you're able to talk coherently and have refused a lawyer, maybe you can answer some questions to help clear all this up?"

With calm dignity, Morbius held up his hand. "I noticed some coffee in your office. Might we go back inside and discuss this like gentlemen? Better still, perhaps you have some tea?"

Cort looked at the ground and tried not to grin. The older man behaved impeccably. Morbius might be pulling his leg and might even harbor a hidden disdain for those in power. Still, he maintained the proper gentlemanly attitude. "All right, Mr. Nightshade. Tea it is."

As they walked back inside, Morbius stared at Cort's nametag. The stripes on his sleeves told anyone who was half aware of uniform standards what his rank was, but his name only appeared on the silver plate over his right breast pocket.

"Ah, O'Leary. That's a grand Irish name," Morbius gaily announced.

It was Cort's turn to simply raise his own brow, but he said nothing.

"Since we're to be cloistered together for the nonce, might we dispense with the use of surnames and call each other by our given names?" Morbius asked. "It seems the civilized thing to do under the circumstances. I, as you know, am Morbius."

He took the hand the older man offered. "I'm Cort." He was surprised to find himself warming to the other man's friendliness. It had been a very long time since anyone had gotten under his skin, but Nightshade had a strange air about him. It was almost as if the man was more than he appeared. His very appropriate attitude and his even, bright smile were both a bit compelling. Simply put, Morbius could draw even a hardened cuss like him out. His prisoner, although both refined and educated, didn't have the fault of being pretentious.

"Ah! Perhaps your name is a derivation of *Cearbhall,* which means champion or warrior in Gaelic. And Leary is an Anglicized word for one who herds."

Once more, Cort found it almost impossible not to smile.

Morbius scratched his head. "I say, old chap…has your family ever had a background in that sort of pursuit?"

Cort pressed his lips together. "Don't know. We're from New York by way of Ireland. Legend has it there was supposed to have been an O'Leary whose cow kicked over a lantern and almost burned a city to the ground."

"I dare say…you're probably not from *that* branch of the O'Leary clan, my good sir!"

He did grin this time. "Why not? How can you be so sure?"

"Because…that incident occurred in Chicago and you've just said your family was from New York," Morbius countered. "Unless one or more parts of your family moved west, the episode had nothing to do with you. Now, let's have that tea."

Cort actually found himself feeling better than he had in a long time. He wondered if the man's niece was going to be as interesting. But, as he boiled water for their tea, the smile left his face and his mood turned sour again. He could feel the glee instilled by his arrested companion slipping away.

The strangest sensation suddenly overtook him. The hair on the back of his neck stood up, and he lifted a hand to rub the spot. Cort could almost swear someone other than his prisoner was watching him.

When he turned, Morbius stood near the cell window, looking outside.

"What's wrong, Morbius?"

"I don't believe that I should attempt an explanation. The sooner Dawna gets here, the better."

"Dawna?"

"My niece. She'll be here by tomorrow morning, I should imagine," Morbius softly finished before turning his attention back to the cell window. "Did you know that there are people whose auras attract very unsavory powers?"

Cort shook his head in confusion. "*What?* What's that supposed to mean?"

"I'm just saying that we can attract very bad entities by our thoughts and deeds."

Cort walked closer to Morbius and stared at the man.

Morbius snickered. "Oh, don't mind me. I'm a student of human nature. In fact, if you're around me any length of time, you might agree that I tend to read too much into situations."

"Maybe we'd better have our tea, and you can answer some questions," Cort woodenly suggested.

"Yes," Morbius murmured. "Tea would be grand. And…I think it's good that Dawna is coming. She needs to be here before something happens."

"What the hell are you talking about?" Cort blurted as his foul mood suddenly intensified.

"I-I was just thinking that there's a reason for everything, my good young man," Morbius calmly stated. "It was no accident that I pulled off the highway and chose this small village to quench my thirst. No accident at all."

Cort ignored his detainee's cryptic remarks, finished making their tea, and tried to cast off the disturbing sensation edging up his spine.